Streetlam
Shepherd Moons

Katherine Highland

You may quote or reproduce content, but the source
should be acknowledged.
If quoting from any sources included in the Author's
Notes please seek the relevant permissions from those
sources.

This book contains discussion of adult subjects, occasional
swearing and some instances of hate speech. There are
brief references to the issues of suicide and self harm. For
signposting to help with a mental health crisis, please see
the Author's Notes section at the back of the book.

ISBN: 9798700207812

Profits from the sale of this book in printed and electronic
form go to Autism Initiatives (Scotland) to support their
one stop shop for autistic adults in the Scottish Highlands.

Covid19 and the setting of this story

This is a work of fiction, the writing of which was made possible for me by the redefining of schedules which Covid rules brought about. I wrote it in the autumn of 2020, at which time restrictions were still in place which would have made a directly contemporary setting unfeasible for much of the story. As it is in part a sequel to my previous novel, "The House with the Narrow Forks" which was also written during the Covid era, this made it necessary to set it some time after the end of 2019.

At the time of publication in early 2021, the whole of 2020 can be definitively ruled out as a setting for this story; it is still unclear how our lifestyles will look during the rest of 2021 and there are mixed indications for the latter part of the year.

I have therefore decided to go ahead with an implied setting of the events in this novel in the early 2020s at the point when Covid restrictions are on the way out. In the event of reality at the time you are reading the story not being compatible with the options and activities available to the characters, I accept responsibility for all discrepancies. This is, after all, a tale not of Covid but of acceptance, friendship, self-discovery, diversity, inclusivity, integrity, cats, streetlights, laughter, dreams, spirits (of all types!), hope and joy. Thank you for the interest in Diane's story which has led you to be reading this; whatever the real world context in which this moment is embedded, I hope that you will enjoy the book for what it is.

Slainte Mhath / Good Health,

Katherine Highland.

1

Fluorescent lighting throbbed down from above as the whine of air conditioning insinuated itself unbidden into Diane Abercrombie's sensitive ears, working in tandem with the harsh cleaning product fumes invading her nose and throat. She was used to the discomfort of these events; years of experience had taught her to allow herself time to recover afterwards from the fatigue of processing every interaction, feeling and sensory overload which the bigger meetings may throw at her. It was worth it for the sense of achievement on a day like today. Volunteering with Up For Work allowed her to give something back to society and make peace with being unable to sustain mainstream paid employment. Away from the unviable routines which had made her so ill time after time throughout her twenties and early thirties, she had found freedom to use her talents within what was feasible for her to take on. Her autistic attention to detail and intensity of focus were able to come to the fore. Occasions such as this represented the pinnacle of all the good this had brought to her life. The online support scheme for neurodivergent jobseekers which had been her initial suggestion and into which she had poured hours of research was being officially launched. Even more thrillingly, the estimable Verena James was about to publicly acknowledge her for it.

Owning the podium at which she stood in a crisp trouser suit the colour of rich coffee with a hint of milk, the charity's outreach manager was describing the months of hard work which had gone into making this scheme possible. Verena's diction flowed from one succinct point to another with the opulent clarity of cut crystal turned facet by facet in the spotlight. Diane's nagging inner voice insisted that in comparison, her own presentation would be more like the jagged, unmodulated gush of a bottle bank being emptied. Yet again she checked the notes she clutched in tense, trembling hands to make sure that she had not blurred any of her thoroughly rehearsed words in their sweaty-palmed grip. On stage, Verena instinctively held exactly the right stance for the light to catch her immaculate salt-and-pepper hair, making eye contact with the audience as she graciously credited this groundbreaking new scheme to the innovation and creative thinking of her team.

The moment was coming; the validation which would make all the extra hours, tired evenings and postponed plans worth it. Diane's heart pounded as she drank in every nuance of this confident performance by the colleague she worshipped. Somehow, in addition to getting her words out flawlessly in this pressured and uncomfortable setting, she must remember to keep looking at the audience as Verena was. She must rely on her memory with her notes merely a prompt, not to be stared at and woodenly read out at the expense of engaging with the roomful of listeners. With the acknowledgement to come, joyous as it was, the hard work of impressing Verena James would begin all over again. With someone so accomplished, it was necessary to prove herself on an ongoing basis in order to get into her favoured circle and stay there; resting on laurels was not a luxury she could afford.

Today was a celebration; she must remember that. Once the mental exertion of giving her speech was over with, she would be able to let herself feel the joy she had been building towards for months since the day she first suggested an online forum and buddy scheme for neurodivergent people who were looking for work. It would be discreet; no-one but the clients of the scheme and those supervising their jobseeking would ever need to know. It would give them a chance to talk things through with someone in similar circumstances and make informed choices about things like whether and how much to disclose their neurodivergence at all stages of applying for jobs. It would give them the confidence of knowing they were not alone, plus the benefits of learning from one another's experiences, good or bad. Verena and Sally had been cautious at first, looking at all the reasons it could go wrong and coming up with examples of people it would not help. Eventually, Arthur had come to the rescue by pointing out that there were lots of people it would help and nobody it would harm if run properly; that it was important not to let what couldn't be done or what might go wrong prevent them from even trying. The management had come around to the idea once Sally had spoken with some contacts at the local jobsearch hub; it had been all systems go from there with Diane researching other schemes, designing publicity, doing the mundane photocopying, dealing with petty cash and all necessary background tasks. She had also put a lot of time and emotional labour into writing up a detailed presentation of how such a scheme would have been beneficial to her as an autistic woman, including some painful personal experiences which she would rather not have relived and had potential funders read about but was willing to endure that for the sake of helping people. Today was about restoring the self-belief which had been shaken by the bad memories she had to disturb; the approval of her superiors, especially Verena, making up for the frustration and guilt about her limitations in this socially energised world she had to navigate.

Diane looked good today; even she had to admit that. Her dark blonde hair with its natural pale streaks framed her oval face just right; her fringe the length she liked it, long enough to sweep to the sides and the rest falling in layers to skim below the level of her shoulders. Her grey eyes were enhanced by a light touch of mascara and a clear gloss gave a subtle shine to her lips; this was as much make-up as she could tolerate but her skin was naturally clearer for it. Wearing her favourite business colour combination, a plain navy blue top and matching open blouse over a pair of burnt-orange trousers with classic low heeled navy blue court shoes, she felt as near to attractive as she ever could. Running her fingers over the tactile edge of the cognac diamond drop pendant which nestled at the base of her collarbone, she took several deep breaths to calm and centre herself as Verena drew towards her concluding remarks before she was scheduled to hand over to Diane as the next speaker.

"...Most of all, I have to thank one colleague in particular who has been instrumental in making this happen. It began with her and would not have happened without her. I am proud not only to work with her but to call her a friend..."

This was more than she could have ever expected! The rawness of putting so much of her vulnerable self out there on display to get this done lay quietly soothed by the balm of this moment. Beaming with pride, Diane began to rise from her seat.

"...Sally Howe."

What?

For a moment, the too-bright overhead lights froze at the height of the flickering which it often seemed no-one but Diane could see; the air conditioning reached an intrusive crescendo and hung there, squealing with the same harsh discord that had crashed into her brain. She felt as though her skull would shatter with the combined resonance. What exactly had just happened?

Sally was on the stage with Verena, shaking her hand and being clapped on the shoulder. Verena was saying something about how Sally's liaising with the jobsearch hub had started this whole process. With a sudden, horrible blast of adrenalin-fuelled awareness, Diane remembered that she was standing up. Too soon, making it obvious to everyone that she had thought she was the colleague Verena was about to single out. Willing her muscles to move for what felt like several minutes, she plumped back down into her chair; awkward, undignified, humiliated. After all this, she still had to get up and face these people and give a speech!

Sally was walking off the stage to enthusiastic applause which Verena appeared in no hurry to quell in order to move on, despite the tight timescale per segment which had been emphasised throughout the planning of the launch. Eventually the echoing applause abated and Verena, her voice becoming clipped and formal once more, announced that there would now be a brief presentation from Diane Abercrombie; a volunteer with Up For Work. She needed to move; to somehow make herself go through with this.

Stepping up to the podium gave Diane the sensation of walking on stilts; detached from the immediate feeling of her own footsteps and standing taller than felt safe or natural. Resting her notes in the place where Verena's own papers had been seconds earlier, the twist of inadequacy in her gut was followed by a punch of heartache; after that came the rising fury of injustice which unlocked her vocal chords just as the pause was becoming long enough for puzzled looks to begin spreading through the audience.

"Good afternoon. I have been a volunteer with Up For Work for four years now and it has been a joy to be involved with this exciting and much needed new scheme, which was in fact my own idea."

The part about it being her idea was not in her script; in her peripheral vision Verena and Sally exchanged glances.

"As an autistic woman who has had experience of applying for jobs in the past, I would have found it very helpful to have someone to share the process with me; somebody who knew a lot about how I felt and what I needed because they had a similar story to mine. Somebody I could have helped in turn, thereby feeling stronger and more confident about my own usefulness and having something to contribute, just as helping me would have made them feel needed and worthwhile. They might even have suggested I shouldn't give a name to a hypothetical criminal when getting creative with sample scenarios at an interview, because knowing my luck it would turn out to be the name of the head of the panel's new grandchild!"

As she had hoped, this example adapted from her own experience drew sympathetic laughter; though Verena had seen and approved the text of her presentation including this anecdote, her expression was more of a grimace. Diane could hardly blame her; the discomfort she felt at telling a story against herself now after the snub she had received minutes earlier must surely be showing in her face and her perpetually awkward body language.

"Of course, particularly in smaller communities, having someone local knowing details of your personal business and vulnerabilities doesn't always feel safe or appropriate. In human rights based social ethics, dignity and privacy are as much key elements as are equality and freedom from discrimination. However, we now have the technology available to connect on an everyday basis more than ever with people who are geographically further away. We also have scope for secure systems which enable controlled access and allow for sensitive communications to be safe and compliant with data protection law. So with accessibility advice from disabled people's user groups, the much appreciated help of our colleagues at the local jobsearch hub and input from their team of online security experts, we have arrived where we are today."

Too many emotions were churning around beneath the surface of Diane's measured and rehearsed words. Looking over towards her vacated seat with her favourite tan suede jacket draped over the back of it, she longed for the comfort of slipping her arms into the sleeves and feeling it mould itself around her as it had from the first time she tried it on. Pulling her mind away from the poignancy of that rewarding safety, she imagined herself once again practising her speech in front of her friends. Kate would be watching now on the video link from her office, unless a client happened to turn up at the centre with a crisis. Diane's fondest memories, though, were of rehearsing in front of Des and Jason in their cheery, welcoming flat with its organised chaos of plants, music magazines and the impressive arrangement of technology around the TV which Diane nicknamed Mission Control. Appreciated even more keenly in the aftermath of the bewildering, heartbreaking period when Covid restrictions had prevented their cherished times together, picturing being with her best friends studded her amplified emotions with the searing brilliance and cutting edge of diamond. Making sure that Jason could follow what she was saying by lipreading as much as he needed to had been a vital enhancement to her preparation in keeping her from rushing her words in order to get the speech finished. She had felt guilt-stricken at first when he asked her to slow down a couple of times; she felt she had betrayed the disabled community by not instinctively avoiding this pitfall, especially given the extra stress caused to Jason during Covid by having the option of lipreading when out and about impeded by the need for face coverings. Des had assured her that it went a long way towards replenishing his younger brother's confidence and self-esteem to be able to help her to make her presentation accessible. Being consulted and his input acted upon had, as Des pointed out, in many ways an even bigger impact in trust building than someone instinctively getting everything right from the start, which in the real world seldom happens. Recalling the warm sense of belonging and acceptance in the lads' relaxed home brought the lump in Diane's throat dangerously close to the safety limit; she forced herself to clear her mind and focus on the present as she continued her speech.

"We are finally ready to launch a trial version of a secure website which can provide password protected access to a mentoring or 'buddy' system and moderated online forum for neurodivergent jobseekers. Members will be allowed and indeed encouraged to stay on the site after securing employment or other placements in order to continue giving the benefit of their experience; we hope that the scope of the site will naturally extend to in-work support. The private chat facility will have clear conditions of use; the exchanging of any personal contact details will be subject to an 'at your own risk' disclaimer and will be discouraged until the parties have been communicating regularly on the website for at least six months. We are saying 'discouraged' rather than 'forbidden'; our ethos is to work towards enabling autonomy and choice."

It had been quite a battle to get that one through. Diane's protests against the prevailing risk-averse culture which was happy to push people into taking on the pressures and responsibilities of mainstream employment yet presumed to dictate with whom they may or may not strike up a friendship had been frustratingly waved aside again and again. Even when she suggested the compromise of "discouraged" along with a clear disclaimer, it once again took Arthur's backing to persuade Verena to accept it. Unassuming, uninterested in plaudits and close to a well-earned retirement, Arthur's logical, common sense thinking and empathic, fair-minded approach had won him respect among his more ambitious colleagues whilst his calmly appreciative attitude made him a rock and staunch ally to Diane. It seemed that he could consistently hear her whilst the others were operating at an entirely different frequency; more than that, he endorsed that she ought to be heard when she fell into doubting it. He bridged a gulf which ought not to exist; if only she could do better, prove herself, fix whatever was lacking in her that made Arthur's advocacy necessary even though she already had the privilege of being able to utilise her own voice. She appreciated his support wholeheartedly and felt no resentment towards him for succeeding where she failed with her own words; he never made her feel that her words had been taken away from her.

"I would like to thank the rest of the outreach team for supporting me to volunteer with them, in general and on this project. I also thank all of the people who have collaborated to develop my idea into something feasible which is now a reality: the Up For Work Together website. Thank you!"

Diane remembered with a hot rush of panic to grab her notes before walking thankfully back to her seat; for the last few sentences, she had been gripping the sides of the lectern and not even looking at the page. "My idea" had been "this concept" in the approved draft; she had already made the point once that it was her idea. Had she overdone it? How much of an edge had she allowed into her voice as she said it the second time? Overwrought and frantic with anxiety, she began going over the speech again in her head; the clarity of recollection she desperately sought eluded her. She scarcely took in anything of the jobsearch hub IT representative's demonstration and screenshots of the website; an aspect of the launch which she had been keenly anticipating, observing people's reactions. Zara was an engaging speaker who elicited a few laughs from the audience when the power point technology did not quite work as expected. Diane wished that she could have concentrated well enough to share in that as she knew it would have been entertaining; freely amusing with no cringe factor, unlike her interview anecdote. Had she truly been brave and altruistic to include that story, or did it come into the category of oversharing and making people uncomfortable? She reminded herself that Verena had approved it. Of course she had! She must have gotten a kick out of it!

She needed to get a grip on these angry thoughts before they showed on her face and got her into bother. Verena was now taking questions; the rattle of clean cups and saucers being brought in at the back of the conference room foreshadowed the informal networking session to come. Diane had been looking forward to that too; she enjoyed catching up with their various contacts and today she should have been doing so in triumph. Instead, she was tired. There was a newly blasted hole in the structure of how today should have felt; caught in the creeping shockwave of unfiltered autistic emotions, she desperately needed to get away and process it all. Back in their office, Arthur would be pottering around making the most of the peace and quiet in between phone calls; Diane would have given anything to be sitting with him having a cup of tea and listening to his stories about golfing or fishing. In the conference room, the carpet now seemed to have an iridescence verging on the psychedelic; at the beginning of the launch it had simply been dark blue with a pattern in shades of cream and gold. Now, it shimmered and undulated like a warped fairground funhouse illusion, disorientating her and straining her eyes. Each cup rattling on its saucer pebbledashed her ears with machine-gun sharp slivers of sound.

Recognising that a hot drink would nonetheless help, Diane joined the queue, which was mercifully short. The tea urn was almost empty; it sputtered and splashed as she tried to manoeuvre herself out of the way of the droplets, awkward with her notes still under her arm and no space wide enough to set them down. She did not even register the presence of the woman approaching her until the cup was abruptly pulled out of her hand.

"What the...?!"

Diane jumped with fright, her notes slithering to the floor despite her best efforts. The woman, whom she recognised as being involved in an Integrations role in the learning disability sector and a regular fixture at networking events, spoke slowly and loudly leaning into her personal space.

"It's all right, pet, I'll do it for you. You're having such a struggle there and I don't want you to burn your hands."

Diane flinched away; the smell of the woman's breath was one sensory input too many. She didn't even have bad breath; it was merely too close and too intrusive.

"Couldn't you have asked me first rather than snatch things out of my hands? The urn is nearly empty and there's nowhere to put my notes down, that's all! This is what I get for admitting I'm autistic on stage! I'm not helpless; I wish people would ask before touching me or grabbing things from me, and not shout in my face. There's a difference between discreetly offering to help in a constructive, respectful way and confiscating someone's autonomy; judging them as less than you for needing a bit of extra time or for looking ungainly. I wish people would listen to me about how mentally damaging these belittling actions are."

Having finished filling the cup, the woman turned back to her, looking through her with eyes already glazed over in wilful dismissal of the points she was making. "Silly girl", she tutted, shaking her head with a patronising laugh as she stepped once more into the personal space Diane had reclaimed whilst the woman was ostentatiously performing her good deed for the day.

"Please don't crowd me; you're too close and it's extremely uncomfortable!", Diane urged her. Electricity began to arc through the icy prickle of adrenalin as the dark swell of shutdown fought the rearing crimson magma of meltdown; ripping open her façade with livid wounds as she clung to the fraying thread of her scripted pleas for the listening and acceptance which she feared would never come.

"I'm trying to help you; you were all fingers and thumbs there, weren't you! You clearly can't manage for yourself;

11

accept it and don't be ungrateful. See, there you go, dear; watch now, it's hot. Can you manage to take hold of it? Don't drop it!"

"Please lower your voice and give me space!"

The woman - Brenda Culper, that was the name Diane's memory was trying to grasp - followed her as she backed away, pushing the cup towards her, still jabbering "Here! Here!"; her shrill words needle-sharp. The barrage of condescension, assumptions about her capabilities and refusal to hear her, on top of the by now physical pain of being talked at loudly and at such close quarters while putting pressure on her, plus the sting of how inadequate she obviously appeared were all too much. This could not happen with Verena in the same building. How was she ever going to prove herself to her idol now; why did this have to happen today, when she was meant to feel good enough in herself for once? She no longer wanted the tea; not when she hadn't managed the basic task of getting it for herself without someone staging an intervention, not to mention thinking she looked as though she needed to be told that liquid newly poured from a heated urn right in front of her would be hot. Still backing away as her stress level rose, things were about to get even worse; Diane temporarily forgot her cardinal rule of never stepping back without looking and collided with someone. Her tormentor's eyes widened with judgemental horror.

"Ooh, CAREFUL!"

Brenda Culper's hands were coming at her yet again. All Diane's life it had been this way; hands coming at her because she had failed, because she was clumsy and awkward, not quick enough, not doing what was expected or in the approved way, not like normal people. Her much needed bubble of personal space; the air she could breathe unmolested shrank to nothing. She could not breathe.

"NO! Please back OFF!"

Still the hands came at her. Diane put out her own hand to stop the invasion of her space; her sole chance of preventing a meltdown right here in front of whoever was watching. She was dimly aware of her fingers glancing off the cup, splashing tea over the pristine carpet. Gasping an apology to the gathering spectators hoping that it would register with the person with whom she had collided, she turned and fled the social area. Grabbing her bag and jacket, she did not even stop to wrap that comforting suede around herself as she ran out of the hotel; her speech lay abandoned under her colleagues' feet.

2

Fresh air. No more harsh lighting; no air conditioning; most importantly, nobody anywhere near her. Diane could breathe again; the threatening meltdown was averted, for now anyway. She had bought enough time to get herself safely home. Once there, the events of the day would come crashing down on her; that hung inexorably in her future, a darker cloud across the grey East Coast sky. The traffic and bustle of Dundee buzzed in the background, impersonal and unthreatening in a space big enough to accommodate it. Crossing the road to the wide, sweeping entrance of the railway station, Diane paused to put on her jacket as the chill of the breeze straight off the North Sea began to register. Getting her ticket and Railcard out of her meticulously organised handbag after having used her hand sanitiser, she smiled at the gateline supervisor in relief as the barrier opened without a hitch; another awkward issue, in public at that, would have been too much. Fortunately her home station, twenty minutes up the coast in the small town of Inverbrudock, did not yet have this additional stress factor. As she descended the escalator from the soaring glass-roofed concourse, someone was playing the piano which had recently been installed for public use; she smiled at him too as the melody swirled around her. His music was brightening her day and he had not seen her fail. She had a clean slate with every one of these strangers around her; they were letting her be and her wounded soul loved them for it.

The ScotRail Inter7City high speed train glided between the high brick walls into Dock Street Tunnel, its power cloaked in its pragmatically confident diesel purr. Being cradled and whisked homeward in its warm interior with its gentle colours and the friendly swish of its interconnecting carriages calmed Diane's fraught mind with each mile it put between her and the event which ought to have been so validating for her. She knew she would have to face updating her social media before too long; her friends would be expecting it and the longer she stayed quiet, the more they would begin to feel concerned. She got out her phone, took it off the silent setting and tried to think what she could bring herself to write. The guard checking her ticket briefly distracted her; fortunately it was one of the regulars who knew that there was no need to ask her if she needed help because of her Railcard, which always made her feel exposed and belittled. She recognised that this was internalised ableism and that the staff were trained to ask this when someone had a Railcard; at the same time, she always prayed that they would be discreet and that they would accept her answer. Surely she was not in the wrong, as some people insisted she was, for not wanting it to be disclosed in front of other passengers that there was something different and potentially vulnerable about her? She understood that having the option of keeping her disability private at all and having any choice in who else got to know and when was in itself an example of privilege; many disabled people had no chance of hiding their vulnerability and had to face the associated ableism and security risks all the time. Still, awareness of privilege should not negate anyone's right to confidentiality. Today, she was glad that the guard assumed she had been out for a jaunt around the shops in Dundee; she did not enlighten him as to why she had really been in the city. By the time she managed to bring her mind back to thinking what to put on her status update, the train was pulling into Arbroath; with a mere five minutes between there and Inverbrudock, this was where she always packed away anything she had taken out of her bag during the journey in readiness for getting off. Her update would have to wait a little longer.

There would be all the usual things to do at home after having been out; in any case she was not quite ready to face the flat she had left feeling so happy and excited hours earlier. Once she was in the sanctuary of her own home and had done everything she needed to, the emotions and overwhelm of the day would take some time to deal with. Although she didn't drink alcohol when feeling so fragile, the Fulmar's Nest with its big first floor bay windows overlooking the sea was highly appealing. She could have a cup of tea there, served in their lovely neat well-made teapots which held enough for a still warm top-up and did not dribble all over the table. She was safe there; she would savour her tea which she would be allowed to pour for herself as the adult she was and would not make a cackhanded hash of it. The thought spread through her, easing her mind the way the tea would soon soothe her stressed and aching stomach as she walked thankfully through the still sea air, inhaling the subtle seaweed tang of home.

The stairs up to the Fulmar's Nest always smelled vaguely of cigarette smoke since the law had changed requiring those who wished to smoke to come outside, where they inevitably congregated as near as possible to the doorway in deference to the Scottish weather. Even as the wind whipped the tendrils of smoke into nothingness, traces of tobacco scent found their way into the dark wood panelling of the stairwell; a faint memory of the olden days. With the actual eye-stinging smoke in a confined space no longer an issue, Diane liked the subtle aroma. She never used the lift which had been installed at the other end of the building to spare elderly and disabled people the slight of having to use the service lift; it was often discreetly suggested to anyone who may be unsteady on the stairs at the end of the night that they use the lift but Diane had never been in that situation. It was a secret joy she hugged to herself whenever she came here; that this was one rare but reliable scenario in which she was not the one being assessed for whether or not she was capable and could make her own choices. If people chose to drink to the extent that they would be advised - with good reason - to use the lift rather than the stairs, that was up to them, so Diane felt no guilt about appreciating not being on the receiving end for once. The frustration caused by people's reactions to that indefinable otherness she apparently projected irrespective of how responsibly and effectively she was going about her business had to be balanced out somewhere. She had no moral qualms over alcohol; in fact she enjoyed it too much to ever let it become a problem and she quite simply detested the sensory aspect of drunkenness and hangovers after a few misjudgements in her full time working days when the pressure had become too much. She had always been trying to keep up with colleagues in the city, often drinking more than she meant to not deliberately for the alcohol content but to give her something to do instead of merely sitting there as the conversation swirled around her like that long ago cigarette smoke. Background noise plus social anxiety was the worst combination for her auditory processing; by the time she pieced together what had been said, thought of a reply or contribution and painstakingly filtered it for any possible offence or unintended amusement, the conversation would invariably have moved on. She had been labelled as quiet, mousey Diane for over a decade despite the depth and breadth of her thoughts, the vastness of her empathy and emotions and the frequent noisy chaos of her inner world. Although, to her mortification, she would still at times experience what she now knew to be situational mutism (a much more accurate and fair description than "selective mutism" which implied a deliberate choice) and be unable to form words, those fractiously camouflaging working days were long gone. So, sadly, was her relationship with her family since she admitted that she could not cope, began seeking her autism diagnosis and embarked upon the long battle to claim disability benefits before her savings ran out. Paying rent to her parents for the flat in which they had invested, benefit rules dictated that because she had close relatives as her landlords she could not claim any state help with that upon being medically advised to leave her job. It had been made clear to her that she was not welcome either to stay in the Arbroath flat or return to the family home in Stirling if she was going to live on benefits. The only help her parents would give her was to provide a letter to the council confirming that she had to leave their property. After accepting her tenancy, she had looked once out of curiosity and seen her parents' flat advertised for rent; her emotions had been so chaotic then, she could barely sort through and name each feeling and hadn't known whether to laugh or cry at the terse, all too familiar "No DSS" caveat. As far as she could recall, she had ended up doing a bit of both. A case worker at a local advice centre who happened to be autistic himself had helped her through the soul destroying process of claiming her benefits, dredging up her very worst moments as examples; Diane knew that she was incredibly lucky to have sourced such well-informed support as she faced her greatest flaws and darkest memories right when she most needed to be strong and positive in order to build herself a new life. She was profoundly aided in this by the liberating answers and vindication which her diagnosis brought her, to the extent that she quietly celebrated the anniversary of the date on which it was confirmed she was autistic. The privilege of getting relatively quick access to this enlightening process and support to rebuild her life was one reason why she was keen to do what volunteering she could in order to give back and help others; this was what today should have been about. She was so ready for that pot of tea.

Helen was wiping down tables in the almost empty pub as Diane walked in; her dark brown hair, marginally too short to tie back, tucked neatly behind her ears as she worked. Two older men sat at the bar and a young couple who looked like students pored over the small ads in a magazine in the corner.

"Hey there! Red or white today?"; Helen glanced at her watch; "Or perhaps amber?"

Diane laughed. "Hey, Helen. Actually brown this time if you don't mind; I'm gasping for a lovely pot of tea!"

"No problem at all; I'll bring it over to you. It was your website launch today, wasn't it?"

"That's right. It was pretty well received, though it was announced as somebody else's idea!"

"Oh, you're kidding? You've put so much effort into that! I remember when you first got the go-ahead; I had to reload a few of the optics sooner than I'd expected to that week!"

"Ha! Yes, I remember that day well. This place hadn't long reopened and it was still restricted to table service. I think you said you were getting your exercise for the week! Everybody was so happy to have some sense of things getting back to normal; not having to wear masks everywhere and keep such strict social distancing. It truly was a new era."

"It was that. I had to double-check that the hand sanitiser dispensers were well stocked in case we ran out of whisky and you started buzzing the alcohol in that!"

Diane offered up silent thanks for Helen's good-natured, funny banter and simultaneous lack of any awkward questions as to why she was drinking tea today of all days instead of celebrating with a few drams as she had before. Helen also knew her well enough to know that she would want to pay for her tea immediately rather than settle up as she left; the fear of her executive functioning failing her in public made her terrified of walking out and forgetting to pay. Once she had paid, she could relax. She put the money on the bar as Helen finished wiping the tables and came around to see to her order.

"So I hope you did still get to do your presentation?"

"Oh yes, I did that; in fact I ad-libbed a couple of times about it having been my idea, so there might be an awkward conversation next time I'm in Dundee! It was Verena who suddenly decided to say that this began with Sally, another one of the team who is a friend of hers, and got her up on stage. It's so sad because at first I got on well with Verena; it's not an anti-autism thing, she knew that about me from the start and was so excited to have an autistic volunteer bring their life experience. She said that anything she could do to make things better or easier for me, she would. Oh, obviously I know that anyone can say the correct things and not necessarily follow them through by their actions, but she always checked with me things like if the light was too bright or if anything noisy was going to be a problem, until she had enough of an idea of my tolerance levels not to need to ask. She once asked the chairman of the Council to take the batteries out of a ticking clock in a meeting I was at! I used to like ticking clocks but they do bother me more now. She used to look so proud when I got up to speak at events. As time went on, she's changed towards me. It's hard to pin down exactly what it is that's changed; she's still surface friendly but now it feels as though that's all it is. It's like the more she gets to know me, the more she sees me on my bad days when I'm slow and clumsy and not so smiley and don't say 'I'm fine' convincingly enough when people ask me how I am, the more she wants to put distance between us. I wouldn't have expected her to give somebody else credit for my work, though. She's too good for that; she doesn't do mistakes. If she says it, she means it; if it hurts, she intends it to or I deserve it to."

"Hmm. I don't know, Diane; she sounds a bit shallow and showy to me. I bet she does make mistakes but does a good job of glossing over them. Look, I don't know this woman and it's not my place to judge her but I've been in the bar trade for long enough to know what a fair weather relationship of any sort looks like, and this doesn't sound like a manager who has your back. I don't like what she's done to you today; you did not deserve that. Now, you relax and enjoy your tea and don't let anyone take away from what you've achieved. It's going to help so many people, remember that!"

"I know it will; I honestly am excited that it's going ahead and that's the important thing. Thanks, Helen; I'll be sitting over there by the window."

Helen was right; she must be happy that the website was going to help people, she knew that. Internally she chided herself for caring more about getting the glory than about the good the project would do. Well, she reasoned with herself, it wasn't that she cared more; it simply made her feel more intensely because of how much Verena's approval meant to her. Helping others gave her an incentive and purpose, but the prospect of being in Verena's good books and of being around the buzz she created gave her the adrenalin rush which beat back the constant fatigue enough for her to get going and work towards that purpose. Pouring the much anticipated cup of tea, she savoured its calming, grounding warmth as she took out her phone and typed her overdue status update; all about being in a whirl of happiness and excitement about the website becoming a reality and the good it would do. If only she could convince the hollowness in her chest to catch up with her online sentiments.

Returning the empty teapot, milk jug and cup to the bar, Diane waved goodbye to Helen as she set off on the ten minute walk home. She had maxed out her coping and performing skills today; the payment would be taken in a tidal wave of exhaustion, mental replays and emotion once she was back in the privacy of home. As she put her key in the door, visions sprang to mind of TV commercials involving people coming in from stormy weather; effortlessly discarding coats and baggage, switching the kettle on and flopping onto cosy sofas with their refreshment securely held in evenly-hued nimble fingers which gloves had made a perceptible job of protecting from the cold. She chuckled sarcastically as she envisaged their unfeasibly dry and immaculately styled hair - no stubbornly soaked fringes or ends escaping hats and scarves - and relaxed, camera-friendly smiling faces. How luxurious if her reality could be like that; coming home, however much the day's activities had depleted her, was merely the start of all the unpacking, checking and sorting she needed to do in order that the next day would not hold the pressure of feeling behind schedule from the off. She rarely had a hot drink within an hour of coming in even on the bitterest of days; if she made one before she got everything else done, it would be left to go cold. Today, she staunchly reminded herself, it was merely grey and unremarkably chilly; the tea which she had already drank still bathed her fraught nerves in silken warmth. She gave thanks for it lubricating the raw, grating shift as she faced the transition from her outer, thinly coping self to its inexorably rising, clamouring inner counterpart.

A long, raucous yowl melted into a torrent of purring as Farolita ran to wind herself around Diane's ankles. The backed up tears were already threatening as she scooped up her cat, burying her face in her ivory and slate grey fur. Blue point Siamese cats were not exactly ten a penny in Inverbrudock and when Diane came across one rubbing against the meagre warmth of a lamp post on one of her twilight walks eighteen months earlier, she thought at first that she was imagining things. The insistent miaows as the whip-slender young cat looked pleadingly up at her, the glow of the streetlight reflected in her ice-blue eyes, soon convinced her otherwise. Accepting the strokes tenderly and cautiously offered by Diane's outstretched hand, rubbing her face against it before looking up at her again with a plea for help in those captivating eyes, the cat had trotted off towards nearby bushes. Stopping to turn around and cry again, she had given Diane the impression that she needed her to follow; her suspicions as to why a cat like this had ended up outside apparently fending for itself were given credence as the cries of her single surviving kitten reached her ears and her heart from under the shrubbery. Taking off her scarf and wrapping up the tiny scrap of grey fur safe and warm, her walk was abandoned for that day as she turned back homewards, the mother cat following her softening the evening chill with relieved purring. Maria the vet had shared her suspicion that the mother cat had most likely been abandoned after escaping and becoming pregnant; with experience of having had Siamese cats in the family home when she was a child, Diane had agreed to foster her and her kitten with a view to adopting them both if the owner was not traced. No blue point Siamese cat was registered at the practice and the mother cat was not microchipped but checks had to be made on national missing pet sites in case she had climbed into a vehicle somewhere else. In honour of Maria's Spanish heritage and the respectful, reassuring and never patronising guidance she gave as Diane nursed her charges back to health, once she was given the all clear to adopt them she had them neutered and microchipped. She named the mother cat Farola; "streetlight" in Spanish, since her eyes would always remind Diane of the lamplight in which she so loved to walk. The diminutive nickname Farolita, translating as "little streetlight" or "little lantern", soon became the name by which she was known. She named the kitten Luz; Spanish for "light". She intended to keep him too but on one of Des and Jason's visits to help with socialising him, the kitten had scrambled up onto Jason's shoulder and snuggled against his ear as a periodic recurrence of pain from the childhood infection which had taken its toll on his hearing flared up. Seeing the fuzzy grey bundle of unconditional love rubbing his pixie face against Jason's smooth dark skin, Diane knew instantly where the kitten belonged. Preferring the clarity of a name with a hard consonant in it, with her blessing Jason renamed him Luke; as soon as the kitten was old enough Diane had updated the details on his microchip and with the vet practice and he had moved to his new forever home. Both cats were frequently taken to visit the other household, enhancing the depth of the bond between the friends.

Enjoyable though they were to recall, the happy memories were superseded by the more pressing matter of food. Setting the wriggling but still purring Farolita gently down on the laminate kitchen floor, Diane washed her hands then mashed up a sachet of cat food in her bowl, changed her drinking water and topped up the kibble. Her own stomach still jangling with stress, she braced herself to scoop out the used cat litter from the tray in the hall, taking in the balancing sensory benefit of a further thorough hand wash under warm soapy water. Whatever it was about the flow of gently cleansing water over her skin, in the same way as the shower often did, it finally released the looming backlog of tears. Hanging her head over the sink as waves of shame broke over her, she could no longer put off reliving the ugly incident with Brenda Culper; the claws of amplified flashback sharpened and acid-tipped with the preceding hurt which had set her up to crash and burn.

Verena.

All these months of hard work and build-up; all the dazzling smiles as she gave updates on her research and added to her original idea, building in safeguards, potential selling points and accessibility considerations. All of the crumbs Verena had thrown her way; always conveying that she was in with a chance of the reciprocal friendship she craved, if only she could do a little bit more; reach a little bit higher; be that bit less who she was and more who she

24

wanted to be. How far had she set herself back today? Had Verena been one of the shocked, cringing onlookers as she unravelled, her illusions of progress and equality shattered in the brutal reality of coming unstuck on something so mundane as getting herself a hot drink? On this day too; her day, for which she had worked as hard as her fatigue would allow? She could scarcely begin to imagine how she was supposed to talk about today with her friends, whose replies to her forced out status update must surely be coming in by now. Both explaining and pretending were beyond her; the remaining option was silence, and that cut her off even further from whatever "right" was meant to feel like.

As her tears subsided, she drank some water then made her way on trembling legs to the small, green tiled bathroom where she washed and moisturised the tender skin of her face. The sight of the miniature bottle of whisky she had set out beside her special occasion crystal glass, in her glass-fronted living room corner unit safe from home alone feline interaction, made her swollen eyes well up again; she turned away, sensibly leaving it untouched for the better time she knew would eventually follow. She always bounced back from these hurts and humiliations; after all, what other choice did she have? For now, she busied herself heating some soup and plating up a portion of oatcakes to give herself an easy, nourishing meal; undemanding TV viewing with Farolita on her lap would fill the rest of her evening as well as allowing her enough space to reply briefly to any comments or messages which required it. She could always attribute her sparse words to a combination of tiredness and her pet's insistence on catching up on several hours' worth of attention. Kissing the cat's silky head, she thanked and affectionately apologised to her for the scapegoating; even the snuggles she got in return felt fraudulently obtained.

25

3

Waking up the day after a crisis was in some ways worse than the crisis itself. There were those merciful few moments filled with no more than the warmth of her chestnut-brown and gold leaf patterned duvet and the unmissable sound of a Siamese cat wanting breakfast, which was enough sensory input in itself first thing in the morning; as Diane stirred to get up and attend to the food, kibble and water, everything else began to slither back into place. Cold tendrils of recollection squeezed around her heart and into the pit of her stomach as resentment prickled in her throat; this was how she had felt in the past after she had said and done things she regretted on those work nights out which she handled so badly, drinking too much, getting emotional in front of the wrong people and staying in situations which were toxic to her. She had learned from that time and put it behind her; yesterday should not have left her with that old familiar creeping shame. She was due the next of her fortnightly sessions with Wilma, her counsellor whose accredited details had been passed to her by a local contact, in two days' time; the thought of telling her about the way the launch event had ended for her made Diane feel queasy. Wilma had a tendency to see everyone else's point of view except her client's. Considering different perspectives was one thing, but Diane was often left with a feeling that Wilma considered her wrong by default and had come to be automatically biased in favour of anyone who hurt or annoyed her. She was beginning to suspect that Wilma resented her for being on benefits, perceiving her as thereby having an "easier" life than someone who was going out to work at a job which included helping her as a client. Her volunteering had certainly appeared to improve the general atmosphere at the sessions and on the few occasions when she had needed to take a break for a few weeks, there had been a distinct undercurrent of scepticism and pressure. Diane would have been happy to bring the sessions to a close; her life now that she had fully settled in Inverbrudock was much more manageable because she had a stable routine without the demands of full time work making her ill. She had good friends, was invested in making a contribution through volunteering as and when she could and had enough time and energy left over to manage looking after herself, her cat and her home. The trouble was, any loss of that stability and safety would instantly see her mental and physical health deteriorate, yet if the periodic review of her benefits suggested that her health had improved it would bring about that destructive change. She kept up the sessions with Wilma for the times when things inevitably did go wrong and for when her mood lowered and she wanted to talk it through with someone who was not a friend, therefore would not be burdened or upset. Even though the sessions often left her feeling worse, she knew that to stop them would look on paper as though she no longer had the same level of need.

Farolita stretched out contentedly on the cappuccino-coloured carpet washing her paws as Diane settled on one of her two matching rust coloured two-seater sofas with a strong cup of coffee and a light breakfast of cereal bars. The sun shone in through the wooden blinds which she kept slightly angled to brighten the room without the light being too harsh. Her original battered three-seater sofa, part of a starter pack when she got the tenancy from the council after the breakdown of her relationship with her parents, had stood along the back wall of the compact living room opposite the window with an armchair at the side opposite the TV. She now had her two smaller low-backed sofas opposite one another so that Jason could lipread more easily when he and Des came round. A second hand wicker chair, draped in a throw in muted shades of orange to protect the chair from cat claws, stood at right angles to the sofa which had its back to the TV so that the three of them could just as easily sit and watch a programme or a football match. Although she struggled to concentrate watching sport on her own, Diane loved watching the brothers' Chelsea or Aberdeen games with them. The structure, set amount of time and lack of requirement for constant conversation made it a particularly helpful thing to share when her social energy was low; watching anything on TV with them, she found that having the subtitles on for Jason helped her too as it lessened the fatigue of auditory processing. She chuckled to herself remembering the time Chelsea had played a televised friendly against Sunborough and Des had taken a swig of lager at the exact moment when she said that the other team was doing so much diving they were going to need a decompression chamber in the tunnel. Des had splurted out his drink laughing; Jason had not caught on as he was watching the screen and when Des repeated it and showed him the droplets on the coffee table as she went to get a cloth, he had laughed until he got the hiccups. During half time, they had all been doubled over laughing again as Jason speculated as to whether the opponents would come back out in wetsuits. Chelsea had won; she remembered that much. These happy times were what she wanted to focus on; what she wanted people to know her for and associate her with. Arthur had thoroughly appreciated that story; she would rather eat raw tripe than even contemplate telling it to the exalted Verena.

Verena. Every thought seemed to be leading back to her. She wanted Verena to see the best of her; to see whatever it would take to make her promote Diane into her inner circle of true friendship alongside the likes of Sally Howe. She had no wish to bring Verena into her personal life but if she were to keep on going out into an often incompatible world, all year round in all weathers to volunteer enough to make a real impact, she needed the energy rush which the prospect of earning her praise always brought. Verena was the light and the incentive she needed to pick herself up and go back into the fray after glitches such as what happened with Brenda Culper; to do enough, regardless of her fatigue and brain fog, to forgive herself for being on benefits and for her life being better than before despite her past mistakes. She must keep doing enough to stave off the constant fear that karma was going to catch up with her and force her back into the hell of full time unsupported working life, cutting her off from the beneficial interaction with her friends with whom she would become too drained and depleted to spend any meaningful time.

Today had been set aside for recovery time after the launch, which even if it had gone to plan would have left her tired and spaced out for a while afterwards. With an inner jolt she realised that as far as the Up For Work Together project itself was concerned, it had indeed gone to plan; it was she who had been knocked off course and failed to recover. The website was launched, out there now and her colleagues had gotten everything out of the day that they would out of any successful event. Even Brenda Culper would no doubt remember an overall interesting and constructive day mildly and peripherally blighted by one strange episode with an awkward woman in the refreshments queue. Diane knew perfectly well that she was not the centre of anyone's universe; she had been told as much innumerable times. The upside of this; of the unimportance to anyone else of what had been such a huge personal setback for her, was that it did not harm her project itself nor change her involvement with it either historically in the planning or going forward with it up and running. She would soon be starting some online training to be one of the forum's volunteer moderators; a task which she could carry out at home, further increasing the breadth of her volunteering portfolio. She would not need to reduce or give anything else up in order to take that on. Being willing to become involved on an ongoing basis with the finished product had been a useful selling point in pitching her idea in the first place; it was noted and remarked upon favourably by Verena, which of course gave it added appeal for Diane as she prepared for what was still a significant change to her routine in tackling the online training. She doubted that there would be anything sent through as soon as today though; she had her much needed head space.

Padding through to the sunny kitchen, she washed her plate and made herself another coffee. As the kettle boiled, she looked out at the view over the trees towards the Brudock Burn and the Angus fields beyond. Perhaps later on she would take her favourite walk along Caberfeidh Road. The long, gently winding street was dotted on both sides with apple and wild cherry trees which held the kaleidoscope of changing seasons at a cellular level in distinctive, beautiful displays of blossom and colourful foliage; horse chestnut, rowan and Scots pine trees grew in many of the gardens which fronted it. Diane's favourite time to walk there was when the streetlights were coming on. The road still had the sodium lights which came on red and warmed to a rich orange, seeming to both contrast and complement the natural shades of the trees. Popular with dog walkers, it was a safe area and the walk always made her feel calm, grounded and mindful.

It had been one of the few enduring constants through the worst days of Covid lockdown and enforced change. Although Diane had never lost sight of how fortunate she was to have uninterrupted financial stability through her benefits and to have nobody cooped up with her at home, the stress of having to judge her distance from other people in a constantly shifting environment when she had to go out and the effects of the general ongoing uncertainty had taken a greater toll than she expected or felt she had any right to acknowledge. The demands upon her autistic processing of every familiar place looking different with new rules and directions left her overwhelmed with shame at her slowness in taking in those instructions, which the wider world perceived as clear and elementary. In addition to her own response to the utterly alien circumstances, she had struggled with heightened empathy about the vastness of others' distress combined with guilt at not being able to drive or manage phone calls well, narrowing her options for community volunteering. A daily routine of cleaning the entryphone panels and communal door handles in the flats where she lived and setting aside time each day to share verified and positive online information and to reply sensitively and encouragingly to posts by people feeling isolated had been her contribution. She was unable to feel that it had been enough; her sense of indebtedness to society was stronger than ever. She had found herself making mistakes and forgetting things more often, having expected that to diminish as the need to travel around was replaced by a much more simple and less time-intensive routine. No amount of evidence that other people were experiencing the same trends as a consequence of a pervasive "pandemic fatigue" infused throughout society could convince her that there was any mitigation in her own inner arraignment. Resuming her former activities had brought even more secret shame; it resembled learning from scratch how to be herself again as even loved and familiar activities became a displaced child's first day at school in a foreign land. She had feared that she would not be welcome in local businesses because her difficulty in judging distance and terror of being publicly chastised for getting it wrong, as well as not wanting to put others at risk or worsen the anxiety of people who were frightened of catching the virus, had kept her from supporting them when they first reopened with restrictions still in place, except for the Fulmar's Nest where she had felt safe enough because of having built up trust with Helen and the other staff. She had a lot of residual guilt to work through about that period of time; a lot of reacclimatising still to do. A day of reading and relaxing followed by her favourite walk was something she could still manage without having to think about it; exactly what she needed to refocus her energy.

Diane's tablet chimed with an incoming email as she was about to make her usual daily check of the news and weather apps. The name of Maurice Thurlowe in the From field; the branch manager, Verena's boss; surprised her viscerally almost as though he had actually walked uninvited into her home. It was unusual for him to contact a volunteer directly and Diane began to feel an uncomfortable quiver of apprehension. The message was brief and gave nothing away; he was asking her to come in for a meeting the next day, the single word "Meeting" forming the subject line of the email. If she could not attend, she was to get in touch with his PA; in the meantime she was instructed not to contact any other colleague.

This looked bad.

She had been accused of catastrophising many times; was she guilty of it yet again? A project had just been launched which grew from her idea; there had to be many positive reasons why a manager would request a meeting with her following on from that. Why, though, would she be told not to contact any other colleague and why was the meeting so urgent, managing by the narrowest of margins to give her twenty four hours' notice? The part about not contacting anyone was the most disturbing. It may be down to confidentiality without it being anything bad, she told herself. The worst part was not knowing. Uncertainty had always been something with which she struggled, especially when it meant she may be in trouble. However hard she tried to reason with herself and to give credence to a lifetime of being told that her perspectives including her gut instinct were at best unreliable and at worst plain wrong, every cell in her body was telling her that this summons was not good news and she was right to feel afraid. The sole good thing was that she had a single day, and no doubt sleepless night, to wait. There was nothing to be gained from asking for any clarification. Diane had long since resigned herself to the likelihood that her tone, even through the written word, becoming unintentionally harsh under stress as with many autistic people and the palpable urgency of her enhanced need for clear information about what lay ahead would see any query dismissed as impatience. Often the people who showed off the most about their progressive attitude to reasonable adjustments, cloaking what should be the baseline in an aura of ostentatious benevolence, were among the worst offenders for labelling disability traits as character flaws and fair questions, understandable anxiety or reasonable requests as challenging behaviour. "So much for having a relaxing day", she told the supine, sleepy-eyed Farolita as the cat stretched out with a soft responsive mew. Diane replied to the email with a single sentence confirming that she would be attending the meeting as requested, then swiped to delete Maurice Thurlowe's message with a shudder as though swatting away a germ-laden bluebottle.

Absorbing herself in TV crime shows, science documentaries and a thrilling mystery novel served to take her mind off the coming meeting, but for no more than short periods. Each time the awareness crashed back in on her was worse than the last. When the sky began to darken, for all it brought the fateful journey closer it still came as a relief as it was the time she had planned to take her walk. She fed Farolita before setting out, topped up the drinking water and kibble, then put on her trainers and her jacket and let herself out. Locking the door of her first floor flat, she walked down the enclosed but still draughty stone stairs to the outside door. Fresh air helped after the full day indoors; the softened atmosphere of twilight and the sound of her own footsteps lulled her into a soothing rhythm as she regulated her breathing and walked off in the direction of Caberfeidh Road. She had deliberately slowed down her walking pace in recent years after becoming so fed up of being teased, often by complete strangers, about how fast she walked. Some people did exaggerated impersonations right in front of her. Although she had always valued brisk walking as an easily accessible, healthy and free way of taking important exercise, the time had come when the demoralising frustration of being teased over and over about the same wretched thing which should not even be considered remarkable in the first place was too high a price to pay. She refused to overcompensate by adjusting her pace so far as to mooch along slowly gaining no fitness benefit at all, but walking more slowly than she was accustomed to did at least allow her more opportunity for mindfulness and relaxation as she took in her surroundings.

She had timed it well. The streetlights were coming on as she reached Caberfeidh Road; points of soft cherry red punctuating the grey dusk, marking out an orderly succession of moments ahead in silent, welcoming witness to her treasured routine. The trees were beginning to turn; the rich tones of autumn beginning their unhurried progress through the leaves, appearing to absorb the warm spectrum of brightening orange as the sodium lights went through their own nightly procession of colour. Some of the lamp posts gave off a subtle electrical hum at the very edge of Diane's hearing as she passed them; others a feeling of energy vibrating at a level which was just below being perceptible as sound. She acknowledged them one by one; not aloud, not counting, simply taking in the rise and fall of light as she travelled through them and noticing the individual lamps in turn. Right from her childhood, whenever Diane went to a place she had not been to before she looked at the streetlights. What shape the lantern part was; what the posts were made of; what colour they shone, or would be likely to once they came on if it was daylight when she arrived. There was something about the latticed network of ordered points of illumination which she found compelling; for her, they gave any scene an added dimension of life. Her close friends, acquainted with the aesthetic fascination which streetlights held for her would send her photographs whenever they went anywhere new. Diane was critical of the irritating tendency some people had to label anything mentioned with the slightest bit of enthusiasm by an autistic person as a "special interest", but she was happy to own this as one. Indeed, more than once when she had mentioned it to people they had acknowledged that they hadn't thought of streetlights as anything other than functional before but could see where she was coming from and appreciated the idea of finding beauty in something so prolific and mundane. It always brought her deep satisfaction to have enhanced someone else's day to day routine with her different way of looking at things.

At its far end, Caberfeidh Road gave way to a less interesting through route towards the tired end of the High Street where places to go were tapering off. A former newsagent's, now a betting shop, stood at the junction perhaps a hundred metres away. Diane rarely bothered to make it a circular walk and head home via the High Street unless she was calling in at the Fulmar's Nest, which she did not want to become so much of a habit that the walk would feel incomplete without it; she preferred to keep this physical exercise and mental grounding distinct in its own right. This was definitely not an evening for the pub. She turned back, pausing for a long look down the winding length of Caberfeidh Road, now fully lit by beacons of vivid orange as the trees kept their autumn colours on hold within their black silhouettes; the leaves and pavements patched with uniform gold where the glow of the streetlights reached. Once again the dread of tomorrow clutched at her insides as she began the walk home. At least she did not have the fear of losing a paid job, with all that would have implied for her financial security. With a substantial pang, she wondered whether she would ever even see Verena again.

Bedtime came around slowly. Diane envied the contented platinum curve of Farolita in her cream fleece cat bed as she walked past her on the way to turn in for the night. She did not expect to sleep but knew she should at least try. After hours of tossing and turning, playing word games in her head which often did the trick of sending her off, she punched her pillow and sighed with frustration. Tomorrow would be daunting enough without being fuzzy through lack of sleep as she faced the outside world and whatever was coming to her. She turned over yet again and began thinking of episode titles from 'The X-Files' beginning with successive letters of the alphabet.

She was in a sleek, modern building somewhere on the sea front. People were bustling about with folders and clipboards, evidently engaged in some kind of high powered office work but she had the sense that it was late at night. A deep fiery sunset was painting the sky uniformly red; she could see people dressed up for a smart evening do congregating on an observation deck in front of floor to ceiling glass to watch it. She must not get distracted; she had to find the person she was meant to be meeting. Their name and position and why she was meeting them were hazy; hovering somewhere just outside of her grasp. She had to get to a different floor to meet them but she could not see any stairs or other means of getting away from the level on which she was currently. Verena was standing beside a group of opulent fawn and cream leather sofas, talking to some other people who looked like managers; they wore dark coloured suits while Verena looked like Alexis Carrington from 'Dynasty' in a sequinned black cocktail dress. Diane was reluctant to interrupt but Verena was the one person she could see whom she recognised. Trancelike, she glided over to her.

"Verena!"

There was no response. Her idol continued her conversation, oblivious to Diane's ephemeral presence.

"Verena! I'm so sorry to interrupt, but I need your help! I need to get to the meeting room but I can't find any way to get off this level!"

The people with whom Verena was in conversation were beginning to register her intrusion; several of them turned to look in her direction as Verena continued with whatever she was saying. One lady, her face a study in incredulity, raised an elegantly manicured hand with deep scarlet nails to point to a suddenly obvious bank of lifts.

"Right there, dear! Can't you even see the sign?"

Diane began to stammer out an apology; not to the lady who had directed her but to Verena, who had finally turned around. Shaking her head, she simply said her name: "Diane"; both syllables heavy with contempt. The lead crystal of her scathing enunciation weighed down Diane's identity like icicles testing a weakened gutter; she turned and fled towards the lifts.

Over by the glass wall, her attention was caught by something happening in the water. Clear globes apparently made of some kind of plastic bobbed on the gentle waves, each translucent sphere was filled with lights. They were all imaginable colours; a silent festival of all the primary and secondary hues in various shades plus endless permutations. Teal, violet, cerise, peach, amber, chartreuse and aqua, even the spectral shimmer of that distinct purple marking the last outpost of visible light on the edge of ultraviolet, ebbed and flowed on the black nocturnal sea. The beauty of it caught at her soul, compelling her to stop and look despite the urgency of her situation. As some globes floated away out of sight, others washed closer to the shore. Diane's heart swelled with the emotion she had come to identify as "too muchness"; impossible to pin down to one category, it was a gestalt, intensely amplified response with everything from joy to deepest sadness, calling at all stations in between. She wanted to stay locked in place; unreachable in a crystal forcefield, among but untouched by these beautiful people who asked nothing of her, watching alongside her the dance of these captivating lights in the eternal flow of the sea. But she couldn't; she had to go. Aching and hollowed out inside, she wrenched herself away and resumed her quest to locate where she needed to be.

One of the lifts arrived as she got to them, its Up arrow illuminating. This was good; this would get her on track to find the elusive meeting room. The doors opened and a couple of people got out, leaving the lift empty. She got in, turning to see other people hurrying over intending to get in. Panicked, she whirled around looking for the panel of buttons to find the one to hold the doors open for them; the buttons all had symbols which she could not understand and did not appear to correspond logically to any door operation or floor selection. The doors slammed closed as the prospective passengers shouted out indignantly at her; before she could make any more sense of the buttons, the lift began to descend rapidly. Down and down, not in freefall but faster than any ordinary lift had any right to be. Heading in the wrong direction for her meeting was not even an issue any more; she had been descending faster and for longer than was remotely feasible from the few storeys above ground where she got in. What was this; where in the world, or out of it, was she going to end up?

Diane awoke with a tidal wave of shock. So she had slept after all. She often had vivid dreams but that one was a belter. Most of the symbolism was obvious, but those mystical spheres of light! She felt an unaccountable ache of loss, knowing that the idyllic scene which had so moved her was not real and not something to which she could ever choose to return. Steadying her breathing and swallowing the lump in her throat, she got up, switching off the alarm which was no longer necessary. Yawning and stretching, she rubbed her eyes as she walked through to the kitchen accompanied by Farolita who was surfing her own wave of feelings in typically loud, vocal Siamese fashion; the desire for petting and pleasure at seeing her human awake competing with the associated allure of breakfast. This was one area where Diane could deliver on all counts; smiling at this therapeutic truth, she gave her cat an extra hug before going about the business of feeding them both. That was the easy part; now, the rest of her day remained to be faced.

4

Pale grey light made barely perceptible shadows on the platform as Diane waited for her train to Dundee. The sun was trying its hardest to break through but the clouds were winning the battle. The three-carriage commuter train was busier than she was comfortable with for this particular journey; people too close to her felt like a sandpaper wrap even if they were not touching her when she was out in stressful circumstances, more so now that she had become unaccustomed to coping with it through the era of social distancing. Reminding herself once again that nobody could be expected to know how she was feeling and it was nobody else's problem, she nodded to the lady who got on at Arbroath and took the seat next to her, warning her in advance that she would need to disturb her to get out at Dundee if she were going further than that. Wrapping her suede jacket tighter around herself, she was thankful that the lady did not try to draw her into any further conversation; there were times when she enjoyed chatting to people on her travels but this was not one of them. She needed all of her resources to cope with the meeting.

The building where Up For Work had its Dundee base looked different somehow as Diane walked up to the front door. Outwardly it looked exactly the same, but it seemed as though an invisible netting of barbed wire had been strung around it since she was last there. The familiar light brown stone had an indefinable hint of menace as she steeled herself to turn left towards the branch manager's office instead of right to her accustomed, more relaxed work space where Arthur would be making his mid-morning cup of tea round about now. Gisela, Maurice Thurlowe's PA, greeted her with practiced efficiency; her navy suit and cream blouse model-perfect, making it remarkable to think that there was a living being moving around in the pristine shell they formed. She was civil but her smile appeared not quite to reach her impeccably shadowed eyes. Whenever Diane was in a formal setting like this, the memory of an encounter almost ten years ago when she had less experience of reading the subtleties of workplace conversation would come back to taunt her. Asking a highly elegant PA whom she had not met before how she kept her collar so free of foundation had felt like a "normal" woman to woman topic to bring up; the frisson of unspoken shock and disapproval had as it so often did taken her by surprise, leaving her to figure out for herself where she had gone wrong. She never again asked a personal question out of context with someone she didn't know, but the misjudgement stayed with her; hanging around her, as she said when relating the story to Des after a few glasses of wine years later, like a fart in a taxi. Memories like this were definitely not helpful right now; Diane forced herself to push away both the hideous incident from her past and the cathartic, fuzzy-edged conversation with Des. She could not afford to be vulnerable to her self-doubt, nor could she risk a nervous bout of inappropriate giggling, if she were to give a good account of herself at this meeting and come through it with her dignity intact. She often wondered whether science would ever come up with a way of measuring quite how much energy autistic and other neurodivergent people used up every waking hour pushing away unwanted or forbidden thoughts and memories; that was before they even got as far as monitoring their tone of voice and facial expressions for acceptability to the rest of society.

Gisela called her to go through to Mr Thurlowe's inner office, her manner and voice giving nothing away. Diane recognised that this was Gisela's professionalism, not her own inability to read her; another of the many things into which she put so much mental effort was resisting the trap of attributing every issue, anomaly or mistake to autism. Even as the flicker of satisfaction at having remembered to filter despite the situation she was in came tentatively to her mind, she stamped that out too; any feeling of having done well carried a risk of dropping her guard and making a faux pas which would leave her worse off overall. With her energy and concentration focused on making her mind neutral, she bumped against the doorframe as she walked in; she had failed to leave enough resources free for proprioception, and Gisela's reflexive "Ooh!" in the background confirmed that she had not gotten away with it even as she registered the brief flare of disdain in Maurice Thurlowe's eyes. She heaved the frustration away with aching mental muscles.

"Sit down"; the manager did not bother to stand up or keep looking at her as he waved her towards the chair opposite his imposing mahogany desk. "Thank you, Gisela."

The door to the outer office closed, leaving Diane alone with her fate. Maurice Thurlowe shuffled some papers; somewhere outside the sound and vibration of a road worker's drill shattered china inside her head.

"So, I'm concerned and disappointed to hear that you had a physical altercation with one of our valued associates, Brenda Culper, at the event on Monday. I don't need to tell you that this is entirely unacceptable and highly embarrassing for Up For Work. Would you care to explain your actions?"

The floor seemed to drop away from underneath the rough grey plastic chair, leaving Diane spinning end over end as the worn sides chafed her gripping hands. A vision of the astronaut Frank Poole tumbling away into space after Hal 9000's malfunction in '2001; A Space Odyssey' swam incongruously into her mind. So it was as bad as she had feared. The horror of being in trouble and anticipating punishment churned acid-bright deep in her gut as the logic and verbal ability which she needed in order to advocate for herself threatened to dissolve.

"A… a physical altercation? Somebody's saying what, that I was in a fight?"

"I understand that you tried to knock a hot cup of coffee out of her hand because she was trying to help you and you didn't like it."

"It was tea!"

The factual correction was out of her mouth before her spiralling brain could catch up; Maurice Thurlowe's face darkened with fury.

"I'm sorry; of course that's beside the point. I'm just… I didn't try to knock it out of her hand! She was coming at me; being so loud and pushing it at me and I'd asked her three times to give me space but she wouldn't. I was on the point of a meltdown and I put my hand out to try to stop her. I couldn't breathe and she kept on coming at me!"

"Coming at you. How ridiculous. You were being clumsy and she was trying to help. Even if you didn't intend to make contact with the cup, you still flung your hand out towards her knowing she was holding hot liquid."

"I… Oh God, was she scalded?"

"Young lady, if she had been, this would be an entirely different conversation. I would have strongly encouraged her to press charges."

"Charges? With the police? But I didn't mean… I was just…"

"You have to realise that actions have consequences. You may be a volunteer, and I appreciate that you have, ah, issues, but you are a grown adult and responsible for what you do. You cannot go around throwing temper tantrums just because your pride is wounded or your feelings are hurt."

"An autistic meltdown is not a temper tantrum, Mr Thurlowe! I was trying to remove myself from the situation. I was physically trying to get away so that I would have

43

enough space for the overload to subside, but she kept following me, ignored my pleas for space and was thrusting the cup at me!"

"Oh, don't be so silly. You're nothing but a drama queen who thinks she's something special when she's not. The reality is you're a mere appendage to a highly qualified professional team. I am well aware that you also took umbrage at the initiation of the website project having been credited to Sally Howe, to the extent of deviating from the agreed text of your presentation."

"It WAS my idea!"

"And precisely how far do you think that idea would have gotten without Sally, who has the skills and connections to take it further?"

"I'm not disputing what Sally did and I appreciated it a lot, but that doesn't change the fact that it was my idea and I did a lot of the groundwork! What happened with Brenda was nothing to do with anything I felt about this; I've nothing against Sally! I rarely deliberately touch anybody, even my best friends but I gave her a huge hug when she got the go-ahead for us with the jobsearch hub. And by the way, I do not think I'm 'something special'. That is too much! I cannot cope with being accused of that when I feel the exact opposite!"

"So we're back to your hurt feelings again. You really are acting like a spoiled little princess."

"Mr Thurlowe, please be aware of your terminology here. You wouldn't call a man a spoiled little prince because his feelings ran high…"

"Oh, we're playing the female victim card in addition to the autism card now, are we? We might as well have the full deck on the table because I think we both know what your problem was on Monday, that you took out on Brenda Culper in such a reckless, dangerous and uncalled-for fashion. It wasn't about Sally getting the credit; it was about Verena not giving you the attention you want from her."

Diane began to think she might faint. The sting of the same old misinterpretations of her responses to overload as mere hurt feelings, vanity and thinking she was "special" faded into insignificance beside this full scale invasion into the most private reaches of her inner life. And "the full deck on the table"; what was he implying there? What "card" was he suggesting pertained to Verena?

"Don't imagine for a moment that any of us, including Verena, are unaware of your obvious fixation with her. Now, I don't care if you're that way inclined; it would make no odds to me if you chose to sleep with aliens from outer space. But Verena has the right to do her job without feeling uncomfortable because some silly little re... childlike female is mooning around with an obvious crush on her. In many ways we should have addressed this before now; political correctness has a lot to answer for, but it's high time we curtailed that indulgence. I am instructing you to take some time out; at least three months, after which we will review the situation in light of the work you have done and your input into the Up For Work Together project. Make no mistake, if you were a paid employee you would be being dismissed right now; if and when you do come back we will expect to be able to have full confidence that you have gotten over your immature infatuation with Verena. Is that understood?"

Diane pressed her fingertips to her temples, closing her eyes for a moment as she strove to process everything she had heard, knowing that Maurice Thurlowe was not about to allow her any extra time. The meaning of the gesture was evidently lost on him.

"Do not even think about turning on the waterworks."

The beige walls were closing in. She had to respond to something, to keep the dialogue open until she could frame the questions she needed to ask.

"Mr Thurlowe, what were you about to call me before?"

"I beg your pardon?"

"You changed it to 'childlike female', but you were going to say something else. I think it was 're' something. What were you going to say?"

"I chose not to say it, so it is none of your concern."

"That's all right; I think I can work it out anyway. Like 'regard' but with a T instead of a G. Am I in the right ballpark there? Whatever your own feelings about political correctness, you do know that's absolutely not OK? Anyway, I am much more concerned at being accused of being some sort of bunny boiler! I don't deny that I have hero-worshipped Verena James for a long time; it would be fair to say I idolise her, but to suggest that I have committed some kind of predatory offence against her? And with a sexual motive? I have never touched her, approached her outside of work, gone out of my way to hang around where she might be or given her gifts. I certainly haven't sexually propositioned her! I don't think of her in that way!"

Maurice Thurlowe held up his hand, distaste written all over his face. "As I said, your - predilections are of no concern and definitely no interest to me. Nobody is accusing you of any form of stalking, and I can assure you that our stance on this issue would be the same if it were a male colleague, so do not try to hide behind your rainbow flag. The fact is, you look and interact with an obvious devotion which Verena finds unsettling. It is not within the realms of criminal activity, but it is inappropriate in the workplace and she did not feel safe approaching you about it in case it did tip you over into stalking behaviour. It is well known that people with your particular problems have a tendency towards unhealthy attachments. It must be obvious to you that Verena would never reciprocate these feelings, whatever you want to call them. You have been blatantly foolish in letting it show and you have no-one but yourself to blame. Now, please leave the building and do not come back or make contact with any of the team until Gisela invites you to a further meeting."

"The training; what about my supervision for that? I'd be doing that at home, so…"

"What training are you talking about?"

"To become one of the moderators on the forum?"

"That will not be happening until I am satisfied you have learned to manage your volatile emotions and be professional."

"I'm an intense person; that's not a crime! You said yourself I haven't committed any offence! This is essentially about punishing me for, what, my private thoughts, or at least what other people have imagined them to be?"

"It's about Verena being uncomfortable with your pathetic puppy-dog adoration. I have told you not to attempt to make this a gay rights issue. Now, please…"

"I'm not talking about gay anything here! I'm talking about the fact this is based on nothing more than people's interpretation of my thoughts! Does Verena really hate me that much?"

"Hate you? You don't register on her radar enough for her to hate you. Now, go home, stop living in cloud cuckoo land and learn to behave like a normal adult."

"Like a non-autistic person, you mean? If I don't even register on her radar, why is she so bothered by me that I have to be thrown out like a sack of rubbish? Well, good luck with Up For Work Together, which you lot evidently think you can run successfully for neurodivergent people as long as you don't have to actually work with or be around any. You tell me I'm living in cloud cuckoo land? If you think that's going to go well with your attitude, you'd need a parachute to get back down to cloud cuckoo land from where you're living!"

"I will not tell you again; leave. Now."

Diane walked out on a tectonic shift of adrenalin; Gisela, who could not have failed to hear the raised voices, made a heroic job of appearing nonchalant for which Diane had to give her credit. She turned to thank and say goodbye to her.

"Arthur!"

The sudden thought had sucker-punched her right in her already bruised soul. Gisela looked up, puzzled.

"Sorry?"

"Arthur is retiring soon and I probably won't…"

Her poise began to waver; the dam was creaking; bulging from the pressure within. She had to get out of there.

"Could someone… please let me know how I can contribute, or may I leave something now for his collection? Will I be allowed to send a card?"

Hearing her voice, Maurice Thurlowe appeared in the doorway of his inner office. Gisela, a hitherto unseen compassion in her eyes, deftly stepped in between them and addressed her boss confidently.

"Diane was most thoughtfully enquiring as to how she may contribute to Arthur Douglas's retirement collection. She has worked closely with him for some time. I'm sure it will not be a problem for her to send a card to him here with a donation?"

The manager huffed, spots of red appearing on his cheekbones. "I suppose not, but right now, Ms Abercrombie is required to leave the premises without further communication with any personnel. See that she does, Gisela."

He watched as Gisela walked with Diane to the lobby, sensible not to touch her. "Use the Ladies' room if you need to", she said quietly. After the raging torrent of cruel words, it was this knowing, understated act of kindness that was Diane's undoing. Unable to look at Gisela as she gulped her thanks, she fled through the door next to the main exit and into the first cubicle where she could no longer hold back what Maurice Thurlowe had so sneeringly referred to as "the waterworks". The unmitigated awfulness of everything that had been said to her, the implications on so many levels, fought a churning war in the gnawing implosion of her insides with the knowledge that she still had to get herself home; to walk out on busy streets and use public transport.

She was a reckless lout who had almost become a violent criminal; the sort of person to lash out at somebody when they were holding a hot drink.

Everybody knew about how much Verena meant to her; something she had thought was more private. People were not only laughing at her and discussing her innermost feelings behind her back but reframing them to reflect their own understanding of attachment; entertaining a mental picture of her imagining a sexual relationship with Verena.

She was off the project which she had created, because she was too emotionally dysfunctional.

She no longer had a voluntary job to balance out being on benefits. Whatever Maurice Thurlowe was obliged to say, her coming back was not going to work out. Not after this humiliation.

She was seen as immature; childlike; a pathetic puppy-dog; a drama queen; a silly spoiled little princess living in cloud cuckoo land. Oh, and the other thing. The word she wouldn't say; the R word. She had no dignity. She had been deluding herself.

She was so insignificant that she didn't even register on the radar of people who meant the world to her and her ideas were nothing unless somebody else took them forward. What was the wording he had used? A mere appendage.

She was worthless.

She was nothing.

Carrying all of these revelations, she had to go outside where people could see her, in order to get home. And she had to do it now; she must not take advantage of the empathy Gisela had shown and risk getting her into trouble by remaining in the building for too long. Anyone would think by now she'd had enough time for a bit of a cry, a quick use of the toilet and to regroup. To somehow go on, despite the body blows she had been dealt. After all, she had no-one but herself to blame. Thinking herself through each step, she forced herself to fight the overwhelming need for stillness in which to process; a need which was rapidly growing towards a full shutdown. She must get out of the building.

Dundee still looked much as it had when she arrived; there was something off, something surprising about that. She felt, illogically, as though the world should look different. The thought of dealing with the journey home was still too much; she knew that she must look distressed and could not face anyone approaching her, even if they did it in the most gentle and respectful way. She reminded herself that she did not deserve respect; asking people to listen to her about her sensory overload or stop crowding her was spoiled brat behaviour. All she had needed during that episode at the launch event was a little bit more time and a little bit more space; the problems getting her drink were not even all to do with her autism. She was hampered by papers under her arm with nowhere to set them down; the urn was sputtering and taking longer as it was nearly empty. Yet asking for that time and space as opposed to having things pulled out of her hands and being loudly, relentlessly talked at when she was already in sensory overload was being a little princess. Her disability was merely wounded pride and hurt feelings. Her experiences counted for nothing. Which meant that she deserved no support; worse, she had nothing with which to support and empower others.

And she was walking along a city centre street in the middle of the day looking increasingly angry, tears still drying on her face.

"Cheer up, love; it can't be that bad! Give us a smile!"

50

Well, it was inevitable, wasn't it.

"Actually, it is; I've just had some bad news, which isn't any of your concern so please back off."

"Oh! Well, I am SO sorry, darling, for trying to be nice!" She thought of all the lessons she had so painfully learned today; something stretched out and snapped back inside her as she painted on an exaggerated smile.

"Of course, it is SO nice of you to heckle women in the street about their appearance! No, I am so sorry for my choice of words! I meant to say FUCK OFF, and hold the please!"

If she was as bad as she'd been told she was, she might as well truly own it; do it in style. In a way, the heckler had done her a favour; she raised a hand in salute as she turned away and walked off with a renewed spring in her step.

Except that turning away had caused her to head in the opposite direction from the station. Crap. She couldn't change direction again; it would ruin her drama queen exit. She was unravelling; she could feel it. Cogs were disengaging, whirling out of control and threads unspooling inside her, slithering into her toes, her fingertips, the roots of her hair. She had to find somewhere to go; somewhere safe where she could do a better job of gathering herself into a coherent whole again. As long as she could see the tall masts of the 'Discovery', she would be able to find her way back to the right area.

Kate! She could go to the advocacy firm where her good friend worked. Even if she were with a client, Diane could explain that she was a friend of hers, autistic and in crisis and needed somewhere safe to go for a short while. Maybe she didn't deserve that shelter; maybe her urge to seek it was not valid but she was taking responsibility for her safety. Surely she could still justify that.

5

The entrance to Tay Bridge Advocacy was discreetly signposted along a side street; Diane had been there before, though the woman on reception today was someone she had not previously met. Rubbing sanitiser into her shaking hands, her whole body still trembling, she approached the desk.

"Hi, would it be possible for me to speak with Katelyn Russell, please? I don't have an appointment but I am a friend of hers. My name is Diane Abercrombie. I am autistic and have had a crisis situation today."

The receptionist, whose name badge identified her as Olivia, smiled at her with calm reassurance.

"Oh, I am sorry to hear that. Yes, I believe Katelyn will be free in around half an hour; let me double-check for you. Please have a seat on the couch over there; would you like a glass of water or a warm drink?"

It occurred to Diane that she had not even been offered a drink of water at the meeting. She realised that she was incredibly thirsty.

"A glass of water would be wonderful, please!"

"No trouble at all; I'll get that for you right away. You relax and take all the time you need; when Katelyn's client leaves I'll make sure she gets a few minutes with you and even if she's busy after that, you can sit and get yourself hydrated and have some peace and quiet."

"Thank you so much. I sincerely appreciate all of this."

As Olivia returned with the tall, chunky glass, she noticed Diane's trembling hands and moved smoothly to get a coaster and place the drink on the side table instead of handing it to her. She smiled again and went back to her desk. No barrage of warnings; no running commentary about how incapable Diane looked; no too fast, too loud intrusion into her space. Why couldn't it always be like this? Her heart sank again as she wondered whether Kate would have heard through her professional connections about the incident with Brenda Culper; no, the "altercation", she reminded herself; her almost acquisition of a criminal record. Another wave of nausea passed over her. As slowly as she needed to, undisturbed, she picked up the glass with both hands and took a long, welcome refreshing draught of the slightly chilled water. Olivia sat at her desk working away on her computer; her presence companionable whilst instinctively unobtrusive. Diane noted that she had been helped via another person's initiative, her state of heightened stress clearly noted and adjusted for in the way she was served her drink of water, yet she had no diva feelings or compulsion to behave like a monster. Interesting. Taking another sip and setting the glass down, she sat back, looked around her and let the quietness begin to wash her clean.

She had not looked at Kate's workplace from the perspective of a client before. A tall climbing plant reached halfway to the ceiling from a dark terracotta pot in one corner of the square reception area; the large, low pine table in the middle of the seating area usually held a variety of magazines for all age groups and would again as soon as Covid restrictions on handling things in communal areas were fully lifted. A wooden puzzle with brightly coloured blocks lay ready to be used again once it was permitted, in a plastic box on the other side table which matched the one on which Diane's glass stood. The walls were painted a soothing light green which complemented the dusky blue carpet with its flecks of green and grey. Uplighters on the wall and a standing lamp in the corner opposite the plant pot provided illumination which was subtly diffused yet bright enough to ensure safety. Diane gave silent thanks that places such as this existed; what limited faith she had in non-disabled professionals serving vulnerable clients for a living had been so badly shaken. She may have deserved everything she got today, but aspects of Maurice Thurlowe's language and attitude told her that no individual belonging to any minority was safe under the shadow of his leadership.

"Diane?"

Kate was standing next to the sofa where she sat, concern etched on her face as she pushed back strands of auburn hair and reflexively smoothed the jacket of her burgundy trouser suit. At the sight of her close friend, Diane's treacherous tear ducts threatened to stir into action once again.

"Whatever's happened? Liv said you had a crisis; you look terribly upset! Come on through to my room; I've got this hour free. Do you want to bring your water with you or would you like a cup of tea? You can have both if you want!"

Picking up her glass, Diane smiled at Olivia who was awaiting refreshment orders. "She's encouraging me to mix my drinks!", she chuckled, grasping at the easy normality of a bit of banter; her self-image shattered, she did not want this kind soul to remember her in no other context than as a person in crisis. Olivia and Kate both laughed; Diane told them she would take the water with her and would also love a cup of tea with milk. Kate wanted a cup of tea as well; Olivia assured them she would bring the drinks right along and then leave them to talk in private.

Kate's room was decorated and lit in the same way as the reception area; it had two green armchairs at right angles around a light brown table on which lay two plain purple coasters as well as a box of tissues that Diane fervently hoped not to need. Kate's desk stood in the corner opposite the door; she closed the lid of her laptop and came to sit at the round table with Diane.

"OK, Liv will be in with the tea any minute so do you want to wait until after that to tell me what's happened?"

Again giving thanks for a sensible and empathic approach, Diane nodded, taking another drink of water. She put the glass down on one of the coasters, then moved it to leave it free for the hot cup, giving Kate a wavering smile. A good decision involving a hot cup of tea felt like some kind of redemption; she was not ready to talk about that particular episode with Kate, who was being gentle and concerned right now but Diane knew from experience would not hesitate to tell her when she was wrong. If Kate did not mention it, neither would she. The pertinent crisis was having found herself in such trouble for her hero-worship of Verena. A knock at the door heralded Olivia's arrival with the tea; accustomed to clients waiting for complete privacy before starting to talk, she was unfazed by the silence in the room, nodding respectfully as she tactfully made her errand as brief as possible before softly closing the door behind her.

"All right, we won't be disturbed now; so what's up?"

"I was called in today for a meeting with…"; Diane shuddered to say the name; "Maurice Thurlowe, the branch manager. He said…" She thought frantically how to explain all of this to Kate without having to mention the tea urn episode. "He basically accused me of being in love with Verena, and said it makes me too emotionally volatile and I'm off my own project and barred from the premises until further notice! They're reviewing it after three months."

Kate groaned, closing her eyes for a moment.

"Oh, no. I was afraid… I wish I'd talked about this with you before now. You don't have to keep it secret from your friends, you know."

"What? You too? I am not in love with her! Not in the way you're implying, anyway. If I were gay I'd say so! I know perfectly well that none of my friends are prejudiced against gay people; I wouldn't be friends with them if they were. I wouldn't call myself hetero or bi either; I don't feel that way about anybody. I don't talk about it because I'm sick to death of people not believing me or thinking there has to be some cliched cowardice behind it which they can be the hero and correct me out of!"

"Diane, if there were no evidence to the contrary then of course I'd believe you. However, you have to admit you have some kind of intense attachment to Verena. Her approval matters so much to you and you've said before that you worship the ground she walks on. Although you don't mention her directly on social media, when you talk about the approval you seek or get for your work, I know you well enough to recognise the same emphasis as when you mention her in conversation."

"That doesn't mean I've got some wild fantasy about a sexual relationship with her!"

"No, technically it doesn't and you've never said anything of that nature. The thing is, it looks to me as though the problem has arisen with the intensity of your attachment to her, not with whether or not your feelings for her are of a sexual nature. The reason I wish I'd raised this with you before is nothing to do with her being a woman, or with judging you in any way. I'm concerned because I can see how much this is draining you, and she's not someone who's ever going to be part of your life other than in her role as a manager."

"You mean she's too good for me even if I did fancy her."

"No! You and she move in completely different circles; she's not perfect. Yes, she's good at her job, but she's got a vastly different, highly socialite and quite conventional lifestyle. She's very confident and relates best to projected confidence from other people, but that's not necessarily the same as being more interesting. She's nowhere near as deep and intense as you! You're drawn to the idea of her; to the thrill of the chase, I suppose. Which wouldn't be an issue if it weren't making you unhappy, and now it's come to this with your work. I'm sorry to ask, but did something happen to bring this to a head?"

"Well, apparently people picked up on my reaction to her introducing Up For Work Together as having started with Sally Howe, when it was my idea. I mentioned it having been my idea a couple of times in my speech when that wasn't in the agreed script. I guess I showed my emotions too much, and the company considered it embarrassing."

It was the nearest she was going to come to admitting the whole truth about what had happened. In any case, Maurice Thurlowe had been incorrect in attributing her reaction to Brenda Culper entirely to her feelings about Verena. Perhaps that context had depleted her ability to appear capable and to cope with the events which ensued, but those genuinely had been down to a combination of sensory overload with the general emotions of the day, fatigue and Brenda's stress-inducing way of intervening.

"I see. As you know, I was watching via a video link from here with a couple of the team; I must admit I was surprised when Verena said that about it starting with Sally and called her up on stage. I said to the others then that it had been your idea and that you had driven the development of it. Yes, there was an edge to your delivery when you referred to it being your idea but we were all saying 'good on her'!"

"I'd already stood up when she started to say about one particular colleague who she was proud to call a friend. How sad and pathetic must I have looked? It was the time for her to hand over to me; I knew she was introducing me at the end of her segment. So I thought this was it and got up. Then she said Sally's name and beckoned her up! Kate, please tell me it wasn't on the video link when I stood up too soon."

"No! No, I absolutely assure you it wasn't; the camera was focused in on the stage. Oh Di. No wonder you were so unsettled! You see, this is what I mean about Verena not being good for you! That was a highly unprofessional and actually rather shitty thing for her to do especially to a volunteer. It was perfectly logical for you to have been ready to get up when you were expecting her to introduce you and it was the time for it as set out in your agenda. Anybody would be put out by that and your feelings about it are completely valid. I still sense, though, that it's her not reciprocating your affection for her that upsets you way more than the slight to your work. That's what concerns me. That and the fact it's been picked up on by other colleagues and the distress that's bound to cause you. Again I'm sorry to ask, but has Verena made a complaint?"

"Not as such; even Maurice Thurlowe admitted I haven't technically done anything wrong in the eyes of the law. He said I'm not being accused of stalking. But he said I'm making her uncomfortable with my pathetic puppy-dog devotion, mooning around with an obvious crush, and that she has the right to come to work without feeling that way and she didn't feel safe to discuss it with me because she was afraid it would tip me over the edge and I would then become a stalker! Why do people think I'm such an evil monster? Ugh, it's all so humiliating!"

"Oh Diane. I truly am so sorry this has happened to you. Did he actually use those words? Pathetic, puppy-dog, mooning around with a crush?"

"Yes, and a whole lot more. I was 'playing the autism card', and when I called him out for using the term 'spoiled little princess' because he wouldn't call a man whose feelings ran high a spoiled little prince, I was 'playing the female victim card'. Then he said something weird about 'might as well have the whole deck on the table', and that's when he accused me of my feelings for Verena being sexual. As in he wouldn't care if I wanted to sleep with Martians; no, what was it, aliens from outer space, and I was to be clear that they would be taking the same stance if it were a male colleague, so I wasn't to 'hide behind my rainbow flag' or 'make it a gay rights issue' because he wasn't interested in my 'predilections'. My work isn't valid unless someone else takes it forward because I'm 'a mere appendage', but I 'think I'm something special'. Oh, and how could I forget? He stopped himself after the first syllable and changed it to 'childlike female', but he almost called me the R word."

Kate's face was white with rage.

"My God. That is absolutely outrageous. Did anyone hear any of this?"

"There was nobody else in the room; not being a paid employee it's not as though I could ask for a union rep, and I barely had twenty four hours' notice of the meeting anyway. Gisela, that's his PA, would have probably heard most of it in her part of his office; the door was closed but we both ended up speaking pretty loudly and she was extra nice to me when I came out. She was told to see that I left the building immediately without speaking to anybody else, but she discreetly told me to use the Ladies' room if I needed to, because she could see I was distressed. I wouldn't want to ask her to witness anything; can you imagine the position that would put her in?"

"Right. I respect your consideration for others, but I would strongly suggest that you do not agree to attend any further meetings with this man without having a witness present. Because we are friends, I cannot act as your advocate but I can refer you to one of the others."

"Kate, I didn't even know what the meeting was about; I got a basic email asking me to come in today at eleven and let Gisela know if I couldn't make that time but I wasn't to contact anybody else. I was trying desperately hard not to catastrophise; I'd seen my project launched the day before and I was telling myself it might be to do with that and the no contact part was to do with confidentiality! Because that's what people tell me to do; stop catastrophising! Now

I'm wrong for having gone in without arranging for someone to hold my hand? Sorry but I can't seem to please people whatever I do!"

"Hey, I'm not criticising you, and it's not a question of needing somebody to hold your hand; the fact is, people like Maurice Thurlowe get away with this sort of behaviour because there are no witnesses, however competent the recipient of the behaviour is. Look, I know how much time and effort you've put into Up For Work Together, and not just because of Verena. But are you sure you even want to go back to that setting?"

"I don't want to lose my involvement with the project; I was hoping I could move towards working from home, being one of the moderators on the forum, that kind of thing. I was supposed to be one of the moderators anyway but even my online training for that is suspended until Himself is satisfied I can control my emotions and no longer have feelings for Verena. You know, when I first started to read '1984' years ago, I found the idea of the Thought Police almost funny; it sounded like a slapstick sci-fi comedy concept, something of a cross between 'Dr Who' and 'The Keystone Kops'. Now it doesn't seem so funny or so fictitious any more! Can you imagine how violated I feel knowing that people have had formal conversations, even meetings, about my innermost thoughts? Finding out that people are picturing me imagining intimate scenarios in lurid detail?"

"Oh Di, I know. It is an invasion of your privacy. Speaking as an advocate; yes, you have a case on many counts about the way this has all been handled. It's ludicrous to suggest that Verena had any reason to be afraid of having an honest conversation with you. Yes, it would have been awkward and toe-curlingly embarrassing for you, and I wish there were no need for it. But Diane, you do need to get over her, and the first step towards that is to admit the attachment in the first place."

"Ah. So you still don't believe that it's not about wanting to have sex with her. This whole thing is disgusting. Not because she's a woman; because you believe my feelings are something other people need to 'handle' as though I lacked the rights to my own mind, or the capacity to make decisions. You and others are picturing my private thoughts and ascribing something carnal to how I feel about someone who is so far above me, it would be wrong of me to even think about that. The gender combination involved is irrelevant."

"And there we have the real problem. This is all about your low self-esteem and internalised ableism. It isn't a question of whether or not this is a sexual attraction."

"I have to disagree with you there, because whether or not it is perceived as a sexually motivated issue influences how people react and the extent to which my autonomy and privacy are undermined. Sex is what our society gets so worked up about; that's what makes people so squeamish. The idea of someone like me even thinking about sex. Although I'm not thinking that way, it still makes me angry as an autistic woman that we're so stigmatised for something which is perfectly natural, again in any gender combination, and which many autistic people do desire. It doesn't help matters that reciprocation of whatever kind is not something to which anyone, disabled or not, is automatically entitled. You cannot legislate for being liked or desired. We have no underlying right to it, therefore no associated claim on the support we genuinely need when lack of any type of reciprocation hurts us. Reaching out for that support is interpreted as feeling an unjust sense of entitlement. Whether it's regarding friends, lovers or work connections, we're tersely told to stay in our lane and stop getting ideas above our station; to Adjust Our Expectations way downwards to take into account what a chore it is to relate to people like ourselves, because WE are such a hard slog! Some people, especially professionals working with us, think they're so progressive because they approve of us having relationships as long as it's with someone they see as being 'down at our level'; usually someone with the same disability, be it autism or any other neurodivergence. Not that there's anything wrong with two people who happen to have the same type of disability getting together if they want to. The issue is how that is then viewed by elements of their support network. Some of these professionals love to see us shyly and awkwardly get together, clumsily holding hands looking at the floor. They think it's cute and sweet; innocent and resolutely non-sexual, like those revolting images of small children kissing on the lips on old-fashioned chocolate boxes and sweetie tins. Something twee from another time, distanced from their reality. They see it as a triumph, because they can be all 'oh, bless' knowing they're going home to their presumed better love lives. As for Verena, I'm not denying that I have an attachment to her; it's just hard to know what to call it, how to define it in a society where everything is so sexualised. Maybe you could call it romantic, but these days that's assumed to incorporate a sexual element too, and if you say it doesn't you're repressed or in the closet. I get a high from being around her; I feel more energised when I have to push myself to cope with going to work or an event if she's going to be there. I recognise elements of what I feel in descriptions of being in love the way that's broadly understood. But it doesn't feel right or honest or fair to either of us to say, or allow other people to say, that I'm in love with her or feel romantically for her. When I make that clear, though, I'm lying or in denial and I'm a project to be conventionalised!"

"You make a lot of good and valid points there about society being sexualised and about attitudes to sex and relationships and disability. It interests me though that the attitude you describe, about professionals seeing disabled people's relationships as some sort of cutesy PG-rated version of their own, bothers you so much if you truly don't want a partner of your own."

"Does it also interest you that racism bothers me, a white person, as much as you know fine well it does?"

"OK, fair point. But the fact remains, I wouldn't be true to myself or a good friend if I didn't push you to break away from this particular attachment and yes, there's a part of me that suspects you're downplaying what you feel, not because you're in denial but because you don't want to take on the hard work of getting over Verena and finding another prospect for the connection you clearly want."

"I see. So now I'm lazy too. Do you have any idea how much it is to ask of an autistic person, to completely tear down and rebuild their entire mental landscape? When someone is so important to them, although that person's presence is confined to one area of their life and they do have plenty of other interests and people around them, that most exciting person is like a watermark through every part of their life. It's one thing to advise someone to avoid seeing or pursuing a particular person; it's quite another to order them to push away every single thought of them. Can you even begin to comprehend the mental energy that would take, and that's added to coping with fatigue and sensory overload, social anxiety and everything else that goes along with autism while keeping on top of everything I have to get done as an adult, sole householder and volunteer? It's back to George Orwell and '1984' again! Where Winston Smith has to watch his thoughts and facial expressions even in his own apartment with nobody around, because the Thought Police are onto him! How can anyone think that's a reasonable or feasible thing to demand of someone? I don't have the energy for any more uphill battles; not ones I have to fight twenty-four seven with no breaks, no relief, no right to take leave or go off sick from it if it gets too much or too exhausting; not even something I can go home from at the end of the working day!"

"Diane! I'm not calling you lazy, nor am I personally demanding anything of you! I'm not making the rules here. Of course you'll still think about Verena, for a long time. But the fact is, she's not right for you; whatever it is you feel for her, no good can come of it. I'm not the one deciding that. This isn't about me. I feel for you, I honestly do. I would take the burden off your shoulders if I could, believe me. I'm not saying you have to push away every single thought. You do need to recognise, though, that the thoughts aren't going to lead to anything good for you, and consider making a choice to look for a different focus for all that wonderful intensity of yours. Now, I'm sure you'd love me to say it's fine; since you're not doing anything legally wrong, your feelings are your own business and give you my blessing not to try to get over Verena. Indeed, you could make that choice. You're right; nobody has the authority to dictate your thoughts. However, I think we both know that you would end up isolating yourself more and more; that all the good things in your life would eventually be poisoned. You may even end up doing things you never expected to do as the feelings take more and more of a hold on you. Without disclosing anything confidential, I've known of instances where that has happened. So no, I'm not giving you orders, but neither can I give you the affirmation you'd like me to."

"So what am I supposed to do now? Not just about her. Believe it or not, she's not the be all and end all of my life; she's present in the background all the time and the foreground some of the time. I mean, how do I, I don't know, adjust? Process everything that's happened? How do I simply be?"

"Well, you've touched on one particularly important point there, in that you need to process. You've had a lot happen in a short space of time. You need to be gentle with yourself; take your walks, go to see Des and Jason, read, listen to music, cuddle that gorgeous cat of yours. 'Simply be' is actually an excellent description of what you need to do right now. Are you still having counselling sessions?"

"Yes; I've got one tomorrow."

"Oh, good! I'd suggest you talk this through with - Norma, was it?"

"Wilma."

"Ah yes, of course. Wilma. Be honest with her, and don't try to think too far ahead right now. There is a lot of good stuff on the other side of this, honest."

"I'm just so tired, and I still need to go out there and get on a train home. I need some air, some more time in a quiet space before travelling but the trains will soon start getting busier and I cannot face that today so I can't wait too long. I left plenty of kibble out for Farolita but I still don't like to leave her for a full day when she's not used to being on her own for that long; Siamese cats don't like that. I'd have taken her to Des and Jason's if I'd intended it to be a full day. I've got a key if they're not in and at least Luke is there. So I need to leave well before the peak, but the thought of rushing out there now…"

"Look, I've got a few bits and pieces to finish up here but I'm leaving early today. If you can hang on for an hour or so, I'll run you home. It's not that much further from Arbroath; it's no bother."

"I don't want to cut into your time at home with Peter after you've both been working all day."

"He won't be back until later anyway. I'll text and let him know but I should still be home first. Seriously, I'll be worried about you if you travel on public transport on your own after such a traumatic day. You're welcome to chill out in Reception, though I'm sorry it will be a bit boring as we still can't have magazines out. I'll let Liv know."

"Thanks so much, Kate. Liv is a diamond; she was lovely and respectful right from the moment I walked in looking like a hapless disaster. I'm so glad you've got somebody like that to welcome your clients."

"She's a star, and you didn't look like any kind of disaster. You're allowed to be upset and show it after the ordeal you've been through."

Diane felt a pang of guilt remembering the details she had kept from Kate; the rest of the story about the event and why she had been summoned for the meeting, not to mention allowing a heckler to provoke her into shrieking the F word in a busy street where children or people intimidated by swearing might have heard. She swore without a second thought indoors with receptive adult company, but normally kept a closer guard on her potty mouth in public. Damn, it had felt good though.

The conversation was kept light and neutral as Kate drove her home; they both knew that she had been given enough to deal with and think about. Thanking her friend profusely, Diane got straight out of the car leaving Kate to head home to the house she shared with her partner in Arbroath. Mindful of everything thrown at her today about Verena, she examined her feelings for any trace of jealousy; there was none. All she felt was relief to get home to one Siamese cat and zero requirement to sustain conversation. Of course she was not in love with Verena! She must remember that she knew her own mind and not allow anyone to make her doubt it. Kate was right, though; she was attached. As the heartbreak of Maurice Thurlowe's revelations about how Verena felt came thundering back from the safe place where she had stashed it during the convivial warmth of the car journey, she knew there was no escaping there being a hard road ahead to even begin to heal from this.

6

Diane's laptop was all set for the online counselling session; she draped a dry flannel over the corner of the screen where her own face would appear. In this way, she could afford Wilma the courtesy of being able to see her by having her camera on but not have to watch herself talking about sensitive matters, especially if she became upset. She made herself comfortable at her small drop leaf dining table at the end of the room behind the sofa which faced the television, preferring the more businesslike setting. The table was for working, filling in forms and suchlike as well as eating; her sofas were for relaxing. This session was definitely not going to be relaxing.

Wilma's face appeared on the screen, her make-up flawless and blonde hair precisely styled as always.

"So, Diane, how have the past two weeks been for you?"

Diane told her. Despite Kate's exhortation to be honest and this being confidential therapy, she once again left out the part about Brenda Culper and hoped that word had not reached Wilma through the professional grapevine. The shame and mortification were too great. Usually the horror of these glitches subsided with time and distance but the magnitude of that one had grown since her meeting with Maurice Thurlowe. The revelation that it could so easily have become a police matter had shaken Diane badly and she was beginning to remember it as though she had deliberately knocked a cup of hot tea towards Brenda. The world truly felt less safe a place than ever in which to be autistic or otherwise disabled, and she was white. The consequences of Jason, for example, being involved in any escalated misunderstanding arising from his hearing loss could be deadly serious. She must become more able to advocate for change; to be a stronger ally. She had to achieve more.

Wilma listened intently to her words, her reactions carefully controlled. Diane could not tell how her therapist reacted to the news of her feelings for Verena having been brought into the spotlight; she had her eyes closed with mortification at that point as she confessed to the situation in which she had ended up. As she had when talking with Kate, she asserted that her feelings were not sexual; she anticipated a sceptical response from the counsellor even more than she had expected one from her friend.

"Now, Diane, you do know there's no shame in having feelings for another woman; not these days anyway?"

Oh, here we go.

"I don't..."

"But we have to find someone who is within reach; someone with whom we can build a real relationship, not a fantasy."

"I don't want a relationship! The thought of somebody sharing my space; no! I don't even want a housemate! I do not want Verena in that way; why won't anyone believe that? And yes, I'm well aware that IF I did feel that way about her, she would be out of my league; thank you very much."

"So I'm hearing that you're not ready to talk about your sexuality yet."

"That's not what I'm saying; you're hearing what you've already decided you expect to hear. Does it matter at all what I say? I may as well sit here repeating 'Mary had a little lamb; she also had a budgie, and when it popped its feathered clogs, she flushed it down the cludgie' over and over again for an hour!"

The conversations she had with Des and Jason which led off in hilariously surreal directions, in that instance about a cousin of theirs who had never heard that Scots word for 'toilet' and insisted on hearing it used in a cultural reference before they would believe it, did her far more good than yet another round of this head / brick wall interface. If only she could call it a day and still be allowed to get on with her life in peace.

"Let's not be facetious here, please. These sessions are about moving your life forward and working to overcome unhealthy habits. Your attachment to Verena clearly falls into that category and the way we're going to overcome this is to get you out there actively looking for an appropriate partner."

"Are you actually being serious right now? You want to police my personal life and make me go through some charade for something which I don't want? Look, I admit I have an attachment to Verena. I wish, though, that everyone would get their minds above their waistline, or at least above mine, and stop making it into something it isn't. Even if it were, nobody has the right to force me into a relationship I don't even remotely want to be in. You can't say to someone, 'right; you will settle for this person and be grateful because some arbitrary box ticking exercise has decided you should'. The thought of having an intimate relationship against my will makes me feel sick!"

"Diane, has something happened in your past which has made you so afraid of a sexual relationship?"

"I'm not afraid of it! I don't want it, that's not the same thing! This is another reason I don't talk about it; when people jump to that conclusion it dilutes and minimises the experiences of people who have had terrible things happen to them, and that makes me feel incredibly guilty!"

"We've discussed your lack of contact with your parents…"

"Seriously, do not even go there. My parents disowned me because while they could just about cope with my seeking an autism diagnosis, having offspring on benefits does not fit with their world view. That makes them shallow and bigoted, but not paedophiles; I will not have them accused of that. My sister and brother, being ten and twelve years older than me and working long hours in successful careers, were amiable acquaintances by that point; they haven't come looking for me, I've left well alone and I consider the chapter closed. Verena is not a substitute for my relationship with them either. Do you think that possibility hasn't already occurred to me? With Verena or any of the other people whose approval and acceptance I've craved over the years? No; the buzz of trying to impress Verena is my line of defence against being too damned tired to keep on getting up, getting ready and putting myself out there day after day running the gauntlet of sensory overload, slow processing, brain fog, misunderstandings, ableism and humiliating glitches, trying to make a difference and live a laudable life! It is drummed into everyone that only a constantly hectic life is enough to justify our being. Being too busy for our friends is becoming a badge of honour, not a sign that we need to look again at the balance in our lives. How often does the word 'tireless' crop up as a measure of how much someone is worth? Where does that leave those of us who fight fatigue every day; who need all of our energy reserves to make the series of palpable transitions, because that's what they are, to start the day? To progress from sleeping to waking, then from waking up to getting up, then from getting up to getting ready and so on before we begin to tackle the even more significant transition from home to outside world with its change of air, temperature, sound, light, smell and everything? And all of that before you factor in the unpredictable social, interpersonal and external elements; meanwhile everything we've done purely to get ourselves to that starting point is discounted as incidental, not even registering on most people's energy output scale? Are you seriously judging me for needing some sort of adrenalin boost to help me with that; do you actually need my estrangement from my birth family or any other supplementary explanation to let you understand why I can't do all of that on my own over and over again without a bit of added incentive? I'm sure someone will let me know if anything happens to any of my biological family; beyond that, I did my grieving a long time ago and I have a chosen family here now which is way more meaningful and close."

"Ah yes, your friends…"; Wilma glanced down, presumably at her file; "Des and Jason. Do you feel that you need to impress them to get the buzz you describe yourself as needing in order to get through the things you have to do?"

"No; it's a different relationship I have with them."

"They're not exciting like Verena, then? They're not enough?"

"I did not say that! Please don't use Des and Jason to back me into a corner to force your own agenda. Don't make me be disloyal to them! No, they don't meet that particular need. Are you happy now that you've made me say that and betray them? Because I feel physically sick having to say such a thing; I would never have volunteered that, nor do I think of them in terms of not meeting any need. They meet many other needs and of course I love my time with them. But it's not possible for them, or anyone, to meet both sets of needs. They're not out of my league; they're there without me needing to strive for it. Which I cherish, and without the need to justify my existence by going out to work in some capacity, perhaps that would be enough. I genuinely want to give back to society and help other people who are going through struggles similar to my own; to spare them some of what I've been through. If I could do that effectively without it costing me quite so much energy and still not be such a pariah in the eyes of society, maybe I wouldn't need the kind of thrill I get from punching above my weight with the likes of Verena in my life. What I have with Des and Jason is equally valuable and never taken for granted, especially since Covid rules kept us apart for so long; Jason's immune system is compromised and he had to face people directly with their masks off in order to lipread so I wasn't prepared to take risks by being in a support bubble with them. By definition, though, that relationship being so close at hand and freely given to me does not provide the adrenalin rush I need to get me through making myself go into environments which are not conducive to my energy and wellbeing. That does not mean that Des and Jason are not exciting or interesting! What it means is that I cannot fit them or any accessible friends into the role Verena fulfils in my life and make them a substitute for her."

"But being available and not 'out of your league' as you put it, is what friendship is. It's not supposed to be the thrill-seeking rush you describe. It's about having common ground."

"Yes, but it's the thrill-seeking rush not the common ground that gets me going in the mornings and lets me keep up commitments which drain me. Des and Jason are the harbour, not the open sea I have to face in order to contribute to society! Don't make that a flaw or imply I don't love them, Wilma! I would not be without them. They are my family now. They know more than my white, middle class, privileged parents could ever dream of about living in the real world and how those of us in minorities of any kind have to support one another. Especially with Jason being partially deaf; intersecting minorities are..."

"Wait a minute; are you saying that Des and Jason are..."

"They are black, yes."

"Ah! I didn't know that. I can see how that would feel like a gesture of defiance to your parents' rejection and perhaps provide you with some of that missing excitement."

"Excuse me? Des and Jason are my best friends, because of who they are! If you think I've latched onto black friends to make some kind of point, then we have a problem."

"All right; I hear you." (Diane doubted that.) "I simply hadn't realised that your friends were of a different ethnicity."

"Black. I need to know that you are able to bring yourself to say that my friends Des and Jason are black, otherwise we are not going to be able to sustain any relationship of trust."

"Very well; I hadn't realised that Des and Jason are black."

"Thank you, though I'm not sure why it should even come up or make any difference in the context of their role in my life."

"No, of course it doesn't, and we need to get back to the point at issue here. I want you to start making a proactive effort to meet someone with whom you can form a solid relationship; the real kind that has to be built. Not hearts and flowers and romance; hard work, communication and making yourself learn to love them if that's what it takes. Nothing worthwhile is easy. I want you to join a dating site."

"No way. Absolutely not."

"I understand that it's a big step and it's scary…"

"It would be wasting my time and that of any people with whom I went out. It would be unfair to people who have joined these sites because they do want to meet someone, to string someone along simply to please you! I won't do it. It would be completely wrong."

"Look, Diane, the deal here is that you engage with me in order to work on making changes for the better. It's not supposed to be easy. It's about your deeper needs, not what you think you want right now. You are not stringing people along if you choose to make the effort to embrace this. You will thank me one day for pushing you to challenge yourself and face your fears."

"You can not force me into something like this!"

"No; you're right, I can not. However, you should bear in mind that if you refuse to move forward, there will be no point in continuing with our sessions."

"Fair enough; I'm sure you will have referrals waiting, so if you feel it's best to end the sessions I will abide by that and thank you for your time so far. As long as it's put in writing that this is your decision because we could not agree on a way forward."

"Yes, I could do that, but I must warn you that it would be recorded as your not having complied with the counselling process; refusing to face up to your issues. Which may be taken into account when your benefits are reviewed as that is what I would have to tell them if they contacted me."

"Wilma! That's blackmail!"

"Nonsense. It's the way the system functions and it's my job to push you to work towards fulfilling your needs, including asking you to do things which you find daunting or do not like. It's normal to resist change, but it is for your own good."

"So what, I have to go on dates to make sure I can get money to live? There's a word for that, you know!"

"Oh, now you're being silly and deliberately obstructive. Nobody is saying you have to have sex with anyone before you get to know them properly and establish a relationship, or that you have to stick with the first person you meet. The point is that you have to make yourself get over your misplaced feelings for Verena, and that means approaching this with a willingness to meet someone new. It may not happen immediately, but it will happen, unless of course you don't commit to trying."

"So if I don't find myself wanting a type of relationship which I have never wanted in my entire life, it's my fault and I get punished? How many people am I allowed to turn down before you cut me off? Is it a bit like the council housing offers?"

"I can see that we're not going to get anywhere today, Diane. You need some time to think over what I've said. I think we should end the session for this time. I will send you an email with a link to a dating site which I know to be run with a strong emphasis on personal safety; you must read and agree to the safety and security policies in order to use it. Remember, you have to be careful on these online sites, even the reputable ones; there are some dangerous people out there. The email will have a receipt request so that I know you have opened it; I expect you to accept the prompt for the receipt being sent to me. I will also send you some literature on getting over crushes. It's written for teenagers but is equally appropriate to autistic people like you who experience emotional dysregulation. When we talk again next session, by which time I trust you will be thinking more clearly and maturely, I expect you to have set up a profile on the site. It's inexpensive and entirely non-discriminatory. This is your chance to have a healthy, real future instead of living in an adolescent fantasy world. It's up to you now."

"Wilma, please don't assume that I'm unaware of good practice in online safety and why it's needed, especially in this context. I get that you need to protect yourself from liability in case something like this should go wrong for a client, but highlighting that the site has safety advice is enough to cover that. I do not need to be told that there are Bad People Out There. I am so tired of telling and showing people how much thought and effort I put into everything I do and still being bombarded with 'careful careful careful'. Even when I try to head it off by blethering away about the precautions I'm about to take, people still say it; either they don't believe me or they think my credibility so nebulous that they see it as an opportunity to be one up on me regardless of anything I say. It's either that or I'm 'overthinking'. Who the hell has the right to dictate the boundaries of another person's thoughts anyway? I certainly don't consider myself to have the right to impose that judgement on anyone else! When I point out the eternal tightrope I'm being made to walk between 'be careful' and 'you're overthinking', I'm 'oversensitive'. I cannot bloody well win and I'm getting more pissed off about it with every passing year! The same goes for lumping autistic adults in with teenagers because we happen to feel many things intensely. It's inappropriate and highly discriminatory. This perception of autistic people as perpetual children needing to be treated as though we were legally underage or needed our relationships vetted has to stop."

"Well, Diane, you're hardly proving otherwise, are you? I hope that we can talk about this rationally next time."

Diane cut the connection and let out a howl of frustration, apologising to the startled Farolita whom it had woken. What did she have to do to get people to listen to her; to properly hear her and believe her reality? Grabbing her phone from the coffee table and taking it off the silent setting, she tapped out a message to Kate, saying that she was now being blackmailed by her counsellor to go out on dates or risk losing her benefits. Stomping through to the kitchen, she opened a rare midweek bottle of wine, opening the window and looking out as she took a long sip. She could really do with a walk but knew she needed to let her anger subside first; it would be counterproductive if her flushed countenance and irate fast walking attracted any hecklers. As the fresh air cooled her face, her fury began to be replaced by a cold dread. How had it come to this; to being forced into seeking a sexual relationship?

Her phone chimed with a notification; taking her glass of wine with her, she went to look, hoping it was a reply from Kate. Of course, it was the promised email from Wilma. Grinding her teeth painfully, she forced herself to click on the button to send the read receipt, feeling as though she had sold her soul. Nothing had been said about it being a condition of her continued financial stability to read the pamphlet her counsellor had mentioned on the demeaning theme of getting over crushes; Diane felt some relief in at least being able to delete the PDF file attached to the email. Sending a leaflet intended for teenagers to a woman in her late thirties was plain insulting. Scrolling down, she took another long swig of her wine as she read the last line of Wilma's brief message. With no evident trace of awareness or irony, she had typed "Any problem with attachment let me know." The wine, fortunately a Pinot Grigio rather than her weekend Shiraz, which Diane had just tipped into her mouth was propelled across the room with a force not usually seen outside of comedy films; Des's lager splurt over Sunborough and their diving paled in comparison. Setting her glass down hurriedly on the coffee table, she leaned on the arm of the couch and gave way to a much needed bout of hysterical laughter. Problem with attachment indeed?! The lads would love this story and so would Kate. Wiping her eyes as she rubbed the welcome ache in her side, the thought of telling her friends that at least she now had a funny story to tell to break the ice on dates set her off again. The thought of those dates soon made her healing laughter die away. Why couldn't she be left alone to live her life her way? She wasn't harming anyone; apart from her frustrated efforts to impress Verena, nothing untoward had even been happening. With her work shifting more towards home based, that would most likely have fizzled out naturally anyway. It wasn't the first time she had hero-worshipped an older authority figure.

Her phone pinged again, this time with Kate's reply, which consisted of a series of question marks. She summarised the discussion which had taken place with Wilma; three dots appeared below her sent message, indicating that Kate was responding immediately.

"I agree she shouldn't have put it that way about jeopardising your benefits; I can appreciate how you feel blackmailed by that. I have to say though, Di, is it such a terrible idea?"

It was Diane's turn to send a string of question marks in reply.

"Lots of people are reluctant to go on dating sites or apps because they think it's all about being desperate, but they end up meeting someone they click with. It honestly would be so much better than clinging to your fixation with Verena. I know you do have a longing for some kind of connection to a special someone. I saw the wistful look on your face when you waved me off after I gave you a lift home, right after you'd been talking about not keeping me from Peter."

"Kate! Haven't I convinced you yet that autistic people's facial expressions often don't indicate what people think they do? If I looked wistful it was because you'd gone out of your way to drive me home after a crisis and I felt bad about there not being time to invite you up for a cup of tea and to see Farolita! I know what you think about Verena, and about my wish that I could have had her approval and yes, been able to be part of her circle, but you cannot expect me to switch those feelings off like flicking a light switch. And one more time for the people at the back: I do not want a sexual relationship, with her or anybody else! Especially going out, spending loads of money I might add, trying to force non-existent attraction with a succession of complete strangers in order to be able to keep my benefits! As I said to Wilma, that's practically prostitution. Not that I've anything against sex workers. I actually think their job should be legalised so that it can be done safely with the right control measures in place to protect them and make sure all they do is consensual and involves people who are not underage. I admire them for being able to do what they do; it is a lifeline to a lot of lonely people who do get overlooked! But it's not a line of work in which I could ever see myself! Yes, Wilma said that nobody is expecting me to drop my knickers for the first person I meet. Well, OK, she put it more politely than that. But she also said I have to "make myself learn to love someone if that's what it takes"! That feels like sexual coercion by proxy; every cell in my body is screaming that this is wrong, and that it's taking away a choice which should be mine alone! She said that if I don't end up meeting someone with whom I can bring myself to contemplate an intimate relationship, it will mean that I'm failing to commit to it and that it must be because I'm stubbornly refusing to get over Verena. So I've got a certain amount of time but at some point fairly soon I'm expected to be in a relationship which my body does not want. Not wishing to be crude here but I'm the one who would have to force myself into consenting to have something I don't want put right up inside me, be it a body part or anything else people use in that context. Something bigger than a tampon anyway. My body is the one which would have to try to "learn" to enjoy that; being intruded into in the most intimate way possible. Not yours, not Wilma's, not Maurice flipping Thurlowe's. Nobody should ever have to do that when they don't want to. Don't you realise how much forcing myself into that would hurt me, physically as well as mentally? Don't you get the magnitude of what you're asking of me?"

"Is that why you've always been so reluctant to look for a real relationship? You're afraid that having sex will be painful?"

"You still don't believe me do you, and I don't know how to convince you. Yes, it would be painful, because I don't want it. I'm not secretly longing for it whilst harbouring a conveniently textbook fear so that some do-gooder can put me right!"

"I'm not being a do-gooder, Diane. I'm trying to be your friend by not being afraid to challenge you when you need

79

it, same as Wilma is trying to do her job although I agree that she went about it the wrong way. I want to see you happy, and to get there you're going to have to bite the bullet and meet people."

"Kate, I bite the bullet facing other people every time I walk out of my front door! I've bitten so many bullets living my daily life, it's a wonder Dr Fletcher hasn't put me on a bullet free diet! I've been telling you all along what would and wouldn't make me happy and you're throwing it back in my face because it doesn't fit with your world view. Yes, I do believe you want to see me happy, but I'm beginning to wonder if it's not mainly because you want to get to say you told me so. I'm sad to think that being right is more important to you than our friendship, but it's starting to feel that way."

"I'm disappointed that you would think that of me but I also get that you're hitting out because you're so daunted by the idea of moving forward. Which suggests to me that you know deep down it's the right thing to do. You don't like someone else telling you, and I get that too because your self-esteem has taken a lot of knocks over the years. Like when you were compulsively watching all those derogatory programmes about people on benefits and it was upsetting you so much. I told you straight that you had to break the habit or stop leaning on other people about it, and you did break the habit, but you didn't speak to me for weeks because I had given you a bit of tough love by being hard on you about it. You're terrified to have to admit that once in a while someone else can see things more clearly than you can about what's best for you, because you have this need to be in control and to be perfect to make up for having made mistakes in the past like we all did."

"Wow. Much appreciate you bringing that up right now and gloating about it. If kicking people when they're down were an Olympic sport, you could represent Scotland. Yes, I did need to stop watching those toxic programmes, but the fact that you won that one doesn't give you the right to use it as leverage to take ownership of me and control the rest of my life, especially my choices regarding my own body. There's a big difference between making alternative TV viewing plans and having to sleep with somebody!"

"It wasn't my intention to gloat or kick you when you're down. It would be much easier if we were having this conversation face to face and I could explain myself better. I feel as though you are personally attacking me now because you resent your own situation of knowing that you need to be getting yourself out there and meeting somebody to share your life with. When you meet the right person, you will want the physical aspect. It will not be the monstrous ordeal you're building it up to in your mind. Why are you assuming that you won't feel attracted to people you haven't met yet?"

"Because I don't feel attracted to anybody, and I don't find the prospect of sex appealing. I think my attachments to Verena and people like her in the past are the product of my intense emotions needing somewhere to go, for the very reason that I don't fall in love the way you normal couples do, while needing a high of some sort to combat my fatigue. To be honest as I head towards forty I'm getting too tired for all this inner drama and I'm fed up with even what I feel about Verena. I want different things out of life. The last thing I want is to be forcing any feelings with somebody else, losing my independence and personal space in the process. Look, I don't want to lose your friendship and you clearly don't accept that I know my own mind on this so I think it's better we don't discuss it any further."

"As you wish. It's your decision whether or not you go ahead with Wilma's suggestion; I didn't mean to imply otherwise."

"Well, not quite my decision if I have to do it in order to keep covering my basic living expenses, so yes, I probably will have to go ahead with it and I wouldn't exactly call it a suggestion. Please do one thing for me though. If and when I do meet people from this website, trust me to know and follow the safety protocols. I do not need infantilising lectures undermining my sense of credibility if I'm going to have to be convincing as adult relationship material to the people I meet. You so often pull me up for things when I'm already doing, or intending to do, what's in line with your unsolicited instructions. For example, when I'd found the cats and I'd agreed to foster them. You were right in there: DON'T get attached. DON'T give them names. DON'T spend too much time bonding with them until you know for sure you can keep them. It may surprise you but I'd already figured all that out for myself as a competent, responsible grown woman. I did everything by the book but I felt as though I was being machine-gunned with "don't"s, and I often feel like a naughty child pre-emptively scolded because of a bad track record, constantly protesting "I know! I am / I'm not!", by which time you've already taken the credit and I have no way to prove I was already on the right track of my own volition and not because of what anyone told me. I'm not saying you're the worst example of doing this to me in my life, and I'm not saying it's entirely because of my autism, though I do believe there's something about being autistic which marks me out as a target for constant pre-emptive criticism. It's exhausting, Kate, and I hate myself for not being able to make people listen, even as far as to say "I didn't know I was making you feel that way; I can see that must be frustrating and hurtful and I will remember to give you more credit for being the competent adult you are." Is it any wonder I'm such a perfectionist when I'm given so little credit even by some of my closest friends?"

"I just didn't want you to get hurt if Farolita turned out to have an owner who was looking for her and wanted her back and to take in her kitten too. I'm sorry if that offended you."

"Not the POINT, Kate! My point is that you assumed that possibility wouldn't have occurred to naïve little airhead me!"

"I wasn't assuming anything; I wanted to make absolutely sure, because I care about you."

"And here comes the Because I / They Care guilt trip. I'm telling you that it hurt me, and why, perfectly calmly and clearly. All I'm getting here is sorry-not-sorries, invalidation of my perspective, and guilt trips. Do you know, although obviously I did not officially name the cats until it was confirmed I could keep them, their names popped into my head uninvited and for weeks I was stressing out because I had unintentionally disobeyed your instructions; feeling worthless and confirming your low opinion of my common sense, because an idea popped into my head? It's good old George Orwell and the Thought Police yet again! Can you imagine how stressful that was; how much that added to the fear that if an owner did come forward and I showed the tiniest bit of sadness because of them having been living in my home and in my care for a while, as anyone fostering animals would be entitled to feel, you would come down on me like a ton of bricks and be even more of a headmistress in future?"

"No, I did not know that; I am genuinely sorry to hear it, Di."

"Thank you. I appreciate that."

"I think maybe you're the one who has a need to be right all the time and you're projecting that onto others a bit, but I am beginning to have more comprehension of why you feel that need. I will try to sound less as though I'm giving orders in future. I have to go now, but please stay in touch; I honestly do want you to be happy and I have your best interests at heart."

"I know you do, and I sincerely appreciate that you have listened. I will be in touch soon."

Diane leaned back against the sofa, closing her eyes in exhaustion. She was emotionally drained by the conversation, for all it had ended well and she felt she had made some progress in making herself heard. She knew that Kate had a point about her needing to be in the right; she also recognised that she had been unfair both to Kate and to Wilma by expecting them to fully empathise whilst not telling them the whole story of the events at the project launch. No wonder people were placing so much importance on her feelings about Verena. She had the right to choose what to share and what not to share, but she could not expect fully informed understanding of her perspective if she kept parts of it back. The familiar waves of internalised shame washed over her. She deserved this anguish; she deserved to have to do things which hurt her.

7

Diane supposed she might as well get this dating profile over and done with. She would not do the embellishing which she was sure, without anyone needing to tell her, that many people on the site would have done. If she got no offers then surely that would be that. Pouring another glass of wine, she opened Wilma's email and clicked on the link; another thing she did not have to be told only to do when she knew for certain that the email was authentic even if it appeared to be from someone she knew! Any security doubt over this email would have been welcome. Ah, but she was not supposed to think like that; she was supposed to be enthusiastic about it! Surely she must be on the Thought Police's Ten Most Wanted list by now! Wilma had been wrong about the website being fully inclusive; there were options to be matched with men or women or either, but there was no obvious accommodation of non-binary people in the options for creating her own profile and they could so easily have used "any" as opposed to "either" as a more inclusive third option. Perhaps it would count as wholehearted participation when Diane emailed the site administrators about that. She selected the option of interest in either men or women; it felt like the least dishonest choice, since she was equally uninterested in dating men and women. Oh well; it might perhaps be possible that she could come out of this with a new friend or two. She still intended to be honest with anyone she did arrange to meet and tell them that she was looking for no more than friendship; the circumstances under which she was signing up were not suitable for disclosure to people she didn't know but she refused to deliberately waste anyone's time, not to mention the money all these dates were going to cost.

There was another thought; where on Earth was she going to suggest going to on these dates? Not the Fulmar's Nest. She was not going to do this in front of people she knew, in places where she was in the habit of going. The well-meaning jollity and encouragement would be too galling. There were a couple of local restaurants; she was not in the habit of eating out, finding it stressful because of the tendency to be leaned over and asked if the meal was OK when her mouth was full, and because maddeningly she was one of these people whom waiting staff often judged to be in need of a loud warning about plates and dishes being hot even when it was obvious. Eating out on her own was becoming more fraught with pitfalls than it was worth.

She still cringed to remember an occasion when she was staying in a hotel on a training course in her employed days and ate in the restaurant; lack of communication among the waiting staff had led to her being asked three times in five minutes by three different people whether her food was OK, always when her mouth was full. The worst part had been the obvious amusement of the middle-aged couple at the next table and the man's pointed remarks about how "SHE's not too happy". Having swallowed her food, which she would have enjoyed had she been left in peace, she had reminded the man that "She is the cat's mother" and suggested he pay more attention to his wife instead of watching her before draping her napkin over the plate and leaving as they both laughed and imitated her Scottish accent; her appetite ruined along with her confidence for the following day's networking. The strain on her as yet undiagnosed autistic brain had already exceeded what she could manage without there being a trade-off somewhere else; finding her way around a new place, coping with the unfamiliar sounds and smells, bright lights, lurid patterned décor and having to use a keycard to get into her room which required the handle to be simultaneously turned exactly the right amount at exactly the right pace had depleted her too much for her to be able to laugh this incident off or brazen it out. She was well aware that she had probably been judged as a miserable harridan; that it would be thought she was the problem, not the other guests' rudeness nor the overly intrusive staff. This was the way it was in a primarily non-autistic world.

Perhaps there was a positive to be gained in having the opportunity to try these local restaurants with someone else. Des and Jason rarely ate out; Des loved cooking too much and his meals were as good as any restaurant could provide. She would not be trying to impress anyone so it wouldn't matter any more than usual if she were made to look bad in front of her "date" by being singled out as looking too inept to have the sense to know when something would be too hot to touch; another bugbear she had learned there was no point in talking about with most people because she would be slated for ingratitude, lack of humility or failure to accommodate the intentions and perspective of others. Yes, litigation culture had a lot to do with these warnings; her issue was with being warned when others being served hot dishes were not. Why couldn't people understand that?

Having someone else at the table might help by taking the spotlight off her; all she needed was to be sure there were enough options on the menu for her to select something which was not messy or unfamiliar to eat. There were some dishes which she knew she would have no idea how to tackle, never having seen in detail how people went about getting at the edible part. The thought of having to be instructed on a life skill as basic as eating a meal made Diane's blood run cold; knowing that she lacked the instincts which other people evidently possessed with regard to anything which needed more technique than using cutlery in a straightforward way was one of her deepest areas of shame.

She loathed touching greasy or wet food with her bare hands; even chips from the chip shop had to be of a dry enough consistency for her to touch. Fortunately, Vinnic who ran the seafront chippy in Inverbrudock made beautiful golden chips which definitely fit into that category. There had been situations when, as an adult, she would be awkwardly picking at or moving something using cutlery and someone would advise her to use her fingers. The shame of being instructed how to eat at her age and fear that explaining would come across as criticising the food prevented her from admitting that she didn't want to touch it with her bare hands, leaving her mortified as she struggled to continue eating with all eyes on her. In the same way when cutlery was appropriate but looked awkward in her often dysfunctional hands, or when her difficulty in judging how much pressure to apply resulted in food crumbling away as she endeavoured to get it onto the cutlery, she would be told to use a different piece which she had overlooked or thought was for another course. Having been banned from ordering scones in cafes throughout her childhood because she had become distressed and embarrassed her parents with the scattering of crumbs as she tried to spread pats of chilled butter was mortifying enough; being told as an adult what to use at the table in front of other people shamed and terrified her.

Then there was the issue of her sensitive throat being prone to even the plainest food catching and irritating it, making her cough as though it had gone down the wrong way. In addition to the embarrassment, it brought painful physical contact as well-meaning people slapped her hard on the back; explaining as soon as she could speak again that it wasn't what she needed, her strained voice sounded ungracious and the criticism of her "tetchy" character piled on again. Even without physical contact, the attention it drew to her in the vulnerable moment was distressing in itself and because the attention was generally motivated by concern, her discomfort was condemned and saw her placed firmly in the Bad Person corner. Eating in front of anyone other than trusted friends was becoming too fraught with anxiety, which in turn made the bad things more likely to happen. It increased the instances of painfully biting the inside of her mouth when chewing and sustaining raw patches on her tongue from it catching her teeth. She never ate clumsily, however much it may appear that way; quite the opposite, yet these issues plagued her. The implications for her capacity, how she was viewed by others and her future ability to maintain her independence and personal living space loomed in menacing shadows as the anxiety brought her to the edge of shutdown, worsening the humiliation by rendering her unable to articulate in any meaningful or socially passable way.

With this as with many issues, of course, to explain how she felt would so often bring indignant reproof for not appreciating the niceness of basically everyone who wasn't Diane Felizia Abercrombie. Not that this lambasting her lack of appreciation of universal human benevolence prevented the same people from lecturing her about all the badness and questionable motivation in the world, automatically ascribing rose-tinted naivety to her thought processes the moment she dared to show enthusiasm and look on the positive side of something new. She retained a steady and consistent sense of logic and justice in her reactions yet felt charged with spending her life continually ricocheting between Princess and Pollyanna if the feedback she received was anything to go by; no wonder her brain hurt from this endless game of social squash.

She seemed simultaneously to be walking a perpetual thin line between "arrogant" and "need to be more self-confident", as she tried frantically to correct her tone and bearing after each bit of negative feedback. In the days before Covid had rendered the ritual of shaking hands with strangers almost obsolete, her handshake was either too weak or too strong; it felt wrong to be grateful to a global pandemic for anything but she could not deny her relief at having one fewer social pitfall to worry about even though she used to enjoy the feeling of connection a handshake gave her within its parameters of brief, not too close contact.

How was someone so chronically out of step with what the world expected of her supposed to navigate dates which she didn't want to be on in the first place? She had to acknowledge that there was an awkwardness to her movements and manual dexterity which was an integral part of her autism and that this was impossible to hide from other people; nowadays, her hatred of this and the unwanted interactions it brought was frowned upon as internalised ableism. Yet another reason for her to feel shame! Surely she was allowed to feel exasperated by it, in the same way as Jason was entitled to get frustrated when he misheard or couldn't keep up. She had never disputed that although some people wanted to score points, others did sincerely want to help. She yearned for a world where those intentions were not automatically perceived to invalidate her own feelings of equally genuine distress.

Was this really worth it for all these negative feelings and memories it was bringing back? Diane reminded herself that it was necessary if she were to minimise the stress of her next benefit review.

Another unwanted memory came to the surface. She had been attending a course with a colleague, Ted. She had always gotten on well enough with him and as there was a break of an hour and a half in between the morning and afternoon sessions, they had gone to a pizzeria for lunch. It was not a dating scenario; the atmosphere between them had always been that of amicable colleagues. Yet somehow that convenient lunch break had taken on the format of an excruciatingly awkward date. She had ended up apologising profusely to a concerned waitress who thought there must be something wrong with her barely touched meal because whenever she was about to take a bite, Ted asked her a question. He asked her why she didn't make much eye contact (that flaming old chestnut again; she simply found it tiring to force it and generally forgot altogether, it was no reflection of a lack of personality). Whether she had a gambling habit because her gaze flicked momentarily towards the rippling lights of a fruit machine in the corner (she had overcome an addiction in her student days; this coupled with being on permanent red alert when out and about plus having restless eyes since focusing made her tired all meant she would never be at the stage of not noticing a fruit machine). Whether she'd ever thought of having the small mole on her neck removed (she was prepared to cut him some slack over that one because of the legitimate issue of skin cancer). Why she ate her pizza from the outside inwards (she didn't like to leave the rim as she always felt it made her look finicky but the dry hardness of it was uncomfortable to her mouth so she liked to get it out of the way while she was at her hungriest). Whether she was wishing she could be having a proper drink (when she picked up her glass of sparkling water and set it down again because it was still fizzing and she knew the bubbles would feel like tiny drawing pins and make her sneeze if they got up her nose). Why she held her glass in both hands (she had to think about that one; an especially stressful and embarrassing question. She didn't always do so, nor did she need to for any physical reason, and at the time she had no answer. Caught being eccentric, and tongue-tied when put on the spot about it; urgh! Years later, she eventually figured out that she merely liked the symmetry of it. Why had she not known that about herself?) And so on. By the time they returned for the afternoon session, Diane had felt she may as well be caged and tickets sold for people to come and observe her many peculiarities.

Sure, she was aware that one bad date which wasn't even a date seven years ago was not a reason to refuse to join this dating website now. The fact that it was against her will and she did not want a partner was reason enough for that. She had told one former friend about that lunch; his take on it had been that all the questions meant Ted had been interested in her and appeared quite offended on behalf of this man he had never met that Diane had the temerity not to gratefully fall at his feet. The same "friend" had tried to hold her hand walking back to the station after their catch-up. When she explained that she did not want to hold hands, he told her that she needed to stop being so uptight and thinking she was better than everybody else.

"So", she had put to him, "when you get home tonight and go out in the morning and you lock your door, does that mean you think you're better than everybody else, or that your house is worth protecting more than any other?"

Her soon to be ex-friend had looked blank.

"Or is it simply that it's your house, and quite rightly you want to decide for yourself who you let in and when? Do you fail to invite every passing stranger in because you think you're better than them, or is it because the house is yours and not theirs? And when you see your neighbours go out and lock their doors behind them, do you think 'ooh, there goes that Joe Bloggs locking up his house; who does he think he is, does he think his house is better than anyone else's; he's so uptight'? Or do you accept it as normal boundaries?"

She couldn't exactly recall the rest of the conversation but she knew she had not been successful in making her point. She wondered how many times she was going to have to explain to people over the coming months that not welcoming physical contact did not mean that she was shy; that her physical boundaries were not indicative of a lack of personality and that she did not need to be saved by anyone.

Diane finished creating her profile, emailed the site administrators with her feedback and suggestions on inclusion of non-binary people then shut down her laptop. She needed to go for a walk; the usually calm space of her own home, now crackling with eerie uncertainty as she contemplated the enforced loss of control of it and the ending of her essential degree of solitude which presumably lay not far ahead, was uncharacteristically closing in on her. She put her unfinished glass of wine in the fridge for when she got home; after a day like this and the huge concession of joining the dating site, she had surely earned a detour via the Fulmar's Nest.

8

There they were, as steady and welcoming as ever; those beautiful trees and the silent orange pageant of the streetlights. The leaves were beginning to fall; Caberfeidh Road was lightly carpeted with the same golden brown and soft subtle absorbency of contact as her favourite jacket which cocooned her in a gentle sense of wellbeing. Diane looked to the shadowed tops of the mighty trees and listened to the ephemeral buzz of the lights' electricity in the quickening autumn air, hoping for answers as to how she was supposed to navigate this new set of conditions under which she must live. Too many people now had told her, some more politely than others, that her lack of any wish to seek out and throw every bit of energy she had into a manufactured relationship was a flaw in her character and that she was missing out on something which despite being openly described as a chore was meant to be in some way wonderful and essential. From what she could glean from Wilma and Kate's advice, if she did the right thing, she would eventually end up in a sexual relationship though she must not expect to be in love with the person because that wasn't challenging enough to satisfy whatever intangible hierarchy was in charge of all this. Intense attachment was the bad Diane who didn't deserve the ongoing security of her benefits but artificially manufacturing a relationship with hard graft and renouncing attraction as a frivolous and irrelevant criterion was the good Diane who did. If this was the way it had to be, how could she prepare for it? Perhaps her doctor's surgery could help. She knew that there were women who wanted to be sexually active but found it painful for medical reasons and that there were ways of helping them with that; perhaps the same could apply to someone who found the act unappealing but had to

94

overcome being wrong in their mindset by forcing it. She was better at setting out sensitive enquiries in writing than trying to put the words together in person; she would make an appointment with a female doctor at the practice and write a letter in advance outlining what she needed to investigate. Feeling better for having clawed back a bit of control in this suddenly foreign land of her day to day life, Diane looked back from the end of Caberfeidh Road and quietly saluted the sentinel streetlights before turning to walk along past the betting shop onto the High Street. She made her way with a lighter step towards the convivial glow of the Fulmar's Nest.

"A house white please, Helen; just a small one."

"One small house Pinot Grigio; here you are, that's £3.95 please. Have you heard any more about your website project?"

"Thereby hangs a tale. It's all a bit chaotic right now; suffice to say I'm having to take a step back for a bit; until after Christmas anyway, then who knows. There's been something of a parting of the ways."

"No! Oh Diane, you worked so hard! I am so sorry to hear that. Look, I can see you don't want to talk about it and I respect that, but it's always good to see you in here and I'm here if you want to sound off."

"Thanks; that means a lot. Actually there is one thing you might be able to help me with. Nothing to worry about, but do you know which of the female doctors at the local surgery is most likely to be autism friendly? I usually see Dr Fletcher but there's something I'd rather discuss with a woman. It's routine; nothing sinister but, you know, private."

"Of course, I understand. I see Dr Blake and she's excellent; she has a good reputation for listening and being sensitive. I know of a couple of people who've found her particularly helpful with mental health issues. I know autism is not a mental health condition, but they're both things that other people can't see and treat physically like a broken leg or asthma."

"You're right, Helen; that is exactly the kind of recommendation I need. Thank you so much. So many of us autistic people end up with mental health problems anyway; myself included, I have no issue with being open about that. My aim is to contribute towards a society where people can talk freely about their mental health and the adaptations they need."

"I know, and I get how much courage it must take you to keep on working towards that. Whatever it is that's happened with your project, please don't lose sight of how much you're giving by doing so."

Diane could merely nod and smile; her emotions still hummed with the excess of feeling that had gotten her into so much trouble. She paid for her wine and took it to one of the tables overlooking the sea. Although it was now dark, the occasional pinpoint flash from a distant lighthouse punctuated the steady blackness with its endless ongoing saga of watchfulness over the water and all the ways of life it sustained. She took her time over her wine, watching out for a glimpse of the moon through the unseen clouds.

The bar was quiet again as she returned her empty glass, turning as usual to head for the stairs at the other end of the long sweep of tables from where she had been sitting. Thanking her for returning the glass, Helen called out, "Why don't you treat yourself and use the lift for a change?"

The world lurched to a juddering halt. She knew what that meant in this pub. Helen, who a short while ago had been right on her wavelength, had joined the legion of people who felt she needed to be guided to a better decision in her impaired state.

"The... the lift? But I've only had one small glass; yes, I had a couple in the house but I didn't even finish the second one; it's in the fridge for when I get back!"

"What?! Oh Diane, I didn't mean that! No! I always thought you didn't want to use the lift because you saw it as being for people who need it; I know how strongly you feel about accessibility issues. I thought you always used the stairs even when you'd been sitting at the other end of the bar from that door as a matter of principle! You've had a tough week and I wanted to give you a bit of a treat; let you pamper yourself a bit, because you wouldn't make that call for yourself!"

She had gotten it wrong; so wrong. This was, for once, a straightforward instance of someone authentically trying to be nice, in a context which was in no way insulting or condescending. She had mentioned having to take time out from her volunteering and asked about the doctors. It was so obvious now that Helen was discreetly trying to give her a break. How could she not have seen that? Because she, Diane, was a truly horrible person and everyone who had criticised her over the years was absolutely right; she was the problem.

"Helen, I'm so sorry. My defences are on red alert right now and I've often seen you and Mark and Krista encourage people to use the lift when they've had too much to drink and wouldn't be safe on the stairs. You were trying to do something so lovely and thoughtful and I completely misunderstood!"

"Oh, don't worry about it; I know, we do tend to do that with the drunk ones don't we! I suppose it's never occurred to us that people notice it as a kind of Fulmar's Nest tradition."

"The truth is, it's always been a constant in my life that however much people assume about me because of my differences, I could always come here and know that because I do stick to making responsible choices about alcohol, this was one place where I wouldn't be one of the ones being monitored, if that makes any sense. That sounds bizarre out loud!"

"No, I can see where you're coming from there! Rest assured, you are a highly valued customer whose courtesy, friendliness and helpfulness are always noted. Krista said to me one day in the summer that your genuine smile and thanks made her feel appreciated again after she'd had some obnoxious tourists in that lunchtime who'd clicked their fingers at her, talked down to her and generally made her feel like something they'd scraped off their shoes. She said that you have such a warmth about you it can turn somebody's day around. People do tend to say these things about people rather than to them; we should be more forthcoming because it can make such a difference. See, you would say that directly to somebody. You would want them to know it because you know how it feels to be down, and you have the natural gift of being able to circumvent that reticence."

"Krista actually said that about me? I'm so angry that people came in here and treated her that way! She's so welcoming and helpful to the tourists. I'm so glad you told me that. And yes, I would love to use the lift for once; I'm so wiped out this week. Thank you."

The compact lift had been designed with that end of the night feeling in mind. Tactfully tinted mirrors, light diffused through heavily frosted panels on the ceiling and floored with an easily mopped surface in a soothing dark brown which complemented a broad brass rail around the wood effect panelled walls, it glided smoothly and sedately down to street level. Diane smiled with a thankfulness so profound it ached, for Helen's instincts and her absolute generosity of spirit in understanding so completely and continuing to give when those instincts were so crudely misinterpreted. She should feel foolish, abashed, mortified and of course ashamed; somehow she felt none of those things. She felt cradled and valued.

She arrived home in a calmer frame of mind than she would have thought possible. Farolita purred around her ankles as she opened the fridge, taking out her unfinished glass of wine and wiping the condensation off before taking a sip and raising the glass to her peaceful, empty flat. "I've finally been in the lift at the Fulmar's Nest!", she told the cat, who looked up at her with an inquisitive "Prrp". Setting the glass on the kitchen counter, she scooped up her pet who snuggled in to her, tucking her head under Diane's chin as her purrs became even louder.

She would have to make the most of this while she still could; of having access to the tranquil oasis of her own living space. According to the new conditions which she must meet in order to be allowed to keep her life and health stable and manageable, she would eventually be sharing everything; even her bed. That may be a long way in the future but Diane shuddered at the prospect. The thought of never being able to routinely sleep alone again was incomprehensible; her mind would not process it. She remembered sharing a room with her sister when she was around six years old and her own room was being redecorated. That had entailed sleeping on a camp bed on the other side of the room, not even in the same bed, yet she had felt as though Georgie must surely be able to hear her thoughts. The presence of another person breathing the same hushed, intimate air of the room in which she was settled down to sleep made her so tense, she had lain awake stock still long after her sister had fallen asleep. She was terrified of disturbing her even as she wished, with the paper-cut keenness of an autistic child's longing, to be back in her own familiar bed in her own room, alone. As a child who would not receive her autism diagnosis until adulthood, such intense emotional responses had no context in which to understand them even as they and the disapproval they elicited doubly pummelled her tender, developing psyche.

Diane rarely thought about her parents now; the raw shock and grief of their rejection had faded but the wound still lay roughly stitched with a nebulous yet iron-hard discomfort at which she had no desire to pick. With another effort of will, she returned her mind to the present moment; to the silky warmth of Farolita's fur against her neck and the muscular sleekness of her Siamese form cradled to her chest. As if sensing the return of her human's full attention, the cat stirred and let out a raspy miaow; Diane set her down next to her food bowl and went to check her phone for any notifications before switching it off for the night. Her heart sank when she saw an email from the dating website; she was not ready to deal with the reality of other people asking anything of her on there quite yet. To her relief it was merely a confirmation of her profile having been registered and that she would be notified once it was live when the standard security checks had been made. Switching off her phone and tablet, she went back into the kitchen and finished off her wine standing at the window. The clouds were breaking up; moonlight spread through the gaps from a point somewhere out of view as though reaching across the night sky from another time.

9

Too tired to sleep, Diane lay staring up at the ceiling. She tensed and relaxed her muscles in turn as various articles read over the years had suggested; it helped her to unwind a little but sleep still eluded her. She thought again about what Helen had told her Krista had said. It had been so reassuring to think that something as basic as a smile and a thank you had made such a difference to someone's day; especially because it had been received as notably warm and genuine. She seemed to be unknowingly bad a lot of the time, according to the unexpected responses she received; it was a novelty to find herself to have been unknowingly good. There had to be a new way for her to build on this; a new setting for her to do her bit within what was manageable to her and still make a difference. The thought soothed her; the timeless stillness of the night stole around her.

She was walking along Caberfeidh Road but the streetlights were different. The trees were much as she knew them; somehow in an unfamiliar light they looked slightly younger, less tall against the end of twilight sky. It must be because this light was a fresh white, like moonlight. The illumination came from round glass bowls below conical metal pendants on the end of swan neck posts, which curved back and around to dangle the icy brilliance of their lanterns into the open space above where the straight part of the posts ended. Diane had not seen streetlamps like this for years; it felt more fitting to her to call these old style designs streetlamps as opposed to the more modern streetlights. They were her favourite kind and they certainly suited Caberfeidh Road. The steady poise of each suspended lamp shining out into the space around it; the graceful pattern of all the points of light dappling the road ahead shone into her inner soul, awakening a raw enhanced response of feeling alive and needing to be there. Sure-footed as a cat; silent as the night itself, Diane proceeded along this new incarnation of her favourite walk. She seemed at once to be walking as usual and floating above herself, level with the ghostly sheen of silver light on the inner curve of the swan necks. At the end of the road, she looked back almost expecting to see the usual orange; still, the white glow held its quiet vigil over the deserted pavements. She turned to see how far the different lights extended; they led all the way to the High Street, and something else had altered about the scene she knew. The drab betting shop with its rusty-grilled facade was now a café; warm light the colour of butter shone from curtained windows which conveyed the promise of welcoming cushioned seats, fresh home baking and the cosy sensory hug of the lightly steamed-up indoors after being out on a chilly evening. She started along the path towards it, keen to have a closer look; her footsteps suddenly heavy, she strained to walk against a sense of her consciousness shifting and changing. She tried to focus; to stay on her mission to reach the curious presence and beckoning cheer of the café, to no avail. Warm cotton supplanted the cool air on her face; her already wide and seeing eyes opened again.

That one was vivid even by her standards. Diane blinked a few times, trying to adjust; after intense dreams like this, she needed an extra few moments to realign herself to her waking world. A Siamese cat clamouring for breakfast was always an effective anchor to convince her, and possibly the neighbours, of being well and truly present in the reality of a new day; she stored the beautiful dream away in the tranquil attic rooms of her mind and went to attend to the urgent business at hand.

Once breakfast was over and the empty dishes washed and put away, Diane put on an upbeat CD and tackled the day's portion of housework. She found it helpful to break the tasks down room by room over the week; fatigue could crash down on her at any time and removing the stress of facing a big heavy blitz of physical effort suited her well. Singing along with Andy Bell's rich, soaring vocals, she recalled the pleasant surprise when she saw a new release announcement from Erasure after a long gap. She usually downloaded her music these days so that she could save storage space in the flat and select her favourites track by track but "The Neon" was one of those releases which warranted buying the CD as well as adding it to her digital library. The particular pitch, tone and resonance of 1980s synth pop had always seemed to vibrate in harmony with the frequency of her brain; depending on how she was feeling, it could uplift her or calm her.

Dusting the bookcase in her bedroom, she winced as her thumb jabbed painfully into the edge of the shelf. Relieved that she had trimmed her nails a couple of days ago, she examined the faint white line where yet again her thumbnail had bent backwards. "You useless klutz; you never learn", she chided herself. She used to like having longer fingernails but the constant breakages and pain of bending them back when she misjudged and caught the edges of things had forced her to give in and keep them short; a few millimetres above the quick. It was a fine balancing act; if her nails were even slightly too short, she found herself struggling to pick things up and the ends of her thumbs were sore from the lack of protection.

At least there was nobody here to shrill out "Ooh!" or "Careful!", compounding her frustration with the knowledge that she had been seen messing up and had added to people's reasons to judge her. She was truly doing her best to take care; she could not help the fact that her brain often gave her the wrong information about how much space she had and where the edges of things were in relation to her fumbling hands. She would love to be without not only the frustration and the extra energy demand of any clearing up after these incidents, but the sensory pain of the unexpected noise and jarring impact. Her anger against herself never diminished; any one incidence taken in isolation may well appear trivial but people often failed to appreciate the cumulative effect of a lifetime of them, and of the searing injustice of the mishaps invariably being noticed but not the continuous background effort into which she poured her energy. She knew that her truly close friends were concerned about the extent of her self-criticism; at the same time, society's obsession with image and being 'normal' made it difficult for her to contemplate easing up on it when she had to work so hard simply to reach the baseline and earn respect even in some friendships. She had come to terms with the conclusion that she was not psychologically safe with some people and drifted out of a few unhealthy routines over the past few years. It was not a question of turning against the people, nor did it negate the good memories and the positives which they had once brought to her life. It was a matter of recognising toxic traits even when they were embedded in friendships which had genuinely good elements and knowing when a line needed to be drawn because the negative aspects were harming her and could not be resolved or mitigated by the positive aspects. Despite her rigidity and loyalty, Diane had learned to move on from people who wilfully disregarded her boundaries. Refusal to listen or change things they did and said which she told them hurt her, insisting that her perspective was wrong and merely a social deficit, oversensitivity or part of the disability which she was "letting define her", now meant a calm but final goodbye.

Interestingly, she had far fewer instances of clumsiness - either physical or social - in Des and Jason's flat than anywhere else including her own home; no more than anybody else might, given that nobody at all, not even the

Verena James types of the world got to go through life entirely escaping ugly moments. Yes, she spent more time in her own home than anywhere else so there were bound to be more glitches there, but she surmised that wasn't the sole reason. Des and Jason made her feel fully relaxed in a way which could not be forced or manufactured. They were her true family and they focused on her strengths in a somehow purer form than any other relationship she had ever had, shielding her from the relentless onslaught of her demons and their self-fulfilling prophecies.

In between tracks on the CD she heard her phone and tablet's email notifications; she finished up in the bedroom then went to check it out. It was a response from the administrators of the dating site, thanking her for her feedback on inclusion of non-binary people and confirming that they were going to implement her suggestions. "Result!", she declared to Farolita as she punched the air in a brief spike of inner triumph before the dull throb in her stubbed thumb reminded her not to allow herself too much praise; the subsiding physical pain lingering just long enough to keep her self-esteem firmly in check even as her cat regarded her with unconditional love in her ice-blue eyes.

Diane found telephone calls extremely awkward; her lack of filtering in audio processing made it difficult to focus on a conversation if there were even minimal background noise and she struggled with having nothing but the other person's voice to provide social cues, which in any circumstances she had to work hard to discern and process in a timely enough manner for "live" interaction. However, once her CD had finished playing, the brief and formulaic telephone call required to make a doctor's appointment from the privacy of her living room was not too demanding. She was pleased to learn that Dr Blake had a cancellation for the following week; that would allow time for a letter to reach her ahead of the appointment.

Although, she thought wryly, it might take her that long to figure out quite how she was going to phrase what she needed to ask the doctor about.

"Dear Dr Blake,

I am writing this letter in advance of our appointment next week since it concerns a delicate matter and as I am autistic, I find it easier to put difficult and sensitive concerns across in writing in my own time. I am therefore doing this in order to maximise efficient use of time at the appointment itself."

So far, so good. Now for the difficult part.

"I have recently been removed from a project on which I was volunteering because one of my colleagues became uncomfortable about my attachment to her, although I wish to make it clear to you as the branch manager made it clear to me that I have not been accused of any wrongdoing towards her. This attachment is not sexual in nature and I do not have any wish for a relationship of that type, but neither my colleagues, my counsellor nor a close friend with whom I have discussed the issue believe me about this. My manager has stated that if I am to be allowed any further involvement in the project, which grew from my own idea, after a suspension of at least three months then I will have to satisfy him that I am over my attachment to my colleague. My counsellor has ordered me to join a dating site; if I did not agree to this, she was going to terminate our sessions and she reminded me that the reason for this would be recorded as non-compliance and potentially jeopardise my benefits when they are next reviewed. Both the counsellor and my close friend are insisting that my lack of interest in sex is down to some flaw in my thinking; that it is because I am too lazy and stubborn to get over the fantasy and build a relationship which is real, hard work and entails forcing myself to learn to love someone against my instincts. If this is what my future holds and if I must put my body through this in order to avoid losing the stability of my benefits, which allows me to function well enough to volunteer as and when I am able, I need to establish whether there is any medical solution to help me when the time comes that I have to go through with the physical act. I cannot envisage it being anything other than extremely painful because my body does not naturally desire it (I rarely even hug!) and I will be unable to muster enough willpower to prevent myself from tensing up."

Reading over what she had written so far, the whole situation looked ludicrous. Diane had a fair idea what Des and Jason were going to make of all this. Yet how many times in her life had she had the "Telling You What You Want To Hear" cliché thrown at her? How many times had the people telling her what she didn't want to hear turned out to be right, and boy had they ever made sure she registered that their perspective trumped hers? How many times had she baulked at hard work, whether academic, professional or psychological, because of the underlying fatigue for which she didn't yet know any name other than laziness? Sometimes that work had paid off, the times when it hadn't left her so ill and depleted she had to think and talk herself through each step simply to cross a room anyway. She had been younger then and had more energy in general than she did now. Was she being nothing but an entitled brat by asking a doctor for help with this, considering how many women had input from others into the course of their intimate lives to varying degrees even today? Though many cultural arranged marriages did still hold an element of choice and many people entered into them with free will and ultimately wanted to make a marriage, so many women were still being denied any choice in what happened to their bodies and young girls were being physically and mentally scarred. Maurice Thurlowe had accused her of behaving like a spoiled little princess; she thought with a tug of compassion how many young princesses, actual children, in history had been sent off to foreign countries to not only marry against their wishes but never see their loved people and places again. Who was to say that some of those cloistered, utterly owned and controlled little girls weren't also autistic? The fact it wasn't known in their time did not mean it hadn't existed. Autism had existed for as long as human brains had. What right did she have to any help with this, comfortable and privileged in her modern first world life? She was no victim of circumstances; she was in this situation because she attached herself emotionally to someone out of her league and failed to manage or hide it adequately. She should cancel the appointment, apologise for wasting the surgery's time and face the consequences of being the way she was.

Diane moved the cursor to hover over the "Close" button at the top right corner of her unsaved document.

Over on the coffee table, her phone pinged with another message alert, making her jump. She left the document as it was while she went to check the alert, glad of the distraction. The message was from Des, inviting her over for curry and the Aberdeen match the next day. She could bring Farolita with her and make an evening of it. The prospect of a convivial afternoon with her dearest friends, the cats and the sensory treat of Des's cooking; he knew how to use spices and to get consistency exactly right, gave her a rush of warmth and belonging which swept away her doubts about allowing herself to ask a doctor for help and advice. After all, making a martyr of herself would not help anyone. The past was gone. Nothing could change for the many undiagnosed autistic people and oppressed women throughout history, whereas any help she was able to obtain now could give her a resource to pass on in turn to others. Accepting Des's invitation, she returned to her letter, moving the cursor well away from the "Close" button.

"I look forward to speaking with you and thank you for taking the time to read this. Yours sincerely, Diane Abercrombie."

She printed the letter off, signed it in the space she had left above her typed name and added her date of birth to aid the matching of it to her medical records. Feeling determined now, she put it in the stamped envelope she had ready, marked "Confidential" and addressed to Dr Blake at the surgery. She would go out to post it later on; there was a box she passed on the way to Caberfeidh Road.

Evening came. Diane had spent much of the afternoon reminding herself to pick up the letter on the way out; a further significant portion of the time had been spent imagining her frustration if she were still to manage to forget. Despite having a less busy schedule since leaving full time paid work, she had been disappointed to find that her executive functioning was still letting her down. Nothing with any consequences of note, it was small things such as forgetting to put the plugs in the basin and sink overnight to keep spiders from coming up, which meant a bad start to the following day as the maddening realisation hit her upon going into the bathroom or kitchen when she got up. "It's just concentration; you'd remember if you really tried", she had been mercilessly told so many times. It was not even unknown for her thinking memory and motor memory to be so disconnected that she would forget to do something even as she was in the process of reminding herself, for instance putting ready one of her regular supplements for the next day even as her mind was registering that it was not one of the days on which she took it. The rapidity with which something could slip her mind after resolving to remember it alarmed her. She winced as she recalled another humiliating instance from her past when she had just agreed to pick up a file from a colleague's desk to put in the cabinet near the door as she was at that moment on her way out of the building; somehow the single minded determination with which she filled her mind with the will to remember and the knowledge of how much it would hurt her if she didn't was supplanted by another thought which, because she was so focused on her thoughts, was enough to distract her within seconds and make her walk right past the desk without picking up the file. She had no knowledge of terms such as motor memory and executive functioning at that time and no clue as to how she had managed to do something so woolly-headed and asinine. Even if she had been in possession of the tools to explain, it would have been unlikely to mitigate her then colleagues' howls of derisive laughter. She had begun to self-harm after incidents like those; furious with herself, unable to comprehend why she was making such risible mistakes despite knowing full well the anguish and disdain it would bring.

Making a conscious effort to breathe, slow her pounding heart and pull herself back to the present from yet another unplanned trip to a bad place in her mind, this time Diane remembered to pick up the letter after putting on her much-loved tan suede jacket. She ran her fingers over it, against the barely perceptible nap of the baby-soft material then smoothing it back down, several times to calm and centre herself. This favourite jacket represented the present; she had not owned it at the time when she made that infuriating error. Those people were no longer in her life; they were not laughing at her now. Her cat was purring contentedly in her basket with a full tummy and had a clean litter tray in the hall thanks to her being on top of her responsibilities. She was taking ownership of her health by sending this letter which she held in her hand, would grip between her teeth as she locked up on her way out and would hold in her hand again until it was posted; pockets were too risky.

The letter susurrated reassuringly over the lip of the post box with a glide of paper over metal, the sound dissipating into the hushed night air; her part in its journey fulfilled. The lights of Caberfeidh Road beamed their usual cheery orange welcome as Diane walked into their glow. "You lot looked totally different in my dream last night", she silently

110

told them; half expecting to see a café lit up in the distance as she reached the far end. The tattered signage and darkened grilles of the betting shop looked even more depressing now; it being Friday evening, sounds of drunken revelry and overexcited teenage girls who flaunted shrieking as a skill to show off to a world which appeared not to mind emanated from the High Street. Diane shuddered, glad that she was "boring" and wanted nothing more than to go back through the restful, soul-deep joy of silhouetted trees and amber-lit stillness to the recharging solitude of home.

10

The cat carrier held no fear as Farolita sauntered in, turning around and settling on the warm brown fleece blanket as she tucked her long, slender blue-grey tail around herself. Diane double-checked the fastenings, well aware that for all the cat was capable of learning to follow her the short distance to and from Des and Jason's flat, anything unexpected such as a dog off the leash or someone setting off fireworks could frighten her into running away. Being regularly seen outside with a Siamese cat, especially one with colouring rarer than the most usual seal point, could also lead to attempts to steal her. "Right then, let's go and see your son!", Diane smiled affectionately, stroking Farolita's face through the carrier's front grille as the cat rubbed against the bars.

Des was putting the finishing touches to preparing his curry as Diane arrived. She let Farolita out in the living room, put her carrier in the hallway next to Luke's and took the bottle of wine she had brought through to the kitchen. The aroma of perfectly balanced spices, rich sauce and the savoury hint of lentils cooking wafted through the flat despite the door being closed to keep the cats out while food was being prepared. She called out and tapped on the door, waiting a moment so that Des could alert Jason if he was in there too; she did not want to startle him if he was handling hot pans and had not heard her. As she walked in quickly closing the door behind her, Des greeted her warmly, handing her a glass of wine.

"Hey, it's good to see you, Di. Jason's at the gym; he'll be back in half an hour or so."

"Cool. Can I do anything here?"

"Nah, you're all right; it's all under control. That's the last pan on now; I'll set the timer and we're done. Cheers."

"Cheers! Oh boy, am I ready for this."

"So you haven't been online much since your big event on Monday; are things good there?"

Des knew her well enough to know that she would have planned out free time after a big event and had it gone as brilliantly as she gave the impression it had in her sole update on the day, she would have been much more active on social media during the week. Even if she were busy, she would have been updating more than she had. Sometimes she kept up the pretence when things were difficult; at times like this past week, she would simply go quiet. Des also knew that she would have to be prompted to talk about it, however much she needed to.

"Well, not really, Des. I'm here to have a happy day and hear all about your week, not be a downer, but it's not good there at all. In fact, I'm off the project and suspended from my volunteering."

She related most of the events of the week, again leaving out the part involving Brenda Culper. She knew that she could trust Des more than any other person not to be appalled and judge her, but it was too deep a shame to bring into this house where she needed to feel she deserved the acceptance and belonging she had found. She edited out some of the worst quotes from Maurice Thurlowe too, knowing how much those would enrage and upset her best friend and that he would struggle to keep quiet while she got out the whole ugly tale. She needed to do that in one go and keep her focus. As she came to the part about being coerced into joining the dating site, apprehension twinged at the edge of her mind; no-one could ever be one hundred per cent certain how another person would react to something which had no precedent in their interactions. Was it possible that even Des might have the same views as Kate on the subject and add to the pressure on her, and could she cope with that?

"So I've got an appointment with Dr Blake next week and the site got back to me about the non-binary issue; they're going to change their terminology and options to be inclusive, which is something." She preferred to end on a positive note.

Des stood perfectly still, the shock of what he had heard plain on his face.

"Oh my God, Di. I wish we'd known about all this! So, what, your manager treated you like a stalker even while admitting you're not one, and your counsellor basically blackmailed you?"

"Well, yes, that's certainly how it feels, despite Kate insisting that she's actually doing her job in pushing me to mend my ways!"

"No way; that is blackmail you've described to me. I don't get what the big deal is with how you feel about this Verena person anyway; yeah, you've mentioned her a few times and you obviously think a lot of her and her opinion maybe matters a bit too much to you for your own good, but why is she making out you're obsessed with her when you're not doing anything except maybe value her approval more than other people's and look up to her? I mean, if you were following her around, sending her messages all the time, giving her presents, going out of your way to try to see her or contact her outside of work that would be different. Or if you'd told her or said to somebody else that you had feelings for her and it got back to her, that would give this some context, but you haven't done any of those things and nobody's even saying you have!"

"Seemingly I'm dysfunctional enough that they think I might do those things if they don't deal with me. They need to protect her from me and I've forfeited my right to privacy of my own thoughts. Can you imagine how that feels? Knowing that I'm such a liability it raises red flags all over the place that I hero-worship someone within the context in which I know them, just because I feel things intensely and am socially awkward because I'm autistic? I guess I truly am a monster."

Diane often found other people's eyes unreadable but she saw a burst of sadness and deep emotion in Des's expressive brown gaze.

"A monster? It kills me that anyone has made you think that about yourself! Girl, you arranged your own living room furniture so that my brother can lipread more easily when we come over. You gave him a kitten you had raised from a few weeks old and were planning to keep, because you saw that Luke was good for him. You noticed, despite the pressure you were under and it not being an issue for you personally, that the dating site wasn't inclusive of non-binary people, and you did something about it! And I could go on. I will not have anyone making you believe you're a monster!"

Des's original South London accent always came out more strongly when his feelings ran high. Diane knew that he was absolutely sincere and, factually, everything he had said was correct; she had indeed done all of the things he listed and they were good deeds. Yet even as his words balanced her interpretation of how the wider world viewed her, the rawness of having learned the full extent of how uneasy and victimised she had managed to make Verena feel simply by being herself tightened its grip on her psyche. In any case, she reminded herself, Des did not have the full picture; she had been selective, only allowing him to see the best of her. He had no idea that she had almost ended up with an assault charge after risking scalding someone through her lack of self-control. So how could his view of her truly count at all, not being properly informed?

"I'm surprised at Kate too", Des was continuing. "I mean, I don't know her that well but she definitely knows you. What was she thinking pressuring you into this dating business when you so obviously don't want it?"

"I guess because she's so happy and settled with Peter, she cannot get her head around somebody needing to be in their own space, not to mention the lack of any desire to have a sexual relationship. I can see why people want to have a partner; the company, someone to confide in and share the work and responsibility of running a household, having a family for those who want that, plus of course how good it must feel to fall in love with someone in every sense and have them feel the same way. Of course I can appreciate why all of that would appeal to someone, and even why they might feel that it's somehow missing from my life because they see me seeking reciprocity in other ways. I don't think Kate has ever lived on her own; she comes from a big family and then she moved in with Peter. Maybe she fears being on her own in the same way I fear being forced to have people around me all the time. She's an advocate though; she should be able to separate her own ideal outcomes from other people's and base her response on their needs, not her own! I mean, I'm sure she does with her clients, because there is that bit of detachment there. It shouldn't be so big a leap to transfer that skill to listening to her friends."

"No, it shouldn't. She could take a leaf out of your book in terms of seeing the other person's point of view! So what's going to happen with your project then; with Up For Work Together?"

"Well, it's still going ahead; I'm going to be called in again after three months and my own ability to be involved is to be reviewed then. They have to be satisfied that I'm not too much of an overemotional loose cannon to be professional on the forum, and more importantly that I'm 'over' Verena. How I'm meant to prove that I have no idea, given that this is all about my private thoughts."

"Jeez, Di. I know you've worked so hard on developing that project, but do you really even want to stay involved with those people?"

"Not particularly, no. Especially with Arthur retiring at Christmas. Ideally I would like to be able to go ahead with becoming one of the forum moderators; that would be done from home, as would the training for it. I would be going in for occasional meetings. I could live with that to stay on the project. The question is whether Verena can bring herself to be contaminated by my sporadic presence, even if I could have supervision with Sally instead of her, which they'll probably insist on anyway."

"And the dating site; what do you want to do about that?"

"Run a country mile, but I'll need to wait and see what the doctor says and if there's any way she can step in with regard to the threat to jeopardise my benefits."

"Man, I seriously cannot get my head around this. It's like you said, practically asking you to be an escort!"

"See, it's not even a case of people saying, 'you've got to have sex whether you like it or not'. They're saying if I start thinking correctly, I will want it, since obviously deep down I do, as evidenced by my inappropriate attachment to Verena; that I don't know what's best for me. If people were trying to force me to go and have sex with anybody who'd have me, then of course I could say 'bugger off; my body, my choice'. But they're being so particular about staying clear of anything that would give me the right to say no to what it is they are asking of me. They're making sure to say that no, I don't have to sleep with anyone against my will; that the issue is that my will itself is wrong or that I'm not facing up to it and as soon as I do what they ask and do it properly, what I want will fall into line with that. They're avoiding any appearance of pushing me specifically towards men, so I cannot claim discrimination. Maurice Thurlowe himself told me not to try to make my suspension a gay rights issue or hide behind my rainbow flag."

"Thurlowe said WHAT?!"

"I know. He is a vile, repugnant glob of bigoted sputum. Sorry Des; that's gross when you're cooking! As well as all the stuff he said about my autism merely being a matter of hurt feelings and wounded pride, and about being bound by political correctness making it difficult for them to protect Verena from me, he said I was acting like a spoiled little princess and… well, he didn't, he stopped himself in time and changed it to 'childlike female', but he almost called me something else. A certain word beginning with R."

Des's hands clenched into fists. "Oh, that's crossing a line. Even if he did stop himself, I swear…"

"He's not worth anyone getting themselves into trouble over. Anyway, even if I do go back I'll hardly ever have to see him. It would be in passing at most."

"I don't like the idea of you having to even see him in passing, but it's your choice and I understand it given the work you've done. You know Jason and I will support you whatever you decide to do. Come on, let's refill our glasses and get through to the living room; see what these cats are up to. Do you want me to bring Jason up to speed when he gets home; save you going through it all again?"

"Yes please," Once again Diane marvelled at how well Des read her; recognising how tiring it would be for her to go through that whole sorry saga all over again. Picking up her glass, she went to the door and opened it a little way; satisfied that the cats were occupied with their play tunnel, she nodded to Des that it was safe to fully open the door. They sat on one of the sofas, relaxing into the soft dark green leather.

Luke came running, his greeting miaow showing his Siamese heritage. Though completely grey with yellow-green eyes, he had his mother's lithe Oriental shape and strident voice. He was at that adorable stage in between kitten and cat, still growing into his long legs. He jumped up into Diane's lap, already purring loudly before his paws even left the laminate floor; with a practiced motion she deftly moved her wine glass out of the way, stroking him with her free hand as he affectionately headbutted her under the chin before curling into a warm ball on her long dark red dress. Farolita was occupied with a shiny purple catnip fish which dangled on a rod from halfway up the multi-level climbing tree at the side of the big room.

"Jason fixed that up there; Luke plays with it for hours. Ah - speaking of Jason, here he comes now."

The front door opened and Jason breezed in, his face breaking into a wide smile as he greeted Diane. Dumping his gym bag on the floor out of the way, he held up another bottle of red wine.

"I got us some extra!", he declared in his precise intonation, his soft consonants slightly blurred and faded by the difficulty he had in hearing them as he enunciated them.

"Brilliant; thanks, Jason! How was your workout?"

"Good, thanks. I was mostly working on my shoulders today." He rolled them and flexed his arms. "I'm ready for a curry. Des, I went by the market and picked up some spices and curry powder you were running low on."

"Oh, nice one, thanks!"

"The guy who served me though! I said my brother was making a big curry today for us and our best mate. He said 'I thought it was the Asians who made curry'!"

"What?!", Des and Diane exploded simultaneously.

"So I said, 'Hey, I'm a bit hard of hearing; could you say that again?' Like, I couldn't quite believe he'd actually said it. And he sort of backed away behind the counter, like he thought I was starting something but I think he could tell by my voice that I genuinely am deaf."

Diane's heart ached to think of the risks Jason ran every day as a black man with partial hearing. Her own auditory processing, though it was to do with filtering rather than hearing, had caused issues when she either misinterpreted something or failed to assert herself because she couldn't be sure of her own senses and feared the awkwardness an

119

inappropriate response would generate. Jason, however, faced an enhanced possibility of violence or of being accused of being a threat and ending up in trouble because of the colour of his skin whenever he was in a situation like this.

"Anyway", Jason was continuing his tale; "he said it again and yeah, I had definitely heard him right. So I told him, 'Dude, you should try my brother's Cullen Skink; it's even whiter than you are'!"

Diane and Des roared with laughter, congratulating Jason on putting the ignorant cashier in his place. Even as Des laughed and beamed with pride in his younger brother, Diane could sense in him the fatigue of yet another incidence of casual racism. How anyone could believe that it was no longer a problem, or exclusively an American thing, was beyond her.

Des's Cullen Skink! He hadn't made it for a while but Diane could almost smell its rich, seaside goodness and feel the satisfying fullness of her stomach after a bowlful of it; the milky depths of flavour, the melt of potato and flaking of fish as she ate.

"Right bro, Diane's had quite a week, so she's going to chill out in here with the cats while I fill you in on all the details in the kitchen. You relax and enjoy your Merlot, Di; see you in a bit."

Diane let herself sink into the padded luxury of the sofa, savouring the velvety wine as Luke continued to purr contentedly in her lap and Farolita, finally tiring of chasing the catnip toy, leapt stealthily up to snuggle beside them resting her head on the silky curve of her son's back. She petted both cats, smiling to think of how pro-Diane the conversation in the kitchen would be. Just for a little while, she allowed herself to absorb the feeling; to take at face value the unconditional love and support of these two brothers who were her best friends and chosen family.

"No WAY!"; Jason's voice carried from the kitchen, followed by a few choice words which some people were still surprised to find a disabled person knowing and using. She supposed Des had gotten to the Maurice Thurlowe part of the story. Luke's big pointed ears pricked up and he lifted his head. "It's OK, wee man; nothing but a rancid bigot you will never need to know about", she murmured as she stroked him again, his purring going up a notch in response.

Minutes later, the kitchen door opened and the brothers emerged with the cats' dinners served early to keep them occupied, followed by their own deep plates heaped with aromatically steaming curry and rice. Diane got out the lap trays as Des switched on the TV; the football match was about to start. Savoury with a subtle, rounded sweetness filling it out, the tantalising smell reaching her nostrils made Diane's mouth water in anticipation as she raised her glass, making a toast to friendship and a win for the Dons; thanking Jason as he handed round the cutlery.

"Oh Di, I can't believe what you've had going on this week! I'm so glad you're here with us today to have a good time. You deserve it."

Jason's words warmed her as much as the flavours and gentle heat of the curry as she tucked in. All three of them turned their attention to the large TV screen as the various lights of Mission Control blinked around it and two teams of men filed onto the vivid green pitch, the red on the Aberdeen home strips and in the waving scarves of the Pittodrie crowd standing out proudly. The friends ate, drank and cheered their way through the match; Des dished up seconds at half time and Diane took a small helping, relaxed in the knowledge that nobody would push her to eat any more then she wanted to and had she not had room for seconds it would not have been taken amiss or made an issue of. She was even blessed with fortunate timing for once; all three of Aberdeen's goals came when she did not have her mouth full and could cheer unimpeded.

None of them wanted to move as the match concluded and the full time analysis began. The dishwasher was loaded, the few covered leftovers judged cool enough to transfer to the fridge and the wine glasses refilled; the trio settled on the sofas again and Jason flicked through the on-screen TV guide to see what else was of interest as Des switched on the minimalist upright bar of rainbow-hued mood lighting in the corner. The light spread from the corner across the plain walls leaving the narrow bar itself in stark silhouette; it reminded Diane of Caberfeidh Road.

"There's a documentary on here about astronomy; we all good for that? New images of Saturn's rings; more detailed than ever before." Both brothers were interested in astronomy; they knew that it was a subject Diane found comforting and absorbing when she needed a bit of perspective and a distraction from the pressures of life.

"Perfect!"

Jason selected the channel and the screen was filled with a blaze of stars.

"Why can't a so-called counsellor respect that my life is good the way it is?" Diane realised she had thought out loud when Des looked in her direction. "I cannot think of anything I'd rather be doing with my Saturday evening. OK, there's nothing to say that dates always have to be at the weekend, but I'm talking about the disruption to my routine; asking me to make room for something I don't want, at the expense of things I do, because I've struggled with a psychological attachment to one person who has nothing to do with my private life."

The combination of the wine and her newly lightened spirits made the whole situation with the dating site seem suddenly, ridiculously amusing. Waves of mirth rose up and she began to laugh uncontrollably.

"Can you believe Wilma actually included a PDF of a leaflet about getting over teenage crushes in her email with the link to the site?"

The incredulous looks on her friends' faces set her off even more.

"And she put in the email, about opening the PDF, 'Any problems with attachment let me know'! I spat my drink right across the living room!"

Des and Jason erupted into laughter.

"Do you think she even noticed the double meaning?", spluttered Des.

"Goodness knows. I couldn't actually care less. The laugh it gave me probably did me more good than months of her therapy anyway! Sorry Jason, I'm making you look away from the screen."

On the TV, the presenter's voiceover was explaining about the stabilising gravitational effect certain of the smaller moons had on Saturn's rings. The subtitles, for once, were doing an accurate job. Watching for unintentionally hilarious mistranslations had become an incidental pastime; the favourite so far was when a politician being criticised was referred to as "that man" and the subtitle had read "Batman". The backdrop of distant stars wheeled behind the mysterious cloudy swirl of Saturn and the ethereal sweep of its angled rings as the presenter continued to explain that after the break, we would learn more about how these shepherd moons kept the rings intact and distinct from one another with clear space around them.

"You know, it occurs to me"; Diane spoke from a crystal clear mind through the comfortable fug of absolute repleteness, "That's exactly what you guys are to me. You are my shepherd moons. You keep all the strung-out pieces of me together within the space I need; always alongside, never intrusive, and you keep what doesn't belong at bay, validating my reality when nobody else is."

Des quietly raised his glass in salute; Jason blamed his suddenly watering eyes on the onions from a meal whose raw ingredients had been dealt with while he wasn't even in the flat. Nobody was going to contradict him.

The time hazily came to coax Farolita into her carrier and walk the few hundred metres home. Still wrapped up warm in the joy of an evening in the most compatible and validating company she knew, the familiar nagging voice which urged "What if they're wrong? It generally is wrong when it's What You Want To Hear" was unusually faint but not silenced, promising its return to full strength soon enough. Diane debated with herself whether she should take down her profile from the dating site there and then before her faith in her own instincts evaporated again. She looked at her closed laptop and shook her head; too tired, too cocooned in a rare ceasefire of her inner battles to be stirring it all up again by looking at the site. Tonight, she would leave it all alone and trust that things were going to work out.

11

The restful night air cooled to an almost winter-like chill, diamond-edged with millions of droplets of water vapour on the cusp of freezing; too small to see, they sparkled on her sensitive skin and shimmered around the hanging white lanterns of the streetlamps along Caberfeidh Road. Dreamlike, her breath invisible despite the cold, Diane's consciousness dimly registered the difference in the lighting; not a surprise this time, rather a feeling of revisiting a location seen once before by chance and returned to out of interest. At the end of the road, her movements remained unhindered this time as she turned gladly towards the enticing lights of the café.

The warm smell of freshly brewed tea and a waft of sweet cinnamon greeted her as she opened the sepia-coloured wooden door, which had a steaming cup engraved in the glass pane and a sign above it reading "The Haven Café" in white letters on a mid-blue background. Inside, the linoleum floor was chequered in cream and chocolate brown. A long counter ran along the wall at right angles to the High Street side windows, topped with dainty cake stands full of classic home-baked favourites; a Victoria sponge which looked so light it could have floated upwards had pride of place on a silver tray, several slices having been cut already exposing a sumptuous layer of butter icing on a rich red base of jam in the middle. Deliciously tempting as the prominent cake looked, it was the seating arrangements that grabbed Diane's attention. Along the two windowed walls and continuing past the end of the smaller windows which overlooked the road along which she had come, tables draped in light blue cloths sat in the middle of high, toffee-brown wooden booths with darker blue and gold curtains at the windows and matching cushions plumped up on the long dark red padded seats. The individual booths somehow made Diane think of cosy attic rooms. What a perfect place this would be to come and relax or have a conversation in private! The café certainly appeared to live up to its name. Diane started to walk towards the counter as the dread heaviness returned to her limbs; fighting to stay, she tried her hardest to focus to no avail. The world shifted again as her eyes opened.

Scrambling out of bed, Diane impatiently rubbed the sleep from her eyes as she hurried through to the living room and rummaged through her tote bag for the notebook she always kept to hand. Keen to write down all the details of the café while the dream was still fresh in her mind, she did not even pause to make the first cup of strong coffee without which she rarely started her day. Reading over her notes to ensure she had not missed anything, she switched on her phone and tablet, made her coffee, fed Farolita and settled down to pull up her search engine homepage, typing in "The Haven Café, Inverbrudock". She didn't expect to get any results but the dream having been so vivid and having occurred more than once, her natural curiosity insisted she look it up.

The surprise she felt when the article came up on the Bygone Inverbrudock site was tinged with an odd sense of familiarity; of having already known on some level that the café had been a real place. Had she come upon mention of it at some point when she was reading up about Inverbrudock before accepting this tenancy after the breakdown of her relationship with her parents and retained it in her subconscious mind? Whatever the reason for it having appeared in her dreams, there it was; a faded photograph showed it there on the corner, the door with its engraved glass and welcoming sign exactly as she had seen it. She knew that she had not looked at this site when she was researching the town as a place to live; she had been concentrating on what it was like right then, not in the past.

126

Des and Jason wouldn't have mentioned it either, being relative newcomers themselves arriving a couple of years before Diane when Des got a job in Dundee after having worked offshore for a time and Jason moved up to live with him in a less fraught and hectic environment.

"The Haven Café, Inverbrudock: This popular café was owned and run by Joan Morley between 1955 and 1968. It is believed to have been sold when her husband Leonard's gambling debts got out of control; the couple, who had no children, subsequently moved away. The premises became a haberdasher's emporium then a newsagent's and, in an ironic twist of fate, the current occupant is a betting shop."

Poor Joan! Diane was glad that she had presumably left the area well before seeing that come to pass; what a slap in the face it would have been. How heartbroken she must have been to lock up her beautiful, lovingly crafted life's work and walk away for the last time. Diane could hardly bear to think about it. The betting shop had always looked depressing to her; she put it down to her own brush with gambling addiction. How much more stark and cruel those metal grilles appeared in her mind's eye now after having seen the welcoming glow of the café. She thought again of her own project, Up For Work Together. At least that was still ongoing and would help people; she was free to choose whatever was right for her own life in a way in which Joan Morley had not been. Taking her coffee cup through to the kitchen for a leisurely Sunday refill, Diane felt a renewed determination to aim towards becoming involved once again as a forum moderator; she would, however, do the preparation for that in her own way, not by being railroaded into seeking a relationship purely out of fearing the consequences if she didn't.

She would need her laptop for going in to remove her dating profile; she had resisted having anything to do with the site on her mobile devices. It felt too jarring and too overbearing to have it on anything she would have with her when out and about. Logging in, she was dismayed to see that she had a suggested match which had already been accepted by the other person. She had hoped it would not happen before she at least had a chance to speak with Dr Blake and begin to come to terms with having to contemplate doing this whole dating thing. She truly didn't want to waste anyone's time or rebuff them if they expressed an interest in her in good faith. She should at least do this person the courtesy of responding; taking down her profile now might make them think they had scared her off. Who knew how much courage it must take people to join these sites when they were invested in looking for a partner and had not found one easily; how much their life experiences may have dented their confidence?

Her name was Priya and she lived in Montrose. Not too far to travel then. Her profile photo showed a friendly smile and kind eyes; a deep cerise pink streak adorned the front of her dark hair, sweeping over her head in a sleek modern style from a side parting down to her jawline. As it had always been for her irrespective of the other individual's gender, Diane admired an attractive person but felt no sexual desire whatsoever. Wilma and Kate's assertions that this was merely her own wrong-headedness rose to the forefront of her thoughts; she tried to open her mind and see if the change would come but there was nothing and she knew that this was simply how she was. Priya had listed her interests as local history, travel and equality issues. Would she be willing to meet up on the basis of making a new friend? Familiar guilt stabbed at Diane's soul as she recognised that was most likely not what this Priya had signed up for; she had already misled someone by allowing herself to be herded into this, just so that she could keep her benefits and not have her own life destabilised. She knew one thing for certain; whatever Wilma had said about needing to make herself participate as a person looking for a partner, she could not bring herself to specifically deceive this woman who had played no part whatsoever in the bad choices which had led Diane to have to be on this site. Sighing at the mess she had caused, Diane began composing a message.

"Hi Priya. Thank you so much for taking the time to look at my profile and for reaching out to invite me to meet up. I agree that we have some good common ground here. I need to be honest with you from the outset; I joined this site against my better judgement as a result of intense peer pressure and I am not seeking a partner, but I am always open to the possibility of making new friends. I will completely understand if you do not wish to meet up with someone who is not looking for the type of relationship you want but if you would like to meet and have a chat with a potential new friend, I would be happy to go ahead with arranging something. I would be willing to come to Montrose; it's the least I can do when I've misled you by being on here when I'm not offering what you and others on the site are looking for. I wish you all the best with your search and truly hope that you soon go on to find the happiness you deserve. Sincerely, Diane in Inverbrudock."

Sending the message, she cringed to think how weak-willed saying that she had joined because of peer pressure made her appear. That was what she got for letting it come to this; disclosing the full story to a complete stranger would be entirely inappropriate and if the alternative made her look bad, it was her own fault. To her surprise, Priya replied within minutes saying that she understood, thanking her for her honesty and assuring her that she would still like to meet. She was coming to Inverbrudock a week on Wednesday to meet with a colleague from Arbroath so would it be convenient to meet up for a drink after that on her way home? She would be getting the train so driving would not be an issue. Replying in the affirmative, Diane explained that she was autistic and that she did not like physical contact. Neither of them needed the stress of an

129

awkward start to their meeting, which she refused to call a date. Priya's response somehow made her feel even more wretchedly guilty even as it warmed her with its sincerity: "Got it; no problem, I appreciate you telling me and please let me know if anything feels uncomfortable or needs to be done differently when we meet. Looking forward to a good chat! Best, Priya."

She so did not deserve this!

Still, she would be happy to take Priya to the Fulmar's Nest; there was no need to cope with an unfamiliar venue in order to authentically meet a new friend.

12

Dr Marsaili Blake looked up from her computer screen on which a scanned copy of Diane's letter was displayed. She took off her fine-rimmed spectacles, laying them neatly on the desk as she turned to her new patient.

"Well, Diane, I have to say I have never heard anything quite like this in all the years I have been practicing medicine and that is more years than I care to admit!"

Diane chuckled, responding to the empathy she sensed in the doctor who was clearly trying to put her at ease.

"I have read your letter over several times as I wanted to be sure I had the facts correct here. Your counsellor has effectively threatened to jeopardise your benefits if you don't start going out on dates against your wishes?"

"That's the long and short of it, yes. I guess I could withdraw consent for the benefits people to contact her and say the counselling relationship broke down which in itself is an example of my being an interpersonal disaster zone, but it would still look bad; as though I had something to hide, and I don't have any other recent involvement with medical professionals to back me up. Wilma, that's my counsellor, thinks I need to be pushed because I don't know what's best for me and that I'll thank her for it one day. The friend with whom I had discussed the situation at the point when I wrote the letter shares her view that I need to be pushed and that I'm simply scared of intimacy or not thinking clearly. Though I have since spoken about it with my best friends, who feel strongly that I should not be coerced into something like this. The problem is, I do have an attachment to someone and in every way except the physical, it could be described as the same genre of feeling as being in love. Because she's a woman, people are assuming that I'm in denial or in the closet. I've told them

131

over and over again that if I were gay I wouldn't have a problem with it, nor with disclosing it whenever the context called for it. So my counsellor believes that I need to be treated harshly to shake me out of my feelings and force me to direct them towards someone 'appropriate' and my friend thinks I need tough love and railroading into a relationship which takes away all of my personal space and prevents me from getting the time to myself which I need. My social energy is so limited, I need more alone time than most people; even my closest friends, much as I love seeing them, I could not cope with them permanently sharing my living space. Yes, I crave the buzz I get from whatever you wish to call what I feel for my colleague Verena; it gives me the adrenalin rush I need to break through my fatigue and challenge myself with a volunteering role, but it isn't about sex. I just cannot get anybody to believe me; it's like I'm right there in front of them being completely honest with them about my feelings, and they can't even hear me. Or they hear me but insist I'm wrong, and how can I prove otherwise when there's this issue with Verena? So I'm being forced into something I know in my bones isn't right for me and I don't know what to do!"

The tears seemed to come from nowhere as all the anxiety and frustration of her dilemma poured out. Dr Blake sat calmly listening, discreetly moving a box of tissues towards Diane without looking away from her.

"I hear you, Diane, and I believe you."

Simple, uncomplicated words yet they said and meant so much.

"First and foremost, I can assure you that your benefits will not be jeopardised if you refuse to go out on dates against your will. With your consent, I would like to contact this counsellor and let them know this is completely unacceptable. I have all your notes here from your dealings with Dr Fletcher and I am more than satisfied that you need to be on these benefits; I will provide any medical evidence required. I would also recommend that we look at other ways of supporting you. Would you say that you are getting anything out of this counselling?"

"Not any more. I stuck with it because I was afraid it would look as though I no longer had the same level of needs when it came to the benefit reviews. I am only in a better and more stable place because I am able to limit my activities and interactions to a level way below mainstream employed life."

"I absolutely get that; the system is not fit for purpose. The fact you were contemplating forcing these actions upon yourself in your letter proves exactly how much you need a safe and supported lifestyle, but your overall needs are not going to change and your recorded reason for discontinuing this particular counselling arrangement will be my medical recommendation, not any non-compliance on your part."

"Oh, thank you so much. I can safely take down my profile on the dating site without fear of reprisals then?"

"Absolutely."

"I have had a reply already but I couldn't bring myself to string her along. I put down seeking men and women, see, because I'm equally uninterested in both with regard to sex! So I told her that I joined as a result of peer pressure and don't want a partner at all but offered to meet up as a potential new friend. It brought it home to me seeing her photo; there she is genuinely looking for a relationship on a website which is intended purely for that purpose, and here I am misleading her by being on there at all. It's not right. Fortunately she was entirely understanding."

"That is excellent, Diane; you handled that extremely well. I must admit I am concerned that you have believed the feedback from others over your own gut instincts about something like this; something so intimate and personal, when you are clearly so articulate and self-aware. Can you tell me a little more about why you think that is?"

"I suppose it's because I've so often been wrong, or told I'm wrong, and always seem to be on the outside of the accepted social norms and ways of thinking. I've had to try so hard at everything, whether due to fatigue or sensory overload or all the intensive learning I have to do about the social side of things which comes naturally to other people. Not all other people; I'm not claiming to be the only one with issues! See, that's another thing; I mention that something is difficult and somehow the standard reaction is that I'm claiming to be unique in finding it so, when I'm not saying anything of the sort! I'm constantly having to defend my perspective. When someone sees whatever it is that people perceive as not quite right about me, whether because of my autism or because of the whole package of 'me' whatever that is, and tries to grab something out of my hands and talk loudly right in my face, I'm a horrible cow for not simpering with gratitude and I'm an evil person because They Were Trying To Be Nice. It doesn't matter that it hurt me; again, that is never heard or acknowledged even by some of my friends. It doesn't matter to them that it terrifies as well as frustrates me that someone could see me that way, as needing forced physical interventions with no right to autonomy or even to have an opinion about it. As in, what it says about my prospects in life and about my future if I am as inept as people judge me to be; what's my life going to be like when I get old? And why couldn't even some of my own friends have had a bit of compassion when I said that something hurt me instead of taking the side of some random stranger over me and piling on more criticism, then getting angry with me when that hurt me even more? It all makes me feel that I must indeed be a monster and deserve to suffer. It doesn't help that I struggle to process in real time and things people say to me often don't fully hit me until afterwards when it's too damned late to assert myself as I should have at the time. I told a friend once; not anyone I'm still in contact with now, that I was at that time feeling suicidal though I had no plans to act on the feelings. She ripped into me; I was not allowed to talk like that, I was so selfish and inconsiderate because she and other people would be left wondering if there was some way they could have stopped me! Why didn't I have the wits to point out that a) I had specifically said I was not planning to die by suicide but had the feelings and was trying to reach out for the support I needed by admitting it and opening up a dialogue, and b) if she wanted to know how to stop me, maybe not tearing me to shreds at my lowest point would be a useful tip for starters? But no, pathetic mug Diane stood there like the proverbial piece of citrus fruit and took the bollocking, then slunk off home with her tail between her legs, alone in the dark on public transport. Why can't I stick up for myself quickly enough, so that people have grounds for believing I have no personality? I don't deserve any support if I can't even string a sentence together in those circumstances when, as you've already seen, I do have the capacity to do so. There's always this standard of 'normal' that I have to claw my way up towards, whatever it takes; doing my own thing is being lazy or uncooperative or antisocial, because We All Have To Do Things We Don't Want To. So I guess I've come to expect that if something isn't a mountain to climb and doesn't make me utterly miserable and exhausted, it's wrong, and vice versa."

"There is a lot to unpack there, Diane. First of all, I need to check since you have mentioned suicidal feelings albeit in the past. Are you feeling that way now?"

"No, not now, and I swear I would not act on it. Maybe I shouldn't have told you that; I couldn't cope with being sectioned and cooped up somewhere with bright lights, noise and other people around me twenty-four seven!"

"That is not going to happen. You did the right thing in being open about it; both today and in the past, and I am deeply sorry to hear that you had that experience. A person would only be sectioned as a very last resort if they were considered to be an imminent danger to themself or others. You have spoken about your feelings in order to progress away from them and keep yourself safe, which in itself is an indication that sectioning would not be appropriate. The shame and stigma around these feelings, and indeed a lot of the issues you have described, needs to be addressed and removed so that people can be better understood and helped appropriately. I see you as a person who, with the right support and boundaries in place to prevent you from becoming overloaded and distressed, could play a significant role towards that societal shift. You need to know that it is allowed, indeed essential, for you to say no when something doesn't feel right. I suspect that you've struggled and camouflaged while beating yourself up inside so much throughout your life, the sort of tasks people mean when they say that we all have to do things we don't want to do probably don't even register as the most individually challenging to you. The difficulties with processing and putting together a response in pressured circumstances, as you describe, are a part of your autism and do not negate your skills at all, nor do they have any bearing on your personality and how much you have to offer."

Diane dabbed at her eyes which were stinging with tears once again. Could what Dr Blake was saying be true; could she, dare she believe it? Yet again she was holding back the incident with Brenda Culper; referring in general terms to people taking away her autonomy and not hearing her, leaving out the part where she recklessly pushed hot liquid at Brenda. And how much of her previous notes had Dr Blake seen? GPs were so notoriously busy; she couldn't have had time to read all that far back.

"I've made some awfully bad judgements in the past though; gotten emotional at work, ranted in front of customers, spoken rudely, made people uncomfortable, drank too much on office nights out and picked arguments or let myself get too maudlin and generally been a pain in the backside, snapped at people more times than I can count even when I didn't know I was being aggressive. I'm not talking about committing crime when I say aggressive; I just seem to have a nastiness about me that makes things I say wrong when they would be reasonable coming from other people. Like, for instance, when a new guy at one workplace called me Diana as he was on his way out, so I called after him, 'Diane!' Because that is my name, not Diana. I was stating a fact. To me, Diane and Diana are entirely different names; it feels no more accurate to answer to Diana than it would to Madonna or Peggy Sue! OK, so perhaps that's my autistic pedantry, but honestly you would have thought I had put him in the stocks and thrown rotten tomatoes at him while simultaneously smearing the good name of every Diana in history including the late Princess of Wales! 'Poor guy, he's only been here a week, he's still learning everyone's names, you're so up yourself, so tactless, so self-centred! Can't you let something go and be normal for once?' All I did was call out, quickly because he was about to go out of earshot, that my name is Diane! Was I supposed to patronise him by not doing him the courtesy of telling him my correct name? To me, that would have been equally bad. But My Tone Of Voice. It happens again and again and I honestly don't know how to pre-empt it and make sure it comes out right; I have a hard enough time figuring out what to say quickly enough! As a compromise because of how I come across, I have to let it go when people call me Di, when I'd really prefer that to be reserved for the people close to me. Not because I think I'm better than everybody else and too up myself to have my name abbreviated, but because it takes something away from how warm and connected and cherished it makes me feel when I hear it from my best friends if I then hear it from somebody I met five minutes ago at a conference and with whom I have nothing in common. I've forfeited that choice in my own identity by being a snooty cow. I tried being self-effacing the next time someone called me Diana after that new guy; I said 'just Diane'. I thought that sounded less 'tetchy', but then I had six months of him thinking he was hilarious by calling me 'Just Diane' from then on. 'Just Diane, there's a phone call for you! Just Diane, are you finished with the photocopier? Just Diane, has the newsletter come out yet?' Six months! With all the others smirking at me then turning to one another laughing at me getting what I deserved! My facial expressions are a problem too; I have found myself in dangerous situations because I've apparently looked at somebody the wrong way. Sometimes I guess I did; I have misophonia so cannot tolerate certain noises like chewing loudly or slurping kissing sounds, which has gotten me accused of being jealous when in fact it's the sound itself turning each cell in my body into a miniature blackboard having microscopic chalk scraped down it. Anyway, I'm going on about trivial examples and I must be overrunning my time slot. To get back to my worst mistakes, getting drunk and running off at the mouth offending people or crying about my problems and getting into potentially dangerous situations, although I learned from those days and made changes to my drinking habits especially around people who aren't my friends, I don't know if I've finished paying for those mistakes or indeed if I ever will. After all, the whole point of punishment is that the person who has done wrong doesn't get to decide when the punishment ends; when they've been punished enough."

"Diane, first of all, the cancellation into which you were booked was a double appointment and when I received your letter, I had your booking extended to the other half of it as I sensed from the content that there was a lot you would need to confide. For you to come to the conclusion that you could be justifiably forced into a sexual relationship against your own wishes, there had to have been a significant, long-term breakdown in your ability both to trust yourself and to question the views of others, especially those in positions of authority. Secondly, what you have described to me here is a combination of a lack of autism understanding and outright bullying which has clearly damaged you. I accept that you have made mistakes and bad choices in the past; there are mitigating factors for a lot of that and you have made the necessary adjustments of your own initiative, which is in many ways even more commendable than someone going through life without making the same errors. I want to work on that with you; on getting you to a point where you can feel free of this sense that you haven't been punished enough and that you owe some enormous debt to society. Now, you have mentioned some friends to whom you are particularly close and who disagreed with your being pressured into dating. Are you in regular contact with those friends; are they close by?"

"Yes. Des and Jason; they're brothers. They live in the next lot of flats and I see them or message them at least once a week. They are... They are my shepherd moons..."

She was off again! How could she have any more tears left? She took another tissue and blew her nose.

"Sorry about that. I don't know, I can talk about some of the most difficult and painful experiences and not get upset, then as soon as I talk about something or someone that is so precious to me, I dissolve into an undignified snivelling mess! Anyway, yeah, we were watching a programme about Saturn and the presenter was explaining how some of its satellites act as shepherd moons by their gravitational influence keeping the rings in shape; keeping their particles together and the space around them clear. Which is precisely what Des and Jason do for me; holding me together in the space I need, always beside me but never intrusive."

"Shepherd moons. Hmm, I like that concept a lot. You have an authentic gift with words and insights, Diane. So am I right in thinking that you found it hard to go along with Des and Jason's assurances and allow yourself to walk away from this dating site because it didn't fit with your ingrained understanding that for a thing to be right it has to be painful and that your punishment isn't over yet?"

"That's pretty much it, yes, though the prospect of losing my benefits had a lot to do with it too. I actually said to Wilma, and my friend Kate who is the one pushing me to go along with it for my own good, that it was essentially making me go out with people in order to keep getting the money I need to live on and that it felt like joining the world's oldest profession. I was allegedly being silly, obstructive, not wanting to move forward; too lazy to get over Verena. With whom I did not want to have a sexual relationship in the first place! To be fair to Kate, she did say that Wilma was wrong to use my benefits as a threat."

"Which she absolutely was. That was unconscionable. I am still not quite clear on how a problem arose with your colleague Verena when you were specifically told you were not being accused of any offence?"

"Oh, I did my trademark, my signature move: I made her uncomfortable. By hero-worshipping her; by allegedly mooning around like a teenager with a crush; my pathetic puppy-dog adoration, and they couldn't address it because they were tied by political correctness and she couldn't speak to me about it because she was so afraid I would be tipped over the edge and start stalking her. Yes, I always made it clear how much her approval meant to me and I guess my admiration showed too much when I looked at her. I didn't need to behave improperly or unlawfully to freak her out; my emotionally intense autistic self was enough. Are you absolutely sure I'm not a monster, Dr Blake? After all, making someone uncomfortable is becoming recognised as serious misconduct; a victim-defined offence, sexual or not. I genuinely don't want to harm anyone yet I'm a predator simply by liking someone too much!"

"Again, you are applying criteria here which were designed to tackle actions and behaviours that don't fit those aspects of your own life to which you are applying them. You are judging yourself as though you had harassed Verena. Your managers are making you responsible for their own shortcomings in supporting an autistic volunteer, which is reprehensible. You mentioned that you were removed from the work which brought you into contact with Verena. Are you still volunteering there in another capacity?"

"No; I'm suspended for at least three months. They are going to review it after that; call me in for a meeting and I have to satisfy them that I'm over her. I guess the counsellor thought forcing me to join a dating site would help with that, though she made it clear that she felt it was what I needed anyway. I really want to stay on the project because it was my idea and I put so much into it; I'm passionate about it and I was intending to become one of the moderators on an online forum which is part of it. That can be done from home as can the training for it, but they won't even let me do that until I can prove I can keep my emotions under control. You see, when we had the launch event for the project, Verena credited the idea to another colleague who is a friend of hers; said she wanted to credit one person in particular with whom the project began and whom she was proud to call a friend. I was due to speak next and she was going to introduce me; it was the time for my own talk to begin. So, mug that I am, I was on cloud nine thinking she'd called me a friend and I stood up all full of myself ready to give my presentation. Then she called Sally up on stage and I had to sit back down again praying nobody had seen or filmed me giving myself too much credit. So when I gave my presentation, I had an approved script but I threw in a couple of references to it having been my idea. It honestly wasn't a dig at Sally; she was a huge help liaising with the jobsearch hub where she has contacts. As Mr Thurlowe, that's the branch manager who suspended me, took great pleasure in pointing out, it wouldn't have gotten any further without her because she has credibility whereas I'm merely an appendage. But my deviating from the script of my presentation and asserting, twice, that it was my idea was evidence of my being out of control and unable to be trusted to moderate a forum in a professional manner."

"You lying hypocrite, Diane", sneered her inner voice; "the evidence of being out of control was your assaulting Brenda Culper with hot tea because of your selfish wounded pride!"

"An appendage?", Dr Blake was saying, barely audible over Diane's demons. "Did this manager, Mr Thurlowe, use that precise term?"

"He did, and that's nothing compared to some of the other terms he used. Spoiled little princess. Hiding behind my rainbow flag. Childlike female, which was a hasty substitute for what he was about to say and stopped himself after 're'. You can probably figure out what the second syllable was going to be. Rhymes with 'bard'. The context was about how my supposedly mooning around comes across; that Verena had the right to come to work without feeling uncomfortable. Which of course she does, and since I didn't need to commit an offence to make her feel that way, it makes my very existence wrong and toxic!"

"Goodness me. What a dilemma for you to have had to cope with. Your existence is not wrong or toxic; it is very important that you know that. It is a powerful testament to your passion and selfless will to help others that you can contemplate remaining involved with these people for the sake of continuing with this project. I will certainly support your case for working exclusively from home on this project and we are going to collaborate on building your self-esteem so that you are not so vulnerable to abuse. I want you to make another double appointment with me for two weeks' time. In the meantime, are you happy for me to contact your counsellor about this? I shall send you a copy of the letter."

"Yes please." Diane handed over the business card with Wilma's contact details. "I cannot thank you enough, Dr Blake."

"It's a pleasure. When is your next appointment with your counsellor?"

"A week on Thursday."

"Right. Good. That gives me plenty of time to contact her. You need not feel any obligation to keep that appointment. If you feel you would like to, I completely understand, but I would recommend that you do not continue with any further sessions. I see that you have been engaging with her for some time. If they were being managed in a way which was conducive to helping you move forward in a suitable fashion, the past events you have spoken of today would not still hold such absolute power over you, especially in terms of your feelings around the right of others to compel you to seek a sexual relationship, and your ongoing sense of punishment."

"Yes, I think I would like to keep the appointment; I need to manage my own closure, if that makes sense."

"It absolutely does, especially given what I know of you from your letter and from speaking with you today. What are your plans for the rest of the day? It is important that you give yourself some quiet space after an intensive appointment like this."

"Agreed; that is precisely my plan. You have lifted such a weight from my shoulders. The activities I have planned for the rest of today involve a certain website and the delete button, plenty of snuggles with my cat, then maybe a walk this evening if I have the energy."

"That's the spirit. I'm glad you have a pet; they are so therapeutic, aren't they?"

"Yes, they are. Farolita is a Siamese and she's so loving. I found her as a stray with a tiny kitten; I fostered them both until enough had been done to establish that nobody was looking for her and I could get her spayed, microchipped and registered to me. Des and Jason have her son. His name is Luke."

"Oh, how lovely! Farolita, did you say? That's not a name I've heard of."

"Well, her official name is Farola; it's Spanish for 'lantern' or 'streetlight'. Farolita is the diminutive form, as in 'little streetlight'. I found her hanging around a lamp post and I love streetlights as an aesthetic interest. Maria the vet is Spanish and she was so helpful to me when I took them in. Luke was originally Luz, as in light. I was going to keep him too but one day Des and Jason were visiting and Jason's ear was hurting; he lost half his hearing from an infection when he was a child and the pain recurs periodically. Anyway, Luz as he was then, scrambled right up onto his shoulder and snuggled in and I knew; this was Jason's cat. He renamed him Luke because the hard consonant is easier for him to hear so the name resonated better with him."

"What a wonderful story. Keep on reaching out to your shepherd moons and let yourself be held together exactly as you are, and I will see you in a couple of weeks."

Diane put her used tissues in the bin which Dr Blake smilingly indicated upon seeing her looking around for it, overwhelmed by her luck in finding such an understanding and empathic doctor. She suspected that the next few patients with appointments that afternoon would wait beyond their booked time and that she would do the same in future; she was more than willing to, knowing that it meant others would access the same immense relief she felt right now. She made the follow-up appointment then walked home via Caberfeidh Road. It was still daylight and the streetlights were off; their elemental power to bejewel the velvet gown of night held dormant within deceptively opaque glass. She smiled knowingly up at them as they kept their secrets; staunchly and quietly waiting their turn to shine again, blending innocuously with the busy daytime world.

13

The feeling of relief was almost worth the stress and angst of the preceding two weeks as Diane clicked on the button to confirm removal of her profile from the dating site. She had messaged Priya first to let her know, assuring her that she still wished to meet and giving the number of the temporary, cheap pay as you go phone she had bought to use for safely conducting any dating site business, in case of any delays or need to change arrangements. She would not normally give out any contact details at all so soon in a new friendship beginning online but these were hardly normal circumstances, her research had confirmed Priya's identity and she owed her that much. Priya was owed that much by the accumulation of circumstances in which she was an innocent bystander, Diane corrected herself, remembering all that Dr Blake had said. As soon as Priya replied confirming that she had saved Diane's number, one final check of her page verifying that there were no further prospective dates to take into account gave her the green light to take back control and put an end to this charade. She messaged Des and Jason with a brief update and promised to tell them more when she saw them next, ate a blissfully unhurried and unobserved dinner then poured herself a dram to quietly celebrate.

She had a well-advised early night and sleep soon claimed her.

There was more activity in the café this time as she soundlessly pushed down the door's brass handle and walked inside. Freshly baked gingerbread filled the air with a warm homecoming embrace as the pages of a newspaper turned with an unhurried sibilance through the events and lives of the day. Voices murmured companionably; a coffee cup was set gently down on a saucer. Behind the counter, a woman of around Diane's age with curled brown hair and wearing a light apron over a pale yellow dress arranged the portions of gingerbread on a two-tiered stand lined with cream, scalloped edged paper doilies. She looked up and smiled as Diane walked over.

"Good evening; what can I get you?"

Diane felt an awareness she did not fully comprehend telling her that she couldn't stay. A dimly lit realisation came that she had no money on her; it seemed to be a far-off knowledge, not the hot embarrassment which such a dawning would normally bring.

"Thank you but I was only passing today; I've found out about this place recently and I wanted to have a look. It's beautifully laid out and feels so relaxing. I hope to have time to stay for a while another day; I live locally and often walk along Caberfeidh Road. I'm Diane, by the way."

"That's no problem; I'll see you then. Thank you for your kind words, Diane, and I hope you will become a regular visitor in the future. Oh, and I'm Joan."

Was this Joan Morley? Diane had pictured her as an older, motherly type. Or her daughter perhaps? No, the article had said that Joan and Leonard Morley had no children. She supposed it was possible that there was someone working at the café who coincidentally was also called Joan, but somehow she knew deep down as she walked back through the white lamplight that this friendly woman who looked to be around her own age was the Joan Morley who owned the café. With that certainty came the added awareness, absolute and utterly calm, that she was dreaming. Her footsteps continued along Caberfeidh Road as solid and real as in her waking hours, but she was walking in a dream along the road as it was around sixty years ago. That explained the younger-looking trees and the beautiful swan neck streetlamps! She was too pragmatic to believe that she had literally gone back in time; not that her mind wasn't open to the possibility of time being something other than linear, but because she would never be chosen by fate for anything so exciting. No, she was being shown this scene because she was open to it and she was meant to learn something from it and to change something in her own time, in the present or near future.

She thought back to her brief conversation with Joan. There had been no sense of being rushed, chivvied or questioned. She must have been looking as she usually did when she walked into an unfamiliar place; the adjustment and processing always showed too clearly on her face and was often mistaken for timidity or being lost, much to her frustration and despair. Yet there was no hint of the endless stream of "Are you sure?"s, or "Don't look so / You look" opening lines which never ended in anything conducive to her self-esteem; those demoralising, recurring utterances that normally flowed through the centre of her life in a turgid river, always on the point of sweeping her away and drowning her self-worth. The relief went deeper than the fact of it not having happened; she had been somehow free of the constant defensive anticipation of it. The entire atmosphere of the place was of somewhere nobody would be rushed, clucked over or their choices questioned; Joan Morley's customers would be safe from having their eating techniques scrutinised, criticised or remarked upon. She had created a sanctuary; a safe space ahead of its time. Diane wondered what life experience had fuelled the insight which she had recognised on an instinctive level in Joan, who had lived and worked in a time when neurodivergence and mental health were not understood and spoken of in the same way as now.

Diane reached the other end of Caberfeidh Road; still dreaming, still fully aware of the fact. She felt no apprehension about not having woken up and not knowing of any technique to make herself do so. She had free will to walk around Inverbrudock in its silver lamplit past. The heady rush of control and power made her feel almost as if she could fly, though she wasn't quite ready to test out that feeling. What she did want to do was take advantage of the opportunity to see whether there had been one of these elegant streetlamps in the same spot as the modern one around which Farolita had been rubbing when she found her. She walked on.

It stood proud, casting its moonlike glow over the corner where another path branched off towards what would in her own era be the flats where she lived; just reaching far enough to drape the ghostly limit of its rays over the foliage of the small, neat shrubs which would grow to shelter a single grey kitten in his time of need. Diane touched the cold iron post, rough under her warm fingertips as she looked up at the hanging light and the vastness of the night sky beyond. "I'm dreaming so I can do whatever I like!", she called out as she swung around the metal standard. "Be at peace with it when your time comes to an end; your successor lights my family cats' way home", she added as she patted its icy surface, thankful that the modern ones held a little warmth in comparison for a small, lost furry body to seek.

What now? Her flat was in a block which had quite possibly not even been built during this era. She must surely do something more profound with this unprecedented opportunity than swing around lamp posts, fun though that indisputably was. Yet even as she searched her mind for a logical response to that question, time was turning the corner and rushing on.

Diane's eyes flew open; the night and the streetlamps yielded to the featureless off-white of her bedroom ceiling.

A lucid dream! She remembered having had those occasionally in the past and it always felt like an exciting privilege to have that knowledge that she was dreaming, but they had seldom been so detailed nor so relevant. Concerns about possible episodes of sleep paralysis made her wary of attempting to bring on lucid dreams and she doubted that she could keep her thoughts focused enough to do so anyway but she remained interested in the phenomenon. There was no doubt in her mind that this one had happened for a reason and there may be more to come. All she needed to do was stay open to the process and welcome it.

14

The swathe of deep pink in Priya Dayal's hair was a blessing in ensuring that Diane could easily recognise her. She had struggled her whole life with prosopagnosia; difficulty in recognising faces. The embarrassment it caused her and the hurt and offence she found herself inflicting on others by appearing not to have paid attention or cared enough to remember them had blighted many a new encounter. It was not always practicable to announce to everyone she met that she may not recognise them easily until she had seen them on several occasions. In this case, to have trouble distinguishing Priya from other similar Asian women would have felt inherently racist even though she had exactly the same issue with white people and it was something which she genuinely could not help. Hair was often her point of reference for recognising someone, whether from a previous encounter, a photograph or even a description. There was certainly no mistaking the vibrant magenta stripe in Priya's hair as she got off the train at Inverbrudock's small, quiet station.

"Hi; I'm Diane! It's lovely to meet you! I hope your day in Arbroath went well; there are some fabulous shops there too."

"Aren't there just! I try to arrange my meetings there for right after payday, especially when I've got birthdays coming up. I can get so many unusual and good quality gifts there. Isn't this a pretty little station! I've seen it so many times from the train but you don't get to appreciate these places until you get off and look around."

"I know; I thought the same when I came to view my flat here. So I take it you don't know Inverbrudock that well? Don't worry; I'll see you back to the station later, I know what it's like finding your way around a new place. It takes me a few visits and all routes look different on the way back or after dark."

"Thank you. So where's this pub we're going to?"

"The Fulmar's Nest, on the High Street. It's upstairs with a great view out to sea. The staff in there are friendly and down to Earth. As a woman on my own in a new town I felt secure and accepted in there from the start. Mark can be a bit harsh with people who've had too much to drink and that can make him appear intimidating; he doesn't always switch that gruffness off easily with the next customer, but at the same time it helps to make the place feel safeguarded. I get the feeling he appreciates it in his unsentimental way when the regulars get to that point of understanding that it's how he is and nothing personal; once I got comfortable enough to ignore it and be chilled out with him, the dynamic settled into something which is, in its way, kind of heartwarming. He's not nasty or out of line; he just doesn't have that switch he can flip to instant sunshine. Helen and Krista are lovely. Now, before we go up, do you want to agree on a story of how we met?" Diane looked around briefly to ensure nobody was in earshot; "I haven't exactly been shouting it from the rooftops that I let myself be harangued into joining a dating site and misleading people on it when it isn't what I want, and I don't know how discreet you want or need to be."

"Oh, I don't mind people knowing that I'm actively looking for a female partner and that I'm on a dating site, though I do appreciate you asking. For your privacy, though, you're right; we should agree on a back story."

"You mentioned that you're into local history? I've been doing a bit of research in that category lately; perhaps we could use that."

"Well, I work at the Angus Records Centre in Montrose, so that would fit perfectly!"

"Excellent! As it happens, I genuinely am interested in finding out a bit more about the history of Inverbrudock so

I'm looking forward to talking more about that. My best friends, Des and Jason, are not originally local either; Des moved here not long before I did and his brother came up from London to join him. Jason is partially deaf and he was finding the city too stressful. Des worked offshore for a while then he got his job in Dundee and rather than find a small one-bedroom place at city prices, he looked at smaller towns round about so that Jason could share with him. So, much as I talk to them about anything and everything, they don't have any more knowledge of local history than I do."

"That's decided then! Right, I'm excited to see this local pub of yours and take in the atmosphere. Ah, here we are, I see! What lovely big bay windows!"

"Oh yes. At this time through the week we shouldn't have any problem getting a window table. Let's go up!"

Krista was tidying up behind the bar, her cropped scarlet hair and the sparkling studs in her ears catching the spotlights as she lined up the opened bottles of house wine and wiped faint streaks of dishwasher tablet residue off a couple of glasses. She waved a cheery welcome as Diane and Priya walked in.

"Hey, Diane! And..."

"Priya. She's a friend of mine in Montrose; she's been in Arbroath today so we're having a catch-up on her way home. Priya, this is Krista."

"Hi, Krista; it's lovely to meet you. What a beautiful pub; no wonder Diane enjoys coming here!"

"Thank you! So what can I get you both? We've got some popular new bottles of house wine at the moment."

Diane and Priya exchanged looks and nodded.

"Are you into red, white or rose wine these days, Priya? I will still take any; I love a warming red in the colder weather, although it's so cosy in here it's not actually needed."

When she was still expecting to have to go through the dating ritual, Diane had been dreading the prospect of endless awkward "you decide, no YOU decide; I'm not bothered, neither am I" type conversations complete with escalating nervous laughter as long-suffering hospitality staff, many of whom would be working their socks off under pressure and for minimum wage, waited patiently for each trying-too-hard pairing to sort themselves out. She had prepared a few scripted openers like this; giving maximum flexibility, deftly including a preferred option while giving the other party a get-out if that option were unsuitable for them. Of course this initial awkwardness didn't apply exclusively to dating scenarios, but Diane was relieved that she was not going to have to go through it over and over again in search of an outcome which she was relentlessly being told by others that she must learn to want. Today was different; she was happy and much less fatigued to be treating Priya with the consideration she would apply to anyone whilst enjoying her company in the context which was right and honest.

"A bottle of red sounds wonderful. Yes please, Krista; we'll take a bottle of house red."

"Merlot or Shiraz?"

Again, the two friends looked at one another. This time it was Priya who was ready with the hack for bypassing an awkward conversation.

"Could you recommend one for us, please?"

Krista opened the rich deep blackcurrant-coloured Shiraz with a flourish, its dark, woody bouquet already reaching their nostrils as she poured it into the glasses. Diane insisted on treating Priya since she had been the one to come to a new place.

"I'll bring the bottle over to your table. I presume you'll be by the window?"

"Of course! Thanks, Krista."

They sat down, taking in the view over the darkening sea. Priya looked around the pub as she ran her hand over the heather-coloured velvet of the chair, admiring the cleanliness of the matching carpet and the polished brass rails along the bar.

"Thanks for saving us from the risk of simultaneously making different choices of wine there!"

"No problem, and Krista has made an excellent recommendation here. This is quite a substantial, complex wine for a house special!"

"See, this is what I love about a red wine. To me, its bouquet and taste have to remind me of the night."

"Yes, I know what you mean. Dark and full of unseen layers. Cheers!"

The two women clinked glasses.

"And here's to your future. I truly hope that you meet someone soon who is exactly what you're looking for and is on the site for the right reasons."

"Thank you! But please don't feel bad about that. As you said, it's always good to meet a new friend. In fact, your honesty and integrity have inspired me to persevere with the site. I was considering at least giving it a break myself after the last one. Even though you and I have agreed this isn't a date, it still feels like bad etiquette to talk about the last one"; Priya grimaced.

"No, feel free!"

"Well, it was awkward from the start; there was no chemistry but we still kept on speaking at the same time then apologising at the same time, ugh. So I took it as a reaching attempt to revive a flagging conversation when she asked me where I was from; I'd already told her. Or, I thought, perhaps she had genuinely forgotten. I reminded her: 'Inverness'. Then she said it; she actually leaned right over the table towards me and asked me it, slowly as though she were talking to a child. 'No, where are you really from?'."

"Urgh! No way! I am so sorry you experienced that."

"I mean, it's not the first time I've been on the receiving end of racism and it won't be the last; it wasn't even nearly the worst. But somehow, I guess, my guard was down a bit as part of me must have thought that if someone were racist they wouldn't have accepted a date with me. I'm not as naïve as that makes me sound; I wasn't conscious of thinking that. Anyway, I leaned in and spoke slowly and clearly as she had to me"; Priya mimicked her movement and tone, emphasising each syllable; "Inverness".

"How demoralising for you! See, this is why people talk about microaggressions, though I'd call that more direct racism. In a way, the term 'microaggression' is misleading as it covers scenarios which are not aggression as in anger or menace. It's more about the effect they have; the way they chip away at people. My friends Des and Jason whom I mentioned earlier are black and they have to deal with all levels of racism too." Diane related the tale of Jason's experience when buying the curry ingredients.

"Nice comeback! And yes, that's exactly the sort of thing. It's not conscious hatred the way people understand racism to be; so many seem to think that racism begins and ends with violence, name calling and deliberate discrimination. All of which are still major issues, but in between there's all the stereotyping, the questioning, the lazy misconceptions. And that, being asked where I'm really from, hurt me as a woman of colour but also as an Invernessian and a Highlander! Inverness is my home town. I was born there; I grew up there; I love and miss it, and here was someone telling me I couldn't possibly belong to it! As if I hadn't had enough of that due to being gay. That's more accepted up there now than it used to be, but there's still a long way to go. In this day and age, some people believe they're being so progressive by not actively objecting to brown and black people living amongst them while still thinking a 'proper' Highland woman must be white and be a Morag or a Mairi, not a Priyanka! Needless to say, there was no question of a second date with that one. I came home, punched a few cushions, had a good cry, made myself a cup of tea and decided I was going to give myself a break from the stress and come off the site for a while. Then I figured I shouldn't make the decision while my feelings were running so high; I would avoid looking at the site for a bit and deal with any notifications as and when, though I was still feeling inclined to come off altogether. And then I got the new potential match notification about your profile."

Diane's eyes filled with tears. "And I shouldn't even have been on there because I'm not looking for what the site is intended for. Oh, Priya. You deserve so much better. Look, I know I said I was on there because of peer pressure and that's partly true, but I feel you deserve the whole truth. I had some trouble over hero-worshipping, not sexually, someone at the organisation where I've been volunteering; nothing untoward happened but the person became uncomfortable with it. So a counsellor with whom I'd been engaging essentially blackmailed me into joining the dating site, saying that she'd cut me off for not complying with therapy and jeopardise my benefits if I didn't join. Then one of my other close friends, also believing that I needed to be pushed for my own good, backed her up; not on the blackmail but on the supposed need for me to force myself into dating. Fortunately I have since spoken with a highly clued-up GP who restored common sense and gave me a way out of the blackmail situation, which is why I've been able to take down my profile and not deceive anybody else who is on that site in good faith. I wouldn't normally dump this sort of personal history onto someone at the first meeting, but after what you've had to put up with and then me not being on the site for the right reasons, it feels wrong to let you go on thinking I strung you along because my mates nagged me to."

"Oh my gosh, Diane, that is horrendous! What sort of therapist coerces someone into dating against their will?"

"One who means well but doesn't listen or believe any mindset seeking outcomes different from her own personal, conventional ideals! I think she genuinely does believe that I'm going to conform and thank her for it and that it's what I need. Not to worry; I have one more session with her and that will be to say goodbye, because my new doctor did more in one appointment than she has in all the sessions I've had with her. My doctor listened, then dug a bit deeper; asked the right questions and made time for me to answer."

"Well, thank Heavens for your new doctor. It means a lot that you have trusted me with this, and please take the burden off your shoulders about feeling you've deceived me or wasted my time! I am delighted to have met you as a friend!"

The wine glasses refilled, the conversation moved on to local history.

"I'm particularly interested in finding out more about a café which used to be up at the far end of the High Street, in the fifties and sixties. It was called 'The Haven Café'. The woman who ran it was named Joan Morley. I read one article about it on the Bygone Inverbrudock site; it said that she had to sell it because of her husband's gambling debts. It made me so sad, especially as that building is now a rather depressing, tacky betting shop."

Krista, clearing the next table, looked up as Diane spoke.

"Sorry to interrupt but I couldn't help hearing you there; Helen might know more about that place. I'm sure I've heard her talking about it with her mum, who remembered it. They were saying the same as you, about how sad it was that the building ended up being a run-down betting shop. Ah yes, I do remember; that betting shop is closing down, that's why they were talking about it. People gamble online these days. I could get Helen to message you if you like?"

"Would you? Thanks, Krista! Please ask her to add me; my surname is Abercrombie and my avatar is a Victorian-style streetlight. You're welcome to add me too."

"I will do. Her surname is Tulloch, and I'm Kristanna Jorgensen."

Priya good-naturedly teased Diane about adding other women on their 'date', sending both of them into peals of laughter.

"I reckon we're way beyond being Jane Austen formulaic on this 'date'!", laughed Diane, reminding Priya that they would also need to add one another on their social media. "Oh my word, could you imagine that lot from 'Pride and Prejudice' with social media accounts?!"

"Status"; they laughingly spoke simultaneously; "It's Complicated!"

"You know", confessed Diane. "after we had to read that at school, I felt so much empathy for Mary Bennet. I never had an imaginary friend as such, but I used to visualise having long conversations with her; getting her out of the shadow of her sisters and giving her the space to say all she had to say. I felt her alienation, her striving, viscerally. Given what I know now, she resonates as autistic to me."

"Yes, I can see where you're coming from there. Trying so hard to keep up and fit in; as you say, to make herself heard in a society which wasn't compatible with how her brain worked and the pace at which she needed to be able to compose her input."

"And get a word in edgeways with Kitty and Lydia around; especially Lydia. I was exhausted by reading any passages with her in!"

"Quite. She must have taken a bit of energy to create as a character!"

"You know, what I find particularly intriguing about that book is that Jane Austen wrote about these five sisters, made the eldest one stand out as the absolute picture perfect ideal of womanhood at the time, in looks, character and all, and named her Jane. Which in itself is not what intrigues me. It's the fact that for all her idealised perfection, Jane comes across as quite dull. She's not the complex and interesting principal female character; Elizabeth is. I find the psychology of that fascinating; I'd love to be able to go back in time and sit Jane Austen down for a proper heart to heart about it."

"As long as that counsellor of yours doesn't follow you through the time portal, otherwise who knows what poor Jane would end up writing!"

"Haha! Excellent point!"

After a couple of hours of wine and laughter, Diane saw Priya off at the station as she had promised; Priya assuring her that she would pass on any information she found out about the café. Back home, Farolita winding herself around her ankles, she accepted the three requests awaiting her from Priya, Krista and Helen; there were also messages from Des and Kate, both seeking to arrange their next get-togethers with her. The next item on her calendar, however, was a queasy necessity; her closing session with Wilma, who would by now have received the uncompromisingly forthright letter recently copied to her from Dr Blake. Much as her belief in her own instincts had been restored, she was not looking forward to finding out how the counsellor would interact with her after having received it.

15

Wilma's face appeared on the screen, composed and impassive as always. Diane had not covered the small square showing the view from her own camera this time.

"So, Diane. I have received a letter from your GP, ah, Marsaili Blake; I understand that she has recommended that we terminate these sessions. Given the impasse we have reached regarding helping you to move forward constructively with your personal life, I am inclined to agree." She pronounced the doctor's first name to rhyme with "Bailey".

"It's 'MAR-sa-lee'; it's the Scottish Gaelic equivalent of Marjorie. 'Dr Blake' to you and me. Yes, Wilma, I agree too. I have kept this appointment because I wanted to have proper closure; we have been working together for some time and I acknowledge that you believed you were acting in my best interests by forcing me to join a dating site. I will never condone the blackmail, and that is what it was. Not the necessary pushing of the wrong-headed client for their own good; not 'being cruel to be kind'; it was blackmail. You didn't listen to me, Wilma; you applied your own understanding of what you believe to be best for everybody, because society as a whole inundates us with constant propaganda and pressure to believe it. The truth is, it is not necessarily best for everyone to be in relationships. Some of us need our own space. This isn't about my being autistic either; plenty of autistic people do want a partner and get one. My enhanced need for alone time and private space is compatible with, not because of, my autism. I believe that my feelings regarding Verena were - and still are, they're not going to go away overnight - a product of that societal expectation; of the fact that my emotional intensity needed an outlet and society tells us that outlet is another person.

That and my needing the buzz of hero-worship to counteract the fatigue of regularly travelling and going into a work environment even as a volunteer. You conflated that with our society's obsession with sex and finding a partner, making both my feelings and the way forward from them into something irrelevant to my reality. As my counsellor, you should have listened and believed me about that reality. That said, I believe that you sincerely thought the course of action you imposed on me would turn out for the good. I don't feel that you intended any harm. In a way, that is even more scary. You made me feel like a bad person for listening to my own instincts and being true to myself."

"I am sorry that you feel that way, Diane, but I resent being accused of blackmail and made out to be corrupt to another professional."

"What else would you call it, Wilma? I do what you ask against my wishes or lose my benefits? And as for your not having come out smelling of roses from a confidential conversation between me and my doctor, well, you know I've had this said to me so many times but for once the boot is on the other foot: This is not about you."

"Diane, if you're not willing to try…"

"Oh, I did. I signed up on that site, which by the way was not quite as inclusive as you said; it made no provision for non-binary people, though it does now after I emailed them about it. I even selected both men and women as an option, since my sexual interest in both is the same; zero. I had a message from a lovely person; I was honest with her and she is now a friend, having agreed to meet me on that basis. On her last date she had ended up experiencing racism from the other party, so it was rather unfair to her that the next woman she contacted turned out to be on the site on false pretences; fortunately she was profoundly understanding when I explained. I knew once and for all after meeting her and having an absolute blast that it wasn't about fearing negative experiences or failing to commit to some mandatory path of righteousness; it was simply not right to force a context which is fundamentally incompatible with me. Oh, one more thing; thank you for the laugh you gave me when you sent that demeaning PDF leaflet intended for teenagers with crushes, and put 'any problems with attachment let me know'. I sprayed a mouthful of my drink right across this room."

Diane thought for a moment that a flicker of amusement may have ever so briefly crossed Wilma's poker face.

"I think our time is up, Wilma; I wish you well."

"Yes. Goodbye, Diane."

The screen went blank. Switching off the computer, Diane smiled with relief, stroking a sleepy Farolita as she picked up her tablet to catch up with her friends.

Having established that Des and Jason would be coming over later on with Luke and a couple of bottles of wine to celebrate her renewed autonomy, Diane bookmarked some pizza delivery menus, got plates and the extra cat bowls ready and settled down to read the longer message from Helen. The content was heartbreaking as well as interesting.

The café, Helen wrote, had a poignant reason for being called "The Haven Café". Joan Morley's mother, Martha Bannerman, had been a member of the Sutherland family who lived in one of the large town houses on the seafront; there had been a tragedy involving a younger sister who was killed by a horse and cart after running out of the house. Martha Sutherland had been engaged to be married at the time; Joan had been born two years later. According to Helen's mother, it was understood that a chance comment by Martha had unwittingly led to their father catching the youngest sister in a place where she was not supposed to be; a room on the other side of a connecting door which she used as a bolthole. This was strictly forbidden as the house had been divided into two properties and the room now belonged to the other half of the dwelling. It was as a result of her punishment for this and the loss of her hideaway that little Harriet ran out into the road distraught and met her fatal accident. She had been ten years old. Even though she had not deliberately told tales, Martha never forgave herself and it cast a long shadow over the rest of her life. Told the full story as an adult, it seemed that Joan had run the café the way she did to recreate the peaceful sanctuary which was taken from the aunt she never knew.

No wonder the café had felt like such an accepting and unpressured environment! Diane surmised that the forbidden room must have been in the attic, the booths had that sense of a cosy space under the rafters. Her heart ached even more keenly to think how it must have devastated Joan when she had to give up the café. Then there was poor Martha Bannerman, already carrying such a grievous burden; how must she have felt if she were still around and knew about it when that positive, nurturing space was lost all over again?

Helen's message went on to recommend that Diane talk to a friend of hers, Sharon Penhaligon, who worked at the Maritime Hotel. Sharon had grown up in the house which was the other half of the Sutherlands' property, though that house had since been sold and she now lived in a flat in town. She was also a close friend of the Sutherlands who still lived in their family home; Charlene and her brother Brandon. Helen didn't know the Sutherlands well as they seldom came into the pub, but Sharon often did especially when her cousin Bethany was visiting from Perth. Helen advised Diane that Sharon would be on early shift at the hotel the next day; Helen would message her and let her know that Diane was interested in researching the café and that she had given her the background. Thanking her, Diane still held back the fact she had been having detailed dreams about the café; at the same time, she sensed more than ever that these dreams had been shown to her for a purpose.

16

Jason took his turn to refill the wine glasses as Diane cleared away the plates and pizza boxes and let the cats back into the living room. As soon as they were all sitting down again, relaxed in the soft illumination from the dimmable lamps she used in place of the bright ceiling light, Luke jumped straight into Jason's lap and began a comprehensive paw cleaning session; Farolita purred contentedly with her chin resting in the crook of Des's arm.

"Thank Goodness you saw that other doctor", Des was saying. "I know you got on all right with Dr Fletcher but this one you saw the other week seems to have completely turned things around for you. Here's to your freedom!"

Three glasses were raised, their contents deep garnet red in the mellow light from the table lamps.

"I have some news of my own too", he continued; "It looks as though I'm going to be made redundant."

"Oh no, Des! I'm so sorry to hear that!"

"Actually, it's not so bad. I'll get a lump sum and I've got some more put by from when I was working offshore; we've been thinking for some time that we'd like to go into business on our own. Probably something in the catering sector. Right, Jase?"

"Yeah, we've been thinking about it for a while and now we're stepping up looking for possibilities."

Diane had already brought them up to speed on her vivid dreams and what she had learned about the café; in that moment, she recalled the other detail which Krista had mentioned, suddenly the most significant. In that moment, she knew.

This was why she had been shown so much in her dreams; why she had been led to find out about the café, about Joan and then about the family history behind it.

The betting shop was closing, Krista had said. That was why Helen had been reminiscing about the building with her mother. It could become a café again, and her best friends were exactly the right people to make that happen in a style which would honour and continue Joan Morley's work.

Des and Jason loved the idea. Of course there were a lot of factors to take into account; change of use and planning permission, whether there were already any arrangements made for the future of the premises, whether they could afford it. They should be in with a good chance though, especially running the business as a community venture with volunteering or work experience opportunities and a focus on being a friendly environment for disabled and vulnerable people. Diane, with some bookkeeping training from her days in mainstream employment, could easily update that knowledge and volunteer to help them out with the accounts.

"Even if we don't get that building, and I totally get why it would be the first choice, there's sure to be somewhere available up at that end. There are a few empty shops up there. We can get on to the Council about it and start making enquiries. I love the idea of an emphasis on making the place a haven. How about you, Jase?"

"It's ideal! I love it, and it would be so good to have you on board doing the books, Di!"

Looking at her friends' enthused faces, Diane saw a future wherein she could do her bit without having to force so much; without having to be so tired and overwrought. She saw a venture in which she could listen to her instincts and pace herself according to what her body and brain were telling her; where she would not need to overdo things in order to become appreciated, accepted and actively wanted, because she already was.

"I'm seeing a theme of what I would call autism friendliness but which is beneficial to everyone. After all, we are all people! So many things which make life easier or more pleasant for us, and I'm talking about ambient style here rather than the reasonable adjustments which are our legal right, make life more comfortable for lots of non-autistic people too though they often don't admit it. Things like gentler lighting and no loud music to contend with when trying to have a conversation. A bit of aesthetic subtlety; cutting down on some of the physical and psychological clutter. I think of it as a kind of autistic hygge. It overlaps with the mainstream Danish concept of hygge but it's expanded to include things like, say, in the context of a café, knowing that nobody's going to bat an eyelid if you like to take the top layer off your cake, eat that separately and savour all the icing on the bottom layer. Or if you eat the various components of your meal separately; the green veg, then the tatties, then the meat. Nobody's going to watch you eat, make comments and add to your stress if you're having the frustration and uphill struggle of an uncoordinated hands day and look a bit awkward with your cutlery. Essentially nobody's going to question you or make remarks if you do things a bit differently."

"Autistic hygge! That's brilliant!"

"Yeah, it's something that's been in my mind for a while. Whether you say it 'hoo-guh' or 'hyoo-guh'; I tend to go for something more like the German U-with-an-umlaut sound. I'm not even convinced there's a definitive right or wrong way. It covers social stuff as well. It can be things like the warm glow of belonging I feel when my closest friends call me Di. That's one of many things I went off on such a tangent about to Dr Blake. When I'm feeling hypersensitive to the point that my skin is tingling and Farolita somehow knows to sit beside me, not on me, or when I'm overwhelmed and a random dog runs up to me and after I ask if it's OK to pet them, the owner says of course and that they never normally go to strangers. That's autistic hygge, which would overlap with mental health

167

hygge and the regular sort. How I feel when I've faded out and missed something and somebody notices and recaps in a way which doesn't make it obvious that it's to catch me up, that's a social form of it. Or when I'm in company where I know I can safely join in and play along with an obvious joke without fear that people will think I've taken it literally and scoff at me; that if I do pick something up wrongly they still won't sneer or correct me in a way that makes me feel worse about it than usual. Where, at the same time, I won't have committed an equally grave offence if I err on the side of caution after a lifetime of being told I'm risibly innocent and treat something with scepticism when it's actually true, like when one of my colleagues years ago told me about having interviewed a local celebrity for our newsletter. See, the day before, she had told me that a senior manager was going to be doing an inspection, which was feasible so I went and fell for it didn't I, and got the usual 'oh Diane, you're so gullible, you'll believe anything' routine. So when she told me about this article she'd written, I said 'yeah, right' and asked her if it would be next to the new wine tasting column by Phil McGlassup. She was so offended; genuinely furious! I asked her if she were familiar with the story of the boy who cried wolf; reminded her of the wind-up about the inspection, but no, it was still my bad for being dense enough to have fallen for that and this article was totally different; much more believable than a manager who actually worked for our company doing an inspection."

"It sucks that ignorant people have treated you that way. Why couldn't she be decent enough to take your point and acknowledge that her wind-up was pointless and unfunny whereas 'Phil McGlassup'; at least that's amusing!"

"Yes, if not exactly original! Ah well, that's all in the past and I'm getting off track as to what autistic hygge means for me, beyond the social aspect. When I walk along Caberfeidh Road and the streetlights are in that transition stage from the dull red when they first come on all the way through to that joyous pure orange, and the trees are shimmering with autumn colours or spring blossom and it's so beautiful my head can't even fit around how amazing it is to be there in that moment, but it's nothing more out of the ordinary than the streetlights coming on and the unusual way that sings in my soul. The feeling of satisfaction when I've made myself go out for a walk and come home feeling less sluggish, and that I can better appreciate my home comforts for having been out; that's actually more in line with the Norwegian koselig, enhancing the pleasure of being cosy indoors by having contrasting time outside in nature. The feeling when I come in and lock my door behind me, knowing that apart from the obvious and welcome Siamese sound effects I am now in complete control of how much noise and other stimuli I have around me. When I read about Scandinavia at the darkest or lightest times of the year and it feels as though there's an ultraviolet thread connecting me to the Far North where those wonderful extremes of day and night are playing out; the Northern Lights, the Midnight Sun, and then I see those colours, feel that crisp clarity, smell that forest resin or warm winter baking somewhere close by and that ultraviolet thread becomes a neon sign telling me I'm already there inside. The fact that 'streetlights' in Norwegian is 'gatelys'; the linguistic beauty and dignity of it, like sentries of light." She savoured the word again: "The sound of it: 'Gah-tu-lease'. When I taste a rich, peaty, sherry cask matured malt whisky and all the layers of warmth spread through me. Then the satisfying clunk of a solid glass tumbler being set down on a wooden surface, releasing a whole chain of memories of travelling and the best times with my friends. All of that and more is my autistic hygge; there will be so many more manifestations of it for other people."

"Wow, Di, you should write a book, you know that?"

"Quite possibly, but I'm not sure who would read it; there'd be no neat, marketing-friendly premise of romance and roses! I guess the main difference between autistic hygge and regular hygge is that the regular kind has its roots in togetherness; the autistic kind is widened out to incorporate as much space and distance as people need. Which does not mean ruling out solidarity or closeness of any kind; it means being together and connected in the format which works best for us at any given time, as well as the gift of being happily self-reliant."

The trio continued to share, laugh and dream as the air outside came alive with the first substantial frost of autumn and the sea change it accompanied.

17

The Maritime Hotel was quiet at this time of year. As Diane walked across the lobby, she was struck by how hushed and relaxing it felt; there was an understated but clear welcome in the meticulously organised stand of local leaflets, well-tended plants and coastal themed ornamental touches around the place. A bowl of shells here, a leaping dolphin-shaped hand sanitiser dispenser there. She was especially glad to see a donation box for the local lifeboat station; always in awe of the sacrifices of volunteers willing to risk their lives and to be permanently on call, she was glad to see their efforts being highlighted and a reminder on show that it was a voluntary service. She was putting a couple of pounds in the donation box when a voice called out "Thanks very much!"; she turned and found herself face to face with a smiling blonde whose name badge identified her as Sharon.

"Hi; are you Sharon Penhaligon? I'm Diane; a friend of Helen at the Fulmar's Nest."

"Yes, that's me; Helen told me you might be stopping by. Pleased to meet you. Helen said that you're interested in researching a café that one of the Sutherland family's descendants used to run?"

"That's right. Helen said you know the Sutherlands?"

"I know the people who are in the family home now, though I didn't know much about the café until Helen mentioned it and I'm not sure Charlene and Brandon know much about that side of the family. Is it a particular project you're doing?"

"Not especially; I moved here a few years ago and I've got a bit of free time right now so I thought it seemed a good time to find out a bit more about the town", she improvised. "I often pass the betting shop that's on that corner now when I'm out for a walk; I love to walk along Caberfeidh Road."

"Oh, it's that building which used to be the café? It's a shame it always looks so grim and run-down. That end of the High Street could do with some regeneration."

Diane did not want to say anything yet about Des and Jason's plans; there were still too many unknown factors. "Yeah, I always walk quickly past that betting shop. I heard it's closing down though, so maybe we will get something a bit more welcoming in its place."

"Yes, I read that in the local paper about it closing. Caberfeidh Road is a lovely place to go for a walk, isn't it."

"It is, particularly when the streetlights are coming on. I've always loved being out for walks at that time. Of course, popping in to the Fulmar's Nest on the way home is always an additional bonus when I decide to treat myself! I'll be going round there next; Helen recommended someone to help me out with an issue and I want to thank her in person. It was her day off last time I was in; Krista got her to message me about the café history."

"Right; I'll probably see you in there, I'll be calling in to catch up with Helen myself after I finish work in half an hour. You're welcome to hang on here and walk round with me if you like; the bar's through there."

"Thanks; that would be good. I'll go and check out your selection of single malts."

"You're a whisky buff too? You'd get on brilliantly with my partner, Paulie. They're a big whisky enthusiast and I've been learning a lot about it since we got together."

"Excellent! Do you and they like peated whiskies?"

Diane noted Sharon's subtle nod of registered solidarity as she smoothly picked up on her use of they / them pronouns for her partner. Inverbrudock was fast becoming a treasure trove of diversity and inclusion when one knew where to look.

"Paulie does; I'm still getting used to them but I do like a sherry cask expression."

"I must admit it's a breath of fresh air to be able to talk to people other than men about whisky, even though my best friends are guys. The women at the project where I've been volunteering would probably think a sherry cask expression was the look on their favourite aunt's face at Christmas."

"Haha, love it! I know what you mean; we women are all supposed to drink gin, though I enjoy that too now and again."

"Stereotypes are such a pain. Well, I like a sherry cask too, as well as a port or Madeira cask; BenRiach have produced some belters. I'll check out this bar and see you in half an hour."

"Perfect!"

"By the way, I should give you a heads up; if I glance at your name badge again when you come back, it won't be because I've drunk the bar dry. I have prosopagnosia; it's connected to my autism and means I need to see a face quite a few times before I retain enough to confidently recognise it after a break. Even when I do believe I recognise a new person I tend to double-check to reassure myself when there's something definite like a name badge I can refer to. I'm telling you this because I don't want to offend you or hurt your feelings, but also because it's kind of my life's work now to set an example of talking about these things in the same way as someone might say 'I need to take my time on the stairs; my arthritis is playing up' or 'I hope there aren't too many tempting chocolate cakes; I'm diabetic'."

"Diane, that is no problem whatsoever and you are so right about the need to normalise these conversations. Thank you; I know it takes a lot of courage and emotional labour. Did Helen mention my cousin, Bethany?"

"Yes, she did; Bethany lives in Perth, is that right?"

"She does. Bethany would be fine with me telling you this because she feels exactly the way you described there; she is autistic too and struggles with recognising people. I know it's not exclusive to autism and not every autistic person has that issue but she does."

"Ah! Does she find it easier to recognise people's hair?"

"Yes, she does! If that applies to you too, you'd have no trouble recognising Bethany; she dyes her hair dark blue."

"That sounds fabulous! I've probably seen her in the Fulmar's Nest with you before; I wouldn't have taken it in with not knowing you then but now you mention it I'm sure I have."

"Probably. Right, I'm going to finish up and I'll be with you in about half an hour; I'll have a blue jacket on but my hair will still be pinned up like it is now."

Making the world safer and less fraught with pitfalls, and disabled people feel valued and equal, could be as simple as that when people listened openly, believed fully then gave a little thought and matter-of-fact accommodation. Diane felt lit up inside as though the Glenmorangie Quinta Ruban she was about to order were already carrying its silky port-pipe richness through her body. Inverbrudock was far enough from the main tourist hotspots to keep its bar prices affordable; getting odd looks for revealing her interest in malt whisky to people who knew she was on benefits was one of the background battles to which Diane had become accustomed. She considered it the least of the prejudices with which she had to cope. Those who "got it" could appreciate that being a whisky enthusiast was a hobby as valid as any other for quality of life and connection with others; a sensory experience, not about getting drunk. A good single malt was to be enjoyed slowly in moderation; a bottle at home would last her for weeks. She raised her glass to the quiet air and closed her eyes in a moment of sheer wellbeing.

"OK, let's go! See you tomorrow, Jen"; Sharon stood in the doorway as Diane finished her dram and put the glass back on the bar, thanking the barmaid who was waving goodnight to them both as they walked out.

"Quinta Ruban! I'm impressed. That's one of my favourites; not that many places have it."

"Paulie likes that one too. They're away for work otherwise they would have come and met up with us; they're always delighted to meet another enthusiast. I'm sorry I don't know much about the café you're researching but I will ask Charlene."

The two women walked up the stairs to the Fulmar's Nest where Helen greeted them warmly.

"Hey, Helen, thank you so much for putting me in contact with Sharon. We're going to be on the drams this evening!"

"I thought you might!"

After they had chosen their whisky, Sharon went to get a table as Diane updated Helen on having seen Dr Blake and had a highly successful consultation; a turning point in her health and peace of mind. She joined Sharon at their table and the conversation soon got around to Bethany's last visit.

"So we'd just come in here; it was busier than it is now, quite a few fellas in. I'd grabbed a table and Bethany was up at the bar getting us a bottle of wine to share. Next thing this guy came in and loudly announced to his pal that he'd had a long day and he could have taken a drink through a shitty cloot. He didn't see me, but he noticed Bethany at the bar and got all embarrassed about having sworn in front of a woman, giving it all the usual 'so sorry, darling'. Well, for a moment I wondered how it was going to go; Bethany is highly sensitive about people seeing her as unworldly or prim, because people sense that she's different or because she's never wanted a relationship. She swears as much as lots of other people and she's definitely no prude; she hates being talked down to and called darling like that. But then without missing a beat, Beth turned to Helen and said, equally loudly, 'A bottle of Shiraz and two shitty cloots, please'!"

Diane hooted with laughter. "She definitely sounds like my kind of drinking companion! I'd love to meet her some time."

"It could actually work out rather well; when she comes to visit she stays at Charlene's because they've got so much room. Brandon, Charlene's brother, is autistic too and he struggled with the change and uncertainty when my mum sold our house next door. I put Charlene in touch with Bethany for a bit of informed support; I'm not suggesting for a moment that all autistic people think the same way, automatically empathise with one another or will get on, but I knew that Beth would give Charlene a lot of insight which only an autistic person could. So she became close to them too. Brandon doesn't go to pubs so Charlene isn't in here all that often but Bethany could take you to visit her and Brandon."

"That would be lovely, if it wouldn't stress Brandon out having a new person turn up with Bethany."

"He's fine when he knows what to expect. He'll come and say hello but most of the time he'll be upstairs reading or working on his model railway layout. I know that's a bit of a stereotype but it's absolutely authentic with them; Charlene's as much into trains as he is and she's quite rightly proud of it too."

"I love trains too! I don't have a layout but I'd be fascinated to see one and I love travelling by train. I was excited when ScotRail took on 125s for their Inter7City services. Although since Covid all my train journeys have been to and from Dundee for volunteering with Up For Work and that's been a tad stressful, not that I'm going to drag us down with all that."

"Helen did mention something about them giving somebody else credit for your work; for something you'd put a huge amount of time and effort into developing from your own idea. She didn't go into detail or give away anything personal, but she was fuming when she was telling me about it."

"Yes, she was when I told her on the day. Not a day I want to remember. Still, onwards and upwards. Another dram? I'll take these shitty cloots back to the bar!"

Helen had already noticed the empty glasses and was coming over to get them; she broke into laughter as she heard the words.

"So Sharon's been telling you that story, has she? I thought that punter was going to need help getting his jaw back up off the floor. I think at first he thought Bethany was going to share her wine with him!"

"Ha, in his dreams."

"Then I was telling Mark about it later that night and these two French students had come in and one of them said 'What is this sheety cloot; is it a Scottish thing?' I had to explain the best I could that it's an expression people use about desperately wanting a drink; so much so that they'd drink it filtered through a shitty cloot, but that it's not to be taken literally because that actually means a soiled nappy. They couldn't believe it; they were so grossed out I was surprised they still ordered food!"

"Oh no! It is pretty revolting when you think about what it really means, isn't it. Poor you having to explain that!"

It had been a long time since Diane laughed so much in new company and had stories like these to tell Des and Jason next time she saw them. She had been worried that she might run out of things to talk about with them as she cut back to the quieter life she needed, even temporarily, and saw only her most trusted friends. She knew that her basic energy levels had not changed and that she would once again need a few quiet days after socialising for several evenings in one week including two in a row, however fun and accessible those evenings had been. Feeling a happy but inevitable fatigue creeping around the edges of her contented thoughts, she shared one more drink with another new friend before leaving her and Helen to catch up. Home, recharging and a spell of routine unbroken except for her follow-up appointment with the highly approving Dr Blake saw her fresh and ready when the time came for Bethany's next visit.

18

Sharon had been right; Bethany Sawyer was instantly recognisable, her dark blue hair guaranteed to bypass the neurological gridlock of prosopagnosia. Diane waved confidently from the large window table which she had been saving as Sharon met her cousin off the train.

"It's so good to meet you at last, Diane; thank you so much for keeping the table for us! The train was delayed for ten minutes outside Dundee; I hope you haven't had any stress holding a table on your own on a Friday."

"It was no problem at all and it's great to meet you too! Sharon was saying that she and Paulie have been introducing you to malt whisky; are you having a dram this time or sticking with wine?"

"Sticking with the wine tonight as that's what Charlene drinks so we'll be having a couple of glasses there. She's really looking forward to meeting you too."

"I gather from her posts that she likes Pinot Grigio so I got a bottle of that to take when we go round there."

"That's lovely of you! We'll have one here with Sharon then make our way to the house."

"That sounds like a plan. I fed my cat before I came out so I don't need to be watching the clock too much. It wouldn't do to have the neighbours complaining about all the yowling if she got too impatient! She's a Siamese and has the voice to go with it."

"You've got a Siamese cat?!"; Bethany exclaimed, her eyes instantly widening as she looked around. Diane instinctively recognised the fear of having inadvertently spoken too loudly in a moment of unguarded enthusiasm and her heart warmed even further towards this fellow autistic woman.

"Yes; she's a blue point." Bethany's response was a more contained "Woah" as her innate social wariness caught up. Diane showed her a photo on her phone. "Farolita."

"What a lovely name! Is that, what, Italian? Spanish?"

"Spanish. It means 'streetlight', or 'lantern'. Well, 'little streetlight'; her registered name is Farola." She told Bethany the back story as Sharon came over with their bottle of wine.

"Beth, did I mention that Diane has a Siamese cat?", she chuckled as she heard the squeals over the photo. "Helen's bringing the shitty cloots over!"

The three women burst into laughter at the shared joke. Diane wondered whether Bethany had waited as long as she had to find this sort of safe, easy camaraderie. Des and Jason had been lights at the end of an extremely long, treacherous tunnel; she would not have been able to embark upon any of her recent connections without the foundation of the ongoing bond she had discovered with them. Once again she reflected upon how good can sometimes come out of bad. It had begun with her furious calling out of a racist remark in the post office queue and paying for the registered letter which Des in a moment of uncharacteristic vulnerability on a bad day had left on the counter as he stormed out. She had taken the certificate of posting out to him and gained the new family she hadn't even realised she wanted, right when they both needed it most. Now he and Jason were forging ahead with the plans to lease the premises currently occupied by the betting shop when the Council took it over, returning it to the inclusive, welcoming café which it was crying out to be. Priya's research at work had turned up a further Sutherland family connection; another sister, Amelia McKechanie, who had been closest in age to Harriet and profoundly affected by her tragic death had established a trust fund for projects which provided what would now be termed a safe space.

Hopes were cautiously rising that this would solidify the feasibility of the business; the trustees had been enthused by the family connection of the building together with the relevance of the friends' ethos at a time when society had been thoroughly awakened to issues of isolation and the importance of accessible public spaces.

"...and Mum actually managed to walk past the Samantha Fox poster in our hallway without making a comment about LGBTQIA political statements!", Sharon was saying, eliciting comically exaggerated applause from her cousin. Diane smiled and joined in, glowing with the warmth of their shared confidence. Carole Penhaligon had come a long way since the era when she presided over family Christmas dinners in Sharon and Bethany's childhood; occasions which had proven painfully overwhelming to Bethany as an overawed infrequent visitor. It had taken a serious crisis in the life of Sharon's niece Lucy, the daughter of her sister Louise, along with Bethany's staunch advocacy to shake both Carole and Louise out of their conventional and ableist mindset. Severely bullied at school in Edinburgh, Lucy, also autistic, had been harangued to the point of a meltdown and run away; finding her way to the bookshop in Perth where Bethany worked. Now a peer mentor for other bullied teenagers, Lucy was rebuilding her life and growing in confidence. Around the same time, Sharon had begun to fall in love with Paulie; a regular guest at the hotel and already a friend. Carole's response to her eldest daughter's non-binary partner was one of well-meaning overcompensation which was patiently accommodated for its good intent and learning curve; gently lampooned in trusted company.

"Diane, in case you're wondering; pleased as we were to hear that Samantha Fox found happiness with another lovely woman after the heartache of losing her long-term partner, the reason Paulie and I have her poster in our hallway is simply because her cover of 'I Only Wanna Be

With You' is our song. When Lucy had been missing and I heard that she was safe with Beth, I went back to work to let them all know, including Paulie who was staying at the time. I walked into the bar and saw them there and knew that they were the person with whom I most needed to share that moment. I'd already messaged everybody but they were the reason I went back to finish my shift when nobody expected me to. Jen had some eighties music on random play in the bar that night and that song came on."

"That's a beautiful memory to cherish! It must be tough for you when someone close to you politicises something so personal. I'd forgotten that Samantha Fox covered that song; now I think about it, that's the version of it I like best. I love eighties synth pop. There's a vastness of celebration in that version which could make the lyrics relevant for me to any happy time in my life. I've never had nor wanted a life partner, but I completely get why that song appeals to couples and I can picture the lights coming on in your soul when you walked into that bar."

Diane was conscious of the need not to get carried away and overdo criticism of her new friends' family members so she held back from any further comment about Carole's initial interpretation of the poster. She hoped that one day soon, the sole thing Sharon's mother would notice and focus on would be that Paulie treated her daughter well, was her wholehearted choice and made her happy. Everyone in a minority group lived a more politicised life by necessity merely to be equal. Surely some things could be accepted for what they were; personally meaningful.

When the time came to go with Bethany to Charlene and Brandon Sutherland's seafront home, Diane stood back as the cousins hugged. Gathering up her handbag and the tote bag in which the bottle of Pinot Grigio for Charlene was discreetly packed, she followed Bethany towards the door, waving her thanks and goodnights to Sharon and Helen who were talking at the bar. Outside, rain threatened from the suspended black foam of a leaden night sky wistfully tinged with the thinly-scattered illusory warmth of the surplus light from the streetlights. The cutting wind swept the seafront clean of anyone who did not unequivocally need to be there. Diane's sense of purpose pushed away the dull drag of sensory dread about the walk home in this weather; keeping her eyes from blurring through the sting of icy rain, hoping that they would not water or clamp shut at the wrong moment and lead her into a mortifying stumble or jostle. Getting safely inside again would not immediately end the sensory conflict; she would still need to restore the circulation to her fingers which no gloves could adequately protect and brush the windblown tangles out of her hair as her sensitive scalp registered each tug.

"Here we are", Bethany was saying; "this is Charlene and Brandon's. Next door, right there, is where Sharon grew up."

Diane had seen the imposing seafront houses before but she looked with fresh eyes at the elegant stretch of stone buildings with their wide incandescent stippling of lighted windows offering a welcome respite from the East Coast pre-winter night. Her gaze was drawn to the skylight of the house next door where an opalescent parade of colours played out an unobtrusive light show from an attic room to the impassive clouds.

"Jordan's got his sensory room up there"; Bethany's voice swelled with tenderness and empathy. "The difference in that wee boy's life since Lizzie and Michael moved in and brought him and his mum to live with them is incredible. I've met Niamh a few times; that's Jordan's mum, Lizzie and Michael's daughter. They are such a lovely family. It's as though the house was waiting for them. Let's get inside; Charlene's looking forward to meeting you and she'll appreciate that bottle of wine you brought. Brandon's going to be over the moon when he hears you love trains!"

Charlene Sutherland's red hair caught the beam of the security light as she opened the door to greet them. Momentarily recalling her lucid dream, Diane thought she glimpsed a hint of Joan Morley's welcoming spirit in the smiling face of this distant cousin; a timeless glint of light on a thread which ran through generations.

Savouring the welcome respite from the weather, Diane set the gratefully received bottle of wine on the marbled kitchen worktop. A loud miaow echoed as the familiar sensation of a cat around her ankles pleasantly surprised her; she looked down to see a handsome ginger tabby arching his back as he erupted in purrs.

"And so you meet Cheminot!", laughed Charlene as Diane crouched delightedly to pet this orange volcano of affection.

"Well, hello there; aren't you stunning! That name means 'railwayman' in French, doesn't it? Sharon did mention that you and Brandon love trains. I'm a train and cat person too; what do you think of that then, Cheminot, you magnificent creature?"

A chirrup and more purring answered that question. The cat followed as Charlene led Diane and Bethany through to the snugly lit living room, full glasses in hand. A man of around thirty with long dark hair sat in a green leather armchair playing a game on his tablet; utterly at ease in tartan pyjama trousers, well-worn grey slippers and a black T-shirt with an image of an InterCity 125 on the front. He looked up and nodded amiably.

"Brandon, this is Diane. As you can see, she's already gained Cheminot's seal of approval!"

"Hi, Brandon. Is that T-shirt from the farewell tour they did for the 125s when the Azuma trains were taking over on the London services? I read about that on the news."

"No, but I wore it when we went to the station to see it. I've got a mug and a badge from the tour; they're upstairs though, with the rest of my stuff."

"Ah; I'm glad you got some souvenirs of such a landmark changeover. It must have been a very emotional time."

It felt as though she had always been connected to these people. Sitting around the coffee table with Charlene and Bethany, a modern heater designed to look like a wood burning stove adding to the ambience, the conversation turned to the history of the café.

"We didn't know much ourselves about Harriet until recently"; Charlene was saying. "All we knew was that she had died young and that it was a road accident. She was the youngest of eight; Brandon and I are descended from her second oldest brother, Alexander. He and our great-grandmother Mary moved back to live in this house when his parents became too old and frail to manage on their own and the house has stayed in the family ever since. When Carole sold the house next door, the connecting door between our attic and theirs, which had been left as an alternative fire escape route when the house was divided into the two properties, was sealed over. While they were working up there, the builders found Harriet's diary. She had it hidden under a floorboard on the landing between the two attics. Sadly, there were only a few weeks' worth of entries in it before she died but they gave us a lot of insight into what she was like. In fact, we strongly suspect she was autistic too. We knew that she got into trouble at school for a fight with a boy shortly before she was killed; it turns out that he was a bully who had been picking on another boy who was disabled and Harriet was defending him. I was so glad that we found all that out about her. She was looking forward to being able to vote and taking an interest in current affairs. She seems to have been such a character. I vaguely knew about The Haven Café and that it was run by someone who was related to us but it was only when you'd been asking at the pub about it and Helen's mother had remembered it so well that Helen told Sharon exactly who

Joan Morley was. I'm very thankful that you took an interest, Diane; it means a lot to know that there was something positive done as a result of Harriet's death, even if it didn't get to continue."

Diane had not intended to say anything quite yet but the clear emotion on Charlene's face changed her mind.

"Actually, that may not be the end of the story. For the time being I need to ask that you all keep this confidential because nothing is final yet; I won't ask you to keep it from Sharon and Paulie but if it could go no further right now. My best friends Des and Jason are in negotiations to lease the building from the Council when the betting shop closes and turn it into a café again. I will be involved as a volunteer helping with the accounts and we're hoping to make it the same kind of sanctuary that Joan did. Not specific to any named vulnerability; run in a way which is easier for autistic people, cognitively disabled people, those who are hard of hearing or don't get around easily. The ethos will be unhurried, calming to the senses and socially unpressured. After all, so many ways of doing things which make a place more accessible to disabled people actually make it more relaxing and welcoming for everybody. When the time came to tell you about it, it was my intention to ask you how you feel about restoring the name 'The Haven Café'. Des and Jason would love to, and even if we don't get this building, we would still like to do this and would look at other premises nearby."

Charlene stood up, her eyes shining. "Oh, Diane, this is wonderful news! I would love to have the name restored; Brandon, how do you feel?"

Brandon looked up from his game, smiled and nodded.

"I am so touched; do you do hugs?"

Diane wished that she could give the answer Charlene would have enjoyed hearing but knew that she deserved and wanted honesty. "Not as a rule; I find physical contact uncomfortable but I deeply appreciate you asking. On rare occasions it will feel right to give or receive a hug and I think it's fair to say that this is one of those occasions." She relaxed into Charlene's brief, gentle shoulder hug, prevented from standing up by Cheminot being settled on her lap. "The last time I hugged someone was… let me think. Hmm, I guess it would be Sally. Oh - that's a colleague of mine at Up For Work in Dundee. I volunteered with them and we recently launched a project from an idea I had; an associated website with a forum and buddy mentoring scheme for neurodivergent jobseekers. Although it was my idea, office politics being as they are, it wouldn't have gone ahead if Sally hadn't liaised with the jobsearch hubs. When we got the go-ahead, I hugged her. I didn't even think about it; I should have asked her first as you did me! I was so relieved that the project was going to happen! We had the launch a few weeks ago, where the outreach manager promptly credited the whole thing as Sally's initiative. I mentioned a couple of times, unscripted of course, in my presentation that it had been my idea. The next day I was called into a meeting less than 24 hours later with the branch manager and I haven't volunteered with them since, though I'm hoping that after the three months they specified I will get to resume online training at home to be a moderator on the forum."

A shocked Charlene and Bethany were exchanging looks of outraged bafflement. Charlene's brow furrowed as she processed Diane's words.

"Hang on; are you telling us they suspended you for pointing out that this project was your idea?"

"Well, there was a little more to it than that. I admit that I have hero-worshipped Verena, the outreach manager, since I've been working there. Nothing more to it than that and nobody has suggested any wrongdoing but I was told it had made her uncomfortable and the events at the launch were taken as evidence that I couldn't handle my emotions and was dangerously attached to her. So they need to be convinced that I can be professional on the forum and that I've 'gotten over' Verena before they will let me back. It makes me think of '1984'. The George Orwell novel, that is, not the year itself; I'm not quite old enough to have any clear memories of 1984 but I'm sure it wasn't like the Orwell version of it!"

"That was the year the Highland Chieftain started", put in Brandon.

"That's it! I knew there was something very positive I associated with the real 1984. That service is an Azuma now, isn't it, same as the Aberdeen to London trains?"

"Yeah. Some people say it's not the Highland Chieftain any more now that it's not an InterCity 125 and I get why, but it's still the only direct daytime train between Inverness and London, running at the same times as before. I preferred to be able to get fresh air in the vestibule on long journeys but I'd rather have a different sort of train than any service get taken away from the people who use it. It's still the Chieftain."

"Of course it is! It's been a big ask for people to get used to the 125s going from the long-distance routes; it must have been the same when people had to deal with the transition from steam to diesel trains. There's no sense in compounding that wrench by taking away familiar associations that people don't need to lose! I really must organise a train trip up to Inverness; I haven't been for ages and the journey up to there from Perth is magical."

Brandon, Charlene and Bethany were all nodding.

"Anyway, I've got a few things to sort out closer to home before I can focus on planning to travel around again even when Covid is completely in the past and leisure trips become more relaxed and feasible. I have to satisfy the Thought Police that I'm not a risk to society because of my admiration of someone. It makes me feel as though anything I've ever achieved in promoting autism positivity has been wasted; that's what kills me about this whole situation with Up For Work!"

"I'm not surprised you feel that way after what you've told us. You've been treated appallingly for perfectly reasonable ownership of your own hard work. Had anyone actually talked with you about your feelings towards this Verena?"

"Oh, no; they were afraid that would tip me over the edge into stalking behaviour."

"How absolutely ridiculous", put in Bethany. "Why are some people, especially employers, so afraid of autism that they can't talk to us about anything and feel their only option is to make these wild assumptions, then punish and ostracise us as if the assumptions had been proved correct? It adds to the culture of 'them and us'!"

"You are so right, Bethany. Verena was highly vocal about accommodating my autism at first. Any time I was in a meeting with her, the more people there the more overt she would be about asking for adjustments for me. As I told Helen after the launch, one time she asked the chairman of the Council to take the batteries out of a ticking clock. Yet as soon as my autism became more personal and less pragmatic to her, she went from autism champion to 'here be monsters'; nought to bigot in sixty seconds!"

Charlene, Brandon and Bethany chuckled at "nought to bigot in sixty seconds"; a look crossed Bethany's face which Diane rightly interpreted as thoughtful.

"Had you said that the clock was bothering you? Or had she asked you?"

"No; though I don't go for ticking clocks now, I used to find them quite soothing, because the sound was rhythmic, as long as it wasn't too loud. I wouldn't have one in my house because I need that space to have a baseline of absolute quiet, but in a meeting with lots of people I wouldn't have been disturbed by the clock ticking. In fact I didn't notice it that much until Verena declared that 'Diane is autistic so we need the batteries taken out of whichever clock that is ticking, please'!"

"And did she have your explicit consent to announce your autism to the whole room?"

"Not specific to that occasion, no, though she had the knowledge that I am open about it when the context is suitable."

"Well, I don't mean to disrespect your own opinion of her for which you must have your reasons, but she sounds like a self-promoting user to me. It's a great pity you would need to remain involved with these people in order to continue on your project but I get why you would want to. Can you do most of the training and work on it online from home?"

"Fortunately, yes. I am feeling much better about the direction of my life going forward; volunteering from home, and hopefully the café! I won't deny I still feel a few pangs about having made such a bad impression on Verena but I'm relieved not to have to see her. The launch event should have been such a proud and happy day, not something I needed to put behind me and couldn't talk about properly with even my closest friends."

"Of course your esteem for Verena is not going to fade quickly or easily. That's how we are and I hope you're not being put under any pressure about that?"

Diane merely smiled. That was a story for another time.

Charlene returned from getting something out of the rosewood bureau in the corner of the room. It was a notebook; leather bound and aged.

"Diane, I want to show you this; it's Harriet's diary from 1923. You are welcome to read it while I get some snacks together for later. When the builder brought it to me and I read it, I felt so sad that Harriet's voice had been unheard for so long and that we'd known so little about her; we didn't even know that her friends called her Hattie. So many of the details which make up a life, lost in time because she had no time to prepare her legacy. Let me top up these glasses and see to the food while you have a read; as I said, she didn't get to write many entries."

"Charlene, thank you for sharing this with me; it is a privilege. I would love to see what Harriet had to say."

Delicately turning the yellowed pages, Diane read the thoughtfully composed words of the little girl from a century ago. Tears of empathy swelled behind her eyes as she recognised so much in her intense emotional, social and sensory experiences. She gasped as she read how her older sister Martha had almost caught her in the forbidden attic room. Joan Morley's anguished, haunted mother! How her heart ached for both of those innocent girls, knowing as she did the chain of events which that near miss had set in motion. The final entry was wrenchingly poignant; an uplifting account of an ordinary Saturday which was wonderful simply in an everyday convergence of happily optimal activity, environment and connectedness. Diane could not bear to look at the unwritten pages thereafter and picture the brutal cause of their blankness.

Cautiously closing the book and laying it safely on the coffee table, she came to a decision.

"I think, if it's all right with the family, that the café should be called 'Harriet's Haven'. She would have wanted to create something like this; more to the point, she would have made it happen. Obviously I cannot speak for Des and Jason, but I can pretty much guarantee they'll be on board with that when I fill them in on what I've read here."

Brandon nodded again. "Cool", he muttered approvingly. Charlene's smile and her hand stopping short of Diane's shoulder said all of the things which her voice could not quite manage to form.

"You know", said Bethany, her eyes fixed on Diane; "The rain's eased off and some of Vinnie's gorgeous chips would go beautifully with these party snacks Charlene's got in. Do you fancy a walk along there?"

Diane readily agreed, sensing that Bethany had picked up on her lack of opportunities up to now to talk with many other autistic women around her own age with comparable life experience. Pulling their coats, scarves and gloves back on, the two women headed back out into the frosty, washed-clean night.

"I don't think it's going to freeze tonight", observed Diane. "I dread that; not because of the frost and ice themselves but because of people thinking I need to be told to watch my step. I'm frightened to go out in those conditions because of what people might say to me and because I know I can't handle that and in general nobody will be on my side about it. My emotions and my defences are massive; that's an indelible part of me. I'm supposed to be humble about it but a lifetime of put-downs and microaggressions makes humility far too much of a concession on top of all that; how can I afford to be even more vulnerable by being submissive to unwarranted instruction and why should I when I'm already doing what I should be? I'm already trying so hard to walk safely and I do get grumpy about people being so patronising, treating me like a clumsy oaf who isn't even trying when in fact I am putting in all my physical and mental energy. I've got suitable footwear, plus grips when they're needed; what more can I do to prove myself to people?"

"Oh, I agree; I get that too. I don't think it's exclusively an autism thing but it doesn't help that we set off people's alien detectors merely by going about our business appropriately. It's not always men either; women do it too. Maybe they misread our visible apprehension about being infantilised as our being afraid of slipping and think they need to tell us how not to, but surely they can see we're not reckless or ill-equipped?!"

"Yeah. It's definitely not exclusive to autistic people; I've never felt that, but as you say we do appear to be a frequent target. Sometimes it's well-intentioned but sometimes it is done out of a sense of superiority; either way, the impact it has on us is valid! Do people not realise that when they shout out to someone to take the precautions which the person already is taking, they might actually distract them or unbalance them when they have to look up to see who's spoken to them, and that could cause them to fall when they wouldn't have otherwise?"

"You know, that's a thoroughly valid point and I hadn't thought of it like that. You're right; that easily could happen. I'll have to remember that next time I need something more relatable to the non-disabled world than my mere 'wounded pride' when I'm trying to make people hear me about the hurtful impact of these incessant unsolicited warnings which we don't need and certainly don't want."

They walked in companionable silence past the front of Sharon's childhood home; emerging watery moonlight glinted on the railings of the promenade. As they approached the chip shop, Bethany stopped for a moment, turning to Diane with a keenly compassionate look.

"Diane, in the house you said something about the events at your project launch, and that you struggle to talk about that day even with close friends. Please don't feel under pressure to answer this question, but I've lived with enough internalised shame and fear of being judged to recognise it when I see it: Did something else happen at that event, besides you adding to your speech that the project was your idea, that you haven't felt able to tell anybody you trust about?"

The night sky wheeled above them, its cosmic timescale comforting in its vastness and absolute indifference as the mortifying memories rose once more from their accustomed place marginally below the surface of Diane's mind. As the stars shone down and the sea rocked to the ancient beat of the moon, she painfully dragged out the hideous tale of the incident with Brenda Culper; cringing at the words ripped from her soul and mercifully dissipated into the darkness. She dared not look at Bethany as she spoke.

"…and if only I'd thought to set my papers down on my seat before I went to get a drink, it might not even have happened. Such a small thing; such a trivial decision, but I simply didn't think and it made me that bit more awkward; enough to make her think I was completely incapable, physically and mentally. So I ended up doing something so serious and so terrible!"

She finally plucked up the courage to look at Bethany, who was standing stock still and listening intently; a few dark strands highlighted blue in the pale, lofty gleam of the streetlights as the wind whipped her hair around her face.

"So, let me get this straight. She grabbed things from you without asking. You repeatedly asked for space; you clearly said no; you were visibly distressed and trying to get away from her. She kept coming towards you, being loud, denying you that space and preventing you from safely removing yourself when you'd become overwhelmed, and was pushing a hot drink at you as you were approaching a state of meltdown. And you're the one who was reckless and did a terrible thing?"

"Yeah. Being a spoiled little princess having a tantrum because my pride was hurt; taking it out on this poor kindly saint because Verena hadn't given me the attention I wanted."

"My God. Did someone actually say those things to you?"

"Not the saint part but the rest. The manager who suspended me after Brenda reported me. They'd linked it to my obvious disappointment when Verena credited my work to Sally and now I'm banned from contacting any of them!"

"Oh, Diane. You've kept that inside all this time with nobody to support you through the effects of such an awful incident?"

"I couldn't bear to tell anyone; I was so ashamed. So because I didn't tell my friends, the counsellor I was seeing or even my new doctor, they all thought my distress after that event was purely about Verena too and I can't blame them. What strong support I did get, from Des and Jason and Dr Blake, I couldn't let myself fully accept because I hadn't told them the truth about what happened with Brenda. My counsellor said I had to join a dating site to prove I was making an effort to get over Verena, refusing to believe that it's not that sort of attachment. If I didn't join the site and force myself to commit to building a relationship with somebody, she was going to end our sessions due to my lack of compliance and she reminded me that if anyone contacted her for evidence to review my benefits, that was what she'd have to tell them."

Bethany's language was as blue as her hair.

"Fortunately I first saw Dr Blake soon after and she put paid to that; she agreed with me that it was blackmail and completely unacceptable, however much the counsellor may have thought she was pushing me hard to get me to what she believed to be best for me. Nobody but this doctor, and Des and Jason, will believe that I don't want a physical relationship!"

"I believe you. If I may ask, and again there is no pressure to answer this; would you consider yourself to be asexual?"

"I've heard of that, but I'm not absolutely certain it applies to me because I do feel a kind of attraction to people, albeit rarely. It's the excitement I feel being around them; I recognise what I feel in descriptions of being in love, but I don't feel the sexual aspect. I'm not confused about my feelings; I resent it when people imply that, I know my own mind! It's the fitting in to society's arbitrary labels part which is unclear to me."

"That sounds like romantic attraction, and yes, you can experience that and still be asexual. Romantic orientation

195

and sexual orientation are different things, though they often align. Some asexual people do experience attraction but rarely or mildly; it can be rare in terms of very few people sparking it in the ace or aro - that's asexual or aromantic - person's life but highly intense when it does happen and the idea of replacing that person with any other is not only unappealing but intensely distressing. That is a lot like demisexuality or demiromanticism but the attraction can happen without a pre-existing emotional bond; a demi orientation requires that bond first. It causes huge distress, especially to teenagers, to have so much pressure put on them not only to exhaustingly fight against every forbidden thought in such a strong attachment but to force themselves to substitute someone else and be prepared to sign over their heart to a person for whom they feel nothing! There are asexuals who are happy to have a sexual relationship with a partner; they're not bothered about sex but it doesn't distress them, subject of course to the same requirements of consent as any other relationship. Some enjoy the act of having sex although they don't feel attraction towards specific people. Although some asexual people are sex neutral or sex repulsed, it's a myth that asexuality automatically means hating anything to do with sex or being negative about other people's relationships. Being aromantic, as the name suggests, means not experiencing romantic attraction. Romantic is not the same as platonic. It is perfectly possible to be asexual and aromantic or to be one or the other. Romantic attraction can be hetero, homo, bi, demi, pan or any other kind, same as sexual attraction can be; both can fluctuate. A person can be asexual, aromantic and form a partnership which is like a particularly intense friendship; that's a queerplatonic relationship. Experiencing attraction occasionally or mildly can be called greysexual or greyromantic. I'm asexual and occasionally panromantic. I know what you mean about people thinking we're confused. They are the ones who are confused! Some people are highly sceptical about these different types and permutations of orientation being talked about; they accuse aces and aros, particularly younger ones, of 'wanting to be special', when all we're doing is being frank about what we feel; often because someone is trying to coerce us into activity we don't want. Although of course anyone has the right to refuse consent whether or not their orientation is a factor in their not wanting the activity, labelling being upfront about orientation as a character flaw is highly dangerous because it undermines confidence in the right to refuse consent without fear of repercussions, especially in young and vulnerable people. I'm not just talking about direct pressure from someone to have sex; the dilemma your counsellor caused is an example of the kind of harm that can result. Why shouldn't there be so many different sexualities anyway, when people themselves are all individual?"

"Exactly! And that is a massively important point about consent. What is it with these people who attack others, often in marginalised groups and feeling at their lowest and most vulnerable, saying that they want to be or think they are special? It's more than likely they feel the direct polar opposite and could be pushed into serious crisis or suicide by these sneering rebukes. It's no wonder people's defences are up, but it becomes a destructive cycle as those defences are perceived as haughtiness or arrogance when a person has been bullied and ostracised their entire life, blamed for that too especially in childhood, and what they're displaying is in fact trauma. How can a person's orientation be about wanting to be special when it's purely how they feel and not a choice?!"

"Precisely, and proudly owning that part of yourself is nothing to do with feeling special either. The more we can talk about it, the more normalised it will become and the safer young people will feel to accept their orientation and declare it when the circumstances call for it. Same goes for gender identity and pronouns. Which is the opposite of wanting it to be 'special'! Of course quite a lot of that is about the ego of those who cannot believe they're being turned down."

"You're absolutely right about the importance of these things being talked about. Here I am a few months away from turning forty and I hadn't realised about the distinction between sexual and romantic orientation, nor the scope of both until you explained all this to me; thank you so much! Romantic attraction does sound nearer to what I feel; I'd say asexual and occasionally panromantic sounds very close to describing my orientations too. Though I have honestly never wanted a traditional partner relationship, even one without sex. It's more a case of wanting to be emotionally bonded; to be significant to them, valued and wanted by them and have quality time with them to look forward to. The buzz of those feelings is the only effective fatigue management I've ever known, but it's not something I can manufacture; I've felt it for so few people in my life and never gone looking for it. When I don't feel it, I don't feel it, and that's with over 99.9% of the people I meet! So I'd say I'm on the aromantic spectrum in terms of how rarely I experience that enhanced feeling and that even when I do, it's not the same as the romantic aspects of a traditional relationship. I am asexual in that I don't experience sexual attraction at all. Liking someone as a friend or admiring them are entirely different feelings from that rare thrill and cannot be artificially converted to it. I cannot imagine how it would be possible to force it in the way in which people want me to, for the sake of conforming with someone 'appropriate', by which they often mean someone to whom I am not attracted in any way because they're squeamish about autistic or any disabled people having those thoughts. I'd be wary of calling my feelings 'romantic' in unsafe company, especially in a situation like this with Verena where I've been labelled as some kind of predator. 'Romantic' in this day and age is given a lot of sexual overtones too and those feelings are equally likely to be policed. I'd rather not have to discuss it at all; it's private! This is what I mean about '1984'! Not talking about it with you here and now; that's different. It's helpful and mutually respectful. It's the first time I've had the opportunity to go beyond asserting what I don't feel and properly put into words what I do feel! When I say I'd rather not have to discuss it, I mean in terms of being forced to justify my private thoughts to people with whom I wouldn't choose to share what I had for breakfast. I also don't want to give people any more reason to believe that autistic people cannot be sexual or romantic beings. As I said to my counsellor, it's compatible with my autism and need for more quiet space and alone time than other people have, but my not wanting a relationship is not caused by my autism. Autistic people can want and get partners and have families."

"I agree with all of that, and the generic blurring of the lines between sexual and romantic which you mention - particularly by the media - is also harmful to aromantic people by erasing the orientation as one which exists in its own right independent from asexuality. It gets in the way of people understanding the complex truth of their own orientations and having the knowledge to own them: 'I can't be X because I feel, or sometimes feel, Y; therefore the people insisting I don't understand my own needs and should in fact be doing Z must be right'. It's not your responsibility anyway to deny your own truth to fight stereotyping. You put these concepts across so well; that's all any of us can do, be true to ourselves and act as ambassadors for diversity. It is also becoming recognised that a high proportion of autistic people are in the LGBTQIA community. It makes perfect sense to me that asexuality and aromanticism are compatible with autism for some of us."

"That's true. I do feel that I have a responsibility not to perpetuate the myth that autistic people in some way 'suit' being asexual or aromantic; falling into it as the only possibility for us, because we're inevitably unattractive as potential partners or lack the social and interpersonal skills to achieve a relationship."

"First of all, you are not perpetuating anything of the sort; by advocating for your boundaries and identity, you are strengthening our cause, not weakening it. Second, orientation is about what a person does or doesn't feel, not how they act on those feelings or what their chances are of them being reciprocated. Not having pursued a sexual or romantic relationship because the attraction isn't there is not the same as having given up. Never having had such a relationship because the attraction happens so rarely that the chances of feeling it for someone who reciprocates are proportionally reduced is equally valid. It is an authentic life experience on the asexual and aromantic spectra and nobody has the right to deny another person's orientation. To weaponise an occasional experience of attraction, or a different type of attachment, into a means to coerce anyone into activity not of their choosing is as wrong and violating as trying to convert gay people to heterosexuality."

"Yes, it is! I'd never thought of my own experiences of attachment and the lack of success, in that it killed any cordial relationship I had with the person, in those detached mathematical terms before but it's incredibly helpful. My one hundred per cent failure rate doesn't feel quite so shameful or such an indictment of me as a person when I think of it in terms of the odds being lengthened by the rarity of those attachments. If I'd had this insight earlier in life, I may have felt able to seek help in the past when I should have. What I feel for Verena makes me sad but it is manageable; there have been attachments, though they still weren't sexual, when I seriously struggled. I never told a soul and tried to cope on my own with feelings that were way too big for me; I felt that seeking help, however confidentially, would brand me as an evil stalker and see action taken accordingly. That I'd be forced to move to a new area where I didn't know anyone; that the person for whom I had the feelings would be notified and would hate me and demand I be punished for the insult to them; that everybody would find out and I'd be a laughing-stock and a pariah."

"My goodness, you must have been hurt and betrayed badly at some point to think that would happen!"

Diane's eyes briefly misted over; night clouds from long ago passed across a decades-old sky, momentarily waking a frightened inner child with their ominous interruption of the light. The adult she had become hurriedly escorted that young teenage girl back to her own time, safely past and dormant.

"The joys of undiagnosed autism and its emotional intensity, Beth. It doesn't help that so many of us tend to be drawn to older people while at the same time we look younger than we are and have a fight on our hands to be taken seriously as our own age group never mind living up to our charismatic elders."

"I can relate to that. Looking younger is another thing we're expected to be grateful for; because so many non-autistic people focus on hanging on to youth with a level of fixation usually attributed to us, once again the issues it causes us are invalidated because that experience doesn't gel with theirs."

"Spot on! Of course, we're the ones who lack empathy and need to work harder at adjusting. Is it any wonder we burn out?"

"No wonder at all. It's not as though we were asking them to do all of the adjusting either; meeting us halfway would be a start! Of course we need and want to take others' perspectives into account; all we ask is to be listened to, not dismissed and for there to be scope to at least agree to disagree instead of pathologising everything about us with an automatic label of 'broken', 'wrong' or 'dysfunctional'. As you've said, that is the kind of thing which prevents us from reaching out for help when we need it. Especially when it intersects with prejudices about sexual or romantic orientation. Needing support or space to grieve over an unreciprocated attachment is valid; it should not be conditional upon forcing a compromise replacement against your will. That is true of anyone, not only autistic and LGBTQIA people. Staying single is a choice anyone is entitled to make; it has pros and cons like anything else and any support needed with the cons does not invalidate it. When staying single aligns with your orientations anyway, it doesn't even feel right to describe it as a choice; a person's orientations are what they are, not options. It's never a crime to feel intensely or to grieve, Diane. Yes, sometimes people in pain cross the line and do things they shouldn't; of course that's not OK. Those people are entitled to help if they need it as well though; to rebuild their lives and avoid doing harm, and to heal from mitigating circumstances."

"I haven't crossed that particular line but that doesn't excuse my having let myself down by coping badly in general; ending up doing things like attacking Brenda Culper with hot tea!"

"See, this is the self-judgement which results from a lifetime of being told our neurology is wrong one way and another. It concerns me deeply that even after releasing it to me, you've still got this incident with Brenda built up and reframed in your mind to the extent that you describe it as having attacked her."

"Now you mention it, when it happened, raw as it was I had almost convinced myself by the next morning that other people would remember it as a small glitch in an otherwise constructive day. Even Brenda; this was before I knew she'd reported me. All I was doing was trying to stop her coming any closer; to give myself space to breathe and I was sure my hand only glanced off the cup by chance and splashed a few drops on the carpet! The manager said that if she'd been scalded he would have encouraged her to press charges!"

"That is preposterous. He's said that to bully and intimidate you by the sound of things; to prevent you from recognising and exposing their diabolical lack of inclusion and understanding. This is why autistic people need to be able to access opportunities to talk through this kind of thing with others who've been through similar struggles. I've had a lot of help from the Autism Initiatives one stop shop in Perth. I'm not one for groups and activities but I have made some good contacts. I want to try something with you right now, before we go to get these chips. Matt, the project manager for the one stop shops who is based in Edinburgh, was the first person I met when I went to the Perth service; he was there for a meeting and answered the door. I've talked with him a few times since then and he recently told me about an exercise one of his friends who uses their Highland service, based in Inverness, had described to him. I think it might work for what happened to you. What I want you to do is, first of all imagine a society where our way of doing things is the norm; where anything which is part of our coping is accepted and others have to fit in around that the way we have to fit in around them in this world. In this alternative society, when people do something destructive and unhelpful - however well-intentioned - they are the odd ones out who are forced to justify it and berated for the harm they've caused irrespective of their intentions. They are the ones who bear the cumulative effect of a lifetime of being on the outside. Now, bearing that reversed society in mind, you tell me the story in the same way you did, carrying all that shame and self-reproach; but as Brenda. I'll get you started: 'I was waiting behind a woman in the queue for hot drinks and she had some papers under her arm so she was a bit hampered as there was nowhere to set them down. Now, I could have offered to hold the papers while she poured her drink. If the papers had confidential information on them and she didn't want to hand them over, then I could have offered to pour the drink for her, simply because my hands were free. It could have been done discreetly and amiably as an equal. But did I do that; did I show her that respect? Oh, no. I grabbed the cup out of her hands without even asking'."

Diane caught on. "Ah, I get the idea; yes, that could be massively helpful! 'So she asked me, not once but three times, to give her space. I knew she was autistic as she had mentioned it in her presentation. She asked me to lower my voice too. Did I listen? Oh, no; how could I pass up such a golden opportunity to look superior and feel smug with my good works? I kept on talking at her, loudly; I followed her as she tried to get away. I could have set the cup of tea down next to the urn for her to take a breath, gather herself and pick it up in her own time; after all, she was becoming more distressed by this point. No; I had so little common sense, I kept shoving a cup full of hot tea towards her even as she put her hand out to stop me and was visibly close to meltdown. And then as if I hadn't done enough, I reported her, a disabled volunteer, to her manager and made her sound like a lout!' Oh my word, Bethany, that didn't half feel good!"

"I thought it might! The great thing is, it's all about helping you come to terms with whatever happened. It is your personal, private healing. You don't have to bend over backwards to see the other person's point of view. You are not doing them any harm at all. You can take a much needed break from the constant guilt trip about people's intentions having been oh so kind and helpful. Even if you don't capture their actual personality and intent in your therapeutic retelling, it doesn't matter. You don't have to do them justice. You're not talking to their boss or a journalist; you're not splattering it all over social media. It's something to do in private or in trusted confidential company, to help you through something which hurt you; that hurt is valid irrespective of others' intentions. Once you've done that, if their motives were so benign, that will begin to come through once you've let yourself feel and process whatever you need to."

"That is such a tonic; thank you so much! I need to message my friends tonight and tell them what happened, so that they can properly understand my reactions after that day. I will tell my doctor next time I see her too. It's such a relief to be able to do that now, instead of keeping this dark secret! Come on; let's get these chips and go back to get warmed up."

Charlene took the trays of party snacks out of the oven as Diane and Bethany opened the shiny, heat-infused brown paper on the steaming parcels of puffy golden chips, setting the unfolded packets on plates exactly as they were. Harriet's diary had been safely put away out of reach of the food but she was nonetheless in the forefront of their minds.

"I don't know what your views are about ghosts and spirits, Diane, but we all believe that Harriet is still around", Charlene smiled fondly. "We had awful neighbours in between Carole selling up and the O'Sullivans who are there now moving in; they made the house happy again. The last lot were noisy and disrespectful; they set Brandon's peace of mind back years with their loud music and rudeness. Anyway, their blasting music started cutting out without any obvious cause; there were banging doors, problems with the electrics, taps gushing cold water and soaking people. They didn't believe in ghosts at all but they insisted the place was haunted and fled! Needless to say there have been no issues since they left."

"I saw her once, when I was ten", added Bethany. "I'd gone upstairs to use the second floor ensuite bathroom; it was Christmas Day and there was the usual houseful, so somebody was in the main bathroom. To be honest I used to deliberately engineer it that way, to prolong that bit of quiet time away from the social and sensory overload. Anyway, I was looking for something to replace the handwash I'd used up in the bathroom and I found the doorway to the attic stairs, thinking it was a cupboard in the guest bedroom. Naturally I had to have a look. I knew nothing at all about Harriet and it was for the briefest moment but I was convinced I saw a girl. I told myself I'd imagined it but it turned out that Harriet always used to wear a particular coat which exactly matched what I saw this apparition wearing, and there was no way I would have known about that. It was in the room where she used to hide away."

"I definitely have an open mind about ghosts and other phenomena. In fact, since you've told me that, I feel I can share something else with you. Although it is true that I started researching the café as local history, I did so because I've been having vivid dreams about it, before I learned that there really had been a café there. The dreams begin with my favourite walk along Caberfeidh Road, except that the streetlights are different; they're the swan neck sort with white light. I've always noticed streetlights; yes, it could be called a 'special interest', though I have my own thoughts about that label on anything an autistic person happens to enjoy! In the dreams, I get to the end of the road and the café is there instead of that grim betting shop. The detail is incredible and matches the one photo I've seen on the website. In the last dream, which was after I researched the café and read Joan Morley's name, I actually met her. She was so welcoming. She had on a yellow dress and an apron; her hair was a rich brown shade, curled the way women did their hair in the fifties and early sixties. That dream became a lucid one; after I left the café but before I woke up, I became aware that I was dreaming and it continued for some time."

Charlene nodded; this revelation did not seem to surprise her. "Harriet connected to you through Joan. This all feels significant, and I am greatly looking forward to hearing about the progress of your friends Des and Jason's plans, though of course we will keep this confidential amongst ourselves, Sharon and Paulie for now."

19

The rain was coming on again when Diane bade her new friends farewell after a warm, convivial evening, assuring them that she did not have far to walk home. Cold and penetrating though the late October East Coast rain was, tonight it felt cleansing; without its characteristic unhealthy dampness. Letting herself in to the welcoming peace of her flat, her mellow tiredness did not preclude completion of the one final thing she needed to do that day. Unhurriedly making herself a cup of tea, she sat down next to a snuggly, sleepy Farolita and typed out the messages she needed to send; first to Des and Jason adding in what she had learned and asking how they felt about naming the café 'Harriet's Haven', then copying and pasting the part with the too long repressed confiding of the incident at her launch event and how Bethany had helped her tonight to Kate. Lastly she noted a reminder on her calendar to tell Dr Blake about the incident and Bethany's help with coming to terms with it at her next appointment. Wilma would never know; even after having been blackmailed, Diane felt that as an injustice on her own part. There had been a time when she would have considered contacting her; now, she was happy to leave well alone. Deeply satisfied, she switched off her phone and tablet; she drank the last of her tea in utter contentment, the sound of the rain on her windows a gentle prelude to the replenishment of sleep.

There was no time to appreciate the white streetlamps on this occasion. Awareness came with a strong sense of urgency. Diane understood two things; that she was dreaming, and that she needed to hurry. Her footsteps came from far away as she rushed along Caberfeidh Road in the profound stillness of an evening embedded deep within a different night decades away.

As she reached the end of the road, the lights of the café were going out.

She could dimly make out the shape of a woman coming out of the door on the corner. As she ran towards the café, the figure stepped into the glow of the streetlamps; curls of brown hair, now streaked with grey, caught the icy light as the woman stood for a moment looking at the building before moving into its shadow again to lock the door. When Diane approached, the woman turned yet did not appear to see her; as she looked in her direction, a single tear ran down one cheek. The realisation of what she was seeing shattered Diane's heart.

"Joan!"

Evidently not hearing her either, Joan Morley turned back to the business in hand; facing the devastating moment alone as she closed up her beloved café for the last time. The key grated in the lock and an era was unremarkably ended in the mundane dullness of the quiet, shuttered street. Head bravely raised, she turned to walk away.

"Joan, wait! Can you hear me? I need to tell you something!"

The straight-backed dignity of Joan's lonely walk away from her life's work continued; unheeding, achingly fixed in time.

"We're going to make this right, I promise! This is not the end. My friends and I are going to do this together; I assure you. For you, for Martha, for Harriet; for everyone who needs it now, in our time."

How much it asked of Diane's precise and tender soul to accept that she would never know whether any comfort indeed came through to Joan Morley at this most challenging of moments in her life.

"Please know that somehow, Joan, and how thankful I am to have been shown this", she added softly as they disappeared into their separate nights.

Farolita rubbed her head against Diane's chin, sensitive to her anguished mood. Hugging her pet to her chest, Diane reassured her with soothing words.

"It's OK, baby; Mummy needs to be sad for a little while today, but it's going to be all right. Our family is going to make it so."

She knew with unwavering certainty that she would not dream of the café again; not in the same recurring, lucid and meaningful way. It was time to move on now into building on those beautiful dreams; making them a reality which would bring joy and sanctuary in the future.

20

"So you knew you were dreaming while you were still in REM sleep; still having the dream?" Kate sipped her tea, her hand fondly extended to an inquisitive Farolita.

"Yes. It's happened before, but rarely, and the dreams had the usual mixed-up content; nothing meaningful like this."

"And you weren't scared when you realised you were dreaming but didn't wake up immediately?"

"No; it felt like a gift. I was devastated when I had the last dream, seeing Joan closing the café for the last time but once it was confirmed that Des and Jason are definitely taking over the premises and getting a community grant, it all became part of something wonderful. The dreams came for a reason; they were beautiful and unforgettable but that purpose has been fulfilled now. We're still waiting to hear back from the Rafters Trust; that's the fund established by another of the Sutherland sisters for the development of creative safe spaces. We're hoping that by opening up the café as a place where people can spend time doing a bit of therapeutic craft work or having a meeting, subject to making one purchase of refreshments and then a sliding scale of donations to occupy a booth for longer at certain times if not buying more refreshments, we will qualify for a grant from them too. Of course we won't be looking at charging anyone extra for needing a bit longer to destress in a crisis; I'm talking about planned time. I'll be helping with what I can; the accounts, cleaning, taking enquiries. I love cleaning; there's something deeply satisfying about making a place you love all shiny, tidy and hygienic."

"It honestly is so good to see you excited about something productive again. Do you think you'll ever go back to Up For Work?"

"At a distance I would, yes; Up For Work Together is my project after all. I would consider working online from home and attending occasional supervision meetings, which I'm assuming would be with Sally."

"Make sure you don't take on too much though, yeah?"

Diane's voice took on a warning tone. "Kate!"

Kate held up her hands in surrender. "I know, I know; you don't need to be told and it's your decision. You never know; perhaps your involvement with the café will lead to you meeting someone nice on your own terms."

"Katelyn Gloria Russell! Seriously, you are going to have to come to terms with the fact that I am asexual. I didn't know that applied to me until I talked it through with Bethany, because of the fact that, as I have never denied, I do experience a form of attachment. It is not sexual attraction! They are not the same thing. This kind of pressure and insistence on a narrow range of norms is precisely why so many people, especially young people, end up tormented over their identity. Could I form a partnership based solely on a non-sexual attachment? In theory, it's possible; as long as the other party genuinely wanted that too and wasn't compromising. Oh, except for the small matter of what I actually want, which is to always have my own exclusive quiet living space to come home to and recharge at the end of each foray into a world which exhausts me. That is valid, however unpalatable it may seem to you. I know it's not what you want for yourself; that is equally valid and I am deeply glad that you have such a strong relationship with Peter. Can you imagine how you would feel if I kept saying to you that he can't be what you want deep down and you should try to force yourself to want to be on your own, because I couldn't see beyond my own ideal outcomes and projected them onto you?"

"All right, yes, I see your point, but it's not the same thing. It's not a natural human state to want to be on your own; we're not programmed that way."

212

"Sorry but that's crap. Yes, the human race has to survive and it wouldn't work if everybody wanted to be on their own, but I hardly think there are enough people like me to endanger the continuation of the species; we wouldn't be a minority then and I'd be spared the constant justifying of it! Beyond survival, it's convention and stereotyping pushing people into believing in such a narrow range of these outcomes as valid, insisting that anything outside of it can't be accepted. I'm not saying I don't need or want any interaction. Surely my updates these past few weeks have proved otherwise! I need to manage it differently though, and I need to be allowed to be happy in my own way, not told that it's impossible because it doesn't fit some arbitrary profile. Now drink up your tea and I'll make us a fresh one!"

Taking the mug from a resignedly laughing Kate, Diane went into the kitchen, took a deep breath and counted to ten. She knew that her friend genuinely cared but she could be so maddeningly conventional!

"I do wish you'd been prepared to at least give the dating site a try", said Kate, accepting the fresh mug of tea.

"You think I didn't? I asked to see a female doctor so that I could check whether there were some medical means of helping me through it if you and Wilma were right and I was obliged to force myself to have sex in order to learn to want it. That doesn't count as trying?"

"Oh, Diane, I didn't realise! You really are scared, aren't you."

"No, Kate. Not scared. Asexual. The word is asexual. It has nothing to do with fear. I have read up on asexuality and aromanticism since talking with Bethany and learned how diverse they are. There are asexual people who have sex in particular circumstances, on their own terms and with as much emphasis on consent as anyone else. Or they may enjoy sexual fantasies but not want to act on them. It is all legitimate asexual orientation and doesn't mean they are scared, any more than my absolute lack of desire for sex means I am scared. Categorising asexual or aromantic people as being scared, too picky or not having met The Right One is not only erasure of their orientations but also diminishes the different, equally valid experience of people who do have a fear of whatever kind getting in the way of a sex life which they would like to be able to have. Oh, and back to the idea of my 'not even trying', although I shouldn't have to any more than a gay person should be obliged to try straight or vice versa; how exactly did you think I suddenly acquired a new friend in Montrose when the last time I went in that direction the train had manual slam doors?"

All right, that was cheating slightly to make her point; classic InterCity 125 stock with those kind of doors had been in regular use a few years ago when the Inter7City refurbishment programme was taking longer than expected.

"Now, I did see… is that Priya?"

"Yes, Priya. I didn't tell you because I knew you'd be all over it seeing what you wanted to see, but I met her through the site before Dr Blake validated my own instincts, sorted out the blackmail element and made it safe for me to take my profile down. I was honest with Priya from the start when she messaged me; she agreed to meet me as a potential new friend. So no, it wasn't a total waste of time, but meeting her made me see once and for all that I should have believed in my own inclinations, or lack thereof. Having someone reach out to me in good faith when I was on site against my will made me feel so deceitful; meeting her and having a lovely time making a new friend convinced me that it was nothing to do with bad experiences, because I had a good experience and a successful meeting but there was not one iota of chemistry of the sort you and Wilma tried to force upon me."

"Diane! What are you like? Don't you realise that attraction doesn't always happen instantly?"

"I do not have porridge for brains! Yes, of course I realise that! I cannot describe how my own asexuality feels beyond 'I do not experience sexual attraction' which you refuse to accept, and I'm not going to try, because you are never going to believe me. We're both a bit 'my way or the highway' on this one and we're probably going to have to agree to disagree. But Kate, although we've had a bit of banter and generally friendly debate over this, I'm going to be serious now. Priya is my friend. If and when you happen to meet her, I expect you to respect that as you do my friendship with Des and Jason. Priya, unlike me, is looking for a partner and as her friend I fully support her in that. She has chosen of her own volition to do so via a dating site; that does not preclude her meeting someone in another context as she goes about her life including socialising. If you insist on acting as though she were involved with me, pushing to make it so, you could end up standing in the way of her finding the happiness she deserves. I will not have that, and if you cannot respect that I will have to walk away. I do not want it to come to that, so I hope that you think enough of me to bear it in mind."

Kate nodded; clearly disappointed but agreeing to change the subject, she moved on to her other news.

"Anyway, I wanted to catch up with you face to face because I've heard some news from Up For Work and I wanted to prepare you. Maurice Thurlowe is no longer employed by them, since he was caught embezzling money."

"WHAT?! That man is a complete waste of DNA!"

"Which left a vacancy for a new branch manager. You probably won't be too surprised to hear that it's Verena. Sally Howe is now in her old post as outreach manager."

"I see. So I could go back to volunteering with them and have almost nothing to do with Verena? That sounds like a plan. I wouldn't have the embarrassment of her being around every corner. I'd still much prefer to work from home but it would make supervision less stressful all round; poor dear Verena could be safely holed up in her office with no fear of being molested by my puppy-dog adoration."

"Hmm. Clearly no feelings left for her then! Sorry, I'm being a bit sarcastic there but are you sure you're in the right mental place to go back to working with them?"

"First of all, wouldn't you be resentful if you'd had something so demeaning said about you? Second, nobody has asked me to go back and I would expect that the order not to contact them until they contact me still stands; I shall certainly be acting, or rather not acting, on that presumption until I hear otherwise. Third, excuse me for not being a robot. No, my feelings, whatever you want to call them, will not go away easily. Part of me will be hurting for a long time. You should be thankful that I'm not getting all giddy about the prospect of seeing her; quite the opposite. As usual you are pathologising and mistrusting me. I am autistic and intense; not a criminal and not so out of control that I cannot make responsible choices."

"Of course you have every right to be resentful; you were treated disgracefully. I don't mean to diminish that at all. I wish you could see that I'm simply protective towards you; it's not about thinking the worst of you. I'm thinking of the pain you may feel, not the wrong you may do. I am on your side; you seem to think that to be on your side, people need to anticipate you being perfect and making the best choice every single time."

"That's always been what I've had to do though, to compensate for my differences. Of course it's not exclusive to autism either; didn't even Shakespeare say something about only our mistakes being remembered?, and he wasn't talking about disabled people in particular. He was right; people in general focus on and remember the times others get things wrong. Say someone drives through the same set of bollards each day for a year and on one single day knocks one of them over. That's the day people will remember and define them by. They won't look at it as 'this person drove through those bollards daily for a year and only once knocked one of them over.' They will look at it as 'there goes the clumsy oaf who can't drive properly; on such and such a date they knocked a bollard over.' Whenever that person gets in their car; even so much as glances across the room at their car keys, out comes the finger-wagging chorus of 'Now, mind, watch those bollards!' And they have no defence, because the three hundred and sixty four days on which they drove through them perfectly mean nothing. I hear that you struggle to understand me; for my part, I struggle to understand why you and many others can't see how frustrating that is, especially when you factor in people's added anticipation of autistic missteps! You simply hear me talking a load of bollards!"

They both laughed at the entirely intentional pun. "No, I do hear your point. What I'm trying to say is, if I or someone else considers a possible negative scenario it's not an assumption that you would bring about that scenario. It's looking at one of many possibilities and wanting to minimise the chances of it being that negative scenario. Which, yes, might sometimes mean acknowledging the 'possibility' of you making a mistake or not knowing or foreseeing something, and that seems to be complete anathema to you because you feel it would instantly wipe out all the good things people feel for you and all eligibility for the support you need. You've been involved with too many bullies, Di; both personally and professionally. It's given you this mindset of not being able to afford even the tiniest slip, and the pressure that creates for you is desperately unhealthy. If people are looking to your vulnerabilities for their own entertainment and sense of superiority, you need to not have them in your life any more than you can help it. When you have a better proportion of people you trust around you; people who boost you up and make you feel good, you will feel differently about it if they happen to warn you about something or question how you're looking at something."

"I don't know, Kate; I seem to always be at the bottom of the class. It's always other people advising and guiding me, unasked for, and I never get to claw back any points by correcting them!"

"See, that's another sign of a lifetime of bullying and othering affecting your mindset; that you see it as a points system even amongst your close friends. That will take a long time to change; a long time and the right people in your life. Perhaps I have been pushing you too hard about this dating business; you're not in any headspace for something like that right now. I am sorry that I've made you feel so hounded, and I promise that, as you rightly say, I will respect Priya's journey of looking for a partner of her own and not make any attempt to treat you as a couple."

"Thank you. I appreciate that." Diane was wise enough to let the "right now" pass; it was the nearest Kate was going to get, at least for the time being, to accepting her asexuality. That was still too much of a work in progress to contemplate discussing her much more complex romantic orientation yet, keen though she was to do her bit to educate people on its distinctness from sexual orientation. As before, she knew that Kate had made valid points amid her ongoing bullheadedness. She had always been defensive around Kate in a way she wasn't around Des and Jason, though she appreciated that this did not mean Kate was any less sincere a friend. She had a style which jarred with Diane's vulnerable self-esteem, but she was not trying to hurt her or deliberately engaging in one-upmanship. Diane hoped that the day would never come when the ways in which they were incompatible brought them to an impasse which could not be worked through. Sometimes even good and sincere friendships ran their course in that way.

21

November was generally thought of as a dismal month on the cusp of seasons but its liminal shifting greys held layers of veiled beauty for those who sought them, while its share of sharp frosts and crystal skies could bring unexpected bursts of colour and life. The orange streetlights of Caberfeidh Road shone unimpeded through bare branches and the full Frost Moon would be visually shouting its diamond blast of reflected light from the heavens before too long if the skies remained clear enough. Diane started her days in the shelter of still-closed curtains, fairy lights and a gradual building of daylight outside; treasuring the warm awakening of that first cup of coffee before either damp heaviness or the glare of the low winter sun could challenge her energy levels.

Of all the names she expected to see in her email In box, Sally Howe was a long way down the list. Too intrigued to wait until her ambivalent, jumbled feelings about it could sort themselves out, she opened the message.

Its tone was professional as she would expect; neither friendly nor unfriendly. The situation had been reviewed following a change in management and she was invited to a meeting with Sally and Verena to discuss a possible return to some form of volunteering activity.

She knew perfectly well what the change in management had been. For a moment, a habitual emotional response flared into life; Verena wanted her back on the team? She squashed it down even as Kate's warning voice intruded unbidden into her mind; the irrational response of self-reproach because Kate's voice got there before her own had to be dealt with next, reminding herself that her brain was merely making an association and the internal warning system was all her own doing.

Did she truly want to dive back into this emotional whirlpool? Was it worth all this to remain involved with Up For Work Together, especially now that she had the café which was fully confirmed as going ahead?

Whatever she decided, she knew that she did not want to appear too eager; replying immediately could be interpreted as still being overly attached rather than her entirely justifiable wish to continue with her own project. Closing the message, she drew back the curtains to let in the pale but clean morning light.

First cups of coffee were good for waking up; second cups, though never quite so powerfully uplifting as the first, were good for thinking. If she walked away from this, her principal motive would be pettiness rather than self-preservation; the transient satisfaction of telling Up For Work collectively where to go. She knew in her heart that she was now in a much stronger mental place with no disproportionate reliance on them for a sense of purpose. Perhaps this was why her last dream of the café had been so upsetting. Seeing Joan at that heartbreaking moment and not being able to communicate with her had given Diane a whole new level of investment and determination. With that, finding a properly supportive new doctor, making new friendships and strengthening local acquaintanceships into firmer connections, she had shored up her defences beyond recognition. There was no longer the same need for secrecy about glitches which left her dissociated and ashamed; no longer the concern that her relationship with Des and Jason would become weighed down by their being her sole confidants; no longer the level of isolated self-doubt which allowed Kate's well-intentioned but often ill-suited hectoring to ride roughshod over her own unendorsed instincts. That said, one piece of Kate's advice stood out in her mind as concurring with her own thoughts; if she were going to this meeting, she would be taking a witness.

The meeting having been accepted, Des had leave to use up before finishing his current job and although he was planning to dedicate most of it to getting the café ready, he was more than happy to go with her. Diplomatically phrasing it as support but telling rather than asking, Diane emailed Sally to let her know.

The building which had vibrated with menace last time she was there was blandly beige in the subdued afternoon light of a dull November day. Traffic stirred lethargic rainwater to trickle indifferently down silted gutters as umbrellas were cautiously lowered and hooded eyes appraised an uncertain sky. Bringing Des here felt incongruous; he belonged to the part of Diane's world where she could truly be herself. At the same time, his presence shielded her from the keen edge of her worst memories, reminding her as much of her worth as of her rights.

Gisela smiled warmly as she ushered them to the office which held such awful associations. "It's good to see you, Diane", she said sincerely as she accepted the retirement card and gift which Diane had brought for Arthur. The absence of Maurice Thurlowe permeated the building like fresh air let into a long-abandoned cell. Even the plants looked healthier; less cowed.

Sally opened the inner office door, her smile wary but genuine. Walking into the room, Diane's first sight of Verena since the events of the project launch was magnified in its queasy intimidation by the fact that she was sitting in what had been Maurice Thurlowe's chair; where he had sat as he eviscerated Diane about her feelings, issues and character. Nauseous with recollection, she glanced across at Des and the world stabilised again. Coolly, she introduced him to Sally and Verena.

"Congratulations on your promotion, Verena"; an unsmiling Diane spoke politely and evenly, circumspectly making no move to physically approach the woman who had been her idol and whose effect upon her still lingered.

"Thank you, Diane. Sally and I have been made aware of some aspects of your last conversation in this office which were not what we would have wished for and which we do not endorse. Gisela felt unable to speak out at the time but was distressed and highly concerned by what she was unable to avoid overhearing. I am sorry that some unacceptable things were said to you in my name, and that this did not come to light earlier so that checks could be made on your welfare. Although we did have concerns about your attachment to me, those concerns were more about how it may be impacting on you than any anticipation of you engaging in inappropriate behaviour. I ought perhaps to have been clearer when I said that I was concerned about what you might do if the issue was raised with you; I meant what you might do to yourself, not to me, and I certainly never suggested a sexual motive in the way in which it was put to you. I confess that when I heard about the incident with Brenda Culper at the project launch, I jumped to the wrong conclusion about why it happened and I approached it as evidence that your attachment and frustrated wish to present a particular image to impress me had become a problem. I have since had cause to reflect upon how the environment, overload and fatigue affected your level of vulnerability that day in ways which were not related to how you feel about me. We are agreed that there is no reason why you should not be able to resume your involvement with the Up For Work Together project if you wish, with Sally as your line manager."

Diane's mind screamed in protest as it stretched to take in all she was hearing. Verena had not in fact seen her humiliate herself trying to pour a simple cup of tea. She had heard about it, which was bad enough; the thought of that conversation turned Diane's stomach, but it was not as horrific as the mental image of her watching it happen. She

222

had not been behind Maurice Thurlowe's vile hate speech and had not been perceiving her as a potential stalker. She had nonetheless been looking down on her as a rather pathetic creature who was way below her league and she still did not appear to see any problem with having announced Sally as the project's originator.

"I appreciate you clarifying aspects of my last meeting and yes, I would like to continue with Up For Work Together, but in a less intensive capacity and working from home. I am happy to train for and serve as a volunteer moderator on the online forum; I am willing to come here for supervision meetings with Sally. Although you have provided a degree of clarification, I am frankly mortified by your perception of me. I hero-worshipped you; I admit that, but I no longer wish to work closely with you, knowing how you feel about it. I have other interests in my life now; I wish to pursue those and negotiate a reduced role in Up For Work Together. The other thing I ask is that you acknowledge it was inaccurate to say at that launch event that the project began with Sally. I will always remain incredibly thankful for your support in taking the project forward and making it happen, Sally; I have never disputed that it wouldn't have gotten off the ground without you. However, that is in itself a symptom of an organisational culture which does not place equal value on its disabled employees and volunteers. Yes, it was a team effort and rightly so; it should not have been taken forward solely on the strength of another person's input though, to the extent that I was publicly erased as the creator."

Shaking her head, Verena drew breath to speak; unexpectedly, Sally held up a hand to stop her.

"She's right, Vee. That was unfair. Diane, you have conducted yourself with impeccable grace and dignity today and we should be thankful that you want to continue with us. I want to share something with you which no-one but Verena currently knows here and it is not to be repeated to or discussed with any other colleague; I am also autistic. I do not reveal it in my professional life, largely because of the type of issues with which you have had to cope here. I am fortunate in that I can manage a healthy working life, with the support of my husband and family. Seeing and hearing about what you were put through has forced me to check my privilege and think about the courage and tenacity you show by doing what you can and advocating with your authentic autistic voice. A project such as Up For Work Together could not happen without that!"

This was a curve boomerang, never mind a curve ball. Sally Howe was autistic? Verena's poised, polished and respected friend and equal? Diane looked at her anew in the light of this revelation. The subtly softened lines of her business attire; the high heeled shoes which must surely hurt her feet and legs more than seamless clothes could compensate for. Was it this camouflage, her working for a salary, her being older or having a husband which made her autism acceptable to Verena in a way in which Diane's was not? Or was it all of those things? Perhaps it was because she did not need to impress her; she was already up at her level. Yet she had called Diane courageous, tenacious, graceful and dignified! What the actual heck was going on here?

"Sally, I am touched that you have entrusted me with this and I assure you it will go no further; neither will I raise it in private conversation with you unless you mention it first, although I offer you all the solidarity I can. Not that I'm all that great an ambassador for autism given how badly I coped with Brenda Culper's intervention that day."

"Yes, well, Brenda has to take some responsibility for that too. After you bumped into me in your attempt to get away from the situation, I tried to signal to her to back off and to put the cup of tea down by the urn. Had she discussed it with me, it would not have become a more formal conversation higher up the chain. But then, why would she?

224

It is people like you who are prepared to talk about autism and share your experiences openly that are needed to bring about the right kind of conversations."

So it had been Sally with whom she collided when, to her agonising frustration, she let slip her usual meticulous observance of the need to look before stepping back; earning a maddeningly merited rebuke for carelessness and blowing a hole in her credibility which she could so ill afford, giving people just cause to write her off as not even trying when she spent her entire life trying so desperately hard.

"That was you? I knew I bumped into someone; I swear I do try so hard to always remember to look around me but I failed that day and it always bothered me that I owed someone an apology but had no idea who it was. Sally, I am so sorry for making such an inexcusable lapse!"

"Diane, you were so distressed and overloaded nobody could have blamed you if the roof had fallen in without you noticing. Please try to forgive yourself for that. We have not done a good job of discharging our duty of care to you as a volunteer, and a highly productive one at that. If you wish to train and work from home, that can easily be arranged. Right, Verena?"

Verena nodded. "Yes; I support that course of action going forward. I hope that we can all put the past behind us and move on. Diane, I shall make sure that your personnel record reflects that the original idea for Up For Work Together was yours, though I'm fairly certain that it already does."

Diane supposed that this was the nearest she was going to get to a direct acknowledgement; no doubt Verena was still afraid of showing her too much appreciation, even when professionally deserved, in case it "encouraged" her. Would she ever be wholly free of feeling unworthy and humiliated around this woman? The pain was no longer so acute but it jangled up through the roots of her soul from a place at the confluence of many wounds too deep and complex to ever be fully healed.

"I stood up to speak, too soon, in front of everybody."

The words were out before she could weigh up whether they were timely or wise; whether they negated Sally's astonishing praise.

"I'm sorry?"

"At the launch. When you said you were thanking the colleague who made it happen and with whom it began. I was the next to be speaking, I knew you were going to be handing over to me and it was the time you were due to do so. All of that, plus it having been my idea as you've just acknowledged, made it logical for me to stand up. Then you called Sally up on stage, completely unscheduled. Have you any idea how humiliating that was for me, having to sit down again? Then what it took for me to regroup after that and give a speech? I am all for moving forward, but I had to get that out, Verena; I need that closure."

Sally's intake of breath as the veracity of Diane's words hit home appeared to prompt something reluctant in Verena; a giving of permission to herself to do the right thing by Diane, acknowledging that at this moment it ought to take priority over her discomfort at the younger woman's intensity and her own heightened need to establish distance in response to it.

"Yes, I concede that you do have a point there; I had been quite dogmatic about sticking to the agreed script and timescale. It was an unfair position in which to put you; it was unprofessional of me to put my personal friendship with Sally before my responsibility to a vulnerable team member. I apologise for that."

'Nicely done, Verena', thought Diane wryly. 'Widen the gulf between us any further and you can start claiming mileage on expenses whenever you and I have to interact even if we're in the same room.' The dreaded nervous laughter threatened to bubble up as her mind went from there to wondering whether that was how Maurice Thurlowe had been defrauding the company; she hastily pulled her thoughts back to the present. Nodding her acceptance of the answer to her point, she turned her attention back to Sally in order to finalise a timescale for her to begin her forum moderation training.

As the meeting closed, Sally enquired whether there were anything else Diane wanted to say or ask.

"May I see Arthur? I've given his card and gift to Gisela but I would like to thank him in person for the support he has always given me here."

Sally readily agreed; beyond giving a polite thank you for her time, Diane barely looked in Verena's direction as she and Des walked out of the inner office. She had seen a certain disingenuous streak in her today which had not been apparent before; perhaps it was her own shifting priorities, or the disconcerting realisation that Verena responded differently to Sally's autism making it Diane's own autistic profile rather than autism as a whole which was the issue, which felt like much more personal a slight. Perhaps it was a bit of both. There was lots to process; right now, all she wanted was to introduce her best friend to her unofficial mentor and have a cup of tea.

Arthur had, it transpired, just boiled the kettle and he was delighted to see Diane come in as he sat down for his mid-afternoon break. It felt strange being in the small staff kitchen again, even after a comparatively short time. It somehow made the colours seem brighter, even though they were mostly pale blues and greys, and the shapes more sharply defined. By the time she returned with tea for herself and Des, the two men were happily talking about fishing; Diane savoured the rush of affection and belonging it gave her to see two of the most reassuring presences in her life chatting together for the first time, both turning to smile as she walked in. Over tea, she and Des told Arthur about their plans for the café and he promised to look out for news of it; that he would stop by when he were in Inverbrudock. "You've been a miss here, quine", he told Diane; his Aberdeenshire dialect coming through as he fondly regarded the colleague whom he had always appreciated for her genuine, loyal nature, sound judgement and concern for others. "It was all wrong that they took you off that website project after all the work you did. I don't know exactly what happened but I heard you made it clear at that do a couple of months back that it was your idea to start with. Well, good for you; I'm glad you did that. This new café of yours sounds like precisely what people need when they don't even know it these days; none of this fussing and braying and wanting to know your business when all you want is a newspaper, or the news on your phone as it is now, a cup of tea and a bit of peace."

Trust Arthur to hit the nail right on the head in his understated, down to Earth way. Diane had missed their chats and putting the world to rights, even more than she realised. She would not see him in this setting again; his retirement was mere weeks away, but now there was a possibility of his becoming a patron of the café; Arthur would not say that as empty words. If he did not have good reason to anticipate being in Inverbrudock and calling in, he would be saying goodbye and good luck.

The train home was on time, its lights warm and inviting in the gathering dusk. Diane relished the contrast with the last time she had been travelling home after a meeting; in Kate's car still in a state of shock, her world so violently deconstructed that nothing felt as though it could ever be comfortable and familiar again. She and Des were going to pick up some wine at the convenience store near the station then go back to see Jason and Luke; a relaxing evening with her best friends to consolidate a mostly successful day.

"I didn't want to talk about this on the train because you never know who's around and who they know, but I did not see that coming about Sally being autistic!"; Diane clinked glasses with Des as Jason laughingly shooed Luke out of his gym bag which lay open on the floor. "Not that I'm suggesting there's any kind of standard autistic look; I know perfectly well there isn't, but the way Verena has been with and about me, you'd think she hadn't knowingly met an autistic person before. Then we find out she's best friends with one! I was thinking on the train, I wonder how many times when she made a big show of asking for adjustments in my name when they weren't things I'd specifically mentioned, they were in fact for Sally and my being on the scene gave her an opportunity to show off about it because she didn't need to be as discreet about me!"

"I must say, Di, she didn't impress me. Verena, that is. Now Sally, she had a bit of integrity and I respected her for the way she spoke up. She may not be quite ready yet and she's entitled to keep her autism as a private matter after all, but I think she will end up taking something of a lead from you in terms of helping other people to become more accepting. That Verena one, frankly, I don't get why someone like you would be so taken with her. She came across as someone who would sell her granny down the river while strutting about advertising it as laying on a charity cruise for the elderly!"

Diane laughed heartily, raising her glass again. "That's her in a nutshell! She's so two-faced she needed two masks every time she went out during Covid!"

The best friends clinked glasses, roaring with laughter.

"I am beginning to see through her now; I don't admire her the way I did, especially after today, and I'm not convinced she's as innocent as she claimed to be in terms of Maurice Thurlowe. He hardly knew me; where else would all that about my 'predilections' and assuming that what happened with Brenda Culper was a result of my feelings for Verena have come from? Besides which, given that Sally was right there and tried to intervene so insightfully, Verena knowingly had access to an autistic take on it from the start. That's a big ask for me to come to terms with; that I can no longer tell myself that it's autism in general Verena's uncomfortable with as opposed to me personally. Which I realise makes me a selfish person because I should be glad for the sake of other autistic people that she is open enough to be a supportive friend to one, not wishing her ableism onto all of us! Kate said something once about Verena responding well to confidence in other people. Maybe that's what it is; Sally is better at believing in herself, or at least appearing to. I guess that takes a bit of pressure off Verena; it's easier for her to look good by being friends with someone like Sally who is nearer to what she knows and understands in her peers and doesn't require her to go out of her own comfort zone. It also means she doesn't have to expend nearly as much energy as someone like Sally or me; no wonder she can afford to shine so brightly. Which, yes, absolutely makes Verena shallow and I pray Sally doesn't end up getting hurt! I hope - well, I know you will understand that it's going to take my feelings a while to catch up with that perspective though."

"Of course I do. It's not about criticising your feelings and emotions; I wish that you could have been spared all the pain and doubt she's caused you. I think Kate is on to something about Verena responding well to confidence because it's her comfort zone but I would take it further than that in terms of why she doesn't respond favourably to you. Although you lack the self-belief Kate's getting at, it doesn't stop you from flagging up when something is wrong and I think that's the crux of what bothers Verena. You will call her out even from the depths of your self-criticism; that shows her up and scares her. I still can't believe you held back about what happened with that Brenda person because you thought you'd done something so terrible. It broke our hearts getting your message and realising that you were carrying that on your own even while we were all together having a laugh and sharing everything else that was happening for all of us. I'm so glad that you met Bethany. Not being autistic, there will be things Jason and I can't relate to in the same way she can, for all we support you and have your back. You need that connection with other autistic people."

"Des, I'm so sorry that message made you both sad! It's not that I don't trust either of you; I needed to be detached from what happened, not bringing it into the joy and freedom of my time with you. Sometimes when something utterly humiliating has happened which makes my impairments unavoidably the most visible thing about me, leaving my self-esteem at rock bottom - I know that's internalised ableism but it's how I feel and how the world still works - I need to block it out in order to scramble back up to that baseline level of self-worth which allows me to accept the joy and wellbeing your friendship gives me and to have a good time socialising with you both. That's why I don't always tell you things for quite some time after they've happened. Then there's the extra time I need to process and the wrong I do other people because of it. I feel bad sometimes that I don't resolve things at the time because it takes longer for me to even get around to feeling and identifying my emotions when something's been said or done that hurt me. Often it doesn't sink in until after I get home and have enough space and quietness for my reactions to catch up. It looks malicious when I appear to be fine then raise something afterwards; I often do it by email because it's easier and I can take my time, but it comes as a shock to the other person. I truly don't mean to mislead people but it increases the internalised shame and that makes it harder in general for me to let myself confide in my friends, even you and Jason with whom I've never been in the situation of reacting too late because, well, because there hasn't been anything to have a delayed reaction to. You are my shepherd moons and I'm already home. Once I'd gained so much useful new perspective from Bethany, all I wanted was to tell you both so that there wasn't this big looming dark secret between us any more. Kate too, because to be fair, I did give her a pretty hard time for pushing the 'dating to get over Verena' angle when she had no way of knowing there was more to my reactions and distress that day. Not that it's stopped her; I had to get quite firm with her about not insisting on seeing Priya as 'the partner I'm failing to accept that I need', because Priya does want to meet somebody and if Kate sees us socially and insists on treating us as a couple it could complicate things if and when Priya does find someone she likes in that way!"

"Jeez, why is Kate so stuck on this? It may well be what you said before, about her not being able to get her head around somebody not wanting the same things she does and projecting onto them how she would feel if she didn't have Peter, but she seriously needs to wind her neck in before she pushes you away altogether. And you have nothing to be sorry for; you don't owe us any explanations. We hated to think of how tough and lonely it must have been for you, dealing with that on your own when we could have been helping you to see it differently even before Bethany gave you the extra autistic perspective."

"I get that, and if it helps, if I had told you I wouldn't have ended up telling someone I'd only just met and I wouldn't have gained that extra autistic perspective. Bethany got me on my own by suggesting we went to get chips from Vinnie's because she'd picked up on me saying I struggled to talk about that day even with my closest friends; she recognised her own internalised shame in me because she's been there with glitches caused by having to live in a society which is not geared to be accessible to us."

"She sounds like someone you definitely need in your life, Di. I hope we get to meet her one day."

"I'd say that's guaranteed; you should have heard her when I told her I've got a Siamese cat! Perth isn't far and the train service is so frequent; she comes through here often, to visit Sharon and Charlene and Brandon, and Cheminot of course!"

Des chuckled, having heard about the handsome stray ginger cat who had appeared soon after Charlene and Brandon got back from a Eurostar trip. Topping up their wine, he poured a glass for Jason and dished up the cottage pie he had prepared. The trio settled in the living room, their plans for the café's autistic hygge taking shape as they ate the lean, autumn night warming meat and its crisp blanket of potato in the glow of the auroral, turning-leaves sweep of colours from the light in the corner.

22

As winter set in, the icy winds and bone-chilling East Coast rain sweeping the ever darkening days towards the solstice, Diane found herself living something approaching her best life. Her mornings were spent doing her training modules then later in the season once those were completed, working on the rapidly growing Up For Work Together forum. In the afternoons she helped Des and Jason with cleaning, measuring and shaping the interior of the café. Walking home each time via Caberfeidh Road, the alchemy of the streetlights gilding the unforgiving cold and grey with liquid golden orange warmed her with the promise of eventual clear skies, Christmas lights and still air spiced with the tang of mulled wine. The empty building, even before they began work in earnest, had soon lost its drab shuttered misery as the clinging despair of thousands of lost bets dissipated along with the gossamer transience of the rare big wins which hooked people in even nowadays with betting shops moving towards encouraging responsible gambling. As warm pale coral spread across the grey walls and curved wood replaced sharp angular perspex and plastic, Joan Morley's light, busy footsteps seemed to echo more closely in time than the heavy, burdened tread of all who had followed the destructive path of her husband Leonard through the years. Soft cushions and stim toys, books and small tactile coloured mood lights were ordered; some of these touches may have to wait until Covid restrictions were fully lifted but they would be part of everyone's anticipation of that longer term goal. Each booth would have a table lamp giving a warm white light, which customers could switch off if they wished and use the mood lights instead, giving as much choice as could be safely achieved when hot drinks were being served. A friend of Jason's from the gym was a lighting engineer and was, Diane had been told, working on some customised lamps to fit the theme. There would be wide booths with easily movable chairs so that those could be taken out to allow wheelchair access; even those booths with fixed seating would not have steps to catch out customers whose executive functioning had been stretched to the limits going about their day. No patron of Harriet's Haven would ever have to risk the danger and humiliation of being distracted and not seeing, or forgetting, a step. One of the more ambitious features, suggested by Diane, was to be cinema style lighting marking the edges of the aisle in the wood-effect floor; not dazzlingly bright but enough to subconsciously emphasise the boundary which people must remember to treat as a road, looking out for others passing before stepping out of their booth. Priya had tracked down and obtained permission to use prints of some photographs of the surrounding streets from the early 1960s; there were none of Caberfeidh Road itself but some showed the streetlights as they had been in Diane's dreams. It filled her with a powerful sense of connection to picture Joan and her customers going about their lives at the foot of those ornate, yet everyday to them, swan neck lamps as she framed their image to become part of the café's rebirth. Screens on the walls would be linked to the feed from various webcams in Scandinavia, subtly emphasising the hygge and koselig element of the café's theme; their winter weary customers could watch the snow sparkle in the lights of far distant Tromso off the north coast of mainland Norway, or with luck on late opening evenings, be right there in a spiced latte glow as the Aurora Borealis beckoned from a soaring Arctic sky.

Christmas was the time when Diane came closest to feeling the pain of estrangement from her birth family. Des and Jason would be in London with theirs and she wholeheartedly celebrated their excitement with them, especially after Covid restrictions had kept them apart more than usual. Her happiness for them was enhanced by the welcome addition of Luke to her own festive scene. Charlene had invited her to share Christmas lunch, but this was a time when Diane genuinely preferred to be alone. To her relief, Charlene readily agreed to meet another day, unquestioningly accepting that choosing to treat the holidays as a time to stay inside, take stock and be completely free from the self-imposed discipline of the rest of the year did not mean that Diane had any intention of wallowing in maudlin misery. She worked hard at maintaining a routine all year round; not staying in for too many consecutive days, getting up, going to bed and eating meals at fairly regular times; the festive season was the one time she let that go. Of course there would be emotional moments; she would allow herself to feel them, go through them and come out on the other side of them refreshed and ready to move onwards. This year, she would have the added bonus of new friendships and projects which she could look forward to picking up again as routine recommenced.

Christmas Eve when it came was the toughest; worse than Christmas Day. Anticipation, especially remembered from childhood, swung the sharpest of all cutting edges; untempered by what was often a blunted and drained reality. Norman and Hilary Abercrombie's relationship with their children, especially their unplanned but magnanimously accommodated third child, had always been one of provision rather than affection. Christmas had been a tasteful showpiece; Diane recalled it with gratitude for the ample privilege she now knew it had entailed. The memories she kept closest to her heart; those which still held the ache of loss were of holidays with Georgie and Ady home from university, wrapping their pre-pubescent baby sister in the intriguing multicoloured cloak of aloof new adulthood mixed with their own nostalgic indulgence.

The year Diane was ten, Georgie had recently painfully broken up with a boyfriend and threw herself into seeking comfort in the homely cosiness of decorating the tree, baking gingerbread figures and watching feelgood comedy films with her little sister. Huddled together in fleece pyjamas with motifs of reindeer and Scottie dogs in Santa hats, the controlled sparkle of elegant tinsel weaving a slow sensory dance around them with the rich, heady aromas of ripe Christmas cake and cooling gingerbread, the two sisters had never been closer; certainly Diane could not recall ever having felt so needed and relevant in the world of her much older siblings of which she was usually on the outer edge. She had sat alongside Georgie's radiant, unspoken pain, feeling a grave understanding beyond her years; unsure of what to do to help yet paradoxically sensing that her inexperienced, uncertain presence was exactly what her sister needed. Throughout her childhood Diane had longed to be older; to be interacted with as the adult she was in her mind. Talking and acting the age she felt herself to be instead of her chronological age came naturally; the smothered laughter it so often elicited from her adult role models hurt, frustrated and puzzled her betrayed heart to the extent of a physical ache. That Christmas, she had found an unfamiliar peace and rest in being able to allow herself to simply exist as a child in order to help and comfort her sister. She remembered that year with more sadness for Georgie's heartache than anything to do with herself. Of the few people in her current life who had been trusted with that story, Des and Jason alone had not followed the established format of which she despaired; most others seized upon it as their groundbreaking discovery of a reason behind what she now knew to be her asexual and aromantic orientations. So many people had triumphantly appropriated not only her memories but her sister's anguish as evidence of how all-knowing they were; appointing themselves as the worldly-wise wranglers of her alleged repressed sexuality, fettered - they assumed - by the fear of getting her heart broken as Georgie had. Then would come the repeated attempts to "fix" her; the cliched lectures, the unsubtle matchmaking, the engineering of situations where she was put on the spot in front of other people with the expectation that she would be too timorously afraid of offending the other party to say no. Which, at times, she had been, though not for the reasons the would-be matchmakers thought. She was genuinely too considerate to turn anyone down in front of a baying audience, for their sake even if they had been party to the set-up; her fears, however, were of how much fury her tone of voice would cause as the stress caused her control of it to slip away, or the condescending pity if she fell into the horror of becoming situationally mute. The words and sentiments would all be there, but whirled by the storm of anxiety into a formless white noise; their fragmented edges scouring and scratching her overstimulated brain as it vainly strove to slow them into coherence. She had always spoken privately with the other person as soon as she could in order to be honest with them about it not being what she wanted; some had been more accepting than others.

These days, her life was once again her own as she celebrated the seasons of the year. At Hogmanay, much as she empathised with those who enjoyed the buzz of the crowds seeing in the New Year and wished them all a safe and happy celebration which suited them, her own style of marking the occasion had a distinct up side too. She had the advantage of not having to queue for drinks and the toilet, shout to make herself heard, cope with drunks pushing and vomiting then wait hours in the freezing sleet and wind for a taxi which would cost three times as much as usual. At midnight, she would stand at her window to salute the turning of the year with a good dram; give thanks for the good things about the past year and for the opportunities ahead. It was all she felt she needed to mark the ritual. Over the Scottish double bank holiday of the first two days in January, she would put a USB stick with a lifetime's accumulation of almost a thousand favourite songs on random play for longer than usual, never knowing whether the next track would remind her of last week in the Fulmar's Nest, her inner world at school or anything from any time in between.

This was already something she frequently did on routine Saturdays as she relaxed with her Shiraz; every so often there would be a serendipitous coincidence, or perhaps a message of encouragement from somewhere in the dimly perceived realms of electrical energy. After her conversation with Sharon about Samantha Fox's cover of "I Only Wanna Be With You" reminded her how much she loved that version of the classic song as a child, she had downloaded it; when she put her music on random play weeks later and it was the first track to come on, Sharon happened to message her at that moment. She and Paulie had been enjoying a limited edition whisky that Diane had decanted into a ten centilitre bottle for them from her own online purchase after they had missed out when it sold out quickly. It had been a day on which Diane's reserves of morale had been low; yet again a moment's distraction had caught her out on a shopping trip which she had forced herself to take despite feeling tired and depleted. Her perseverance had not been rewarded; she had misheard the bored mumbling cashier and handed over the wrong amount of money, then been laughed at when she cursed her auditory processing problems and fervently wished out loud in that unguarded moment for one day without embarrassing herself. At these moments when she most needed to be heard and taken seriously, unknowing people around her heard it as a joke and laughed even more, jarring her ears and her soul. Spending the rest of the day fighting off the unwanted mental replays, she had been in two minds as to whether she could allow herself her usual music and wine; the impeccably timed song selection and message had felt like the absolution which was as remote and inaccessible as the sun from the surface of Pluto on days like these when her perennial trying backfired on her, chafing her soul raw. "A Harriet moment", Charlene had said, smiling sagely as Diane related the story to her; she firmly believed that her long-dead relative's fervent empathy had continued in some form of ongoing connectivity, harnessing electrical impulses which transcended the corporeal. The theory resonated strongly with Diane; the implication that she had become a part of their extended family wove extra filaments of glinting steel into the frail, tenuous lattice of her sense of place in society.

Raising a specially chosen dram; this year the Islay-born amber miniature ocean of a sherry cask matured Bunnahabhain, every evening from the winter solstice through to the second of January was an integral part of Diane's festive schedule. With each passing year she thought with a more benevolent fondness of Georgie and Ady; she wholeheartedly wished and hoped that both her sister and her brother had found genuine happiness in their conventionally packed-scheduled, pressured lives.

23

The early days of January were tough for many of the Up For Work Together forum's members as the calendar insisted life return to normal irrespective of how burned out neurodivergent brains cried out in protest from the depths of winter and the festive season's own associated overload. Digging deep for words to help, Diane cast her mind back to a particularly cold and damp January Friday when she had been staying to cover the phones at her last job. Her growing lack of stamina to cope with the pub tradition at the end of increasingly exhausting working weeks made her a convenient source of phone cover to allow those who embraced the culture to get away as soon as the flexible hours allowed; the fleeting appreciation it afforded her took the edge off being taken for granted. It had become a bittersweet routine; once past the initial wave of resentment combined with the daunting realisation each time the last colleague from her team left with scarcely a backward glance that she was committed to staying for two more hours however tired she became, those final minutes of her working week took on a distinct stark beauty which she guarded closely to herself. The long, open plan office shed all of its social overload and enough of its sensory excess to feel like a cloak altered to fit, draping itself around her in a temporary truce. Outside, a back road led through a broad underpass where various buskers would take advantage of the acoustics. On Friday afternoons, according to whatever arcane system of etiquette applied and was somehow shared and understood among unconnected individuals with no ambiguity, the pitch belonged to a lone saxophone player whose unhurried notes drifted upwards through turbulent layers of city air to meet and resonate with the winding down of Diane's exhausted brain. Of her drawn out and largely merged memories, this specific January Friday stood out; a bizarrely beautiful dystopia. The tall streetlights were coming on, turning the compact halo of rain around each one to something more colourful and organic-looking than diamonds; the flesh-toned glitz of padparadscha sapphires was nearer the mark. The music spoke to her of a calmer late nightlife that lay out of reach on the faraway shore; across the impassable, churning, ruthlessly loud melee which inflamed the Friday night culture with sensory buffeting and social drowning. Each note mellowed on the saturated atmosphere evoking a long turning of hot, overcrowded summer to the cooling space of autumn. City nights yawned and stretched into a neon sunset of blue and pink jazz club signs at intimate venues, scattering their rays on the liquid surfaces of velvet red wine inside and rain-soaked pavements outside. Heavy-eyed readiness for the tranquil embrace of a mercifully quiet home and bed surfed the invisible waves of social acceptability from scorned and pitied, through amusedly tolerated, all the way to acknowledged and even expected there at the far edge of the indigo shadows.

Reliving that memory in the new light of the forum, it occurred to Diane that it represented an area not often focused on in this context. Incentives to work for those who could do so were clear in terms of outcomes; wages, independence, purpose, structure, interaction, building and using skills. What was missing was an encouraging visualisation of the moments which carried the ongoing journey to those ends beyond bearable to attractive. Real, relatable and palpable instances of working life bringing everyday interludes of joy and energy boosts; examples which could be unexpectedly echoed in anyone's working day at any time as a supplement to those less tangible principles which required the additional energy of constant self-prompting to remember and strive for with gritted teeth.

Opening up a new thread, she invited members to share their own experiences of uplifting moments which happened at work, travelling to and from there or in circumstances which were directly connected to working, including employability courses, jobseeking activity and volunteering. This was not, she asserted, a call for examples about having the money to do or buy things; it was about pleasures experienced in the process of doing the work itself and the examples must not identify anyone or give away any sensitive employer information. She started it off by describing those peaceful Friday late afternoons, the thrill of having the normally hectic office almost completely to herself and the pull of that haunting music.

As she typed, another memory came to mind and she included it too. She had been sent on a training course which entailed an overnight stay in Birmingham; a city she had never visited before. It had been at the time when the trend of winding strings of compact lights around the trunks and main branches of trees was first becoming popular. She had arrived pleasantly surprised by the orderly linear flow of New Street Station; her expectations of Birmingham perhaps coloured by the chaotic asymmetrical trope of Spaghetti Junction, the station had soothed and welcomed her with its easy navigability. She had glancingly admired the fairy light-studded trees outside her hotel before checking in and facing the task of finding her room. Eight floors up, she had taken in the view of the city and unpacked before returning to the window for a more detailed perusal. It was then that she looked downwards as well as outwards from the room which overlooked the trees she had passed on the way in. From that height, the tiny, densely packed ice-white lights blended together into an ethereal luminescence giving the effect of looking directly at the trees' inner life force. She had stood staring for ages, mesmerised; everybody she saw at the training course the following day, including a few of the hotel cleaners, heard about it. She had seen the effect several times since but the novel impact of that first occasion had never left her.

Replies began to trickle in, telling of funny, colourful and rewarding things which people remembered from their ongoing or historic work related experience. The thread steadily climbed up the numbers of views. Reading through it on a morning when a fiery January sunrise had woken her, Diane realised that there could be a booklet in this; published fully anonymised in terms of individuals whilst still attributed to the forum and with no employer identified so as not to give inappropriate advertising, it could help to reach other people as it further raised the profile of Up For Work Together. She posted asking how people felt about it, making it clear that she had not yet discussed the idea with anyone outwith the forum itself. Favourable response and more examples ensued, she emailed Sally to ask whether this could be done, clearly setting out her awareness of the need for anonymity and lack of any impression of advertising. There was a time when she would have copied Verena in on the email, hoping for the thrill of an approving reply from her; Diane cringed as she admitted it to herself. Yes, if Verena did contact her either directly or via Sally about this, she would still feel that rush. She hoped that the fact she was no longer actively seeking it was enough to satisfy the lingering requirement to make amends to some people in her life for finding it too daunting to do what they expected of her. She drew the line at subjecting herself to some kind of exhausting mental boot camp to purge herself of an attachment of which they did not approve. Now that Wilma was off the scene, when she thought about it that disapproval was restricted to Up For Work and to Kate, whose forceful opinions had a way of making her come across as a majority all of her own. Sally replied thanking Diane for her message and suggestion, promising to consider it and discuss it with the team then get back to her. It was enough.

The returning light which began to be perceptible in February as the earth stirred from its hibernation was reaching pale fingers across a dusky blue sky when Diane's phone pinged with a message from Priya. She had some good news to share and would love to meet up with Diane in person, not having seen her since before Christmas. Diane had yet to make the short journey up the coast to Montrose to see her; she was long overdue a train trip for purely social purposes.

The view of water being unexpectedly found on the opposite side of the railway than usual as Montrose Basin glinted under monochrome skies was what Diane had always associated with that part of the East Coast line. Leaving the chilly station with Priya, whose pink highlighted hair brought colour to the stubbornly lingering grey of late winter, Diane laughed into the biting wind as she agreed that talking and listening were going to work much better indoors.

The pub was the kind which appeared small and insular upon walking in but extended back to an open area with an elegant corner bar. Taking their seats at a table which was tucked behind a pillar with flaking ochre paint, Diane began to surmise as she clinked glasses with Priya that her friend's eyes were shining with something other than a physical response to the cold wind.

"I wanted you to be one of the first people I told, because whatever you felt about the circumstances of our first meeting it was your integrity and your lovely company that made me decide to persevere. I've met someone, Di. Her name is Linda and she lives in Aberdeen. I've been seeing her since before Christmas; you may have seen her appear on my friends list but we've been keeping it quiet about being a couple until we'd had some time to establish it to ourselves. I have no doubts though; this is going to last. We both took down our profiles on the site weeks ago."

"Priya, that's wonderful! Such lovely news; congratulations, I am so happy for you both! It is incredibly generous of you to include me in this way; you've made this happen by going for what you want despite the awful experience you had before meeting me and how that made you feel. If it's a suitable time for both of you, I'd love for you to bring her to the café opening; if you're not publicly a couple yet, she's welcome as a friend."

"Thank you; she may be away working but even if she can't make the launch, she will be coming with me to see you at some point. I will certainly be at the launch; I'll take leave for that."

"I do hope you can make it; you've been so helpful, finding out about the Rafters Trust and getting those photos for us. As far as Des, Jason and I are concerned, you're one of the team."

"That means so much. I've been enjoying the updates; this autistic hygge concept is so fresh and relevant."

"I'm glad to hear that from someone who isn't autistic; I hope that it's the kind of thing that will break down barriers and make people see that inclusion and accessibility aren't about pushing non-disabled people out and the two groups don't necessarily need to be seen as incompatible opposites!"

"I think you're on to something, absolutely. How are the plans coming along?"

"It's going well; Jason's friend Mitch from the gym is custom making some table lamps for us and I'm being made to wait until my birthday to see them, but other than that the fixtures are almost complete."

"Of course, your birthday's coming up; it's in March isn't it?"

"That's right; a couple of weeks to wait and we'll be opening soon after that."

The afternoon flew by and a slightly merry though still perfectly responsible Diane caught the sleek dark blue, silver-grey and white Inter7City train back to Inverbrudock as thin, penetrating rain was beginning to spark in the glow of the station lamps coming on. The guard teased her good-naturedly as he came upon her checking her hand mirror and wiping a faint red wine stain off her mouth, still smiling about Priya's welcome news when he came to check the tickets; laughing, she confirmed that yes, it had most definitely been a good session. She reminded herself to hold off until she got home on any feelings of satisfaction that he did not judge her to be in need of any warning to watch her step getting off; there had been times when she had benign conversations while out and about and thought she had passed muster but been brought crashing back down when people came back to add the dreaded pre-emptive strikes, often unnecessarily loudly for all around to hear. She didn't need to have been drinking alcohol at all for it to happen; when she did drink, she was strict about keeping within her safe limits. Society still had some way to go though before the combination of a good day or night out and a Disabled Person's Railcard stopped raising eyebrows. Watching the string of warm lights disappear towards Edinburgh, she smiled as the relief washed over her; even if anything were said to her between the station and home, she had made it through the journey without a glitch. Freedom from social anxiety would never be a feasible goal; the trick was to make the most of, and build upon, the precious times when she did have a successful outing of any kind without any of the demoralising, infuriating belittlement which blighted her life and separated her from those who refused to even try to understand how it made her feel.

The light continued to grow and the days to inexorably lengthen; at the turn of February to March, Sally emailed Diane, copying in Verena. They were highly enthused by the concept of producing a booklet, agreeing with Diane about the need for more tangible everyday incentives to make jobseeking a more friendly and enticing prospect especially to some of the daunted and psychologically scarred people who were referred to Up For Work. Accepting her proposal to seek consent by private message from all individual contributors and acknowledging her prudent stance on anonymity, they were happy for her to compile it and send the content of it to them to have made up into booklet form. They had been planning a six month update on the Up For Work Together project and this would be a positive addition to it. Perhaps they could hold another networking event to launch the booklet as well as marking the six months; Diane would be fully credited and would be welcome to speak.

Six months ago, she would have been dancing around her flat. Staring at the screen, Diane's first reaction was to laugh as she pictured herself replying saying that this time she would bring her own flask of tea. Her second reaction was to hope that this would not clash with the opening of the café. Of course she would be nervous and plagued by bad memories, especially if the same venue was used; she was by no means eager to see Brenda Culper again even when staying safely away from those sputtering urns, but no way was she going to avoid another launch of her own work. Lagging behind all of these thoughts came a nebulous jolt of pleasure at Verena having been included in this email and by implication endorsed the content; it was quickly swamped by the thought of telling her friends, old and new. She replied thanking them, accepting the invitation to do a launch and letting them know the dates on which she was unavailable; she did add that she would be bringing her own tea. No punctuation smileys, no exclamation marks, no friendly chat; merely that plain fact. Sending the email, she made herself a strong cup of coffee and spent an enjoyable hour copying and pasting the examples into a document, messaging each contributor with the generic consent request in Up For Work's approved wording and asking permission for a couple of small changes in order to avoid identifying brand names or companies. There were almost thirty examples including her own; they would make a lovely counterbalance to the daunting dreariness of forms and stark commitments. Within days she had all of the permissions she needed and sent the document to Sally; she would copy Verena into any communication if and when she was specifically asked to, not before. No ambiguity could be allowed to creep in to this fragile truce.

24

With her love of the changing seasons and the natural ceremony inherent in the wheel of the year, Diane would have loved to have been an equinox baby but her birthday fell short of that by over a week. Given the events of the preceding few months, her life had realigned itself with beautiful timing for the milestone of turning forty. The café was to open in time for Easter; her booklet would be launching well before the end of March so there was no conflict of interest. Not only did the two events not clash but they were far enough apart to allow her enough time to recover from one and prepare for the next. Sitting in Charlene's welcoming living room eating a second slice of the delicious birthday cake she had baked with its meltingly soft yellow butter icing, Diane gave thanks in her heart once again that she had been put in contact with the Sutherlands so that they may become involved with the café, continuing Joan and Harriet's legacy. Their involvement would have a palpable impact on the business too; Charlene's offer to bake cakes for it had been received with justified enthusiasm.

"I don't know whether Brandon will be up to coming to the opening day, though he will appreciate having the café as a place for us to go to every now and then for a treat", Charlene was saying. Diane had been invited upstairs to see Brandon when she arrived; she had found him giving some routine maintenance to their model Inter7City train as Cheminot slept contentedly on a cushion in the bay window. His benefits were being reassessed and even though Diane had passed on the details of the advocacy contact who had been so helpful to her, the stressful process made socialising more difficult than usual for Brandon. He had nevertheless asked Charlene to make sure he got to see

Diane on her birthday. Watching him tenderly clean and oil the tiny gears of the pretty little train, Diane's eyes unexpectedly welled up with the heartache of knowing the hell of intrusion, negative focus and suspense he was being put through in order to be able to keep his life the way he needed it to be in order to stay well enough to cope with each new day.

"It's fine, Charlene; you and I will figure out together whatever is the best way to bring the celebration to Brandon. He will be included by association and even if it's no more than saving him a slice of cake, he will be a part of it in whatever way he needs for it to work for him."

"Thank you so much. We are both tremendously excited about this. Ever since Harriet's diary came to light, we have felt that she deserved more of an ongoing memorial than a handful of people reading it. You have given us a blessing beyond words and we're both so happy that you came into our lives. Des and Jason too. I've lived here all this time but we don't tend to go out much locally; we're either travelling or in the house, so a whole new world of Inverbrudock has been opened up for us. I love Des and Jason; they are such wonderful guys."

"They are indeed. They saved me, and I mean that literally. I don't want to do the cliched birthday thing and get all maudlin about my birth family's behaviour but suffice to say I needed a new one and I got one; in fact I got an upgrade."

Charlene nodded, her eyes filled with understanding of both Diane's sentiments and her need for the moment to pass without becoming too intensely emotional.

"So what time are you going round to the café to see these mysterious customised lights then? I am so intrigued!"

"Six o'clock. I'm meeting Sharon and Paulie for a dram at the Fulmar's Nest at five. Oh, I got a lovely card from Bethany with a voucher for the Whisky Shop; Priya says that the Inverness branch is outstanding and I might have myself a trip up there sometime, or I can use it in Edinburgh or Glasgow if I have reason to go there. A trip to Inverness does appeal though. There's a whisky bar called The Malt Room which I would love to check out; it's run by whisky enthusiasts. I can well imagine what the benefits people would make of me having an interest in malt whisky but it isn't something to get drunk on; that's wasteful. It's to be savoured; there's a discipline to it which makes me want to keep it special and take my time. Sharon and Paulie have told me so many stories of chatting with people from all over the world at whisky events."

"Yes, they love their whisky and I know they enjoy sharing that with you. How lovely for you to be able to have a convivial birthday dram with them. Would you like another coffee? There's still plenty in the pot."

An hour later, Diane was heading home with her third and fourth slices of cake on a paper plate wrapped in cling film. She put them safely out of the reach of her extra vocal, purring cat and then spent some time catching up with messages and relaxing before changing out of her forest green blouse into the sparkling red top which matched her smart stone-coloured trousers and perennial tan suede jacket equally well. A costume change in the middle of the day was rare for her but a birthday as good and friendship-packed as this merited it. The andalusite ring she had bought four years earlier on the first anniversary of her autism diagnosis, her private "second birthday" which fell in May, flashed red and orange glints from its olive green depths as her hand moved; complementing most of her special occasion clothes equally. A child of the spring most at home in autumn colours, she was learning to own the perceived contradictions in her life. The matching pendant glinted at her throat; a champagne tourmaline cluster on her other hand completed the ensemble; its fawn and gold sunburst a miniature tableau of the day's festivity.

"Happy birthday!"; Helen smiled as she pointed to the rarer single malts on the top shelf. "Give me a shout if you can't make out any of the labels; I keep meaning to have a list printed of what we've got but it would keep going out of date as we sell out. Sometimes we get one bottle and when it's gone, it's gone."

Paulie nodded with a wry smile. "The specialist whisky bars often have that issue. They have an entire wall of more out of the way malts and they keep these binders with beautifully presented menus but it's hit and miss as to what they still have. I have suggested to several of them that they should keep the menu on a tablet or some other electronic device which can be updated more easily instead of printing out sheets of A4."

"That's a brilliant idea, Paulie!", enthused Diane; "It would save so much embarrassment for people like me who tend to keep picking the wrong ones; the ones they've sold out of!"

Paulie nodded, closing their brown eyes for a moment evidently reliving an unpleasant memory. "That's the feeling I keep telling them their customers don't want to take from their visit. I remember one instance which deeply affected me. I was in a whisky bar, a good one in a prime city centre location on one of my work trips away; it was before I met Sharon."

Squeezing her partner's hand, Sharon clearly knew their pain from whatever they were about to relate.

"It was a special day; the anniversary of when I first came out as non-binary. It should be a proud day and it generally is, but at that time I wasn't so happy about other aspects of my life and I wasn't feeling as upbeat or worthwhile as I felt I ought to on that date. It was one of the years when I doubted myself so much I wondered if I'd done the right thing at all. There's so much more to it than starting to use they / them pronouns; not all non-binary people even use those. Anniversaries, especially of the sort not understood by the rest of society, tend to bring their own pressure. It's not so much about wanting any special sign; it's more about not wanting there to be a negative sign."

Diane understood, feeling the same way about her diagnosis anniversary; she kept quiet though. This was Paulie's story.

"The place wasn't busy; there was one man at the bar who obviously knew the staff and had been talking to them. I had the menu and picked one out of their mid-range section. Sold out. So I picked another one. The only other one on the list of a dozen which was also sold out. And this man looked up, scoffed at me and said 'Well, your instincts are pretty poor, aren't they?' I swear I felt a part of me die right there and then."

It seared Diane's soul to imagine how Paulie must have felt. It didn't matter in the least that they knew, logically, that the man had no idea of the impact of his words; that they were not intended to go deeper than a joshing mockery of the luckless choices of drink order, crass and uncalled-for though that was in itself. Paulie had been on a brittle precipice with no alternative but to keep going; wearing a thin veneer of nonchalance which was all the covering a psyche scoured raw could tolerate. They had needed to pass in that moment; not necessarily to excel but to avoid being noticed for any weakness, including unlucky selection which was no failing on their part but looked hapless and asked more of their tenacity than was damned well fair at such a fragile intersection of time, place and meaning. The other customer could have had no idea as to the needle-sharp, white-hot fall of his casually smug words into the open wound which was their context for Paulie. If people thought before they spoke, particularly heckling or gloating, how much better the world would be. What was to be lost by holding back a remark like that? The trouble was, people couldn't see what was to be gained, because the gain was in what didn't happen. Diane felt a molten rush of thankfulness for Sharon's hand gripping Paulie's, holding them safe in the present as remembered vulnerability seemed almost to visibly ripple across their fine features to the tips of their chestnut hair.

"So I handed the menu back to the barman and insisted that he give me his own recommendation, up to a certain budget. Disclosing in front of other customers how much I could spend was nothing in comparison to the mortification I felt. Fortunately the evening took a turn for the better when a young American couple came in. They hadn't been to Scotland before and were interested in discovering whisky; I bought them a welcome dram and we shared some travel stories. It turned it into the exact type of occasion they wanted and they will never know how profoundly they saved my day. Later on in the hotel I was thinking how the initial scenario with the discrepancy between the menu and the stock could be avoided; not the ignorant heckler, there's no accounting for that, but helping customers to be less likely to be frustrated by making unsuccessful choices. The barman had said to me how it was impractical to keep printed lists up to date and I understood that, but nowadays with information so fast-moving it's logical to find ways to adapt, to enhance the customer experience."

"Good on you for turning something so personally painful into a lovely evening for those Americans and coming up with a constructive idea for other people", Diane praised them gently, her heart still humming with anguish to think of Paulie dealing with that moment alone, far from home and unsupported. What seemed a trivial nudge to many people could be the final blow to send a drowning soul below the waves for the final time. How fortunate that Paulie had held on; that they came through to this much better and happier time. She was internally aware that many people in her past would have made similar gloating comments to her about her blundering tactlessness in invoking such a painful memory; at the time of being around those people she would have had no defence. Now, instead, she felt a calm rightness about having been trusted with that memory and given rare, precious knowing validation to the other person's feelings. "I'm sorry that you had to cope with that pain on such an emotionally charged day, and that I've reminded you of it. The last thing I want to do is add to the stress of dealing with this world for someone else in a minority group." Being autistic did not excuse her from her responsibilities as an ally, after all.

"Oh, don't worry; I'm reminded of it every time I look at a menu", smiled Paulie; their generosity of spirit shining through.

A fiery Highland Park invoked the coming journey of growing daylight, more enhanced the further North one travelled. Diane updated Sharon and Paulie on the progress of the Up For Enjoying Work booklet, as it was now named; Sally's choice, which she liked. The cover design had been emailed to her the day before and she had approved it, no longer caring so much whether it had been Verena's idea to add "By members of the Up For Work Together forum, from a concept by Diane Abercrombie" to the front cover, or what Verena thought of her as a result. Her mind was turning, as inexorably as the progress towards the equinox, to the reveal of the special table lights which awaited her at the café with her chosen family.

Des met her at the door, a huge grin on his face. "Happy birthday! I'm not going to ask you to close your eyes to lead you into the building; I wouldn't expect you to find that comfortable. I'm going to let you walk in like any customer would and you can see the lights as they would discover them."

Marvelling yet again at how perceptive Des showed himself to be, Diane walked into the almost completed interior of what would soon officially become Harriet's Haven. Jason stood next to the row of booths on the side leading away from the High Street, the smile on his own face matching that of his brother. "Happy birthday, Di", he beamed, gesturing to the nearest table on which stood a lamp that took Diane's breath away. The swan neck tops of the old 1960s streetlamps had been reproduced so faithfully, their design must surely have been researched online for the fine detail which could barely be made out in the old photographs. Their hanging lanterns dispensed a dimmable warm white light rather than the brilliant icy tone which had been necessary and in keeping with lighting the streets, but the shape was identical. Diane could scarcely make out the tall giftwrapped box which she rightly guessed contained a bottle of malt whisky and formed the rest of her birthday present on the table through the tears which sprang to her eyes. Jason stepped aside to allow her to see the entire row of secluded booths with their streetlamps glowing amid the warm tones of wood; the restful green curtains and upholstery and the blue and gold cushions they had all chosen, all bordered by the opaque sheen of the cinema aisle lighting in the floor.

"Guys, I don't know what to say; I'm overwhelmed. In a good way! Thank you, thank you so much!" Turning to Jason, she added "You must tell Mitch thanks too; he's done a sterling craftsman's job there. I never expected anything like this!"

Later in the evening, relaxing with a second glass of wine after an informal birthday dinner of Des's chorizo macaroni cheese, she cherished the vibrant affection of Luke's purring in her lap and watched her shepherd moons as they moved in their orbits; reassuringly and uncomplicatedly being themselves. Jason adjusted some settings over in Mission Control as Des tidied and did a quick inventory of his jars and bottles in the kitchen. Enya's voice floated ethereally from the speakers as the light spread its spectrum of colours towards the ceiling. After her birthday was past, she would once again be rehearsing a speech in here; this one was nothing more to her than a task to be done as part of her volunteering. She was not under any illusion that she would find the booklet launch any more accessible than the last event, but she would be coming from an infinitely stronger background now that she had an even wider range of autism informed support and a life of her own, shaped by her true instincts, to come back to.

25

"Oh, my gosh! She is absolutely gorgeous!"

Bethany crouched in the doorway of Diane's living room, staring awestruck at the slender blue-eyed cat who had greeted her with a yawn, arched back, long stretch and run to her with a winning combination of purr and full-throated Siamese miaow.

"Isn't she? Yes, that is La Farolita. I'm so glad you get to meet her at last before we go to this launch."

Diane had been relieved and touched when Bethany offered to take leave from work and stay on an extra night at Charlene's after her latest visit so that she could give her some moral support at the six month event for Up For Work Together. They didn't need to catch the train until mid morning so there had been time for Diane to walk the short distance to Charlene's and bring Bethany to her flat; the least she could do was give her the chance to meet Farolita in real life. They had coffee before bidding a fond farewell to the attention-loving cat and heading for the station.

"Are you feeling OK?", Bethany murmured discreetly as they walked into the conference room which Diane had left in such distress six months earlier. She nodded briefly, taking several deep breaths as she looked around. Many of the same people were milling about; including, to her great discomfort, Brenda Culper. Leaning towards Bethany, she was about to discreetly point her out with a description when the woman scuttled across to one of the volunteers from the jobsearch hub who was setting up a projector. Exactly as she had done to Diane on that awful day, her loud voice shrilled across the entire room as she bustled and clucked around the embarrassed volunteer, barging into his space as he tried to take his time over the various cables and plugs in the unfamiliar setting.

"Can you manage, son? Oh dear, you can't, can you. You've got yourself in a right muddle there. No, dear, see, you do it like this. Careful now, don't trip" (as the young man instinctively tried to dodge out of her way and get some semblance of workspace back). "You're all cackhanded there; let me. Now, see, you insert this one…"

Diane could not bear to watch; Bethany's expression was like thunder.

"Good God, the whole freaking room must have heard her call that poor man cackhanded. I presume that is the famous Brenda? Was she as indiscreet as that with you?"

"I'm afraid so. Though if she'd tried telling me to insert anything anywhere, I wouldn't have known whether to take her up on it in a way she didn't expect or nominate her for a bravery award! Oh, this is too much. She's still at it, announcing that poor lad's struggle to the entire room. Come on, Beth; we're going in!"

The two women walked over to where the painful scene was playing out; the young man looked at them, scarlet-faced and still cringing away from Brenda.

"Hello, Mrs Culper. I'm sure you remember me from six months ago; Diane Abercrombie. This is Bethany Sawyer, a good friend of mine. Now, I had a manual dexterity issue at the last event which played out much like this, ending in a lot of embarrassment and distress. I think there's a learning experience to be had here. The whole room can hear you and that truly isn't necessary. You're telling this gentleman not to trip, making him the problem when he's instinctively flinching away because he needs space. Please step back from him and lower your voice."

As Brenda Culper gaped at Diane in shock, Bethany was unobtrusively and respectfully instructing the young man, having recognised the type of projector from her own work in a bookshop which had hosted a few educational events. The blank white screen burst into life. "Thanks!", he was saying as they exchanged a gentle fist bump.

"Well, what about that? He's got it working perfectly there. Nice one, team! Do enjoy yourself at our event today, Mrs Culper; I'm sure you will take away some food for thought."

Unusually for her, she linked her arm through Bethany's as they made their way over to speak to a beaming Sally who had waved to them. Though Diane rarely sought out touch however close she felt to someone, on her own terms and in the right context it would follow naturally. It was corrective touch, however physically light, that presented the biggest problem for her. A prod in the arm from someone assuming she was merely inattentive when in fact trying frantically to figure out what direction a shout was coming from, for instance, she would still be able to feel hours later. Introducing Bethany to Sally, she went on to tell her about what had occurred with Brenda; getting her own side of the story in first with a witness felt like a prudent self-protecting move. "Don't worry", Sally assured her; "you won't see any repercussions for that. I could hear her myself from the other side of the room and was about to ask Verena to discreetly have a word when I saw you both defusing the situation. You certainly seemed familiar with the projector, Bethany; we might be needing you too!"

As she took in the easy, friendly vibe of Bethany explaining to Sally about her experience with setting up the projector, Diane marvelled at the difference to which she was still getting used; the crucial fact of not being up against it all on her own. The difficulties were still there; the lights and noise of the venue were already making her feel tired, but this time she felt safer in the knowledge that she had been heard and endorsed. She was willing to endure a bit of sensory discomfort which was within the bounds of what she could reasonably cope with, for the sake of her life's work; the ongoing battle for her was to make people realise that accessibility was not always simply a matter of turning down the lights or using an unscented product. It was about appreciating that an autistic person such as herself would be tired and drained as a day like this went on; not condemning or infantilising her for it, not embarrassing her with commentary on her differences and struggles, offering help discreetly if necessary and accepting the answer, and giving her a bit of extra time and space as opposed to getting right up in her face and braying at her.

They took their seats as the time came for Verena to open the proceedings. Once again, bad memories congregated in a tight knot in Diane's stomach; beside her, Bethany's calmly supportive presence anchored her as she listened to the opening speech and prepared to be introduced. She waited until Verena announced her name before standing up, needing an extra moment to be sure that she had processed correctly and not projected what she wanted to hear. A look of irritation flashed momentarily across Verena's face as she registered that infinitesimal pause; did she think that Diane was hesitating to make a petulant point? Setting aside her unease, Diane stepped up to the podium, thanking Verena as impassively as her stretched nerves would allow. Her speech was brief and to the point, describing how the idea for the Up For Enjoying Work booklet came about and thanking Sally for her support and the title suggestion. She had no occasion to change or supplement any of the wording this time; she had the validation she needed. Bethany's presence exuded encouragement; she also caught sight of Kate, in the audience in person this time. Sally was stood right next to Verena; Diane did not want to look in that direction, still afraid of whatever expression her face may show being open to misinterpretation.

At the refreshment break, true to her word Diane had her own flask of tea with her. Kate came over to congratulate her and to meet Bethany; thoughtfully, she offered to get her a cup of tea so that she could stay and talk to Diane instead of having to join the queue. Diane smiled fondly at her friend as she walked over to get the drinks; it was moments like this which reminded her why they were still so close, though she had yet to navigate telling her about Priya and Linda. She could picture herself being told off for having 'missed an opportunity there'.

"Brenda asked me if I was getting an extra drink for 'one of the special needs people'! I told her it was my round at the bar; you're definitely a bad influence on me, Diane!", Kate chuckled as she returned with two cups of tea. She, like Des and Jason, had been saddened by the revelation of what Diane had kept from her and how the effects of that secrecy had rippled outwards, as well as being appalled at the indiscreet behaviour of someone who should have known better.

"Urgh! 'One of the special needs people'? Who still talks like that?", shuddered Bethany; "Uh oh; apparently someone who's heading this way."

"It's so good of you to support Diane here; it's important that people who need extra help can come to these events", Brenda addressed a taken aback Bethany.

"I'm here as a friend who is jolly well proud of Diane's selfless, creative work. Being autistic myself, I can tell you that it's more a case of non-autistic people needing extra help to make these events accessible", she replied, a thinly polite smile fixed on her face.

"YOU'RE autistic? Well, I never would have guessed it. However do you cope with having your hair dyed that colour?"

As Diane and Bethany laughed incredulously and even Kate had no idea what to say, Brenda reached out intending to touch Bethany's hair.

"Whoa; you might want to consider asking for consent first", barked Diane as her friend instinctively leaned away from the unwelcome contact. No doubt she would get tone policed again but nobody got to do that to her friend right in front of her, especially somewhere to which she had brought her as a guest.

"Diane is correct. Please respect the autonomy and personal space of my volunteer and our guest, Brenda; interact with them as you would any other person."

Sally's voice came not loudly but with such authority that for a split second Diane thought it was Verena who had spoken. A small guilty flare of disappointment was quickly superseded by the glow of her pride in Sally and renewed belonging to her role as a volunteer with this organisation, secondary though that now was to her involvement with the café.

The latter half of the event passed unremarkably; Brenda kept her distance and a few people asked Diane to sign their copies of the booklet to themselves or to someone who was going to benefit from it. As she and Bethany helped Sally and Colin, who had taken up the post vacated by Arthur's retirement, pack up at the end, Verena finally came over to speak to Diane. Politely thanking her for her input, she gingerly extended an invitation to join the staff team for a drink.

"That's very kind of you, Verena, and I appreciate it probably wasn't easy for you to say. I'll pass, though. My friend Bethany who came with me today has to get back to Perth as she's been away for a few days and she's working tomorrow. I also have quite a lot I need to get home to, as it happens. So we'll both be heading straight for our trains."

There was no mistaking the relief on Verena's face, though there may have been a subtle hint of dawning respect mixed in.

"Oh? You have something special happening at home?"

Diane smiled enigmatically, not even caring about the vaguely insulting emphasis on "you"; her mind already on her commitments in Inverbrudock.

"Indeed. I have my streetlamps and shepherd moons."

Turning away from a slightly puzzled Verena, Diane walked out of the conference room with Bethany, thanking her once more for giving up leave to come to the event with her.

"I'm buzzing! I know the fatigue will hit me tomorrow but it's good fatigue for once. I envy you going to Perth; I haven't been there in so long. Your status updates from the Station Hotel when you pop in there for coffee or a drink have reminded me how much I always liked that building, and Perth Station is so atmospheric in a dignified, Gothic way. The air feels kinder getting off the train there, I remember; there's a hushed, soft-focus feel to it even when it's cold. There's so much space there; it feels like a respite from sensory harshness and clutter. Sound loses its sharp edges there, if you know what I mean. It's another example of autistic hygge. The hotel too; that feeling of unhurried space manages to embrace you and free you at the same time. I must get back to Perth soon. Covid got me right out of practice at taking unplanned trips out and I need to get that impulsivity going again; it's not something I ever want to lose. Yes, I love having my routines but I miss taking off somewhere completely unplanned. I can talk about these things to you and know you'll get it; so many people are thrown by these apparent contradictions but both routine and impulse are authentic parts of me. Oh, I'm making myself want to go there right now!"

Bethany's eyes gleamed with empathy, Diane's perspective on her adopted home city resonating as strongly as her description of the role impulse played in her life.

"So what's stopping you? Get a ticket! It's only half an hour from here after all. We'll go and have a drink in the Station Hotel and you'll be able to join the return half of the ticket with the one you've already got from here to Inverbrudock to make the through trip home. It will be the ideal reintroduction to spur of the moment trips for you; I know exactly what you mean about being out of the way of it. Brandon and Charlene are feeling the same; needing to build up in stages to what they usually do."

"You know what? I am absolutely going to do this!"

They both jumped up and down squealing with excitement, for once not caring what anyone else thought of two grown women letting their enthusiasm show unchecked.

The train was an Inter7City; busy with the beginning of the early evening passenger flow. Diane and Bethany found a double seat which had been vacated at Dundee and had space for Bethany's overnight bag at their feet.

"I hate having to use the overhead rack", confessed Bethany. "The number of times complete strangers have tried to grab my bag from me to put it up there the minute they see me start to do it, sometimes without even saying a word to me! I don't like to generalise about gender but it has to be said, it's usually men. Another thing we're supposed to be grateful for, even when it's done with such obvious superciliousness; don't people realise it's incredibly rude to grab someone's property and not even speak to them? Apart from the disrespect, a woman could genuinely think she's being mugged!"

"Oh, I know. I get that too. If someone offers, for the simple logical reason that they're taller and have longer arms, that's one thing; as long as they accept a polite refusal! I'm sure I've seen something online about this sort of thing with regard to disabled people; there's a hashtag. 'Just Ask, Don't Grab'; that was it."

"Yes, I've seen that; it was created by Dr Amy Kavanagh. She is autistic and partially sighted. She also created the 'Staying Inn' online virtual pub initiative to connect isolated disabled people during Covid."

"That's right. The value of people being able to share their experiences and be honest about how various aspects of majority behaviour affect them is immeasurable, especially when that honesty goes against what society tells us to think and feel."

"Absolutely. That feeling of swimming against the tide is why it took me a long time to come to terms with knowing I can only do so much; to see the value in potentially helping even one person, whether or not I get to know about any difference I've made. I had to learn to resist the temptation to give up when the end product of all of my energy felt consistently small-time and insignificant. I can't change the world on my own but that doesn't mean that it doesn't count each time I help one person in one small way. That person matters, therefore it counts; in that moment it is enough. Since I made peace with that, I've found I don't feel quite so depleted and I can do that bit more."

"That is interesting; I have a lot of internalised guilt about my limited energy and productivity too. It makes me feel that I have to strain myself unduly to earn every little pleasure. Yet what do you know, here I am gallivanting off on the train to Perth and it feels absolutely in order! So you've certainly helped me."

The evening lights of the Fair City opened out to the calm blue-grey sheen of the River Tay as the train crossed the long silver curve of the viaduct; the impressive spire of St Matthew's Church and the sturdy, wide arches of Perth Bridge to the right. The view was familiar to Diane from memory and many photographs but seeing it in person never lost its capacity to give her a frisson of excitement. Glancing at Bethany, she felt a rush of affection as her friend's love for the city showed in the subtle lift of the corners of her mouth and the glint in her eyes; details which autistic people were not generally thought to be able to read. To be fair to non-autistic people, quite often those kind of details did get missed, to varying degrees depending upon the individual and the situation. In these moments as the Inter7City train bore them in gently hued, well-worn comfort over the tranquil grid of streets to the cathedral-like station, a profoundly thankful Diane silently and knowingly shared in her friend's welcome home.

The sweeping platforms and broad footbridges easily absorbed the footsteps and chatter of their fellow passengers, turning the cacophony of strangers into a companionable murmur of brief and benign coexistence. Passing through the small and modern concourse with its line of ticket barriers, Bethany waved to a staff member who knew her for being a regular traveller as he headed towards the far-flung Platform 7 to meet a passenger who had booked assistance and would soon be arriving on the Highland Chieftain from London. Diane reflexively smiled and waved too; he acknowledged her with a nod in her direction, effortlessly integrating her into the laid-back warmth of Bethany's circle and the instant recognition characteristic of the extended railway interest family.

The Station Hotel cast the inviting glow of high ceiling lights from its tall windows across the car park as the two women walked through the automatic doors of the station's main entrance into the light breeze. A patchwork of illumination along the first and second floors hinted at guests arriving into their welcoming rooms; through the brass-handled revolving door, Diane could make out a group of people with suitcases queuing at the reception desk on the right of the spacious lobby. Walking in, Diane's eyes were drawn straight ahead and left to the elegant rise of the hotel's magnificent staircase; its dark wood and rich carpet complemented by a large stained glass window and the restrained glitz of ornate brass and cream uplighters. She and Bethany turned right past the reception desk and found themselves a table in the small bar which led through to the grander but still relaxed restaurant; its crisp white tablecloths pristine beneath the sparkle of the chandeliers.

Bethany insisted on treating Diane to a double whisky to celebrate her having both faced the work event and made a return to impulsive travelling. Looking around the informal bar, the evening took on a dreamlike quality as Diane savoured her dram. She was only now fully taking in that she was, unexpectedly and wonderfully, in Perth again and with such an important new friendship to give it a fresh context. She understood herself and her energy levels well enough to keep this as a brief visit; it had been a big enough day. One drink whilst chatting about the city and the shops which she hoped to visit again; Exel Wines, the deli Provender Brown and the fascinating independent gift shop Boo Vake (a phonetic rendering of the Gaelic 'Buth Bheag'; 'little shop') to name but a few; it was enough to leave her wanting more as she thanked Bethany once again for a memorable day and returned to the station.

"It's a journey of two halves", she smiled to the guard as she showed him her tickets back to Dundee and on to Inverbrudock, laughing as she explained that she had made an unplanned detour to Perth to celebrate with a friend. She recognised him as a football fan and relished the banter as he jovially told her not to expect a pie at half time. Countering that she hoped the journey would not go into extra time as she had some more celebrating to do in Inverbrudock, his response that such a scenario would end up in penalties had her chuckling long after he moved on through the carriage. Still on an adrenalin high as she disembarked at Inverbrudock, Diane mentally thanked her fatigue for holding off to allow her one more social call.

"Well, it certainly went better than it did six months ago!", she assured Helen as she poured her dram in the Fulmar's Nest. After filling her in on the impulsive flying visit to Perth with Bethany, Diane told her the salient details of the work event.

"Good for you! I bet that felt satisfying!", Helen laughed as she came to the part about turning down Verena's obviously reluctant, diplomatic invitation for a drink.

"It did, though it irks me that she was so obviously relieved, and that she didn't even bother to thank Bethany for mucking in helping with the clearing up when she was there as a guest. Sally was highly appreciative. Verena of course was too busy glad-handing to do any clearing up; it's beneath her. She has no faith in me whatsoever and I know it shouldn't bother me but it's not a nice feeling being on the receiving end."

"No, I can understand that, and I know it's not helpful when people say it's the other person's loss when you're the one feeling the effects. You do seem much happier in yourself though and that's the important thing."

"I suspect that the less she means to me, the happier she will be to be around me, but by the time she's no longer feeling the need to treat me like an unexploded bomb, it won't be a bonus any more! It's a bit of a Catch-22, to be honest. I resent having been expected to work so hard with the aim being to feel nothing. Fortunately I haven't had to force myself the way I was being told to, because my life has naturally taken me in another direction."

"It certainly has; I am looking forward to checking out this café of yours!"

Diane finished her drink and went home to feed an extra noisy but quickly forgiving Farolita, who had been left well supplied with kibble and water for the day. As she looked through the responses to the genuinely happy status updates she had shared on the train and in the pub, she caught sight of the unopened miniature of malt whisky which she had left untouched in her living room cabinet after the disaster six months earlier. The café would be a different celebration; this was perfect for giving her closure on the bad times she had been through with Up For Work. Pouring the contents of the bottle into her special occasion glass, she saluted the subtle shift in texture of the night air as it promised the lighter days, still with lamplit evenings for a while yet, to come.

26

Pink and white blossom had burst into life on the trees along Caberfeidh Road; at dusk it would float in transient haloes around the perennial strident orange of the streetlights. The trees, the lamp posts, even the curve of the road itself seemed to bloom with awareness that this was the day. After the months of planning, making applications, preparing and putting together the finished look, Harriet's Haven was officially opening.

An article had been published in the local paper and online promoting the new business and with her consent, Des had insisted that Diane be credited for her shaping of the general café idea into what it had become. Seeing her name in print alongside everything her friends had achieved brought a lump to Diane's throat, she felt that her own contribution had been small compared to the two brothers who had taken on the risk of starting their own venture. Jason had firmly reminded her that she had been responsible for driving the coming together of a workable plan, bringing in highly useful contacts and putting in several grafting hours of cleaning. "We need to sort out your impostor syndrome", he had gently and caringly chided her.

The weather was a typical mix of sunshine, cloud and showers as a steady flow of customers began to trickle in. Several volunteers had been signed up to serve; the unpressured ethos communicated itself to them too and everyone soon relaxed into a rhythm. The light of the spring day made its journey across the sky, shining in turn through each set of curtained windows and resting on the varnished tabletops. Priya arrived from Montrose at lunchtime; as she had anticipated, Linda was away for work but the couple hoped to be visiting Inverbrudock together soon. Sharon and Paulie came in during the afternoon, instantly recognising Charlene's signature coffee cake which stood in prime position on the counter. It was the second of the two she had baked and they were fortunate that there were still a few slices left. The Fulmar's Nest was busy at the start of the season and Helen and Krista were unable to get away, but both sent messages of congratulations and good luck as did Kate and Bethany. Several customers arrived from the pub, having been told about the new café and come to take a look; Diane smiled as she recalled doing precisely that in the bizarre setting of her lucid dreams. Standing where Joan Morley had stood all those years earlier, she felt a rush of the emotion she called "too muchness" threaten to overwhelm her, albeit with happiness and positive feelings; an unremarked upon, acknowledged and understood few minutes in the quiet shelter of the back doorway brought everything back under control.

As closing time came around, the sky grew overcast and the warm glow of lighted buildings steadily took over from the fickle spring sunshine. The final few customers having left and the volunteers let away home with heartfelt thanks, Des and Diane were going through some receipts in the back when Jason came through calling for Diane.

"There's a man here asking for you; I think he said his name was Gabriel. Sorry, I was shutting the till and I don't know if I heard him right; I asked him but he said could I just get you."

Gabriel? Diane didn't know a Gabriel; perhaps it was someone from the paper wanting to ask some follow-up questions. Protectively, Des, Jason, and Priya who had been in the Ladies' room when the man arrived gathered around her as she walked through to the seating area.

Looking at the tall, fair-haired visitor, a void opened up in the precious new foundations of her security. Trembling, with all the formality befitting this moment, she made her introductions.

272

"It's Adrian. Jason Asante; Desmond Asante; Priyanka Dayal; this is Adrian Abercrombie, my brother."

At Diane's nod, the others tactfully withdrew; Priya turned the sign on the door to "Closed".

"So, Ady, it's been a while. I presume you read about our café in the paper."

"Yes, I did. I am so glad that you have gotten over your phase of wanting to live off the state."

"Excuse me? Are you under the impression that I have become an entrepreneur and is that why you've come here? It is Des and Jason's business; they are my closest friends. In fact, they are my family now, because as you may recall I found myself in need of a new one some time ago. I am heavily involved, but my work here is on a voluntary basis. I cannot manage full time employment especially dealing with the public and I require more downtime due to fatigue and autistic burnout than any paid job would allow. I am paid the benefits for which I qualify and I give back what am able; I am also a volunteer moderator on a forum for neurodivergent people looking for work and have recently launched a booklet of positive stories collated from that forum, but yes, I am still on benefits. If you cannot accept the reality of my life, Adrian, then there is no point in you coming back into it."

"So what, you're volunteering for those people to whom you introduced me?"

"Des and Jason, yes. I work with them, not for them; that's how true family operates. Priya is a good friend who has helped out a lot with this project."

"And you're telling me that the black guy I spoke to when I came in asking to see you, who is obviously a bit slow, is what, one of your bosses?"

Repulsed, Diane stepped back from this man who was somehow closely related to her yet stood there spouting such ignorant drivel.

273

"I see some things haven't changed in this family. You spoke to the only person in the room at the time who immediately came and told me; I was obviously going to know who it was without any description, you didn't need to bring up the colour of his skin. When you do so in the context of him being my boss, I don't think I need tell such a smart man of the world how that comes across. Jason is partially deaf. He was closing the till, which made a noise and prevented him from catching what you said accurately; I'm told you declined to repeat it. Let me make this abundantly clear: If you want to come in here, even as a customer let alone as my relative, you will unlearn your ingrained racism, treat my friends with respect and if Jason needs you to repeat something, you will do so with good grace."

"I'm sorry, Diane; I didn't mean to be racist but I take your point about needing to consider my words more carefully. I didn't realise Jason had a hearing impairment; I admit I jumped to the wrong conclusion there. I'm still disappointed that you're not working, and I have to say I honestly don't understand why you can't."

"Not working? You really need to let go of your prejudice about benefits. This kind of ignorance is why many people struggle on and don't claim what they need, which would allow them to live much more constructive lives. And if Jason were 'slow' in the way in which you thought, are you suggesting that would make him any less worthy of equal status and the adjustments he would need? Oh, Ady, you have an awful lot to get to grips with. It's not going to happen overnight, but if you are willing to open your mind, I'm not ruling out us rebuilding some sort of relationship over time."

"Well, I'm not going to be having the conversation I hoped to be having with our parents, but I know that Gina misses you."

"Gina. I still can't get used to thinking of her by that name."

"Of course; you always called her Georgie. Yes, Georgina goes by Gina to everyone now; it fits better with her professional image. It sounds more mature."

More mature. Even at this delicate juncture, her biological brother managed to make a dig, or at best a crassly ill-judged comment. And she was meant to be the socially clumsy one.

"Right. This is an awful lot for me to process, Ady. You have turned up out of the blue on what is already a highly emotional and tiring day, for all that particular fatigue is from a positive place. If you bothered to try to understand even the rudiments of autism, you would know that was a lot to ask me to cope with. There is not going to be a conventional family reunion and return of the prodigal daughter today; I suspect that's never going to happen, but this has opened up the wounds of my being thrown out of our home for being disabled all over again. And do you know what gets me the most? It's those two guys through in the back who are going to be the ones picking up the pieces, on what should be an entirely happy and upbeat day for them."

Diane dashed away sudden, angry tears.

"After I've had time to come to terms with this, yes, I would dearly love to see my sister, and I am not ruling out seeing you again. Right now though, I would like you to leave, please."

Adrian nodded, taking out a business card and placing it on the counter.

"I agree that my timing was thoughtless. When I saw the article online, I don't know, I thought that…"

"What, that I shook off my autistic burnout, anxiety and fatigue like a cold? It doesn't work that way, Ady. Don't get me wrong; many autistic people can and do have successful careers with the right accommodations, but

275

many of us are so damaged by the time we get our diagnosis we will never be able to manage mainstream full-time work. That does not make us lazy parasites or freeloaders; you need to get that out of your head. It's bigotry. There are countless more people out there who have not been as lucky as I have to access an official diagnosis; it's worse for them having to justify themselves and their needs all the time, and that's because of the exact societal mindset to which you and our parents - even our sister, it pains me to say - subscribe. Neither of you stood by me as Mum and Dad threw me out right when I was coming to terms with the realities of my life! Please do some reading up before you contact me again. Read things written by autistic people, not by so-called experts including non-autistic parents and professionals working with autistic people. However much those people learn, and many of them do, we are the true experts."

"Yes, that is reasonable. I will, and I believe Gina already has been doing that."

As her brother walked out of the door, Diane picked up his business card and sat down in a booth. The soft, comforting glow of the customised lamp wavered and dissolved in her tears of shock and overload. As if by magic, her friends were there; her shepherd moons, close by but allowing her the space she needed, holding the pieces of her in place; intact to all looking from a distance.

A glass of water was set down on the solid wood in front of her.

"We heard most of that, Di", Des was saying gently. "I'm sorry; I know it was private but we wanted to be ready if it got out of hand. By the way, you were absolutely magnificent. You handled yourself like a boss."

"Thank you. I don't mind that you heard, though I'd rather you hadn't had to hear the ingrained racism. It saves me going through the whole tedious story. I'm more annoyed that it's overshadowed our big day!"

"If anything, it's made it bigger. Do you want one of us to ask Charlene to come round half an hour later?"

She had been there for the opening and was due to come back at the end of the day to accompany Diane on a special errand. Determined, she shook her head, drank her water and went to the bathroom to quickly cool her face. There were advantages to not wearing much make-up, she thought to herself as she brushed her hair and reapplied her minimal lip gloss and mascara.

Charlene was basking in the well-deserved feedback on her coffee cake as Diane came back through; the beautiful yellow roses she had brought rustled in their cellophane like the wind in rain-soaked trees. Noting her friend's concern at her reddened eyes, Diane quickly assured Charlene that she was fine. "My brother turned up. My biological brother, not my actual brothers of course"; she indicated a smiling Des and Jason. "It threw me a bit, but I'm with the people who matter now and I am so up for doing this; the day would not be complete without it. I'll fill you in on the details about my brother later. Priya, I know you have to get away for your train soon; thank you so much again, for being here today and for all you've done. Please give my regards to Linda; tell her I'm looking forward to meeting her."

Waving a temporary goodbye to her friends, Diane took the roses and she and Charlene walked the short distance beyond the end of the High Street to their destination.

The cemetery had that aura of enduring peace which could not be taken away even by the sporadic misuse of the sacred space by teenagers looking for a place to drink and smoke. The two women read each headstone with respect for a life lived and the impact of its passing felt, eventually finding the modest grey stone they were looking for. Diane gently placed the bouquet of roses at its base.

"Joan Constance Harriet Morley. Loyal wife of Leonard Morley. Beloved daughter of Seamus and Martha Bannerman. 1925-2010."

"Thank you for setting the path for us to follow, Joan"; she spoke softly and respectfully. "I told you that my friends and I would make it right again; I don't know whether you heard me. I hope you know somehow that you will always be part of Harriet's Haven, and I hope that you and your mother are both at peace now. I sense that you're with Harriet and know she is at peace too. You all deserve it; you are where it all began."

She stepped back, allowing Charlene her own moment with the relative she had never known.

"I don't know whether I'll ever match the Victoria sponge that Diane saw in her dream, but I'll give it my best shot, Joan. I wish that I'd known you and I wish that somebody could have reassured poor Martha that she wasn't to blame for Harriet's death. Thank you both for bringing Diane, Des and Jason into our lives. They are exactly the right people to continue your work and you found them for us; you and Hattie."

"It's such a shame that they never met. Harriet and Joan, that is", mused Diane as she and Charlene walked back to the café. "I think they'd have been such a valuable support to one another."

"Yes, I believe they would have. Poor Joan; she can't have had it easy, with her husband's gambling. I'm glad she came back to Inverbrudock, even if it wasn't in this life. It truly does feel as though she's part of the café."

"She is part of it, and I am one hundred per cent certain that she would fully endorse your cakes."

The grey sky was darkening as they returned to the café, the new season still too much in its infancy to hold off an early dusk on a cloudy evening. The sight of the warm glow from inside tugged hard at Diane's already overstretched emotions.

"Do you mind if I wait out here on my own for a moment? Seeing the place lit up from the street; it's something I need a bit of time to take in, that it's real."

"Of course; I understand. I'll let Des and Jason know you'll be with them shortly."

Charlene walked into the café; through the inviting windows, Diane could see her talking with Des and Jason. She walked around the corner to the end of Caberfeidh Road, turning to see the kindly lights of the café from there as they had first appeared in her dreams. Simultaneously overawed by the magnitude of seeing this in reality and laughing at herself for her fancy, she cast a fond look towards the string of opaque blooms on their metal stems; poised and waiting for dusk to deepen enough to activate them, flooding their orange gleam through the blossom on the rejuvenated trees. All of the beautiful gardens along her favourite street were waking up again with the new growth of spring; she felt their resurgence deep in her soul.

As she began to walk back towards the café, she was brought out of her daze of happy tiredness and iridescent thoughts by the unexpected sight of a woman standing at the door. Quickening her steps, she prepared to explain that they were closed and tell her the opening hours. As the woman turned to face her, Diane realised with a slow inner dawning of pure contentment that there was no need to explain anything to this particular interested party. She had already told her all she needed to know, even if it had not been directly heard at the time. On this same spot, over fifty years ago.

Perhaps she had imagined it, she reasoned; the eerie pre-twilight at this quiet end of town, her overwrought state after an exceptional day plus having come straight from the graveyard amounted to plenty of grounds to support that theory, yet Diane stood firm with the courage of her convictions. Whether it was inside or outside of her imagination, she was meant to see what she saw on that softly lit corner.

Smiling and waving from a past era which had been stolen but was now restored, Joan Morley turned and walked away; her step lighter this time with the lifting of a long-borne burden from her dignifiedly squared shoulders.

27

This was the good kind of exhaustion; the kind which followed a red letter day. Did people still talk about red letter days?, Diane wondered as she waited for the sleep which never came instantly, however ready she was for it. That expression, she remembered learning, had its origins in the marking of holy days in church calendars and became part of everyday language when physical calendars were the hub of planning and organising before computers and mobile devices took over. Within a generation or two, it would probably be obsolete along with the concepts of clockwise and anticlockwise. Time was shifting; so many of the social and psychological settings in which she lived her life were being reconfigured. She smiled to herself; poised on the edge of sleep, even the gentle chuckle at the realisation of how technology-orientated that thought was took noticeable physical effort. The muscles around her mouth relaxed again; her breathing slowed and deepened.

She was walking upstairs to her new room. Excitement and newness fizzed in every sensation; the give of the plush, springy carpet under her feet, the polished glide of the bannister under her hand and the smell of furniture polish fastidiously applied even up here on the seldom-used staircase which ascended to the top floor.

Was she really here? Sight, sound, smell and touch told her that yes, she was in her original family home; it was familiar but palpably different. She recognised it while acknowledging a degree of puzzlement at the aspects of it which were not in keeping with what she recalled. Did she live in this house again? Or still? Questions about the timeline in which she found herself flitted against the edges of her consciousness like bats around the sealed windows of a tower; present, in keeping with the setting but their place was on the periphery of it. As her senses registered more details and acclimatised to the input, the ethereal flutter of questions receded into the background, conceding mental space to her immediate need to process her surroundings. There on the stairway to the highest floor, she seamlessly crossed the border between logic and perception in one prosaic step; she became fully engaged, the guestroom air filling her lungs and the calm, involved banality of here and now settling in her stomach.

The plain white-painted door on the attic landing creaked as she opened it and propped a chunky, faded fabric sand-filled doorstop against it in preparation for her things being carried up. At the far end of the attic, the newly-discovered door to the extra room which she had never known existed swung open into the light which poured through French doors on the opposite side of the roughly hexagonal space. The walls were a blank canvas of magnolia; the light coffee-coloured carpet frothed with patches of sun, the shadow of leaves from bushes in the small terrace garden sprinkled across them like a barista's flourish of chocolate and cinnamon. Diane twirled around in her new domain, picturing where her furniture would go and in a moment of undreamlike clarity looking to see where the plug sockets were. "I love this room!", she rejoiced aloud although there was nobody there to hear her. She floated across to the patio doors, keen to explore her small patch of roof garden.

Following the paved path which led from her door, she was surprised to find that it came to a low wrought-iron gate on the other side of which was a quiet street lined with similar gardens and cottages. Turning around, she realised that her own top floor home looked from here like another cottage; the lower floors of the house and neighbouring properties were built into the side of a hill. This narrow street onto which her garden opened could have been taken straight from a Thomas Kinkade painting. Low sloping grey roofs caught the light of a sky washed clean by a recent shower; roses, hydrangeas and hyacinths bloomed in neat clusters alongside meticulously weeded paths through mown grass in each miniature garden.

Time was rushing onwards again; from the bright new morning of minutes ago, the marbled sky was turning to a cosy dusk. Warm lights in subtle off-white shades came on in cottage windows; outside, resonating on the exact frequency of Diane's soul, a network of moonlight glowed into life from the tops of the intricately detailed wrought iron lamp posts which lined the tranquil street. Pulling out her phone, she began to take photo after photo, increasingly aware of a need to record this scene for posterity. Frustratingly, each press of the button to take the photo took longer to work, requiring her to hold the phone perfectly still for more and more unfeasible lengths of time. Urgency crept into this peaceful twilight; deconstructing its fragile ecosystem, introducing the inevitable march of reality where it did not belong but could never be indefinitely held at bay.

The hidden room dream again! Really? Diane found herself laughing at the cliché even as she hauled herself yawning and rubbing her eyes into a new day. She had experienced variations on that theme in dreams throughout her life; she understood the popular psychology explanation of unfulfilled wishes and potential as well as the more direct and personal relevance to her interest in stories of such discoveries in real buildings. She had recently shared an article on her social media about someone having found a hidden room in their home, commenting that for all the topic fascinated her and haunted her dreams, if she were in that situation for real her first instinct would be to establish whether there were a structural reason for the room to have been sealed off. "While at the same time dancing around all of my known rooms, toasting the new discovery with my best single malt and shrieking with excitement!", she had added, to the knowing amusement of her friends.

It was clear to her that the unexpected encounter with her brother had made her dream of a house based on the family home; she didn't need any dream interpretation book or analysis to make that connection. Laughter which she was not quite awake enough yet to fully appreciate bubbled up at the ridiculously obvious interpretation that she had risen above her family's prejudiced behaviour. Almost embarrassingly textbook it may be, but it was sound. The Thomas Kinkade-esque street at the top of the house in her dream had been inspired by a particularly artistic photo shared by one of her online friends on a permitted visit to Pitlochry during the Covid-restricted summer of 2020. The mechanism driving every part of her dream could be pragmatically compartmentalised and understood. Diane was used to having aesthetically rich dreams which left her saddened, disillusioned, shaken to the core when she awoke and had to detach herself into reality. Yet every so often a dream would stand out in its vividness, calling out to be committed to memory as had been played out in this one with the compulsion to take photos even as the return to consciousness moved actions in the dream state away from her grasp. Sometimes a dream would recall previous ones and reinforce their meaning. As she made a determined effort to hold on to the details of her dream until she could write them down, feeding Farolita and putting fresh water in her bowl, Diane's mind wound back to the dream she had the night before her personal nadir when she attended the horrendous meeting with Maurice Thurlowe. The interchange of lights floating on the dark ocean came into new clarity; as some had receded out of sight, others had come to shore, shimmering with relevance and renewed purpose. They were all exciting; they all fed her enhanced need for energy. The compelling draw of the lights which were drifting away out of her reach was real and valid; so was the homecoming inward rush of those which bobbed unhurriedly in the foreground. Everything she felt was allowed; it was there, so it was entitled to its space. Letting it come and go was so much more constructive than forcing herself into a repressive regime to appease a system which would not give a millimetre to accommodate her neurology.

Where was that notepad and pen? As her cat's purrs echoed from the newly-filled food bowl, Diane wrote down the details of her dream. It didn't need to be teaching her anything to deserve to be captured for future reference; the fact that it had spoken to her and made her feel inspired was enough in itself. Any insight she gained was a bonus. Describing the dream version of her family home, she felt a grey to green shift of peace in her thoughts of Georgina and Adrian; her parents were further down the line of reconciliation, but some calm emotional neutrality regarding her siblings was a positive step. It was on her own terms and it was enough.

She was enough.

28

The online chat with Kate had, for once, not degenerated into an argument over Diane's refusal to conform and seek a partner. She had taken her courage in both hands and told her about Priya and Linda; Kate's response had been to say that she was pleased for them and to acknowledge that she now realised Diane had done the right thing. Having seen how happy Diane clearly was with her new projects and the balance of her life, something had finally fallen into place in her well-intentioned brain.

"I'm sorry I pushed you so hard, Di. I should have listened but I was so focused on how unhappy you were and on wanting to change that. I admit I got stuck in a rut with that even when things had started to turn around for you and it was clearly nothing to do with any relationship, or with Verena. When you told me how you dealt with your brother turning up, and on the day of the café opening of all days, it clicked with me that what you needed in order to thrive was not what I thought it was. Which you'd been telling me all along. You shouldn't have had to be afraid to tell me about Priya getting together with Linda."

They had gone on to discuss her role with Up For Work and how although Sally had proven a better line manager since the departure of Maurice Thurlowe, there had still not been a celebration worthy of Diane's significant contribution; initiating both the Up For Work Together project and the Up For Enjoying Work booklet.

"I would love to organise an informal get-together in the Fulmar's Nest for you. I know you wouldn't get the most out of it if it were done as a surprise, which is why I'm coming out with it here and now. I'm talking about getting as many as possible of your circle of close friends together and us all toasting your achievements."

Kate needed this as much as she did, Diane surmised; her intentions had always been for the best. Besides which, the idea of an easy-going gathering of her friends in a place she loved and properly celebrating her work genuinely appealed to her. It was no longer a matter of craving praise; it was a need to tidy up the messy conclusion to stages of her working life which had been left in limbo by the incompatibility of the official events with the functioning needs of her autistic brain. It was about getting closure on and counteracting the damage done to her by the first event. The recent event which had gone somewhat better was a step in the right direction but not enough to balance out that horrendous day and its after-effects.

So she had readily agreed, and now she was on her way to the pub in the afternoon sunshine. A top the colour of dark chocolate with a fine outer layer of sparkling metallic copper thread perfectly complemented her favourite burnt-orange trousers as it fell to just above the hem of the tan suede jacket she still wore like a second skin; the natural highlights in her dark blonde hair caught the sunlight as she walked.

Miroslav, Des and Jason's employee who had café management experience, was fully trained and insured now to take a shift and let the brothers have more flexibility with their time off; they would be there to celebrate with her, as would Kate and Peter, Sharon and Paulie, Charlene, Bethany, Priya and Linda. The party had begun in the same way as her birthday; with coffee and cake at Charlene and Brandon's house. Brandon, whose benefits had been re-awarded thanks to the help of the advocate Diane had recommended, did not feel up to being in a pub with a group of that size; Diane was above all relieved that he could say so and took it as a compliment, feeling privileged to be invited to begin her celebration in their home so that he could be part of it. Draining the last of her coffee and giving Cheminot one more cuddle, laughing as she remarked that a few ginger cat hairs enhanced her outfit well, she helped Charlene clear away the plates and cups then the two of them and Bethany walked around to the pub.

Helen and Krista had been brought up to speed on the celebration by Sharon and Paulie, who had been the first to arrive. Three tables for four next to one another at the window had been marked as reserved for them, allowing for a more intimate and less socially expansive feel than one big table where crossing conversations could become stressful and a number of people would be boxed in requiring major upheaval whenever someone needed to use the bathroom. As Diane walked in with her friends, Helen announced that the first round was on the house. The five of them cheered; messages were quickly sent to those who were still on their way to ask what drinks to order in for them. Des and Jason arrived next; five minutes later Priya walked in, resplendent in a deep magenta trouser suit and accompanied by a woman in a cornflower blue dress with tiny white polka-dots, her shoulder length mid-brown hair framing a pretty, expressive face. Diane rushed over to meet them and be introduced to Linda, thanking her profusely for coming along and welcoming her to the circle of friends. Kate and Peter arrived last. Diane had met Peter several times before; she introduced them to the others, noting to her relief that Kate could clearly see how right and suited Priya and Linda were as a couple.

"We do have one surprise guest for you, Di", smiled Des as he looked up from answering a message on his phone. "He's on his way up now."

Diane turned to see who would walk through the door.

"Arthur! Des, how did you…"

"I got in touch with him through the fishing club he mentioned. I thought it seemed fitting to have him represent Up For Work, even though he's retired. He was thrilled with the idea and said he would be proud to come and acknowledge your efforts."

Krista brought over the pint Des had surreptitiously ordered for Arthur while Diane had been greeting Priya and Linda.

"It's an honour to be here, Diane. You worked so hard on getting that project together and your booklet was an inspired idea. I feel things will be better for you working with them now; Sally will have your back. I gather she's learned a lot, much of it from you."

Diane merely smiled sagely; however close she had been to Arthur as a mentor, she would still never share what Sally had divulged to her. Who got to know about that was Sally's decision and hers alone; nobody should be obliged to disclose a diagnosis unless they felt entirely comfortable and ready. She motioned him to sit at the spare seat at her table with Peter and Kate; Sharon, Paulie, Charlene and Bethany sat at the middle table with Des, Jason, Priya and Linda at the end so that Jason did not have to contend with conversations on either side. Referring to Brenda Culper by her initials since they were in a public place, Diane filled Arthur in on the events at the latest meeting; Kate joined in with how appalled she had been by her remarks to Bethany and the presumptuous attempt to touch her hair without asking; something which, as Diane pointed out, happens even more regularly to black women. The account of Sally's intervention was met with a knowing nod and wise smile from Arthur; both he and Kate gave delighted clenched fist salutes as Diane came to the part where she had told Verena that she could not stay around to take up her polite invitation to a drink with the staff because she was going home to her streetlamps and shepherd moons.

As Peter and Arthur bonded over golfing techniques, Kate excused herself to go to the Ladies' room, indicating to Diane to come with her. Tearing herself away from a conversation which she was finding interesting in its passion and precision, she was curious as to why Kate would involve her in such a tradition as going to the bathroom in pairs.

"Look, I know you were enjoying the golf talk and I don't mean to go all conventional girls' talk versus lads' talk on you as that is definitely not your style. I won't keep you long. I wanted to tell you again, face to face, how sorry I am for the pressure I put on you about dating. Even though something good came out of it in that you've found a wonderful new friend in Priya, the way it happened was completely wrong and I was a big part of that. Being here today, seeing Priya with Linda and seeing how authentically happy you are with your life and your friends now even though Verena is still on the scene, has finally gotten it through my skull. You were right all along; I was projecting my own feelings about how devastated I would be if I lost Peter. Perhaps there's even a part of me that envied you your self-reliance and made me face how dependent I am upon being in a relationship. I mean, we're fine; there are no issues to make me think I'm at risk of losing him or anything, but there's always that awareness that a lot of my happiness is tied up in the relationship and therefore not wholly within my control."

"Kate, it means a lot that you have been so honest and open with me about this. I always knew that your motives were good; I get defensive and forceful because I've spent so much time being talked over and not listened to or believed, by a whole range of people throughout my life including those with the best intentions. You believe me now and that's what matters."

"I'm glad you had Des and Jason so close by and that you're involved in the café project with them. They have always been more on your wavelength. I love your description of them as your shepherd moons. I'm afraid I haven't even been in the same ring system."

Diane burst out laughing; she could not resist, there was no way she was going to refrain from saying it.

"No, Kate, I'm afraid you've been speaking from Uranus."

"Haha! I must admit that thought had occurred to me too but that good old joke only works in the second person."

Overbearing though she could be at times, Kate was always such a good sport. Following her back through to their table, Diane hoped that her big-hearted friend never would have to face being on her own.

As more drinks were ordered and Helen and Krista brought over the snack plates of chips, sweet potato fries, crisps and dips, Diane asked them to stay for a few moments while she said a few words since there was nobody waiting to be served.

"Right; this is an informal celebration which is exactly what I wanted so I'm not going to make a full speech, but as it is my real project launch event, I can't let it go by without saying something. I want to thank you all for coming here; especially Kate for coming up with the idea and organising it in such a thoughtful manner. Thank you to all of you who have come from outside of Inverbrudock and who have reorganised your schedules or used up leave to be here. Thank you to those who have come here not knowing many of the people you would be meeting; I truly appreciate your efforts. Thank you to Helen and Krista for your wonderful hospitality and for having become my friends too. I'm supremely glad that each one of you is in my life; you have all helped me to appreciate how good that life is and to get myself to a place of strength and awareness to be able to truly own it. To be able to look around at all of you in this lovely town which I am proud to call home, and look up to the sky and out to the power of the sea and know that I have all I need right here. I hereby declare the Up For Work Together project and associated Up For Enjoying Work booklet officially and fittingly launched!"

Everyone cheered and gently applauded before tucking in to the casual buffet. As the afternoon turned to evening and those who had to travel or get back to other commitments began to disperse, with the pub becoming busy Diane, Des, Jason, Sharon and Paulie stacked the empty plates and glasses on the end of the bar and gathered around one table. Paulie and Sharon went up to the bar to get in one more round of drams, having noticed a couple of new whiskies which had been ordered in for the Easter tourist trade. "I think I saw Helen taking a couple of empty bottles down, so you might want to check with her what's still available", Diane suggested, catching Paulie's eye briefly; they nodded with a warm smile at the shared understanding that Diane had remembered their painful story and she had their back. Sharon too cast her a look of pure gratitude. These were the small beacons which spelled out the purpose of Diane's life now; honest sharing of the darkest moments leading to healing ones where the psychologically depleted outsiders coping with living in an incompatible society threw one another a lifeline.

The conversation turned to the café's opening day. Diane explained that she had not heard any more from Adrian; she hoped that it was because he was doing some reading up and soul searching. If he never came around, she admitted, she could deal with it but it greatly saddened her to think she may not see Georgie - no, Gina, she corrected herself - again.

"Is your sister blonde like you and Adrian, or is her hair darker?"

Jason's question was completely unexpected. "She was always naturally blonde like us and the last I knew she was still blonde. If she were going to go dark, I think she would have by the time I last saw her; unless she colours it of course. We do have Spanish relatives on my mother's side; my middle name Felizia is after one of them, it's a Basque name. So some of my cousins are very dark-haired, but none of us inherited that gene."

"I ask because there was a woman who came to the door of the café later that day, right before you came back in after you'd been out with Charlene. She was probably a passer-by looking to see what the new place was, but there was something about the way she was peering in; as though she was looking for something or somebody she'd lost. She looked happy though. Charlene and Des both went towards the door but by the time they got there she had gone, and then you came in. You probably caught a glimpse of her walking away. It's been bothering me that it might have been your sister and you narrowly missed seeing her. She had brown hair though; big curls like they'd been set in rollers or something."

Des, Jason and Charlene had seen her too!

"Don't you worry; I did see her, and it definitely wasn't my sister. It was someone much more relevant to the café. I thought I'd imagined it; I'm so happy that I'm not the only one to have seen her. I suspect everyone at this table is as open-minded about this sort of thing as I am; the woman we all saw was Joan Morley. I believe she was giving us her blessing. I am so glad to be able to tell you, now I know it wasn't my wishful thinking!"

As one, the five friends raised their glasses: to Joan Morley; to Martha Bannerman; to Harriet Sutherland; to everyone for whom the café would figure in the process of their soul gaining a much-needed rest. They silently saluted the understanding that it would be achieved with the pure, unobtrusive helping hand of meeting, perceiving and endorsing each welcome visitor in their own reality.

Plans were made, messages exchanged; invisible but unbreakable threads of friendship woven into the hushed night air as everyone headed for home. The long-quiescent streets of Inverbrudock felt newly awake with an unhurried yet vibrant sense of emergence. Its energy hummed in the roughened stones and sang in the ever-present rolling of the sea as life unfurled into its full range of colours and possibilities once again.

Diane stood in the glow of a streetlight, the yielding memory-foam settle of her familiar home awaiting her. There was no rush; nothing to prove. She turned and went inside. The steady illumination, fulfilling its vital role whether noticed or unseen, went on shining into the receptive twilight.

Author's Notes

My previous novel, "The House with the Narrow Forks", introduces the fictional town of Inverbrudock and the characters of Bethany, Sharon, Paulie, Helen, Brandon, Charlene and Cheminot the cat, as well as giving the back story of Harriet Sutherland in more detail including her diary entries in full. Sharon's teenage niece Lucy, her experiences of bullying at school and her mother Louise's reluctance to accept her autism diagnosis are also featured as a main storyline.

All of my books are written to promote autism acceptance and understanding; all royalties go to Autism Initiatives Scotland's one stop shop for autistic adults in the Scottish Highlands. I am as always thankful to the contacts and friends I have made in this and the other two one stop shops run by Autism Initiatives in Perth and Edinburgh; links to their websites are included at the end of this section.

The travel restrictions at the time my novels were being written ruled out my usual train trips to places I would have liked to research in more detail in order to use them as settings. Hence the invention of Inverbrudock (the "u" is pronounced as in "up"; "brothock", as in Arbroath's old name Aberbrothock, is thought to derive from "brudoc"). The town would be at a point where in reality the Dundee to Aberdeen railway line turns inland north of Arbroath. All businesses in Inverbrudock are fictitious and do not represent any real life organisations including any with similar names. The same applies to Up For Work and associated projects, the jobsearch hubs, Kate and Priya's employers and the Rafters Trust. Brenda Culper's invented role does not equate to any real post and Sunborough is a fictitious football team.

Wilma the counsellor is not based on any real life therapist; I am also fortunate not to have encountered any real people who are quite so horrific as Maurice Thurlowe and Brenda Culper. Those characters are intended to bring home to readers some of what we have to put up with as disabled people as well as showing how even well-intentioned attempts to assist can be damaging, especially when we are not listened to. Brenda's interventions may appear unrealistically over the top to some, but trust me; this is how hustling, space invading "help" enforced without listening and against the recipient's wishes often sounds and feels to people with sensory sensitivity and heightened anxiety. I would like to apologise to anyone who has, or is close to someone who has, the same names as my more challenging characters; they had to be called something!

There are some original ideas in this book which are my own and ascribed to Diane for the purpose of plot development as well as a way of putting them out there. My research at the point of writing has not given me any reason to believe that they correspond to any currently existing initiatives; any omissions or pitfalls are my own. If anyone wishes to incorporate any element of the Up For Work Together project, the Up For Enjoying Work booklet, any features of Harriet's Haven or the concept of autistic hygge into something which helps neurodivergent people, you may; I would appreciate it if you would mention my book as the source and let me know at the email address provided at the end of this section.

All whisky recommendations are my own; The Whisky Shop and The Malt Room in Inverness are real, as are all Perth businesses mentioned by name in this book. I am conscious of the difficulties which many people experience with alcohol and I urge readers to emulate Diane's principles of staying firmly within her limits for health, safety and security whilst embracing the freedom of choice which every adult, disabled or not, should have. Hangovers are no fun; neither are dangerous or regrettable choices made when drunk and their consequences, nor getting to the point of having to give up, entirely and forever, something one genuinely enjoys.

I have used a degree of dramatic licence in giving Diane the words I wish I could have found so quickly and clearly in stressful situations. This has been done for ease of reading and in order to convey the vital elements of autism understanding; it is important to remember that in real life situations, many of us often freeze and struggle to say what we so desperately need and want to. It is important to note that our ability to pick up on non-verbal cues and social subtleties also varies dramatically, from person to person and also from situation to situation for any one of us. For instance, Verena's invitation to Diane to join the staff team for a drink; an autistic person in Diane's situation there may well have taken the invitation at face value. If you are not autistic and are reading in order to seek a greater understanding, please imagine you are in Diane's place and consider the following: Did Verena extend that invitation only to make herself appear magnanimous, or out of a sense of obligation, or did she genuinely want to extend an olive branch? Did she issue the invitation in the hope that Diane would decline, or was it a test to see whether she were rehabilitated from her hero-worship enough and in "control" of her autism enough to know to do so, or would it have been OK for Diane to accept as long as she took it literally enough to stay for that one token drink then leave? Even if she had time to talk this through with a friend, how long would Diane be allowed to spend working out the course of action a) expected of her and b) best for her before being rebuked for overthinking? How exactly can she get all of this right? Do all these hypothetical questions feel exhausting especially when you factor in the pressure to respond quickly? Congratulations; you are beginning to sense what we go through daily.

Aromantic and asexual orientation and hero-worship are also personally relevant. I have aimed to convey how dangerous it can be for people who have been isolated by the incompatibility of conventional society with autistic and / or asexual and aromantic people (autism and sexual / romantic orientations are separate aspects which may or may not intersect!), when self-doubt and inappropriate expectations from others combine. Neither of the people who piled pressure onto Diane to engage in dating meant her any harm; both Wilma and Kate sincerely believed that they were pushing her out of her comfort zone for her own good. Imagine how far this could have gone had she not been fortunate enough to encounter a doctor who not only "got" her but knew the right questions to make time to ask and accommodate the answers. Many people are not so lucky; untold numbers have not even gotten so far as to be able to access an autism diagnosis, especially non-cis-male and non-white people. If there is someone like Diane in your personal or professional life, please listen to them, take them seriously and believe them.

It is also important in any circumstances to fully listen to what someone is telling you and bear in mind how your words may be interpreted before pushing the adage that relationships are supposed to be hard work. You could be reinforcing or coercing something which is not right for the person or even impeding their scope to recognise and escape an abusive situation.

Love and thanks to my own shepherd moons; Matthew, Ann, Jeni, Karen Kaz, Karen Catalina, Sarah, Kathleen and Lyndon "Dins" (the real life inspiration for Charlene and Brandon), Gabi, Bridget, Ian, Kathy, Lynsey, Liz and Tam, and Ruth who was taken from this earth far too soon.

I am blessed too with parents who are nothing like Diane's. My use of a pseudonym has nothing to do with their attitudes and is not indicative of my relationship with them.

Thanks to my publishers, David and Gwen Morrison at PublishNation for all of their support, goodwill, guidance and patience.

https://publishnation.co.uk/

For more information and further reading:

Autism Initiatives Scotland's one stop shops:

Highland:

http://highlandoss.org.uk/

Perth and Kinross:

http://perthoss.org.uk/

Edinburgh, the Lothians and Scottish Borders:

http://www.number6.org.uk/

Autistic led organisations promoting solidarity and understanding:

Autism Rights Group Highland (ARGH):

http://www.arghighland.co.uk/

Autistic Mutual Aid Society Edinburgh (AMASE):

https://amase.org.uk/

Triple A's (Aberdeen):

https://webspace.triplea.uk.com/

Scottish Women's Autism Network (SWAN):

https://swanscotland.org/

Own voice autism fiction; a most enjoyable and informative read: Elle McNicoll:

https://ellemcnicoll.com/home

Other relevant links:

Mental health crisis support:

Where to get urgent help for mental health - NHS (www.nhs.uk)

LGBTQIA in the UK:

https://lgbt.foundation/

Aromanticism:

AUREA - Aromantic-spectrum Union for Recognition, Education, and Advocacy (aromanticism.org)

Asexuality resource (AVEN):

https://www.asexuality.org/

Disability and accessibility, including the #JustAskDontGrab campaign against non-consensual touching of disabled people; blog by Dr Amy Kavanagh:

https://caneadventures.blog/

Deaf Action:

http://www.deafaction.org/

Anti-racism resources (UK based):

https://home.38degrees.org.uk/2020/06/04/a-collection-of-anti-racism-resources/

Gambling addiction:

BeGambleAware®: Gambling Help & Gambling Addiction | BeGambleAware

Online dating safety advice (for those who genuinely want and choose to do so!):

https://www.onlinedatingassociation.org.uk/date-safe.html

Lifeboats in Scotland:

https://www.scotlandinternet.com/lifeboats-in-scotland/

Cat rescue, lost and found advice:

https://www.cats.org.uk/help-and-advice

Hygge, koselig and similar concepts; allthingsnordic.eu:

Join Us - All Things Nordic

Aurora webcams: seetheaurora.com:

Webcams – See The Aurora

Caberfeidh Road was inspired by Dalfaber Road in Aviemore; Diane and her story were "born" on a holiday I took several years ago at Caberfeidh Log Cabin:

Home (log-cabins.biz)

Katherine Highland:

Other works and to give a rating or review (you can do this even if you did not buy the book on Amazon and it is extremely helpful especially to independent authors; much appreciated!):

https://www.amazon.co.uk/Books-Katherine-Highland/s?rh=n%3A266239%2Cp_27%3AKatherine+Highland

Email me (this is not my private email address and is checked weekly):

katherinehighland@pnwriter.org

Printed in Great Britain
by Amazon

56856448R00180